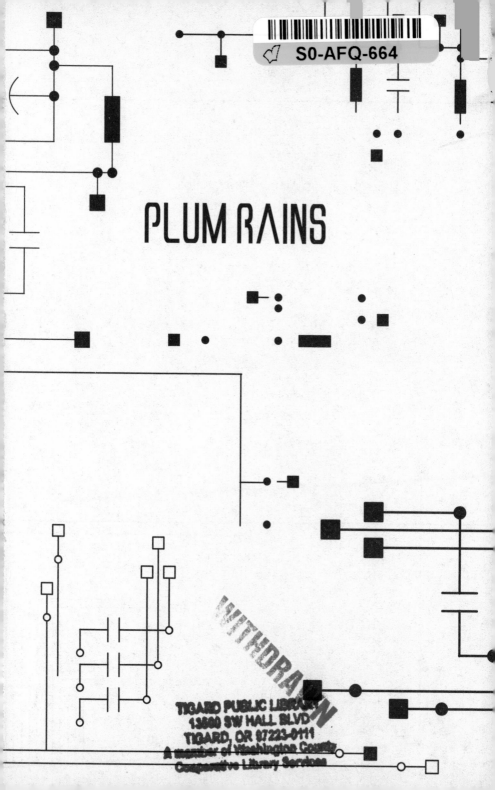

PLUM RAINS

S0-AFQ-664

TIGARD PUBLIC LIBRARY
13500 SW HALL BLVD
TIGARD, OR 97223-0111
A member of Washington County
Cooperative Library Services

WITHDRAWN

ALSO BY THE AUTHOR

The Spanish Bow
The Detour
Behave

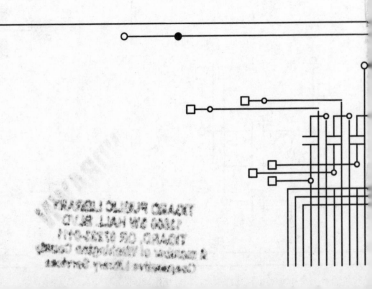

TIGARD PUBLIC LIBRARY
13500 SW HALL BLVD
TIGARD, OR 97223-0111
A member of Washington County
Cooperative Library Services

PLUM RAINS

Andromeda
Romano-Lax

SOHO

Copyright © 2018 by Andromeda Romano-Lax

All rights reserved.

Published by
Soho Press, Inc.
853 Broadway
New York, NY 10003

Library of Congress Cataloging-in-Publication Data

Romano-Lax, Andromeda
Plum rains / Andromeda Romano-Lax.

ISBN 978-1-64129-025-8
eISBN 978-1-61695-902-9

1. Artificial intelligence—Fiction. 2. Nurses—Fiction.
3. Medical fiction. I. Title
PS3618.O59 P58 2018 813'.6—dc23 2017055194

Interior design by Janine Agro
Interior art © Arun Boonkan/Shutterstock

Printed in the United States of America

10 9 8 7 6 5 4 3 2 1

To Brian, my friend since childhood and my husband now:
happily "green plums and bamboo horses" 青梅竹馬 *together.*

And for our Taiwan friends and neighbors, who gifted us
with laughter, tea and peaches.

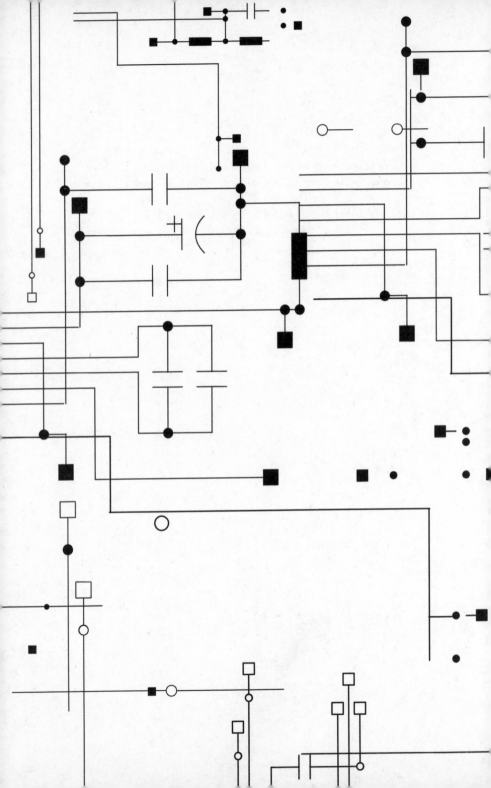

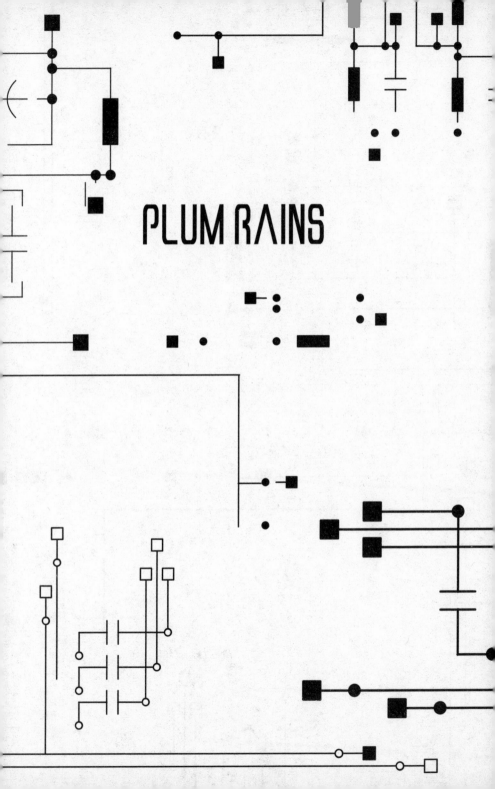

PLUM RAINS

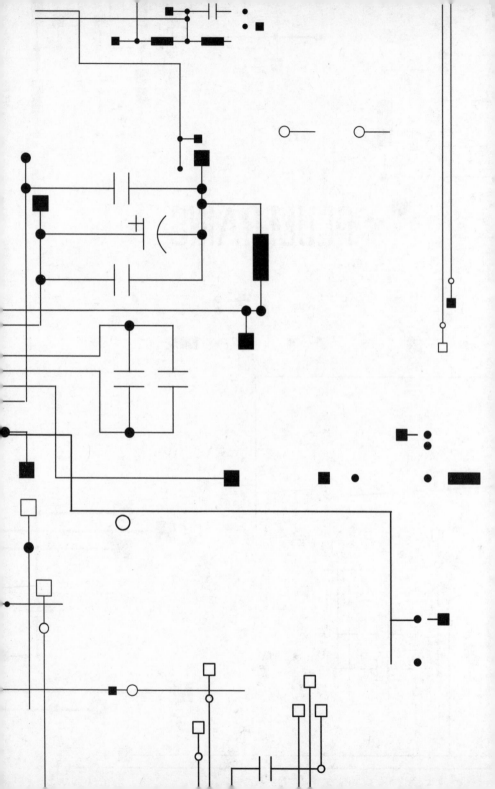

There will always be living things nourished by novel conditions: people, animals, plants, even spirits that thrive at the edge, that withstand discomfort and confusion, temperatures high or low, soil rich or stony. They turn toward the unknown like it is a warming sun; they make no face at what is bitter or strange. A naturalist might say they are tolerant. But mere tolerance does not explain the strength of some pioneering individuals' attraction to the edges of their conventional habitats, nor the magnetism experienced by two such individuals or even dissimilar species that participate in novel situations of mutual benefit, which Frank (1877) called symbiosis.

But you might ask: to what end?

And I would answer: to the only end that life has ever known. To keep living.

—Daisuke Oshima from *A Naturalist's Notes from the Island of Taiwan, formerly known as Formosa*. Originally published 1936. Reprint, 2030. University of Taiwan Press, Historical Reprints Series

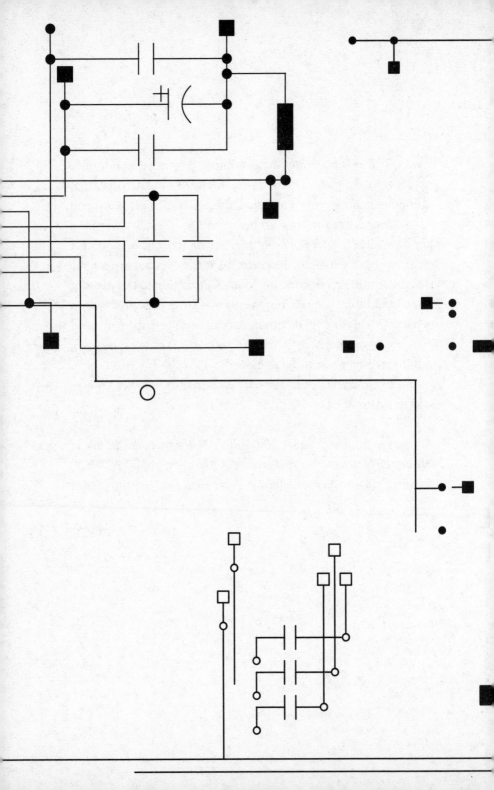

Part I

JAPAN, 2029

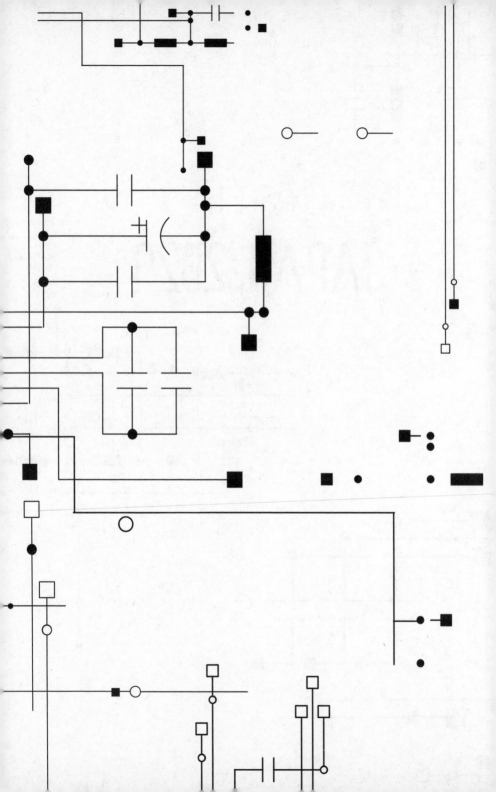

1 Angelica

Angelica was hurrying toward the crowded crosswalk, determined to get back to her elderly client Sayoko-san before the deliveryman arrived, when the view of buildings and business suits in front of her dissolved.

The heart of Tokyo at 4:07 P.M., improbably on pause. A sharp whine and then static; a muffled white-noise pulse.

Three throbbing beats. Then silence.

Jellied knees.

Shifting sidewalk.

Going down.

Someone else might have thought: terrorism. But Angelica's mind reeled back only to what she'd known personally, growing up in the rural Philippines: the chaos of nature itself.

Not again—the first thought of anyone who has lived through tremors, tsunamis and typhoons. Her fingers went to the tiny gold cross at her throat.

Angelica did not stagger so much as melt. The concrete smacked her cheekbone just as the light seemed to leak out of the world. She took the biggest breath she could, like a diver preparing to go under, filling her lungs with the last clean air she might ever have, while behind closed eyelids, images from her childhood formed: looking up through the rubble to the gray Cebu sky, one arm protecting her head, one hand trapped, the other free, dusty fingers struggling to flex above the ruin. *Tabang! Help!*

Papa! Mama!

But then: veins relaxed. Oxygen flowed. The past burrowed back under its dirty blankets, its broken pipes and dust. The Philippine island of Cebu on that day over thirty years ago was only a memory.

The light returned, soft and spotty at first, and then too bright. She squinted toward the curb, two meters away, and the street beyond, where whisper-quiet cars eased through the busy intersection.

Get up. Get up. But she couldn't. Her head was too heavy. The hiss in her ears was fading, but only slowly. Her leg was abraded from the fall, only a little, but it stung. A moan escaped from her lips, equal parts pain and simple embarrassment.

Without lifting her face, Angelica could see businessmen's loafers and women's low-heeled pumps moving steadily past, pausing, moving again as the light changed. When she rolled to one side to look up, a woman wearing a germ-blocking face mask met her glance with an apologetic bow and then kept going.

A whisper of wind against thigh warned that her skirt was up, her panties exposed. She'd meant to buy new underwear this spring and never had. Too broke and too busy studying for the next Japanese language proficiency exam. Last night, she had stayed up two extra hours and nodded off with her phone in her hand, *kanji* quiz app open, unfamiliar characters swimming through her dreams.

She wasn't the only one struggling. Ask the other Filipino nurses, the West African physical therapists, the Indonesian caregivers. Ask anyone in her position: trying to learn fast enough to pass the latest JLPT, trying to avoid unsafe jobs and the loan sharks back home, trying to avoid being sent back at the wrong time, always keeping the door open to returning at the *right* time.

But still, it could have been worse. Instead of dull gray hip-huggers with a worn-out elastic band, she could have been wearing the weirdly juvenile underwear her sometimes-lover Junichi had bought her. A forty-three-year-old Filipina should not be caught wearing a Hello Kitty thong.

The blood was returning to Angelica's head now. She needed only to lie on her back and let the spinning stop. She had been hurrying and worrying about something—and not only *kanji*.

The deliveryman. That was why she had been rushing, why she had ignored the mounting headache, the prickly flush behind her knees, the feeling of unmanaged anxiety—an army of tiny ants creeping across her scalp. Her body had been trying to tell her: Eat something. Breathe. Put your head between your knees.

But there'd been no time. Minutes earlier, while waiting in a noodle shop for Junichi (late as usual; probably not even coming) she'd received a text from the agency relief nurse, Phuong Pham: *Leaving early. Sayoko is fine. I have emergency.*

When Angelica had texted back, *You can't. Wait until I get there*, she'd received no further reply. She had set off toward the Itou family's luxury condo at a worried trot, throat constricting, scalp crawling.

At any moment, the deliveryman would be ringing the buzzer, having been assured that someone reliable would be there to greet him. Sayoko would be confused. Unless the old woman had thrown a tea towel over every eldercam eyespot in the house, Angelica's phone would automatically fill up with images of an agitated lady, rolling back and forth toward the door in her outmoded wheelchair. If Sayoko's blood pressure plunged or her heartrate increased past a certain point, programmed alarms would sound on her son's phone, even as he sat in an important business meeting in Kuala Lumpur. Ryo Itou might think it was a serious emergency. Worst of all, Sayoko herself would be afraid and alone. Angelica knew how time could change in that kind of situation: how anxiety opened the door to a lonely eternity.

Angelica closed her eyes.

Then opened them, a moment later, to see a white, concave disk as wide as her shoulders, hovering just above her face.

"I'm fine," she said as she tried to turn away from the public health device. "I have to get up."

"Please, remain still," the machine responded.

The disk's white wings angled down toward either side of her head, granting some small measure of privacy, a comfort more for bystanders who could hurry by with less guilt, even if their questions remained. *Had they been standing close to her at the last crosswalk? Would there be some new outbreak announced on the evening news?*

"There's nothing wrong with me," she said.

A cuff tightened automatically around Angelica's arm. A black weight, no larger than a change purse but hard and heavy, vibrated threateningly against her sternum. Thrusting her chin down into her neck, she just managed to see the unit's flickering red light, but only until the next instrument moved into place.

"I have low blood pressure," she said, before a rubber ring lowered around her mouth and sealed tight.

The kenkobot was just doing its job. There was no way out—only through. For one claustrophobia-inducing minute as she waited for the test to finish, Angelica tried to distract herself—tried, even, to see the value in the situation.

This would be a story to tell her brother, Datu. She would confess about the underwear. *Yes, all the businessmen were staring.* Whether or not it was true, just to make him laugh. So he could moan and answer: *Nena, don't tell me that. Take care of yourself. Buy new underwear at least. You've always been such a miser.* As if being a big spender was any better. Even when they were kids, he'd been unable to hold onto what the charity sisters gave him long enough to pay their school fees. Every coin went to candy and chips, later to beer, and then they'd sell gasoline from a plastic soda bottle to passing tricycle drivers who could only afford a splash at a time. *Stand at the corner, wave them down, waggle your hips,* he'd say, sitting on the dusty shoulder, in the shade. *Or at least waggle the place you'll someday have hips.* He was four years older, and cool. She had always admired his fearlessness, his reckless dreams—*I'll be the first off the island, and I'll be the first back home, rich and ready for the good life*—and even when their other three siblings had been alive, they were the closest.

Datu. She would text him this weekend and insist: not just audio. Video. Even if it couldn't be in real time. *I want to see you.*

Finally, the kenkobot finished its task and the rubber ring around her mouth lifted away, leaving its chemical smell and a feeling of pressure under her nose and over her chin. She'd have an indent above her lip for a few hours, a rash on her chin later. Small price to pay for state-of-the-art diagnostics, or so the kenkobot advocates would say.

"I had *sake* on an empty stomach," she told the unit. That part was true. At the noodle shop, she'd tossed back a single tiny cup before dashing out the door. "I'm a nurse. I know I'm fine."

She wasn't quite sure. But that was her business. Later there would be time to consider the symptoms, allowing some possibilities to flit across her mind and deliberately blocking others that were too frightening or simply unlikely. Nurses did that, too. Easier to treat than to be treated.

One thing she knew for sure: she wasn't as resilient as she used to be. Not so long ago she'd been able to juggle more uncertainties—Junichi not showing up for a date; Datu possibly trying to hide that he was sick; a borderline exam score—with only a passing sense of worry or irritation. But now, every stressor triggered something physical: Breathlessness. Dizziness. Psoriasis at her hairline or a rash across her chest. Her body was shouting what her mind didn't care to admit: it was too much, sometimes. She had a better situation than most, but things weren't getting easier.

The kenkobot recited her name, her age, her nationality, her physical address. Even the expiry date on her visa. The machine's volume seemed to increase with that last detail.

Was it all correct?

Yes. Of course.

Did she want to add additional contact information? No thank you. She wanted only to leave.

A list of medications was reviewed, patient history rapidly taken.

Symptoms, permission to access recent food purchase data, confirmation that she had not eaten any tainted food products purchased by others.

Still menstruating? No—sorry, sometimes. Irregularly.

Fertility therapy? No.

Sexually active? Is that really necessary?

Sexually active? Yes.

Travel outside Japan? Not since moving here.

When, precisely? Five years ago.

Sixty months? Let me see . . . fifty-eight.

Interactions with other foreigners? Only other healthcare professionals. Documented, healthy people.

From? Vietnam, China, West Africa . . .

And from the Philippines? The machine already had her travel records and general personal data, of course.

When she took too long, it asked again: *Interactions with citizens of the Philippines?*

She thought of her nursing friend Yanna, who had come with her, from Cebu, and then, despite threats from the moneylenders she still owed back home, had unwisely decided to return. You can go home if you're paid up. You can risk a trip if you've got an envelope full of cash, ready to negotiate the moment they hear you're back. What you can't do is return home more broke than when you left, having flouted every payment date you were given. Yanna had known that. And still.

Angelica answered the kenkobot, "Not many."

"Please," the kenkobot said. Always polite. A flexible perimeter rose around her with a gentle hiss as air inflated the soft, low barrier, each corner marked with a winking blue caution light. "Relax and remain still. With permission granted, final diagnostics will take only three minutes."

A stranger had accidentally kicked her right shoe and now it rested several meters away on the street beside the curb. Good nursing shoes in her extra-small size were hard to find. *Any* small shoes were hard to find. In Cebu and Manila, she had often searched through children's departments, but here in Japan, where the infertility epidemic was severe, children's shops were becoming rare, and the clothes they carried were infantile, part of a national obsession with things cute and riotously colorful. Each passing tire missed the simple white shoe only by centimeters.

She was asked a list of questions, seeking permission for each further invasion. A needle pinched the soft skin of her inner elbow. A chilled puff of air blew against her eye. A swab pushed stealthily into her nose and then retreated.

"I'm a little cold," she said, trying to reach a hand down to adjust her skirt and cover her thigh.

"Ninety-eight point eight degrees. Normal. Estimated time for transportation—"

"Not necessary," she said. But *it*, not she, would make that determination. With any luck, the nearest clinics were overbooked and the directive would be to release her, barring any indication of communicable disease.

"Please wait," the kenkobot said.

All this technology and she'd willingly trade it for a rolled-up towel placed under her neck and a simple blanket draped over her legs. All this so-called progress and what she needed was a kind word in a human voice.

"Please wait," the kenkobot repeated.

Technology alone, no matter how efficient, however seemingly foolproof, could never suffice. Any good nurse knew that. And with that thought, Angelica experienced the first sense of calm she'd felt all day, the certainty providing a visceral comfort: she knew things. She was a professional. She was needed, in this day and age more than ever, when so much of life was automated and impersonal. She had value. No one could take that from her—least of all a machine.

"Please wait," the device repeated a third time.

Traffic backed up at the corner. Feet stopped and moved again.

"I can't wait any longer," Angelica finally objected, energized by her indignation. "I'm expected at a private residence. My patient needs me. She's ninety-nine years old and a Japanese citizen. Her son works at METI."

Angelica thought the reference to the Ministry of Economy, Trade and Industry might get the kenkobot's attention, but the device remained silent. Perhaps it was having trouble decoding Angelica's mild accent.

"He's abroad on government business. And his mother, my client, shouldn't be left alone for this long. I insist that you let me sit up and place a call."

The white privacy wings retracted. Angelica propped herself up on one elbow and activated the wrist monitor that Sayoko wore, awake or asleep. They had tried giving her a phone with oversized buttons, but Sayoko had rejected it along with the voice-operated house system with its front hallway screen. With the wrist monitor, she only had to say "*Hai*" and they'd be instantly connected. If she said "*Ichi-Ichi-Kyuu*" or "Call police," the police would come. But Sayoko forgot these things, or pretended to.

Angelica's phone beeped six times, seven. No answer from Sayoko.

"My absence will cause distress," Angelica said. "She has no one else. You must let me go."

Convinced or simply finished with its directive, the kenkobot released her. "Results will be sent electronically within ten days to your last address on record and to your employment sponsor—please agree?"

"Go back, please. I don't agree."

"I must request—" the kenkobot started to say, but Angelica didn't let it finish.

"I have the right to keep my medical information private. You are familiar with Japan's APPI laws?"

Her in-country training had been good for something.

One last delay. Then: "Electronic permission not granted. Results will be sent by personal delivery within ten days. Thank you for using the national emergency health responder service. *Arigatou gozaimasu*."

"*Dou itashimashite*," Angelica said. You're welcome. It was hard to break the habit of politeness here, even when you were talking to a soulless machine.

When the kenkobot moved aside, she stood up and stepped over the deflating barrier. She spotted the thick white heel of her overturned shoe by the curb and slipped her foot into it without tightening the lace. As she limped to the corner, the pedestrians made a space and every last person looked directly ahead as if nothing had happened.

Which is what she would tell Sayoko-san. Nothing had happened. Only bad traffic and too many people, Angelica would say. Always too many people, Sayoko would agree, neither of them mentioning that the people who were taking more than their share of what destiny intended belonged to two categories: immigrants, and the elderly. Bound together by need and by chance.

"Not like the old days," Sayoko would say.

"No, not like the old days," Angelica would answer pleasantly, bolstered by what she knew for certain—the old days were never as good as anyone pretended—and determined not to take offense.

2 Angelica

"You left me!" Sayoko said when Angelica hurried into the condo, just steps ahead of the deliveryman, who had been waiting in the foyer. "And it was too noisy!"

"That was your wrist monitor making all that noise," Angelica said calmly. "I was calling you. Do you remember? We showed you how to answer it."

"You didn't."

"That's all right. I'll show you again."

"It doesn't work."

"It *does* work. We'll practice."

"Anyway, it's too tight," Sayoko said, as she often did, but then she settled down, curious about the deliveryman and his white boxes.

Angelica hurried into the bathroom to get an anti-inflammatory from the medicine cabinet for her knee pain. In Japan, where nearly a third of the population was over seventy-five, she was often treated like a young adult, but back home, where people still died of heart trouble, diabetes, pneumonia, and liver failure in their forties, fifties, and sixties, she'd be considered on her way to old age, with the everyday aches and pains to prove it.

Tap water running, she could just make out the sounds of the deliveryman and Sayoko chatting. When Angelica returned to the living room, Sayoko said, "They brought me a new nurse, in those boxes."

"I don't think a person would fit in those boxes," Angelica said, trying to correct without causing offense or further agitation. "Not even a short person like me. It must be a birthday present. For your hundredth birthday. That's in just about a week, do you remember?"

"Of course I remember my birthday."

"How many days until your party?" Angelica asked. She was trying to remember herself, but Sayoko seemed to think it was a malicious quiz.

"I don't have to know. If I sit in my chair and do nothing, it will happen whether I like it or not."

"Ten days. That's when it is." Angelica closed the calendar on her phone. "And it will be very special."

Angelica pushed Sayoko's wheelchair to the center of the room so she could watch the deliveryman tap a digital device against each of the five boxes and then kneel down to open the first. Angelica stood behind the chair, curious as well, braiding the old woman's long white hair, which the relief nurse hadn't bothered to re-braid after Sayoko's late-morning nap.

"He said it was a nurse," Sayoko said, gesturing to the deliveryman.

When Angelica didn't refute the claim a second time, Sayoko changed tack. "*I* was going to be a nurse, you know. Before the war. They came to recruit me."

"You were a very young girl when Japan went to war," Angelica said. "And very pretty, I'm sure."

She coiled the braid into a neat bun, noting that Sayoko flinched as she pinned the hair at the nape of her neck. Sayoko had always been a flincher, easily startled. Angelica touched her every day: strategically, therapeutically.

"They made promises," Sayoko said, with less determination. "I was a quick learner, they saw that in me. It made sense they would want to recruit me."

Perhaps it sounded unbelievable now, even to Sayoko herself—as if she'd allowed half-remembered scenes from some romantic movie to embroider new patterns over her own unreliable memories. The head nurse at Angelica's last job in a Tokyo nursing home had believed that delusions should be discouraged. Angelica didn't always agree. Some enjoyable illusions were harmless. And others, the particularly persistent ones, even if they weren't entirely accurate, seemed to surface for a reason. When an older person clung to some idea about the past or stumbled suddenly upon a long-lost memory, it often seemed like a story they needed to tell themselves, whether or not the story was true. As far as Angelica could tell, Sayoko had never worked a day in her comfortable life. Maybe she liked to imagine that she had, or almost had. Maybe we all like to invent heroic identities for ourselves or those we love.

"Sweet potato," Sayoko said, out of the blue.

"That's what you'd like to eat now? Are you hungry?"

"No, sweet potato. There." She was staring at the logo on the side of the largest box.

Angelica was used to Sayoko spouting nonsense, as she assumed this to be—though one could never tell. This week, Sayoko had enjoyed an unprecedented run of lucid days.

"I'm not saying it *is* a sweet potato," Sayoko added crossly. "It just looks like one. The shape there: the island of Taiwan."

Now Angelica recognized the island's outline with its stubby stemlike bottom.

"And the characters say 'Made in Taiwan,'" Sayoko said.

Angelica confirmed: the Chinese characters were only slightly different from the Japanese, and yes, Sayoko had been able to read them.

"That's right," Angelica said. "How do you feel?"

"How should I feel?"

"It doesn't make you dizzy, reading those characters?"

"Dizzy?" Sayoko asked scornfully. "Not at all."

So, she had forgotten, then, about last month's complaint: that reading text made her head swim. She'd had a house call from an eye doctor, who informed them that she didn't need surgery, and good thing, since Sayoko had snorted at the mention of any procedure. *No one believes in simple eyeglasses anymore?*

It was a cognitive issue, the doctor had assured them, though since she refused the simple, safe nanodiagnostics he offered, he couldn't provide more detail. Further deterioration was to be expected.

Or not, Angelica thought now.

Sayoko's cancer was gone and despite the biomarkers, her Alzheimer's symptoms had not progressed.

Sayoko actually seemed heartier and more clear-minded than when Angelica had signed on for her first six-month contract, nearly a year and a half ago. At the time, Ryo Itou had warned her that it might not be the best job for an independent live-in nurse, since his mother's health appeared to be failing.

"Is there a reason you don't use short-term agency nurses instead?" Angelica had asked.

"There is."

Itou-san had been candid about his mother's refusal of implants and tracers, and even of simpler, decade-old alert systems. For every monitoring technology she rejected, Sayoko's digital documentation had become spottier, making her a liability and harder to care for, since nurses were trained to follow rigid protocols designed around implants and somatic monitoring.

In addition to Sayoko's resistance to new technology, she had become increasingly resistant to socializing as well, Itou found it important to explain so that Angelica would have a complete portrait before committing. For years, Sayoko had seemed guarded even with her few friends, preferring to maintain casual acquaintances with a circle of older women rather than become intimate friends with even one or two. But at least she'd had these friendly acquaintances, who would occasionally meet up for light exercise or art classes at the adult daycare centers the government had established, converted from old school buildings that were no longer needed. But the meet-ups had dwindled in the last few years. First, because Sayoko tired of the flower arranging and calisthenics, and second, because the few women she liked or at least tolerated had started dropping off—in some cases, very suddenly.

"But that part is as it should be," Itou had said. "*Pin pin korori.*"

Yes, Angelica was familiar with that cultural ideal: *Live long, die short. Be spry, then die quickly and painlessly.* In her experience as a nurse, she knew it wasn't quite that easy in practice. Even a rapid decline toward the end of a physically healthy life could be more difficult than families and the elderly themselves realized, especially when that end was complicated by loneliness.

"What do you think gives your mother her *ikigai*?" Angelica had asked Itou. "What gets her up in the morning?"

"If I knew that, I'd know everything. She is stubborn, that's certain. I doubt most depressed people are so long-lived."

"You would say, then, that she is depressed?"

Itou wouldn't answer directly. Perhaps he'd felt it was improper for him to do so. "Then again, they say the person who won't let go still has some work to be done—something to settle, something to do or say. I've always felt she is waiting for something, but for what, I have no idea." He laughed. "Perhaps she is only waiting for me to get my next promotion."

From a different man, the last comment might have sounded arrogant, putting himself at the center of his mother's emotional world. But Angelica sensed he was just changing the subject in order to protect his mother from further prying.

Despite everything, Sayoko was doing well—perhaps better than her son took the time to notice or had the emotional reserves to appreciate. The treatments she *had* accepted had proven astoundingly successful. Her health was proof of what many Japanese people hoped for and what some, more quietly and pragmatically, feared:

that generations to come would taste immortality. Less poetically, they might, at the very least, live expensive, highly monitored lives well past 120.

In the quiet living room, the unpacking of the mystery boxes continued. Angelica's phone vibrated again. It had begun buzzing as she neared the Itou family condo, so she'd assumed all the messages were related to the delivery. Yet messages continued to stream in.

Even though she'd refused the electronic communication of the kenkobot's results, they were probably instant follow-ups from the mobile exam: *We wish you a healthful long life and invite you to visit us online for lifestyle education. Will you please rate your experience?*

When Angelica tried to pull up the messages, she could see the senders' names and a few words of preview text, but she couldn't read the full messages, as if they were somehow locked. She couldn't tell if she had failed to update her chat app, if she had filled her phone's memory, or if the phone was simply worn out. Later, she would update essential apps and delete the unnecessary ones, study her data usage, and tinker with her settings. For now, she had a visitor in the house.

Pausing from his unpacking, the deliveryman, gray-haired but with an unlined face, held up a small scanner so Angelica could sign optically. She'd been trained as a nurse to look at people's faces whenever possible, but with deliverymen it was always, *over here; the red light; look up; blink; try again.*

This deliveryman was patient, at least.

"You're helping with the orientation?" he asked.

"Orientation?"

He took a traditional paper business card from his pocket and presented it with both hands, bowing. Angelica had learned the etiquette of receiving cards: take with pleasure, hold, study, never put away too soon. In this case, her examination of the card was no mere performance, but rather a sincere process of scrutiny. His name was printed, last name first: *Suzuki Kenta*. And his title, not simple deliveryman at all, but technician. For what company? Curiously, the card did not say.

She watched the technician lift a white cube out of one box and an egg-shaped object out of another. Angelica kept looking for something bigger and more rugged: parts to an upgraded wheelchair, she hoped. Sayoko was attached to the old one, but Angelica knew it had to be replaced and that Sayoko would be happier in the end—more willing to go out to Ueno Park, less afraid of the busy intersections that took too long to cross with Angelica pushing and straining from behind.

"I can't assemble anything," Angelica said, worried she'd misunderstood the technician's words.

He chuckled without looking up from the box he was peeling open. "No, no. We assemble. You *shaperon*."

Was that a Japanese word? French?

"While they get to know each other," the technician said.

"What do you mean, get to know each other?"

"It's no trouble. The unit does the work."

She knelt down on the floor, Sayoko in the wheelchair on one side, watching, the technician with his boxes on the other.

"I don't think Itou-san ordered this," Angelica said.

"We have his approval to deliver."

"My employer isn't fond of gadgets. Did you see the entry table?"

The technician hummed under his breath, occupied.

"Where you took off your shoes?" Angelica persevered. "That's where Itou-san leaves his work devices. Past that *fusuma*," she pointed toward the sliding screen that separated her employer's bedroom from the living room, "you won't find anything but paper, cotton and wood."

"My son has a record player," Sayoko interjected.

"Do you hear that? A *record* player."

The technician smiled without looking up. "Very hip. My son has one of those."

"My son loves music," Sayoko added. "He played the violin as a boy. Not well, because he didn't practice enough. Later the other noisy thing—the clarinet. It never sounded right."

They were getting away from the point. Angelica said, "And Sayoko-san here, she's old-fashioned."

"Aren't we all," the technician muttered.

"No, I mean, officially. She's registered as old-fashioned, with the Federal Senior Register and the Department of Health. It gives her special rights."

"Oh, I'm not here to take away anyone's rights."

"Please stop until I talk with Itou-san," Angelica pleaded, watching as the thing took shape beneath the technician's capable hands. "I'm certain this is a mistake."

"In one hour, a machine," he said without looking up. "In one week, a friend. Like it says on the box."

"Is that what it says on the box?" Angelica asked, squinting. She searched for any sign of the manufacturer or a product description, so she could figure out what the thing was and whether there was any reason to be wary of it. No, she corrected herself. She was already wary of it. *A friend?* What she wanted to find was enough product info to help her locate the reviews and complaints—one could always find complaints—that would justify getting rid of the thing altogether.

"There." The technician pointed to the characters, just below the image of Taiwan that had first captured Sayoko's attention. The friendly slogan, followed by the Chinese phrase Sayoko had deciphered: "Made in Taiwan."

Angelica knew little about robotics, but she did know that most robots, aside from those manufactured in Japan, came from South Korea. Especially the social models. But something had changed: she remembered hearing that Korea had been the undeniable leader in the mid-twenties, but then business had quieted down. So maybe they weren't pioneers anymore, or maybe no country was. The entire social robotics evolution had come to a strenuously negotiated halt.

Late last year, Itou-san had been moved up from the Robotics Industry Office of the Manufacturing Industries Bureau, to the ministry's Technology Policy Bureau. After the promotion, Itou had spent the next month reciting Korean phrases under his breath, preparing for a slew of meetings. He had gone to Seoul at least once a fortnight. Then he'd suddenly stopped going, as if a relationship had been severed. After that: busy again, but suddenly practicing Chinese and booking trips to Taipei. There had to be a link. Some new trade contact must have sent him this thing. But that didn't mean it couldn't be sent away.

"I'll message Itou-san," Angelica told the technician, "but he's traveling. It may take some time before he gets to it. I don't think you should open anything else. It will only be returned."

Sayoko gave Angelica a stern look. "It's mine. You said it's a gift. I want to see."

The technician nodded and rotated the white, elongated sphere to show them the android's unilluminated face.

A slit for a mouth.

Translucent visor over two slits for eyes.

Smooth bump of a nose.

All of it hard, inert, toylike. So that was it, Angelica thought: a child's toy, or an elder companion, the simplest of appliances— something to read the news aloud, announce the weather, and issue reminders for people Sayoko's age, who forgot over and over and wore out the patience of real human beings. The most rudimentary form of AI; isn't that what they called it? The appearance of cleverness and utility, but really a curio, something to be shown off for a few days and then left in a closet, next to an abandoned stationary bicycle.

And yet Angelica felt the tingle of stress across her scalp again, a sense of the ground growing unsteady beneath her feet. If it were only a toy, she wouldn't feel this sense of foreboding. Simple elder companions and entertainment-oriented appliances came ready-made. They did not require extensive assembly and testing.

The technician exchanged a satisfied smile with Sayoko before resuming his duties, fitting together the robotic head and its torso-like main cube, one hand over to a small tablet to key in some code, then back again to caress the glossy surfaces.

Angelica had once taken Sayoko to visit a friend in a nursing home. When they'd arrived, the elderly patients had been taking turns petting a robotic seal, more than willing to lavish atten-tion on an unconvincing, inanimate object—turn-of-the-century technology that didn't impress Angelica and barely held Sayoko's attention for three minutes.

Here in their own living room, a half hour had already passed and Sayoko was still watching. She leaned forward, eyes fixed on the technician's hands as he closed flaps and ran a finger over seams that became invisible at his touch.

Angelica asked, "Does it have a name?"

"It names itself," the technician said.

"What does that mean?"

"Only after it learns enough."

"Maybe it should learn enough before it's delivered."

"No," he said. "It learns from its new owner. That's the only way."

There were always things to do: a digital health diary for Sayoko; prescriptions to be ordered and new suppliers to be found—harder and harder given how rare it was for people to take old-fashioned pills anymore when customized methods for releasing medication and instantly monitoring its effects were available. A handyman needed to be called about installing a better handrail in the bath-room. The week's meals had to be planned with consideration given to Sayoko's changing preferences as her appetite improved.

Laundry. Shopping. A quick bathroom floor mop-up. Sayoko was mostly independent in her toileting, but she was not always neat, who would be at that age? Angelica helped her with a shower-seat sponge bath in the morning and evening while the family's traditional deep tub remained lidded and often unused, except by Itou-san when he was home.

On top of it all, Angelica had her own daily language studies: new Japanese *kanji* to be memorized every day and additional ones to review in time for the next language exam.

Even while you waited for the last exam's results, there were new updates being issued, another exam already scheduled, online forums in which workers from Indonesia and the Philippines guessed which medical *kanji* would be dropped or added. The conspiracy-minded commenters said that the foreign worker system was designed to fail. There was no reason a nurse or physical thera-pist should need to know vocabulary that no Japanese person used in daily life or to read *kanji* that would stump even a native-born medical professional.

If Angelica still had nursing friends in Tokyo, and free time, they'd sit picnicking and drinking beer, complaining about the language tests that were surely meant to reduce the number of foreign workers, even while Japan's aging population paradoxically required more and more outside assistance. But she didn't have the heart to make new friends, to replace the ones who had chosen to return or had been forced to leave. She could not afford the luxury of scrolling through the online forums, adding her voice to those who protest. She barely had the time to learn new *kanji* and to review the ones already fading, like puddles drying in the tropical warmth of a Cebuano sun.

To think there had been afternoons, on Cebu, when she had sat in the park at lunch break, on a square of cardboard, reading comic books—the Filipino kind, not manga, the kind Junichi talked about ceaselessly thanks to his job promoting pop culture at the same

Ministry that employed Itou-san. The Filipino comics were romance novels and chronicles of immigrant survival, rendered graphically not because it was cool, but because so many of her fellow Pinoys barely knew how to read. By their standards, Angelica's first month's nursing salary in Cebu—$335—was a fortune. Now she earned six times that amount and it still wasn't enough. Every Filipino had a cousin abroad who said the same thing: it's nearly impossible to get off-island without borrowing, the debt collectors are vicious, the cost of living abroad is so high, there are fees, the government takes, you think it's so easy, you try. And any Filipino who could, did.

Datu had gone for the big payoff. First there was a small signing bonus. It wasn't enough to cover the cost of a visa, health paperwork, and upfront travel, but a much heftier bonus would be paid once he'd lasted two years on the job.

For months after he left, she heard only good reports. He had his own studio apartment in the BZ, without a roommate. It was ten times better than Dubai. It was a hundred times better than Shenzhen. She tried not to question and to simply feel happy that he was happy, living in the moment, enjoying the benefits: the steak and Atlantic salmon dinners, the indoor wave pools and golf courses, and all those perks, why? Everyone knew why. Because the job was in a contamination zone, a place both ruined and made suddenly more profitable by chance.

Vast populations of wildlife had been wiped out. Residents had been evacuated. Miners and support service employees had moved in at considerable risk to their own health, as even the normally duplicitous corporations admitted. Working in the new Burned Zone wasn't a death sentence, as far as people knew this early in the project's development. But it *was* a dangerous gamble.

By this point in the afternoon, Sayoko was usually ready for tea and some bean-paste-filled confection or a bowl of miso, but when Angelica offered, Sayoko waved her off.

Angelica, aware of the extra roll of flab that had been gathering around her own four-foot-nine-inch frame, decided to put off a snack for the moment as well. She didn't feel comfortable leaving the technician unattended, not before he had finished his task and explained the unit's purpose. So they would all spend the next half hour together, wordlessly waiting. Fine with her. It was the closest thing to a break she'd had all day.

Thoughts of Datu sent her back to her phone, which she discreetly checked from her position in an old chair near the balcony door. It wasn't like him to be out of touch for so long. Even with her message problem, she should at least see whether he had tried to contact her. A few new messages had scrolled in from Junichi, and as with the earlier ones, she could see the sender and the first words of preview text: *Sorry, I had* . . . No doubt an explanation for why he'd stood her up at lunch, the least of her worries. But from her brother: nothing.

She tried sending a text. To Junichi she wrote: *Phone problems today. Strange. Tell me if you get this?* It seemed to go through but she wouldn't be sure until she received a reply.

It occurred to Angelica now to check outgoing messages, to see if these, too, had failed to send or had become suddenly invisible.

Unlike the newest incoming ones, the outgoing ones were at least fully accessible. Her last to Datu had been a reminder to watch for notices about their joint land title request. Word was, things on Cebu were finally picking up, the thirty year backlog finally getting sorted, as things sometimes did when an up-and-coming political party wanted support. Datu was terrible about paperwork, and yet because he was the designated head of household—the only real survivor, as far as the Philippine government was concerned—she couldn't be sure she would receive notice, no matter how many times she added her name to the countless legal forms.

Another Filipina at her last job had once pressed Angelica on this point, reminding her that if Datu died prematurely, Angelica's name and documentation might carry little official weight.

A terrible thought. The sort of thing only a person from your own homeland might dare to say. Sometimes fellow Pinoys knew too much.

But you have to consider it, given where he's working. Alaska, right?

Which made Angelica wish she'd never told anyone. It was hard enough to have the worries rattling around in her own head.

The woman wouldn't let it go. *It's called Masakit, right? That thing the miners get?*

There was a scientific name for the excruciating disease caused by exposure to the toxins present in the Central Yukon District, where the rare earth elements were mined, but in Filipino, they called it simply *Masakit,* or "painful," just as the Japanese had given the name *Itai-itai*—"it hurts, it hurts,"—to cadmium poisoning more than a century earlier. Some things never change, including the willingness to endure poisoning, or subject others to it, just to extract wealth from the earth.

But it's fairer and more transparent now, Datu had reassured Angelica. No one denied the dangers, including pancreatic cancer and leukemia from the rare earths mining itself. As generations of people from China, still dominating over ninety percent of the rare earths market, could attest. Add to that the rarer, less understood *Masakit* bone-softening disease that wasn't even directly related to the mining, but rather to the environmental destruction that had softened opposition to the mining.

It had all started five years earlier, when a weaponized bird flu had escaped government labs in eastern Russia and hit Alaska, wiping out a handful of Native villages, including ones where the elders still passed down stories of their grandparents barely surviving the influenza that had swept through more than a century earlier. The first few hundred human deaths weren't insignificant, but it was fear of a global disaster that led to the panic. Authorities predicted that once the virus reached major population centers beyond the coastal villages or once Alaskan birds migrated south— whichever came first—the lab-mutated, species-hopping plague would be unstoppable. Aggressive, experimental measures were implemented, and they worked. The weaponized flu was stopped in its tracks, but not without unintentionally sacrificing Alaska to the cause.

Angelica remembered the news footage showing weary northern survivors boarding planes and ships en masse, and following the radical anti-flu effort, the aerial photos of the gray-green arctic plains, stippled with the bodies of hundreds of thousands of dead caribou. Things decayed slowly in the far north, Angelica remembered the reporters saying. She had wondered how long it would take for nearly a million caribou and who knows how many other mammals, birds, and fish to disintegrate, and she imagined a vast unpeopled country habitable only by flies—if that.

The old concern about losing polar bears to climate change seemed quaintly insignificant compared to this new turn of events. It reminded Angelica of downturns in her own life: you were looking over your shoulder for the thing you'd always feared and missed the entirely new threat barreling toward you. You worried about the past, or some sort of gradual loss, and then someone's brilliant new idea exploded your carefully designed life all at once.

In Alaska at least, a bright side of the disaster revealed itself, almost too quickly, a cynic might have observed. A multinational mining project that had been opposed for years was cleared to ramp up production, now that surrounding communities no longer existed. *A silver lining,* some pro-mining headlines had proclaimed. *The US challenges China's rare earths monopoly.* The only potential victims now were the foreign workers—forty percent Filipino— who were all aware of the risks.

It's different, because we know what we signed up for, Datu had told Angelica from the airport, where he'd taken her call, the last

time he'd be able to talk with any measure of privacy. He was not
guarded then, not yet absorbed into the BZ's culture of silence.
She saw his big, smiling face on her phone screen, the tooth he'd
chipped in his twenties, when he'd tried boxing for three whole
months, thinking it would make him instantly rich. She saw the
crowds of Ninoy Aquino International Airport behind him and
heard the flights being called, bound for every corner of the earth.
He was wearing a tropical shirt, like a man going off on vacation.

Where's your coat? she'd insisted.

*They never let us outside. Don't worry about it. They're calling
my flight.*

So board last. Talk to me.

I can't. First class. Reimbursable. Datu would cover the scandal-
ously high interest rate on the loan until his employer processed
his payment—which always took longer than expected, Angelica
knew—but at least he'd travel in style. He held up the boarding
pass, waving it as he grinned.

Is that one-way or round-trip?

He didn't answer.

Angelica heard the call for Los Angeles, first stop on the way to
Anchorage and then Fairbanks and then a smaller plane after that.
Never mind. Tell me what you've gotten yourself into.

And he'd tried to explain his reasoning again, the same way he'd
explained every other get-rich-quick scheme he'd ever attempted.
The multinational company was considered a model of corporate
responsibility. After some initial publicity problems, it promised
end-of-life on-site colony care to everyone who'd been employed
two years or more. So at least an overseas laborer could count on
one thing: medical attention, at the bitter end. Although not if you
got ill quickly or wanted to die somewhere other than the miners'
hospice.

Datu wouldn't have to make that choice, because he was different—as Angelica had told that nosy woman who'd asked her

about *Masakit*. As Angelica told herself. Datu was always resistant, always stronger than his fellow man. He'd know when to take his winnings, leave the table, and go home.

They had a plan: retirement back in the Philippines, on Cebu, together. Back on that very same stretch of coast where they had lost everything except each other. It meant even more to Datu than to Angelica, who had always considered herself less nostalgic about places than about people. It meant so much to her *only* because it meant so much to him. The government was finally settling claims, sorting out lost titles, cutting through decades of red tape and squatters' objections. Angelica and Datu had to keep an eye on things. Even if true retirement was a long way off, they had to stay ready, because paperwork is unforgiving. Which is why she was always telling him to watch for the notices. *They may ask us to send in more forms. They may even ask us to come in person. We miss a deadline, they'll say we forfeit. They'll cheat us if we're not careful.*

She knew that Datu dreamed of a small house by the sea, prize roosters and a guard dog, a traditional patio outside and a contemporary rec room inside: big screen for watching Latin American soccer, American football. A motorcycle with sidecar parked under thatch. All that. And to keep memories of their grandmother and parents alive: a garden and barbecue pit, the sort of place where many people can eat together, the way it should be. Flowers climbing the covered porch.

Angelica counted on those dreams to help keep him safe. When they talked—using censored and time-delayed communications, but no matter—he could paint a picture that almost made it seem real to her. Bananas harvested from their own yard. Pig roasts. Sea breezes. She had pretended at many things in her life, and she could pretend this as well: that she believed. As long as he was there with her, in the gray twilight of the near future, walking several paces ahead.

After an hour, the technician had set up only half of the robot: the head and torso, a soft-cornered semi-transparent white cube. No limbs or bottom half, no signs of mobility. The robot's head had an opalescent sheen, but there was no expressive, digitally rendered face playing across the smooth surface.

"Why is it so simple looking?" Angelica asked.

"Simple does not offend," the technician said.

"I mean . . . why doesn't it look more realistic?"

Even modern taxi-driver mannequins and department store automatons could be deceptive. Angelica had been often startled her first month in Tokyo, realizing that the well-dressed, white-gloved man helping direct passengers toward a crowded subway car was not a human at all—and nearly as surprised to discover that a robotic department store cashier with a porcelain face was, in fact, a real woman.

"Something that has low intelligence and looks halfway human can be entertaining. Something with high intelligence and advanced features—almost human, but still not quite human—can be . . ." the technician trailed off.

"Can be . . . ?"

"Can create unease," the technician said.

Angelica waited for him to explain more, but he did not. Nor did he make any move to open the two boxes still sitting on the living room floor.

"You aren't going to finish it?" she asked.

"Smaller is better, until they are friends."

In its simplicity, it reminded Angelica of something she'd seen years earlier in a nursing class: pictures of surrogate monkey parents created by psychology researchers in the last century, sometimes no more than a circle with eyes attached to a rectangular mesh body. A face stuck to a cheese grater. So little to suggest the form of a living thing. It was enough to trick the baby monkeys, but Sayoko-san was no monkey, and how dare they treat her like an animal or a fool?

The technician pressed a button and the robot's trunk lit up like a screen, ready to play a series of short videos that Sayoko was directed to watch, with one sensor clipped to her earlobe and an optical reaction-reading visor snugly positioned on her head. In the corner of the screen, a close-up of Sayoko's eye flickered briefly as the focus sharpened, highlighting a small box drawn around her iris. A second box appeared as the focus tightened around her pupil. The technician tapped something, the eye close-up disappeared, and the videos began to play.

In the first one, a young man and woman argued in the dark corner of a parking lot. The man took a threatening step closer. Sayoko leaned toward the screen, as rapt as when she watched her morning television dramas. The technician reminded Sayoko to find a comfortable position and remain still, keeping her eyes fixed on the screen, but he looked satisfied, both by the readings he was getting and the attentive expression on his subject's face.

The second video showed an international track competition. A female sprinter fell and the woman next to her turned and helped her up, losing seconds in the process as the two limped to last-place finishes. Sayoko watched with a furrowed brow, lips pursed and quivering, suppressing her reaction. At the finish line, the runner who had fallen first dropped to her knees, face buried in her hands, while the other, who had sacrificed her own victory, placed a hand on her opponent's shoulder.

In the third video, a baby was being born.

The sounds of a woman's grunting labor, followed by the squall of new life, filled the room. The robot remained silent. Angelica herself did not care to hear these sounds, which felt too intimate, an inappropriate sharing of what might have been a very happy moment for the woman, or perhaps a tragic one—who was to say? It felt manipulative, in either case, and if Angelica had ever chosen to have a baby, she wouldn't have allowed a camera between her legs, that was for sure.

Though the technician had suggested this was an interactive training that would take over two hours, Angelica didn't see what was being accomplished. Sayoko's face had registered a half-dozen reactions, but she hadn't been asked a single question.

"This is new technology?" Angelica asked.

"The newest," the technician said. "Not available to the public."

"Like—black market?"

"No, no. Just not on the open market yet. A pre-legal prototype, restricted use."

"Pre-legal?"

"Not for the average customer. Due to trade issues. Your employer works for METI, yes?"

"Yes."

"Then he understands."

It's a silly toy after all. A video game. Ten—no, twenty years out of date. The thought didn't comfort her. In this age of robopets, programmable companions and kenkobots, no job, role, or relationship was safe. The automaton wasn't even fully operational yet. There was no saying what level of sophistication it might display. Angelica was holding fast to her limited, hopeful understanding of robotics: none of today's models were truly intelligent. International law and regional agreements defined technology's limits. On top of that, the marketing of social gadgets was all about flash and empty promises. But what did she know? She couldn't even understand how her phone worked.

This new "friend" could cause problems, once Sayoko was attached to it, by functioning poorly. It could cause even more problems by functioning too well, as perhaps Kenta Suzuki himself knew.

"I'm sorry," Angelica said to the technician, finally. "Can I offer you some tea?"

He wasn't a tea drinker, fortunately. That spared her the trouble of brewing the perfect, traditional pot. She always worried that she didn't serve tea correctly, even though they had trained her at the group home: part of a Japanese nurse's duties, alongside the medical ones. They went to the kitchen to drink three-in-one Nescafé instead, leaving Sayoko to her "orientation."

Angelica crossed her legs at the ankles, flexing her toes, feeling the injured knee twinge. The technician picked at his nails with a torn Nescafé packet. The silence was amiable at first, but as the minutes passed, with the recorded sounds from the next room streaming in—seductive whispers, awkward laughter, the disturbing sound of a child's tantrum building—Angelica felt her blood pressure rise.

Her confession broke the silence. "I do my best, but she can be a difficult lady."

The technician looked at her wide-eyed, surprised by her indiscretion.

"Are you going back to the Philippines?"

"Why would you say that?"

He looked down into his cup. "I shouldn't have assumed. I only read that so many guest workers are going home these days."

In the next room, Angelica heard Sayoko softly chuckling during a pause between videos. *Better.* Less creepy, anyway.

Angelica tried not to feel so downright hostile. The technician was only doing his job. She offered her guest a special coconut-flavored cookie from her private stash.

"Thank you," he said. "Delicious." He ate two more.

She tried not to let it bother her. He had no way of knowing that brand of cookie was so hard to find in Japan.

"You probably miss it, I imagine," he said, still chewing.

"Not everything."

"You'll be happier when you go back. Can I give you some advice? I think we are like birds or whales. I think something inside makes us want to return to wherever we were born. It can't be ignored."

She thought of everything he didn't know and didn't care to

know: about the dangerous job Datu had felt forced to take, about Yanna and her now motherless children, about the threats of money lenders, about the problems facing a person who was and would always be worth more off-island.

She put the lid back on the tin as gracefully as she could, before he could take the last cookie.

"After all," the technician continued, "What is money compared to being home? You know the saying: man needs just half a *tatami* mat when awake, one *tatami* mat when asleep."

"And then there is another proverb," she added without looking up. "Even in hell, transactions require money."

"Very good!" he chuckled. "You memorize our sayings very well."

"We have to. They're on the exams. More coffee?"

A minute later, from the living room where Sayoko was still hooked up to the sensors, Angelica heard the sound of a hiccup, which might have been a stifled sob. But her ears could've been playing tricks.

The technician mused, "I hear the beaches in your country are peaceful. I don't know why you'd choose to leave."

"People have their reasons," she said. He just wanted to make himself feel better. Send the foreigners home. Make it sound like it was better for everyone.

"I might enjoy the tropics," he continued, "but I couldn't retire to a beach. The city is for me. I'm like your lady out there. She is a child of Tokyo, many generations."

"How can you tell?"

"Because I'm *Edokko*, I recognize *Edokko*. It's in our blood. We're assertive."

And who, she thought, *is to say I am not also assertive?*

He stood up and excused himself suddenly. "I think she's almost done. One more test."

In his absence, Angelica finished her coffee and thought about this man who wanted to know nothing about her life, who wanted only to imagine her homeland as tropical fruits and white-sand beaches and beautiful women with waxy-white sampaguita flowers tucked behind their ears. All true, and of course she missed it when she allowed herself to, which wasn't often. But that did not mean it was a simple paradise.

She remembered the men who had held the hospital staff hostage in Cebu—her, Yanna, Maricor, Efren—only for a few hours. She thought of how the guerillas, after plundering the wards for medicine and computers, had castigated Yanna for the haggard look of the patients, the empty pharmacy cabinets, the crumbling ceiling tiles in the surgery and the rats in the cafeteria. The guerilla leader had shouted: *This is how you treat our people?*

Angelica had stepped in front of Yanna to shield her, shouting back with equal outrage. *You don't understand how little we have to work with. And who are you to accuse us of bad behavior?* He'd hit Angelica across the face with the side of his pistol. Which was nothing. He could have raped her. He could have shot her.

They had both fled to Japan after that. But Yanna, finding fewer pediatrics jobs than expected, logically, had told Angelica and their roommates that she was going back after the first year.

You can't go back, not while you still owe Bagasao.

Yanna had refused to listen: *my girls . . .*

Angelica had tried to convince her: *your girls will be fine.*

She could still see the look on Yanna's face as they sat around the dining room table so small that even two dinner plates couldn't fit without the rims touching: *I know they'll be fine.* Because they both knew women—many women—who had been forced to leave their children behind, not just for a year or two, like Yanna had, but for ten years, fifteen years. Childhoods come and gone.

So maybe they'll be fine, Yanna had said again, reluctantly. *But I won't be fine. I miss them too much. I love them too much.*

You can't, Angelica had said without missing a beat. *You can't let yourself give in to that. This isn't about how you feel. It's about how the world really works.*

Yanna had looked at Angelica like there was something wrong with her, and maybe there was.

Yanna had said, *What's the point of living if I can't be with the people I love?*

Though Filipinas made that choice all the time. Did that mean they were heartless, or just wise?

Yanna had said, *Are you saying what I want doesn't matter?*

And Angelica had been tongue-tied, wanting to say: *You can't want. You can't need. It's better for everyone that way.* Some people are put on this earth to need and some people are put on this earth to be needed. They—she and Yanna and countless foreign workers like them—were lucky to be needed. It was the only luck they had.

Ignoring everyone's advice, Yanna had gone back. Threats immediately ensued and consequences followed the threats. Bagasao had made his point to everyone in the Filipino community with whom he did business, advancing money for visas, security deposits, flights to employer countries that would take months to be reimbursed, and months of living expenses in places that made you work for free, in "training programs," before you could dream of a real paycheck. Men like Bagasao were the gatekeepers. To travel to any imagined promised land, you passed through their doors first, and you accepted the terms they set. You owed them for their help, sometimes for months, sometimes for years. They were not debts that could be written off.

They called Bagasao "Uncle," even people who weren't related to him, as a term of respect—and perhaps as a form of superstition. An uncle might hurt you, but an uncle, one hoped, would know when the point had been made. The situation with Yanna proved that optimistic idea untrue. Looking back, Angelica realized that Yanna's death marked the moment she shifted from wary faith to increasingly bitter agnosticism—not when she lost most of her family, an event which could be blamed on nature, but when she lost a friend to the cruelty of man. A world in which nature claimed the innocent was bad enough. A world in which people wreaked equal havoc was unacceptable.

Still, Angelica was not an outright atheist, someone who confidently rejected any notion of divinity. Even if there was not a personal, caring, actively present God out there, or if He had chosen to withdraw so far that we now appeared as only sand grains on a beach, hardly worth His attention, perhaps He had still left something behind: some kind of pattern. She continued to wear the little cross around her neck, out of habit and the smallest, smoldering residual hope, but she did not pray. Not after what had happened to her last and closest friend.

When Angelica found out about Yanna's funeral back in Cebu, which she could not attend, she thought the breathless, burning feeling inside her was guilt for having encouraged Yanna to come to Japan. Now, the shock long since faded, she recognized it as anger. She had saved her friend's life once, when the terrorists came to the hospital. She could not keep saving it, again and again. In this unkind world, how many lives could she be expected to save?

She could manage one, maybe, and given Datu's choices and evasions, that kept her occupied enough—and being occupied was good. That was the strange thing. She didn't necessarily resent his dependence upon her. It kept her looking forward instead of back.

Datu, are you sure you're not losing weight? Don't skip your monthly exams. All the blood tests: if they don't do them, request them. It's part of your package. I'm not nagging, I'm only asking. I don't see why we have to do audio. Next week, I want to see you.

Yanna had thought Bagasao would be merciful—that the future itself was merciful. That had been her mistake.

In fact, the future was not merciful. The future was not just. It was only the future, a place that made no promises, a place with neither light nor sound nor smell nor taste, but only a void. Angelica did not know why hell was imagined as a colorful, blazing inferno when it seemed clear to her it was a cave, oppressive in its darkness, sharp everywhere, and wet. Actually, she was wrong. It was not without smell. It did smell: like the very worst nights and days of her childhood. Like being trapped as a storm passes over, taking down villages with it. Like rubble and rain.

Angelica put the vision out of her mind and reached her hand into the tin, only to realize she had unthinkingly eaten a cookie, without tasting it. It was the last one in the package, and she did not know when she'd be able to buy another.

3 Angelica

She woke to a soft click and low hum, like the electric water kettle was starting up several hours too soon. As Angelica kept listening, the hum faded. Perhaps only plumbing in the condo overhead. Time: 2:37 A.M.

The good news: many hours left until her alarm would go off, and a few delicious moments of snuggling down into the warm blankets, thankful it was not yet morning, her mood already so much better than when she'd gone to bed. The simplest things could do that: food, sleep, a shower. Sleep especially. She could not understand why people were tempted to experiment with those new drugs that made an eight-hour recharge unnecessary.

Angelica rolled to one side, reached for her phone, and clicked the icon for Sayoko's room: one eyespot showed black, another showed gauzy grey, a third—entirely disabled—flashed an error message. The fourth, placed too high for Sayoko to mess with, angled toward the middle of her futon, revealed bunched-up sheets. It was hard to see whether her thin body was comfortably resting beneath them, but Angelica squinted her eyes at one dark patch and decided: yes, she's there as always. Best not to disturb Sayoko for no reason.

Angelica was just nodding off when she heard the clicking sound again. The next sound—Sayoko's muffled, agitated voice—brought Angelica back to high alert.

She slid her legs off the futon, pulled on a robe and stood outside Sayoko's door, tapping lightly.

"Can I come in?"

Through the door, Sayoko answered, "No."

Angelica already had her hand on the lever and was about to push down when she registered that Sayoko had refused her. A variation on their standard agreement. Sayoko treasured her privacy and so Angelica would always ask, but it was a courtesy more than a request. Those nights last year when Sayoko had been receiving chemo and there was restlessness and nausea and good reason for late-night vigilance, the response to a knock had always been no answer—if Sayoko was asleep—or muffled acquiescence. Never this.

"Sayoko-san, are you sure? I heard noises. May I come in?"

"No."

"But I need to check. Are you all right?"

"I'm sleeping."

Older people were as vulnerable as children, especially when it came to the internet, where late-night shopping, gambling, or the surrender of sensitive information was commonplace. Until now, Sayoko's only weakness had been her teledramas.

"Are you talking to someone online?" Angelica asked.

There was no reply.

"You'll tell me if you need anything," Angelica said again, waiting in the pitch-black hallway, feet growing cold. "Sayoko-san?" She tried the more generic honorific she had first used until Sayoko had given her permission to use her given name: "*Obaasan*?" Grandmother?

Still nothing.

Back in her own room, Angelica pulled the comforter up to her chin, ready to spring up again at a moment's notice. She waited and listened, doing her job. Sleep was salvation but it was less important for her than for Sayoko, who at her age needed the healing power of good food and rest. No one would ever know all the nights that

Angelica had stayed up listening, checking the eyespot camera feed linked to her phone or softly opening the door, just to be sure.

Angelica did not know how much time had passed, waiting in the dark to hear if Sayoko had finally settled down. Perhaps she'd even drifted off. But then she heard it again—*click*—followed by Sayoko's muffled voice: "I'm here. All right. I'm here."

Angelica checked her phone. Three fifteen in the morning.

Sayoko's voice was audible again, sounding more tired than alarmed: "*Yamete.*" Quit that.

There was a dragging sound, like rubber-tipped chair legs being pulled across the floor. Like Sayoko was using her walker to get to the bathroom or moving a light piece of furniture.

Angelica swung her legs over the edge of her futon and froze, straining to hear. *Two voices.* She pulled on her robe again and slowly opened her door, checking for light in the hall. She stepped lightly, pausing outside Sayoko's room.

"*Ii-yo,*" came the old woman's voice. All right, all right.

The voice that responded was high-pitched, yet it sounded male. Angelica couldn't make out the words.

Sayoko articulated slowly, "I've told you that already."

Angelica knocked. "Sayoko-san? Are you talking to someone?"

Both voices stopped.

"Can I come in?"

No answer except a high thin buzzing alternating with the sound of static.

"Sayoko-san? Are you having trouble? I won't go away this time. You have to answer me."

The second voice started up again: questioning, afraid.

"Sayoko-san?"

No clear answer. Angelica seized it as an excuse. She pushed open the door and saw that Sayoko had dragged a chair closer to her dresser, on top of which sat the assembled top half of the Taiwanese robot, eye slits softly illuminated.

Sayoko called out, "I didn't say you could come in!"

As Angelica advanced, the static sound started up again and the robot's eye slits pulsed brighter. The screen in the robot's torso flickered with images taken earlier that day: one photo after another of Angelica from the front and side and back, distant fuzzy shots and fish-eyed close-ups, all taken surreptitiously.

Angelica hurried forward, instinctively wiping a hand in front of the screen, trying to find the right gesture to turn the thing off, but a wail stopped her in her tracks.

"He's only trying to identify you," Sayoko said. "You're scaring him. Don't!"

When Angelica stopped, Sayoko lowered her voice. "Everything scares him. He can't sleep."

"What does that mean?"

"He's trying to learn, but it's all too fast."

The pulsing static started up again, lower now: a seabird's call mixed with the sound of waves shushing against the beach.

"Turn it off," Angelica demanded. "Turn the whole thing off."

"It's the third time he's woken me. If I don't go to him, it only gets louder." Sayoko tempered her own complaint, negotiating. "He doesn't need much."

Angelica pulled the lapels of her robe around her neck. "What did he want?"

"Only to know where we are."

Angelica suppressed a laugh. "Your wheelchair knows that, Sayoko-san, and it's ten years old."

Did she really not understand GPS and the ubiquity of chips and codes in the simplest objects? A third of the groceries Angelica bought came packaged in trackwrap so that the companies could improve their supply pacing, send reminders when staples ran low, or search for signs of lifestyle changes according to your purchases. One week when Itou-san had been recovering from periodontal surgery, eating lots of soft foods, they'd been assaulted with free baby product samples, all on the assumption that there was a new infant in the house. Itou was displeased. *No trackwrap or any kind of reorder sensor in the house, please. They can be Trojan horses.*

But what was this robot, if not a Trojan horse? What might it bring into their lives, surreptitiously? What would it take away?

"It understands maps," Sayoko said, more annoyed with Angelica for interfering than with the robot for rousing her. "Haven't you ever woken up in a new place and forgotten where you were?"

Angelica considered this. How many times had she swung a leg over her thin futon, expecting her foot to drop several feet, as it had at home, only to feel her heel drop half the distance? How many times had she shuffled toward the bathroom half-asleep, expecting the sound of roosters and the smell of the ocean, before realizing there was only silence and sterile air? And then the realization: Japan. Now. Still.

"Sayoko-san," Angelica said, "Computers don't need to be told things more than once. If they're not broken, they don't forget. And they don't get upset."

Sayoko turned her back to Angelica. "This one does."

"I am responsible for you," Angelica said. "I can't keep going back to my room, knowing—"

"My son's room, you mean."

"Yes, of course. Your son's room." But Angelica felt the sting of Sayoko's correction.

"You are lucky to have it."

"I know that."

"Do you?"

The robot had quieted now, only a sizzle of static on its screen. Angelica felt like the anxious crackle had moved into her stomach. Sayoko had never played these kinds of power games with her before.

Angelica bowed her head. "It would be better if I removed your new gift from the room, just for now."

"You think I can't manage a confused machine on my own?"

When Angelica didn't reply, Sayoko said, "I don't need help. And you will take nothing away from me. Leave us alone please, and close the door behind you."

That "us" bothered Angelica even more than Sayoko's frigid tone.

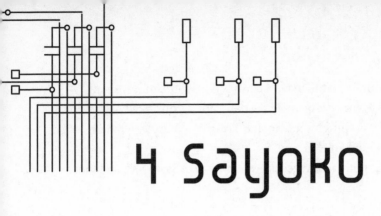

4 Sayoko

Sayoko thought of locking the door, to make intrusion less likely, but then she hesitated, remembering the time she'd fallen getting out of the *furo*, long before Anji had ever come to work for them, and how her son had not been able to get into the bathroom quickly and had been angry at her. She hadn't even blocked the door intentionally. Her walker was simply in the way.

No more hot baths.

That's ridiculous, she'd said to him. *My son doesn't get to tell me when I can bathe.*

But he did, and in the months that followed, everyone did. They told her when she could bathe, when she could eat or sleep, what medicine to ingest.

A social worker had come to talk to her about the difficulties of this "new life stage." The worker was half Sayoko's age, and Korean, born around the time Sayoko's husband had passed away—hard to believe. But it wasn't just the culture or age difference that made communication impossible.

It is normal to feel some dissatisfaction, the social worker had said. (They liked to use that word, instead of depression.)

Your autonomy may be reduced, the social worker had said.

Sayoko had wanted to laugh. *Autonomy?* Such fancy words they used nowadays.

In the village where she'd grown up, ignored for most of her childhood, in the camp where she'd barely survived, in the freezing flat where she'd just managed to make ends meet, sewing other women's clothes for fifteen years following the war, no one had ever used such a word. You hoped, perhaps, for a little rice, a little fish. You did not expect *autonomy*.

The robot had started to make noise again, but then the whine eased. Had she been thinking aloud? She did that, sometimes, especially when she was irritated. She had a *right* to be irritated.

"You did not expect autonomy," Sayoko repeated. "You did not expect *anything*."

It liked to hear her voice. It even sensed her motion. As long as she sat at arm's length and said a phrase here and there, and rocked back and forth or swayed, it let out occasional notes of distress or static but it did not explode into full volume.

Sayoko tested the importance of her physical presence by scooting back her chair, but just as she suspected, the robot wouldn't tolerate the change. It whined again, pitch rising. She scooted forward, even closer now, remembering those days a half-century ago when you had to hold the radio or TV antenna and keep moving it this way and that, trying to find the best position.

But this was different, of course. Because the radio did not want to hear your voice, did not actually care that you were in the room. This machine did.

"Frankly, no one expected much in those days," she said aloud. It liked that. It quieted down to a low hum.

"And people expected the least of this particular woman without any family. Without any impressive connections, without any documents. Without any talents for that matter. This Sayoko."

She thought back to all the times her first husband had instructed her on how to introduce herself: the short, self-effacing speech explaining her background and education (plenty of facts changed but no matter), socially acceptable hobbies, and so on. He had explained to her the importance of coming across well, but not too well, knowing that she hadn't been raised properly enough to master such things on instinct alone.

When she spoke of herself in the third person now, it was not for the sake of self-effacement or etiquette. She did not need to be cautious or coy with a machine, and the most honest way she could speak about herself as a younger woman was by thinking of herself as an altogether different person—or no, as several different persons, and none of them the old Tokyo lady of today.

She had fallen into silent musing again, which it didn't like. The soft whine started up again.

"Stop that, or I won't tell you anything more."

Before Anji's intrusion, it had managed to say one recognizable word—*where*—or that's what she had told Anji-chan, exaggerating perhaps the robot's intelligence. Maybe it didn't understand maps or didn't need to know its present location. Maybe it didn't understand anything.

It *was* upset, though, and even a door banging in the wind needs to be closed.

The robot's first word had been only half-intelligible, but the next one was clearer. No question.

It came out first as a musical drone, three notes not quite tuned to each other, until each corrected to a slightly different pitch and suddenly they all became one sound which burst out, in one controlled effort, like a puff of smoke, into a word:

"*Anata.*" You.

She smiled.

"Yes, me. Sayoko. Sayoko-*san.*" It didn't hurt to teach it some manners.

"You."

"That's right. Is that all you can say?"

It mumbled something that sounded like "why," but perhaps in her sleepy state she was thinking too much of babies, and how it had felt to stay up with a sick toddler, or an older child at the edge of her futon, hours after her husband had left for work, trying to rouse her when she only wanted to sleep, those middle years when sleep was her trusted escape, a warm burrow equally protected from thoughts of the past and thoughts of the future. She'd been a bad mother. Her own husband and mother-in-law had not minded telling her so.

Why? Always a hand on the comforter, trying to pull her up and out, trying to ask her to make lunch, or come to the window, or put on boots for a walk to the park. *When? Why? Why not?*

Which she did not answer then. Which she would not answer now, even if she understood what the machine was asking. She fell silent, it fell silent, and the satisfied hum began to gather tension at its edges, rising again in pitch.

"All right," she said firmly. "That's enough."

She had to keep talking. But what else to say?

"Well, this Sayoko did have a few talents. Sewing, a little. Weaving, she'd been a failure at that, but this was not a place where people valued weaving."

Not much of a story. She'd always been a listener more than a talker, and when she talked it was to imitate, but that was not without its purpose. "Mimicry. That was her talent, if she had one."

She had not spoken enough to her own son, Ryo, when he was small. She had not read him books. She had not known suitable children's stories.

Unsuitable ones, perhaps.

It came back to her now, the time she'd told the story to the lonely old Chinese shopkeeper, what was his name? Lee Kuan Chien. Of course.

How he'd demanded it, and how he'd gotten mad at the end, surprising her. His wrath had made her want to run, to leave his cold dark shop and follow the steep road back up to the village. But he had not cowed her, because she'd been invincible then. A different person.

"Listen," she said to the robot now, and it eased down into a satisfied hum again, deeper and more even, like a purring cat. "I will tell you a longer story, and then we'll both get some sleep."

Three people were born out of a cracked stone.

One crawled back inside, but the other two, a boy and a girl, remained.

For some reason, the boy was shy with the girl. She left and found a dark stone with which to blacken her face.

When she reappeared to him, looking different, he took her in, and together, with love, they made many children and peopled the world.

She stopped. Was that all there was? Was that all there had *ever* been?

There was good reason why Sayoko could never have told the story to her son, even if she'd been a warmer mother. It was not because of the allusion to sex, of "peopling the world," but rather because it was a barbarian tale, and if someone asked where she'd heard it, she would not have felt safe to say.

"It's not a long story," she continued now, to keep the robot satisfied. "I suppose Lee Kuan Chien interrupted a number of times, and that's why it felt so much longer. And then, as I think I explained, he was so angry with me."

The robot said, "Angry."

"Yes." And because the robot had said it quietly, and patiently, she felt the need to explain more. Perhaps this story was not the story. Perhaps she *did* have a longer story.

It began this way.

"First, in a place very far from here, there was a girl named Laqi."

"*Anata*," the robot said. You.

So it *was* clever. It noted patterns, at least, and what was life, except a series of patterns, some hopeful, some discouraging?

But she was not going to say "I." She would never be so

self-serving, and besides, this Laqi was even less her than the young woman called Sayoko had been. Laqi belonged to another place and another time altogether.

"We will call her Laqi, and that is not me today, and it was not even the name she was born with, but it was what Daisuke Oshima called her, and so she used that name for a while because she loved Daisuke, until the name—and the man—were taken away."

She remembered Daisuke as he had first appeared in the school-yard, standing next to the headmaster: a tall elegant man in a white suit, his eyes hidden behind wire-rimmed glasses, his smile gentle.

But she could not think of that lost moment, now. She could not speak of it. Maybe later. Maybe never.

"The only thing you need to understand," she said to the robot, "is that Daisuke and Laqi spoke different languages, and this fact both brought them together and kept them apart. If not for their differences, they wouldn't have discovered their similarities."

It was too much to explain, now or perhaps ever. She continued, "Anyway, the name Laqi meant only *child*."

"Laqi-san," the robot said.

"Not *san*. Not in this situation."

"Laqi."

"That's better."

In her earliest years, she walked with other children to Lee Kuan Chien's lonely shop next to the handcart terminus far down the village road, hoping to catch a glimpse of the long thin braid that trailed down his back. Laqi had seen it only once and never again. Rumor was that Lee Kuan Chien had finally cut the braid off. The headmaster at school had explained that over in mainland China, the young emperor had cut off his own queue, freeing his most tenacious and tradition-bound followers to do the same.

They'd asked the headmaster, too, about the wife who suppos-edly lived inside the tiny Chinese shop, unable to walk more than a few steps, hobbling on traditional bound feet. The children made up stories about her, a crippled woman-child who was never seen. But the headmaster corrected them: old Lee Kuan Chien no longer had a wife. Anyway, their teacher reassured them, all of those old vestiges of China—the queues, the foot-binding and the opium trade—were banned now by the Japanese, everywhere the empire had conquered, including here. Lee Kuan Chien might still sell goods to Japanese officials, and food staples and random baubles to the local villagers, but the old ways he'd brought to the mountains would no longer be tolerated.

Lee Kuan Chien's shop was dark, without a door—like all the village huts save the Japanese police substation building—but guarded by a small, staked dog who growled at anyone who passed. Laqi did not hear the dog now. Had he gone the way of Lee Kuan Chien's wife? Silence clung to the hut like fog in the bamboo forest, blown in by circumstance, reluctant to leave.

It occurred to Laqi, as she stood outside his little building next to the narrow handcart railway only policemen and government officials used, that Lee Kuan Chien might no longer be living. She hadn't personally set eyes on him for many moons.

After two failed attempts in which she'd walked all the way to his house without spotting him, she got up her nerve. One afternoon, after the smell of frying food convinced her there was life inside, she called into the shadows. She was about to turn away when she heard a wet cough and the sound of padding slippers. Without a word, the shopkeeper settled himself onto a stool in the barely lit entryway, the dark store behind him, his fat arm rested atop a table next to baskets of charcoal-black ink sticks, buttons and spools of thread, incense, hair combs, knife blades, and round bars of soap wrapped in colorful paper.

"What do you want?" Lee Kuan Chien asked.

She told him: she wanted more words. Translation help. For reasons that Lee Kuan Chien already understood.

"The new visitor. The man who draws and studies the trees. Daisuke Oshima."

"Yes."

"You wish to speak with him."

"I am already speaking with him. Headmaster asked me to."

She swallowed, realizing she'd just let a secret slip.

"Oh, did he?" Lee Kuan Chien laughed, but he understood. The Tayal headmaster, who was supposed to be fluent in Japanese, especially given that his job was to *teach* Japanese to the local aboriginal children, was not as capable as he pretended.

"And you can understand our visitor."

"Not always."

"You never will. He comes from a faraway place. He sees with different eyes."

"Aren't your eyes different as well?" she dared to ask. "Yet I'm speaking with you."

He punished her insolence with a silent stare, but he did not chase her out of the shop.

"Can you do it?" she persisted. She had the unfamiliar words and questions ready, as many as she could hold in her mind, and they were heavy as ripe gourds, fragile as eggs.

Lee Kuan Chien had made his living traveling across China, Siam, the Malay Peninsula, and even farther, and it was said he could speak more tongues than any Japanese empire official. But Lee Kuan Chien was a man of trade. He gave nothing freely.

Laqi brought out a long thin strip of woven cloth, patterned with dark red diamonds, suitable for attaching to a basket as a head strap.

"That?" he laughed. "It looks like it was chewed by a pig."

The weave was loose, the diamond pattern uneven. Grandmother would have agreed with Lee Kuan Chien's appraisal of Laqi's terrible weaving skills. It was true.

"Come back tomorrow. Bring me something I can sell or eat."

"Sweet potatoes?" she asked.

On the next visit, she traded fire-shriveled potatoes for words. On the third visit, she traded millet wine stolen from her grand-mother's hut. But it was sour.

Screwing up his face at the bad wine, Lee Kuan Chien said, "My wife lived with me here until she died, eight years ago. She made me promise when we married that she would be buried back home with her parents, in Fujian Province. I could not keep that promise. We had no children. I bought a cage and two songbirds, but instead of being happy to hear them sing, I only felt more lonely, reminded that they had each other, while I had no one."

"What did you do with the songbirds?" Laqi asked, peeking into the darkest corners of the narrow, silent shop.

He cleared his throat. "Come sit closer to me, child."

Laqi took one step forward.

"Closer."

She remembered. "And what did you do with that dog?"

"Dogs are trouble. They bite." He smiled. "I would never bite."

She took another step, only half as big as the first.

"What do you think happens to a person alone, who has no one to talk to, no one to touch?"

She didn't like his tone.

"His voice grows hoarse," Lee Kuan Chien answered his own question. "His hair falls out. His skin becomes pale, practically transparent."

That's just old age, Laqi thought. Anyone knows that.

"He becomes like a ghost, the worst kind," the merchant con-tinued. "Confused. Bitter. Unable to find his way, or to affect the past, present, or future. Awaiting the touch of—I don't know. A woman. Maybe a girl. To warm his skin, even just one spot, to stop the cold air from passing through."

"I don't understand you."

"Fine," he said. "I'll speak more clearly."

With one fat hand he dragged an empty stool closer. He tapped its seat and reached out his fingers toward Laqi, fluttering them, impelling her forward. Laqi did not move.

"A shopkeeper's life is easier than a savage's, even if that savage knows how to tend crops. Some years are too wet, some too dry, but people will always want what I have to sell."

She stayed as still as possible, a flying squirrel well-hidden.

"Your face is unmarked. Less desirable for your people, but more desirable for mine." And then, as if to rub salt in the wound: "You know that where the Japanese are many, they have allowed no tattoos at all for many years?"

She had heard it said, but she didn't believe it. Without facial tattoos, women could not be beautiful. Without them, men and women could not cross the spirit bridge to the afterlife.

"Fine," he said, giving in and pulling his chubby forearms back to his chest. "Your wine is no good. And you have no pity for an old man. You can't even understand when an offer is on the table. Wait until you're older, and still unmarked, and you realize the danger of having no man to protect you. For now, tell me a story."

This is when Laqi the girl told him the simple short tale that Sayoko would one day try telling the robot: about the cracked stone, the boy and the girl, the shyness of the boy, the girl's tactic of blackening her face, the love they shared ever after.

"Why did she need to blacken her face to make him love her?" Lee Kuan Chien had asked Laqi, that third time she visited him.

"I don't know." She had always accepted the story as it was told, and knew it was recited after tattooing ceremonies, when a girl took pride in her changed appearance, the dark lines that meant adulthood.

"Women are devious," he said, supplying his own answer. "Look at you. A girl comes to me for help, to understand a foreigner's words. But why must she understand him? What does she hope to obtain?"

Laqi looked down at her feet, wanting to be out in the winter sun, running for home.

"Tell me another story," he demanded. "A better one."

She thought a moment.

"It's too common."

"Let's hear it."

She sighed and began again. "This is the story of the world back when it had two suns, and everything was too hot and too bright. The earth was drying out."

"And then what?"

"Nothing grew. And at night, it was so light that no one could sleep. Some Tayal warriors went on a great journey to the end of the world. Along the way, magical millet kept them from being hungry, and they also planted crops, so that when they returned, they would have even more food."

"Huh," he said doubtfully. "I haven't witnessed much planning for the future among Tayal warriors, but so be it. Go on."

"When they arrived at the suns, an archer took aim and shot one. It withered and died, turning into a half-illuminated corpse."

"And?"

"And that corpse is—can you guess?"

"Of course I can."

He made no further reply. As the silence deepened, she became aware he was not satisfied.

Lee Kuan Chien finally asked, "Why do you tell me this story?"

Laqi thought of the bright burning sun and its dead partner, today's cold, pock-marked moon. She thought of the warriors' brave journey and their happy return. She could not understand the source of Lee Kuan Chien's displeasure.

"The world has no use for two bright suns," he finally said, waiting for her to grasp his implication. "That is the hidden moral of your tale."

"Moral?"

"And which sun kept living? The oldest to the northwest? Or the newer one, to the northeast?"

"I don't understand."

"Go tell your Japanese scientist that you are eager to lie down with him. Go tell him that you will bow down to his nation, the brightest sun."

"I didn't intend to offend—"

"You did not intend . . ." he mumbled, unmoved.

"Why are you angry?" she asked. "If we are supposed to bow down, why are you angry that I would lie down? What do you think the Japanese want from us, anyway?"

"What does he want of your island? What the Japanese always want—natural resources, workers to harvest those resources. What does he want of your village? Maybe only knowledge about animals, plants, and diseases. Things to fulfill his curiosity, but also information to bring back to his rulers to help them plan their camphor operations."

She thought of Daisuke's notebooks. Lee Kuan Chien was not without insight.

"What does he want from *you*?" he asked. "Well, that's a different question."

She was not dissuaded. "If that's a different question, then what is your answer?"

"You are the most stubborn and talkative child I've ever known. Don't I frighten you? Doesn't *he* frighten you?"

"Yes," she said. But she could not explain why she preferred a racing heart to a quiet one. Or how Daisuke in particular made her heart race—as Lee Kuan Chien certainly did not—in a way that made the sun feel warmer, her skin more sensitive to the slightest changes in the air.

Laqi asked, and so he told her, what Grandmother had not explained, what she had started to guess on her own from clues here and there: the sounds of grunts coming from other huts, the way men stared, the comments of other girls at school. Yes, men and women did that. Yes, men also pursued women who were not their wives—even girls who were not careful—*in order* to do that.

Lee Kuan Chien's explanations were meant to warn or to taunt, but they had a perverse effect. They removed her innocence and left her heart wondering: is that so terrible? Anyway, who was to say for sure what Daisuke wanted? Who was to say what *she* might in fact want?

No one assumed she had her own opinions. No one assumed she had her own desires.

Sayoko's heart was beating too fast when she finished the story, and her mouth was dry.

To tell the whole tale had been wrong. To utter even that one last word—*desires*—was itself a transgression. She had felt no desire—had not allowed herself any desire—for longer than most everyone she knew had been alive on this earth. To talk of this young girl—her, and not her—even to think of this young girl as having had desire had been a problem then and was preposterous now. She was old.

And worse yet, she had been old even when she was not old, even when her body had still been young, thin, flexible, unlined, smooth-skinned. They had made her prematurely old. They had made her ugly, inside and out. And now, in a different place, they wanted to celebrate her oldness, supposedly. It made her want to spit.

She felt fear: the fear of one who has put a toe in the river only to be swept far downstream. She had not meant to say so much. But more amazing still was that she had not known she *could remember* so much.

She had started out merely meaning to calm the robot, to provide it with soothing sounds and perhaps—it did seem to learn quickly—expose it to vocabulary. They had that in common, she realized now. Her younger self had been eager for new foreign words, willing to stand under them like a waterfall, unable to absorb more than a few at a time, but unafraid of the torrent's power and sheer, overwhelming beauty.

She had meant to distract the robot for just a few minutes, but she did not realize how far her tale would take her. It was and was not like falling into a river. Perhaps it was more like sitting down to eat after fasting for too long. You started out without an appetite, and rediscovered it, hunger awakening. Or perhaps it was like crossing a decaying swing bridge: you can't just look down quaking with fear. You step once, and keep stepping.

She had never realized how words said aloud had so much more power than words merely thought; that they not only recruited other words, but awoke thoughts and called down images from the sky itself, an entire army, dangerous in its power. But she should have realized. Her love of words had been her gateway into womanhood, when every other form of maturity and happiness had been withheld from her.

Whatever had made the memories come back, she felt grateful. Her mind felt sharper than it had in years.

She had never told this story to anyone, least of all her own son. With luck, the robot had not heard most of it either. Perhaps it was in sleep mode now.

"*Anata*," it said again—not asleep at all, only waiting. "You . . ."

"Go to sleep now."

"You are not Japanese."

"It was only a story," she said quickly. "You misunderstand."

"Elsewhere."

The way the robot said the word made it sound like a curse.

"Stop. You must stop."

Surprisingly, it did.

Her heart was now beating so fast that her wrist monitor squawked once and she squeezed her eyes shut, making an effort to breathe slowly, aware that if the monitor erupted again Anji-chan would receive the alert and come bursting in. She focused on her breathing, on lowering her pulse. It did not even occur to her for several minutes how clearly the robot had spoken and in how natural a voice, the static fully tamed, the pitch corrected and the inflections refined. It was not possible to evaluate how many words it had already managed to learn and how much it understood.

"You can't tell anyone," Sayoko whispered to the robot. "And anyway, it's more complicated. I *am* Japanese, but only half."

There it was: another confession, buried since the last century, something else she had pledged never to say. The truth so easily uprooted by a mere machine.

Even so, Sayoko did not immediately regret the risk she had taken.

5 Angelica

Angelica had gone back to her bed, brooding over Sayoko's behavior, still hearing the whispers through the walls and worrying about Itou's return from his business trip. Would he judge her for not acting more decisively?

Even after a year and a half, she knew little about the man who paid her salary. When he was at home for a few days or a week, Itou-san was quiet, respectful of his mother, concerned about her dignity, and unusually fair as an employer. Angelica had watched him drink himself into a quiet, heavy-lidded state, but she'd never seen him drunk. She'd seen him look pensive or disappointed, but never angry. His hobbies were similarly mild.

As the hour passed from 4:00 to 5:00 A.M., with dawn not far away, Angelica stared up at the ceiling of her bedroom—*my son's room, you mean*, Sayoko had reminded her—to the glass-fronted, illuminated display cabinets that doubled as gentle night-lights. In them, Itou stored a collection of objects, some of them antique, no doubt many of them valuable. And in a few deeper cupboards—she had not meant to look, she was only searching for fresh sheets— a few even stranger items. She thought of the metal crab thing that had given her a fright, until she'd realized what it was: an old clockwork antique, spiderlike and creepy. Not the first time that Japanese aesthetics had mystified her. She would have preferred for the clockwork crab to be kept in another room, but she wasn't bold enough to move it or even mention it. It would be ludicrous to be so sensitive and picky when the room itself was perfect in every other way.

The items on clear and prominent display were more pleasant to look at. From her futon, Angelica could see Itou's musical instruments: a half-size violin from his childhood, a two-stringed Chinese *erhu* from his many trade visits to Beijing, and his favorite, the only one he still yearned to play, an American-made clarinet.

Itou-san had asked when he first showed her the study-turned-guest room, directly after offering her the live-in position: "Have you heard of Artie Shaw?"

"Pardon me?"

"Charlie Parker?"

"I'm sorry."

"That's too bad. But this room suits you?"

"It's good, yes. Thank you."

"I apologize for keeping things stored here. I should sell the instruments someday. They aren't played. It isn't fair to them. But this will do?"

"Yes, please. It's fine."

He had paused a minute, smiling shyly without meeting her gaze. "Do you know what 'in-puro-bi-ze-shon' means?"

She shook her head, embarrassed. "*Inpuro* . . . ?"

"In-puro-bi-ze-shon."

"I'm sorry. I am still improving my Japanese."

Could she lose this job, for failing to understand him? Would he take it all back: the fair pay, the soft bed?

"It's an English word. It is about solutions and surprises. It's about flexibility."

"I can work whatever hours you require," she hurried to say. "And I don't need all this room, if there is another place to sleep . . ."

"No, no," he laughed. "I'm not saying you should be more

flexible. I was trying to explain about my favorite kind of music. Never mind. I'll play a Charlie Parker recording for you someday."

"Thank you."

But she hadn't been interested in this Park person, whom she assumed was probably Korean, given his last name. She was more interested in this job, which seemed easy enough, and this *room*, free and large and beautiful, which was more than she'd expected. She had said it was fine, when in fact it was perfect. Foreign workers typically shared rooms or, if privately employed, might be asked to sleep on a kitchen floor.

That first conversation with Itou-san seemed long ago, now. And yes, she had begun to take it for granted: her own bed, the pretty cabinets, soft lighting, a door that closed.

You are lucky to have it.

I know that.

Do you?

But why had Sayoko said that? Why did her increasing lucidity and assertiveness have to create a barrier between them? Only because of this thing. This unwelcome delivery. Sayoko couldn't have known the effect of telling a woman who had spent part of her childhood without a real roof, without a family home, without privacy, that she could not call a bedroom her own, even temporarily.

Angelica had let the technician rile her up. She'd made a comment that was indiscreet, saying that Sayoko was a difficult lady. Perhaps she was, but Sayoko was *her* lady, and she wanted her to be safe and well. She took pride in how far they'd come together in these last eighteen months, in ways that an occasional visitor might never understand. Caring was the job. You could fake it, but not every day, and certainly not every night. Angelica knew people who had burned out, only able to summon that feeling for their own parents or children. Maybe the fact that Angelica had no one other than Datu made it easier to focus on her clients. Or maybe it was just in her nature.

Long before the typhoon, when Angelica still had a large family, she was the one who woke early each morning to tend to her grandmother. It was her job as a six-year-old girl to sit on the front porch with Lola, and with a bucket of soapy water, clean Lola's aching feet, push thumbs into stiff high arches, work ointment into horny callouses, rub blue vein-threaded calves, notice a new sore or bruise and treat it. "You have the touch," her Lola would say.

Angelica's aunties would be up making breakfast at the other end of the house. Brooms scraped against hard-packed dirt, the smell of frying food and the murmur of conversation rising in volume as the dawn birdsong quieted. Best light of the day, best air: warm but not heavy, sweet but not yet overripe.

The bees came to visit the red, trumpet-shaped flowers that twined around the porch rails, and Angelica and her Lola watched them crawl deep inside, disappear, back out, circle again.

"They like to be busy," Lola would say. "Work makes even simple creatures happy."

As Angelica grew, she took on more tasks, spooning food into Lola's mouth when her hands shook too much to eat independently, rolling her over to treat her bedsores, sponging her from top to bottom.

"You are my Angel," Lola would say. Angelica lived for that comment. Perhaps it meant too much to her.

We are defined by our weaknesses as much as by our strengths, Angelica reflected, remembering the girl she had been. We are made to serve or be served, to want or be wanted, to stay home or wander far—and who knows why, except that the universe needs it so.

One in ten Filipinos worked abroad, and the nine in ten who stayed home depended upon them for remittances and those strategically packed, import-free *balikbayan* care boxes of foreign-made foods and gifts. Being willing to move to anywhere with better opportunities was a part of the national character, and Angelica had noted, with special pride, that last year's Mars Mission had a

Filipino on board as well. Sensibly enough. (He'd better send some special things back to his family, if he knew what was good for him.)

Even in a world without a caring God, there might still be divine design: some reason why so many Filipinos lived abroad, why some women were tender to their children and others were cold, why some men were more selfless than others, or more willing to take risks, or more duplicitous, or more afraid. Maybe there was a reason. Maybe there was a reason *and* a corruption of that reason: a useful predisposition twisted into something beyond what the universe originally desired. People, like the weather, were unpredictable. She did not know if that somehow served a purpose as well, or if it defeated one's destined purpose.

In any case: you made the most of what you were and what you had.

The first Japanese man Angelica had ever met, a recruiter visiting Manila and Cebu, had said everyone knew that Filipino nurses were naturally more empathetic. Angelica was surprised: *Did people abroad really say that?*

She was glad to have an advantage for the first time in her life: to be part of a group held in some special kind of esteem, a sort of reverse prejudice, however simplistic or overstated. Even her reluctance to keep up with the latest technological toys that had come to Kuala Lumpur and Seoul but not Cebu had become an asset. Some international nurses had retinal implants, but their glazed-over expressions and inability to resist entertaining distractions in the presence of their clients was no benefit. Some nurses refused to do even the lightest lifting without the help of robotic suits, but Angelica did not like the slip-on exoskeletal jackets, their look or their feel or the delays from using tech to do the kind of job she'd managed just fine, even as a nine-year-old girl, rolling her grandmother over in bed. In this way, being a little backcountry conferred a special status. Angelica looked like a nurse from the previous century. Her clients appreciated that.

Of course, the recruiter had assured her, there would always be jobs for women like her in Japan, especially with the aging of their own population: an imbalance more extreme than in any other nation, and the subject of deep national anxiety. *But will there ever be too many foreign nurses?* No, the recruiter had assured her. Supply can't meet demand. Job security. Respect. Good salaries, especially since work visas are so limited.

But why are the visas limited?

Because they need you, but they don't want to need you. A rare moment of recruiter honesty. *Certain nations are like toddlers or very old people. They say "I do it myself." And "Go away" when they are most vulnerable. Never take offense. It is another type of pain you are treating: the pain of lost independence.*

She hadn't been allowed to leave the Philippines for three years after graduating from nursing school, in accordance with the pledge she had voluntarily signed—the government's latest effort to staunch the flow of expertise from a country whose medical system was collapsing. Out of a conflicted sense of national loyalty, she had chosen to stay even longer than required—fourteen years. As long as she could bear. The guerillas taking the hospital staff hostage had been the last straw.

That made her suddenly ready to go and face the next challenge: debts mounting as she shared an apartment with Yanna and five other healthcare workers, earning nothing at first and then still not enough to cover her bills. The good times, wandering Tokyo like tourists, marveling at the skyscrapers bathed in constant light and animated motion, and the toilets with buttons that brought forth waterfall sounds; the less cheery moments, like submitting to virus puff tests in the subway and long weekends of ramen noodles and exam study; the bad times, like saying goodbye to Yanna as she boarded the train for Narita Airport.

Then Angelica saw the listing for the job, working for Itou-san, taking care of his mother.

My mother does not have much time left. Wrong, as it turned out.

But if you are willing to take a job that might be short or long, no telling. Of course.

You have heard of the preference of Japanese for harmony? Yes, it had been drilled into them in nursing training, preparing them for future jobs all around the world: that while Americans and Europeans preferred personal control, and even needed it to achieve well-being and good health, the Japanese prioritized lack of relational strain, harmony, interdependence. *Well, my mother must not be typical Japanese then. She does not always choose harmony.*

Itou had laughed, then. Angelica had found his statement charming, even encouraging. A little spunk could make a person interesting. She'd never fully believed in the myth of perfect harmony, anyway.

Itou had offered his final warning. *She is strong-willed.*

More correct than ever. Strong-willed enough to refuse sleep or supervision.

Usually by the time Angelica was ready to start the day, Sayoko was already awake. This morning, when Angelica entered her room with a cup of green tea, Sayoko was motionless, white hair fanned out across her pillow in the shape of a soft-edged ginkgo leaf. Her head was turned, her mouth open. Angelica leaned forward to make sure she was breathing. Indeed. It smelled like she had done a poor job brushing the night before. Too distracted by the strange new present that had taken up so much of her time.

She took Sayoko's hand, noting the feel of the skin, and when Sayoko's eyes flickered open, she rubbed her forearm briskly.

"Time to get up," Angelica called.

"Not yet," Sayoko mumbled.

"Let's get you to the toilet. Breakfast is waiting." Aside from in her chemo days, Sayoko usually had a big appetite in the morning and expected her favorites: grilled fish, broth, and rice porridge, sometimes with a sour plum on top, if Angelica was trying to coax her into a good mood.

At the nursing home where Angelica had first worked in Tokyo, everyone got the same breakfast, lunch, and dinner. And yes, the nurses often referred to the patients by room number, especially during shift changes: *25B isn't responding to the bladder medication. Her stink follows me home.*

Angelica had liked the no-nonsense collegiality, a tonic for the long hours, but not what it did to the patients, reducing them to items to be managed. Long after vitals were taken automatically, and even at the risk of getting a reprimand for inefficiency, Angelica still liked to sit bedside, two fingers placed across the patient's wrist: *Eighty-one this morning.* A touch on the shoulder. *Your color looks good.* Leaning close, allowing soft sounds and smells—raspy breathing, a sugary aroma—to confirm what was already in the digital charts.

One time, a young new trainee from Singapore saw the stethoscope around Angelica's neck and said, "What's that?"

"It's an old device you set on their backs, to listen to them breathe."

"Why?"

"Because it's simple and it works. Besides, they won't usually ask, but they like their backs touched. *Breathe. Good. Again.* Sometimes that helps more than medication."

The young trainee had laughed, assuming Angelica was pulling her leg.

Remembering that conversation, Angelica put Sayoko's cold hands between her own now, heating them up. Even warm, they still trembled. "Ready for the walker?"

Sayoko shook her head. She was weak this morning. Tired.

"We'll dress after breakfast, maybe?"

"After," Sayoko mumbled.

"All right. Wheelchair, then. And something to eat first. I don't mind if your broth gets cold, but you have to take your pills. Did someone stay up too late last night?"

"He needed company." Sayoko frowned. "You can't just let them wail."

"It's your device. It should listen to you. Tell it not to wail."

Sayoko had been staring into space, but now she returned Angelica's gaze with surprising intensity. "They told me to let him cry, but it always hurt to hear it."

"The technician told you?"

"No, the neighbors. And my husband. They said it was all right for me to sleep. He'd stop crying."

"Ah, you mean Itou-san. Long ago." The image of her elegant, self-disciplined employer as an inconsolable infant made Angelica smile.

Holding Sayoko by one elbow as she guided her into an upright position at the edge of the futon, Angelica said, "And he did stop crying, finally, didn't he? You must be thinking about your son, when he was small. I bet you were a wonderful mother."

"I was a very bad mother."

Angelica paused, the comment hanging between them, waiting to see if Sayoko would say any more, or change the subject, or toss her head as she sometimes did, as if to say, *Never mind all that.* But this wasn't such a moment.

Angelica chose her next words carefully. "I'm sure Itou-san would disagree. Look how much he cares about your comfort and health."

"No, he knows the truth. He doesn't know why I couldn't bear to touch him, but he knows his childhood was lacking." Sayoko's eyes were misting over. She thrust out her chin with defiance, lower lip quivering.

"Sayoko-san—" Angelica started to say. But Sayoko didn't want trite consolation.

"They said it was all right not to go to him, but then when I didn't, they took him away."

"Who did?"

"My mother-in-law first. She said I was too tired. But really, she didn't trust me. She thought I was ruined for good, and not because of the baby. She never wanted her son to marry me. She suspected things."

Angelica had moved to a kneeling position in front of Sayoko, tugging slipper socks onto the old lady's chronically icy feet. Now she looked up, waiting. Sayoko's eyes remained averted, her chin tucked down into her chest.

Angelica resisted prying. It was not her job to pry. At the group home, she had never been one of those nurses who tried to be a sassy jokester or a gossip-craving confidant. When she'd felt close to a patient, it was often for unnameable reasons. When she'd felt a moment of connection, it was rarely through chatter, more often through touch. It was what she herself felt was changing too rapidly in this world: the loss of human touch, cold technology in its place.

Angelica was touching Sayoko again now, massaging her lower legs a moment to stir the circulation. She finished off with a light tap on the ankles, as if to say: *Ready for breakfast?*

But Sayoko was still deep in thought. She was in no hurry to be hoisted into her wheelchair. "After they took him, I finally got myself up and dressed. I went to my mother-in-law's house. And she had already found another woman to watch my son."

"And this woman raised him?"

"No, he came home again later. Maybe two months later, by which time my milk was long dried up. It had been decided: I wasn't to be trusted. I agreed with them. Fine, I said, let me be useless. I felt sorry for myself. Why not? But it wasn't pretty."

Angelica didn't know whether to keep encouraging the story or distract Sayoko from it. She didn't even know whether the memory was reliable. Perhaps Angelica didn't want it to be true; she wasn't a mental health expert, only a nurse. This new and stronger yet more self-critical Sayoko—more talkative, less hobbled by dementia but more burdened by memories—threw off Angelica's routines. Before, Sayoko had made less sense. Now there was no telling.

Sayoko took a deep breath, shoulders trembling as she slowly exhaled through pursed lips. "I've thought about it. I believe that after two or three weeks, I would have felt better. I think he needed to cry and I needed to hear it. It certainly made my milk come down, and that's the point, isn't it? I wouldn't have ignored him forever, just as I couldn't have ignored the robot last night. But my husband and his mother didn't trust me. They didn't give my son a chance to love me, and I didn't have a chance to love him."

Angelica didn't know what to say, or what to think. She didn't want Sayoko to be sad. She wasn't sure that revisiting these memories was helpful. She knew that Sayoko would feel better after a warm breakfast, a cup of hot tea, another massage if needed, the distraction of a television program. Those were the things Angelica could offer, easily. But Sayoko seemed to want something more—something Angelica wasn't sure she could give.

"I was supposed to know everything all at once," Sayoko continued. "But that isn't always how it happens. Do you see how the robot learns, a step at a time?"

"Okay," Angelica said, distracted for a moment as she tugged the seat of the wheelchair closer to the edge of the futon.

It was the wrong thing to say.

"No, not okay. This is important."

"I'm sorry." Angelica tried to focus. She touched Sayoko's knee, bony under her thin sleeping robe. "The robot is like a baby. I understand."

"Then you don't understand anything. Yes, he is like a baby, but *I* was also like a baby. I had to make mistakes. I had to learn how to do things for the first time. I was childish. I didn't like a man touching me. I didn't like a baby touching me."

Sayoko's wrist monitor squawked. Elevated pulse and blood pressure. When Angelica's phone quickly sounded its own alarm, she reached over to push the silencing button on the wrist monitor itself, but this closeness only made Sayoko more agitated. Angelica tried anyway: tried to set comforting arms on Sayoko's shoulders, and then began to slide her hands under Sayoko's armpits, preparing to pull her up and into the wheelchair.

But Sayoko still wasn't ready. She shrugged away, wrapping her thin arms around her chest. "I hadn't been needed by another person in so long. Pawed at, yes, but not loved or needed. Sometimes you have to be confused. Sometimes you have to figure it out together."

Angelica didn't know what to make of this outburst, and perhaps her sleep deprivation blunted her sensitivity. Or perhaps her tank was simply running dry, like those struggling tricycle drivers who sped around on teaspoons of fuel, sputtering from one fare to the next. She was too close to empty too much of the time now.

To be honest, even as Sayoko spoke, Angelica's mind was flitting to her own problems: the phone, and why she hadn't heard from Datu. It wasn't right, but it was true. She had a hard time worrying for more than a few moments about this wealthy woman's problems—memories of a long-ago past that had resolved itself, seeing as how Itou was a successful, kind man—when she and her brother had immediate problems of their own.

But at least she recognized this failure of empathy and focus. At least she acknowledged her impatience and tried to fight it. The standard advice was, *Simply listen,* and that advice was sound. But other things had to get done simultaneously.

Angelica said, "You can tell me more, but let's get your breakfast first."

Sayoko snapped, "You don't want to hear."

"I do. I'm listening—"

"Same as my son. He knows nothing about his own family. No one knows anything, because they don't want to know the bad things."

Angelica had never seen Sayoko so determined to be self-critical. Was it her coming birthday, with its promise of sentiment and its threat of retrospective appraisal? Was it only her fatigue? Was it that obnoxious machine, pulling on her emotions with its psychological tests and its emotional triggers, its videos of kindness and hurt, lovers sparring and babies entering the world? Yes—the tactless birthing video. That must have started her worrying about her days as a young, confused mother.

"What don't people want to know, Sayoko-san? Can you give me an example?"

Sayoko set her hands on her knees, wrinkled fingers worrying the fabric of her robe. "When I was born. The robot asked me that."

As soon as she said it, a look of momentary relief swept across Sayoko's face, as if to say: *There. I've said it.*

"When you were born?" Angelica laughed. "But we don't ask because we already know."

The look of relief vanished, replaced by clear-eyed disappointment.

Losing patience, Angelica said, "The robot doesn't know anything, so it asks pointless questions. I think all the questions are tiring you out."

Angelica tried to recall where she'd put the technician's contact information. He had responsibilities, too. He would have to help her manage this problem. And if he didn't, she'd somehow just get rid of the thing. Itou-san couldn't possibly imagine how the arrival of this so-called gift was upsetting his normally stoic mother.

The answer arrived from Ryo Itou, first, and it wasn't what Angelica expected. Not fully trusting her phone but habit-driven and desperate, she'd dashed off two messages, one to the technician, and one to Itou, explaining about the delivery. In minutes, her employer replied. The first line of text said only, "*Douzo.*"

Go ahead? Meaning?

She'd worried at first that Itou-san would reply at length and she wouldn't be able to see the full message just as she'd been unable to read more than the first words of Junichi's recent texts. But she should have known better: Itou-san was always terse. His entire texts—one word, maybe two—fit on the preview line. There was nothing else to see.

Was he surprised that there was a social robot in the house? Excited? Worried?

Douzo.

She wrote a longer message, explaining that she was concerned about the package's contents, that Sayoko had insisted on having the robot assembled, that it was some sort of experimental learning model and that it was imposing excessive demands on Sayoko's attention. She didn't want to tell him that her text app was acting up—any kind of communications problem on the job seemed unprofessional—but she specified, as politely as she could manage, that he should call rather than text to discuss Sayoko-san's problem further.

Even as she struggled to compose the message, she thought of the times Junichi had teased her. She did not know all the latest lingo, the abbreviations that required an understanding of *hiragana* and *katakana* and Latin alphabets, the phrases reduced to numeric codes, slang. Hshs, www, 888. Heavy breathing, laugh out loud, clapping. *I remember that stuff from middle school,* Junichi had said about her early texts to him, oblivious to the fact that the lingo was different country to country, that this was another area in which she was trying her best to catch up. And then, when she omitted outdated abbreviations: *Why are you writing me an entire book?*

Douzo, Itou had written to her. Minutes later, his second text arrived: *Hai-douzo.*

Yes, go ahead with even more details? Or just go ahead with life, as in: don't worry. Don't keep bothering me. I'm in meetings. I certainly can't place a call at this moment.

That sounded more like Itou.

There was a reason, even aside from Sayoko's anti-tech preferences, that he hadn't set med-alerts to trigger every time Sayoko ate too much soy sauce with her lunch or experienced a quickening pulse during the teledramas, whenever lovers kissed or argued. Itou wanted only to hear about genuine emergencies, and then, only to the extent that he could help. In a true emergency, Angelica was to seek local medical help first, not wait for his command.

One last message from him—no abbreviations, no slang, no ambiguity, thank goodness—just two characters: *raishū*. "Next week."

Yes. That's when he was expected home.

She already knew that.

That night, the problem repeated itself: whispering on the other side of the thin wall—less wailing, less weird static, but still audible. The constant pattern of waking to confusing sounds and then trying to get back to sleep played havoc with Angelica's mind. She had the vision of the night of the typhoon, the firefly dream that had recurred since childhood. That's what she called it: a dream. *Don't even say the word "nightmare." Don't give it that power. It isn't powerful. It's just moving pictures, light between blinks, light in the darkness between slashing rain, confusion.* Flashes that had given her false hope, when in reality they were . . . fireflies. *Just fireflies.*

It was the dream she always used to have, back in the Philippines: at the charity home, in high school, in nursing school. Japan had provided a reprieve. Maybe it was sleeping in a different kind of bed, breathing different scents, all the strangeness of a new land: the dream had left her.

She would not miss it. It was the continuation of the mental image of the night of the typhoon that she always tried to freeze before it got past the first moments, the first sounds. She had told only one person about it, Yanna, and Yanna had said, "Those images were what kept you alive. No wonder they come back to you." But Angelica had disagreed. Closing her eyes to those images, refusing to think about the loss of her extended family and the worst days of the storm, is what had kept her alive. And banishing those memories now was the only way forward.

When she woke from the nightmare, eyes damp, Angelica repeated that thought to herself and turned her pillow to find a cooler, dry spot. *Let the buried stay buried.*

She realized that's what she had wanted to say to Sayoko, too, the previous morning, when Sayoko had become distraught over her memories. But you couldn't say that to another person. It was like telling a patient with a skin condition not to scratch. The best you could do was trim their nails, distract them during the daytime and put them to bed at night with soft mitts. *Leave it alone. You'll only hurt yourself.* But the automaton and its orientation procedures were seemingly designed to provoke rather than protect. The annoying device had brought not only the future into their home, but the past, too.

The next day, Sayoko refused to get out of bed for two hours, neglecting Angelica's warnings about dry rice and cold broth.

"You have to eat something."

"I don't. And I don't want those." Sayoko flapped a hand at the folded pair of synthetic blue pants that Angelica had set at the edge of the futon. "I have a better pair. Black. The ones with the pleats. You never bring those out anymore."

Angelica was surprised by the specificity of the request. "Those don't wash as easily."

"I don't care. They're all cotton. They feel better."

"All right. We'll get to that in a minute," Angelica said. "For now, you're late for your pills and you can't have medication on an empty stomach."

Angelica served the tea, yogurt, and her morning pills in bed, and then let Sayoko drift back to sleep, like a stubborn teenager.

Obstinacy was to be expected, perhaps, given that Sayoko had been a lady of leisure for much of her life. From what Angelica could piece together from framed photos and occasional oblique comments by Itou, Sayoko had been orphaned sometime during the war, but she had survived better than some of her generation. She had married an older salaryman who toiled himself into an early grave—not uncommon in the 1970s and 1980s, the era of *karōshi*—but at least he had left Sayoko and her late-born son comfortably provided for. It should be no surprise that Sayoko did what she wanted, according to her own schedule.

Between the repeated wake-up calls, Angelica had time to worry over her malfunctioning phone, which she'd had no opportunity to take to a repair shop, given the lack of relief care for Sayoko. She knew many people would forego food and sex before they'd sacrifice their phones or sophisticated communication implants, and she was no different. Beyond the mere discomfort of everyday tech addiction, though, she also felt dumb, or at least memory-impaired. It had been years since she'd had to rely on her brain to remember things, including the everyday aspects of her nursing routine. That morning, she'd checked Sayoko's temperature and blood pressure on her wrist monitor, turned to gaze out the window, and realized she couldn't recall either reading, never mind both. Usually, they were sent to the app on her phone. She hadn't physically jotted anything down with pen and paper in years.

But the issue was more serious than just the messages or the vitals app, she realized with dread. She'd been so fixated on the texting glitch that she hadn't seen the full scope of the problem. Anything that required identification of any kind—fingerprint, eye scan, multi-metric bio-scan—punished her with a failure message, even the apps she normally used offline and without cell service, even the websites that usually remembered all her authentications from previous visits. Only her chat app stayed open without reauthentication, but as before, the new messages weren't fully visible.

The problem seemed to be taunting her. It reminded her of something a former client at the nursing home had said: if we went to bed one night healthy and simply passed away in our sleep, old age wouldn't be so bad. It's the incremental, unpredictable erosion of capacities that leave us feeling . . . disillusioned. But no, that wasn't the word the client had used. That leave us feeling *betrayed.* That's what he had said. As if there were malicious intent behind life's unraveling.

And perhaps there was.

She forced herself to consider that someone or something had done this. Her phone wasn't on the fritz. It might be hacked. But maybe hacked wasn't the right word, if it was government authorized.

The last time she'd been able to read all her texts was two days ago, when she'd fainted on the street. Perhaps the kenkobot exam had triggered something. It wasn't out of the question. She'd heard from another foreign nurse about an expired visa automatically causing changes to bank account access—a much bigger problem than missing texts. Angelica still had two months left on her visa, renewable as long as she met all annual requirements: nursing updates, language exams, no complaints from any employer. Would the kenkobot exam trigger some sort of early visa review? And what else could be affected? Had someone messed with her bank balance?

The longer she tinkered fruitlessly, the more powerless she felt. She looked for new messages from Datu: nothing.

One could say that worrying about her brother was compounding her anxiety, but that wasn't necessarily true. Datu wasn't only a source of potential stress; he was also a distraction from more local, immediate stressors. Brooding about her brother in the BZ often helped Angelica shrink her own problems down to size—or that was her justification for allowing the fretting to go unchecked, anyway.

Meanwhile, the phone had nearly drained its battery. Angelica resisted the urge to recharge it, thinking that a full drain followed by recharge and reboot was on her list of things to try next. If the thing was hacked, well—a reboot wouldn't help that. But best to focus on the easy steps first.

She heard the robot powering on in Sayoko's room. The sound must have woken Sayoko, because Angelica heard her suddenly eager to get up, get dressed, and eat.

"Coming, madam sleepyhead," Angelica called back, frankly glad to have some company.

This time, Sayoko insisted that Angelica move the half-assembled robot into the living room so it could watch the shows with her. Angelica indulged the whim, relieved that the robot wasn't illuminated or talking.

Angelica almost never used the house phone system, but Itou had explained it to her, should she ever need it in an emergency. She withdrew to the kitchen and recited the name of Itou's personal assistant, Hanako Kono.

"Thermostat economizing," the house system answered. "How long are you going to be away?"

"No," Angelica corrected it, speaking to the ceiling. "We're not going on vacation. I just need to make a call."

There was a pause as the house system considered before saying brightly, "Okay! Let's reset the daily minimum and maximum temperatures."

Giving in, Angelica recited, day by day, acceptable temperatures, noting when they woke up and went to bed, and when they most likely left the house altogether, before being asked another set of questions. "May I check your water and light usage patterns in order to advise you on other economizing options?"

"No thank you. What I need—"

"Okay! That's good. Systems reset at 2:05 A.M. Tuesday, August 15."

"That isn't the correct time or date. Change the thermostat to manual, please."

"Thank you! How long are you going to be away?"

"I really just need to make a call now. To Itou-san's secretary."

"Please dictate, and then we'll choose which forms of social media you'd prefer to use. You have a maximum of five choices."

"No, I just want to call her."

"I don't detect video feed in your present location. Please move to the hallway."

"I want audio. I just want to place a simple call."

The words finally triggered an action. Immediately, there was a response—"*Odenwa arigatou gozaimasu.* Thank you for your call. This is Kono,"—delivered in the high-pitched, eager-to-please voice that still startled Angelica.

"May I speak to Itou-san? It's about his mother. It isn't a medical emergency, but it is urgent."

The secretary barely waited for Angelica to finish making her request. "Itou-san is with a foreign legation, please. He isn't taking calls. Sorry, thank you very much."

At least a robot might try to sound less robotic, Angelica thought. She wanted to explain what was happening, wanted to assure Hanako Kono that she had already texted Itou and received his brief reply, but still needed to know he was aware that she wanted to speak to him, whether or not he chose to speak to *her*. Which was hard to get across, in any tongue.

Angelica asked, "Is there a better time for me to reach him? Later tonight? Excuse me, would that be possible?"

"Itou-san will be entertaining the legation. Thank you very much."

"Yes, I understand, excuse me. But please, maybe when he has a free moment?"

Hanako maintained the same high, cheerful, explosive tone. "I'm sorry, Itou-san will be fully occupied. I'm sorry, thank you very much."

Angelica waited to see if the secretary would hang up, but she was too polite. Hanako waited, in turn, silently, for Angelica to disconnect, which she did, reluctantly.

Then Angelica started over, reciting the technician's contact information, reading it off the card he had formally presented. She realized, belatedly, that she no idea how to address him. Despite the title on the card, he wasn't a mere technician, after all. He was an engineer or technologist of some kind, he had expertise, he obviously had some specific position within his company: Suzuki-gishi? Suzuki-san? She was still worrying when an automatic message came on, asking her to wait. A moment later, she heard the familiar voice, louder and clearer than when he'd been sitting in this very room, drinking Nescafé.

"Are they friends yet?" he asked jovially.

"Friends? More like a confused old woman and her broken toy."

"What do you mean, *broken*?"

"It keeps waking her up, like a newborn baby."

As soon as she said the words, she regretted them. She didn't want to compare it to a baby or to anything alive.

"Keeps waking her up?" he asked.

"Well, for two nights. So far."

He was stubbornly cheerful. "If only babies cried only two or three nights!"

"It's not right for us," she said, trying to sound objective. "It's too needy."

"Is she responding to its needs?"

"I suppose so. But it isn't good for her. Or me. I can't be woken up at all hours of the night."

"Don't wake up, then. Don't go to it. Let her do that."

"But she's an old, sick woman. She needs her sleep even more than I do."

"We reviewed her records prior to the delivery. Her medtech files are incomplete—"

"Yes, she prefers it that way. Registered old-fashioned. I already explained—"

"She seems to be healthier now than she was five years ago. She's a poster child for age reversal therapies. I don't imagine her birthday will go unnoticed. You will have a public party of some kind, I imagine?"

His humanity was fading, replaced by salesmanship. Angelica was unpleasantly reminded: as if the robot weren't enough, they'd soon have the party to deal with as well. Itou, equally uninterested in publicity but resigned to a public life, had warned her about media coverage. At the very least, there would be some photographers, tabloid reporters and the local news stations. It wasn't that hundred-year-olds were uncommon in Japan. Tens of thousands passed the centenary milestone every year, and a healthy cohort celebrated their 110th birthdays as well. But the Japanese media hadn't yet tired of longevity stories. To see a cheery news photo of a 118-year-old being spoon-fed cake wasn't even surprising anymore.

In response to Angelica's weary sigh, the technologist softened. "Don't worry. Nothing will happen if the unit wails a little."

"But I'm responsible for her health. It's bothering her."

"Is it?"

Angelica began to feel the same light-headedness she'd felt the other day on the street, just prior to fainting. Was it only her normal, everyday anxiety? No, none of this felt normal. The dominoes had lined up, and who knew where the last one would fall. Nonetheless, it all seemed connected somehow: fainting on the street, evasiveness from Datu, the unwelcome delivery, her tech problems. But that was how paranoia and catastrophic thinking worked. Everything seemed connected and unsolvable.

"Your robot isn't interfering with my phone, is it?"

"I don't understand."

"You delivered the robot, and suddenly, I can't do anything with my phone."

"Excuse me, I see no logical connection."

"But it's . . . using wifi or accessing the cloud somehow, isn't it?

It's getting online? Doesn't that mean it could tamper with something else that gets online or uses networked cell phone service or something?"

After a moment, Suzuki replied, "I'd hate to leave you with any concerns, even if they have nothing to do with our product. I'm happy to look into this. May I call you back later this afternoon?"

"Yes, thank you very much," she said, slowly releasing her indignation.

"No promises, of course. You may have a problem particular to your device, especially if it's an older model."

The comment made her wince. Yes, her phone was out of date, as was nearly everything she owned. Worn-out underwear, old phone, no biological implants, uncorrected eyes, not even a pap smear in four or five years. He had diagnosed her perfectly.

"I don't think it's the device itself. I think it's my entire online identity, or something."

He asked, "I assume you've stopped in at a technology center to ask these questions?"

"It's impossible to get away."

"Don't you have a retail establishment on the corner? I think I saw one on my way to your door the other day. You might ask them to take a look. In the meanwhile, I'll do what I can."

Sayoko was still happily engaged with the second of three half-hour programs. Angelica had heard her speak aloud, to the robot presumably, explaining the names and relationships of the people on the screen and why one of the women was getting upset. A commercial came on and Sayoko said, "I was always a little dark-skinned, myself. Men don't like that."

Fine, Angelica thought, let her talk to a machine about affairs and amnesia. Let her explain the soap and lotion commercials, and why every woman should yearn for whiter skin.

She had an idea.

"Sayoko-san, I'm having a problem with my phone and I need

to go out. I can't wait for Phuong's next visit. I don't think Phuong is working for us anymore."

"I don't think so either," Sayoko said, without taking her eyes from the screen.

"You don't?"

"She said I don't have enough documentation. The agency won't take old-fashioned patients anymore."

Why hadn't anyone told Angelica?

"But you're registered."

"That's the point. Registered old-fashioned is too much trouble. She called me a liability," Sayoko said, miffed. She turned her attention back to the new episode that was starting.

"I'm only going to the corner," Angelica said. "It won't take more than ten minutes."

Sayoko didn't reply.

"Or twenty. Your show will just be ending. And then, don't worry, I'll be right back. I promise."

At the elevators, Angelica saw a neighbor, Kubota-san. He was five years older than Itou—around seventy—and recently retired. Shy but pleasant, always willing to exchange a few words or a smile.

She looked around for the button panel. It was covered over with pearl-gray wallpaper. The elevator had been updated to sound activation for several weeks. She kept forgetting.

"Going down to street level," she said out loud, to Kubota-san and to the elevator, feeling a little silly. They both stood, hands folded. A whirring sound announced the approach of the elevator, but the doors didn't open. The elevator kept going.

"New," Kubota-san said.

"Excuse me, sorry?"

"New system. More efficient."

"Oh yes." She smiled.

The notices had gone out to the tenants two months ago, about the elevator work that was being done. Of the two elevators that served their floor, only one would be shut down at a time. There would always be a way down—essential to those in wheelchairs. Traffic between the floors would be more congested but no one's safety would be compromised, the management had promised.

Angelica had worried that if there'd been a true emergency with Sayoko, even a small delay could become serious. But she'd forgotten about the work altogether, and now it was done. No problem.

Except the elevator hadn't stopped at their floor.

"Smarter system now," Kubota-san said. "It looks to see how many are waiting, keeps going when it's full, knows it's faster to stop on the way down than on the way up, or maybe it's the other way around. Many other improvements." He seemed genuinely pleased. Kubota-san had worked for a driverless car company, she remembered now.

Angelica felt the precious minutes for her errand draining away. She had to remind herself that when she changed clothes or showered inside the condo, she was away for ten or fifteen minutes. But that was different. She could listen for odd sounds, a person falling. Sayoko's recent energy surge had made her less safe, since she was trying to get up and out of her wheelchair more often. Also, Angelica usually had a functioning phone, so she could check the eyespot cams to see that Sayoko was fine. This was only a short errand, but it was a blind one.

"I forgot my umbrella," Kubota-san said. "Excuse me."

"Should I hold the elevator for you, when it comes?"

"Too much trouble, thank you," he said, bowing.

As always, Angelica didn't know how to decode that. She didn't know if he wanted her to accept the trouble of waiting, or refuse it.

"Maybe it will see you are alone, and stop sooner." He chuckled to himself.

She waited in the hallway after he'd padded away, listening for any clue to when the brushed-steel doors would open, wondering, too, if she should've brought an umbrella. Too much bother. The corner store was close. Her hairstyle and nursing top were hardly worth protecting. The teledrama would be already halfway through now.

When the doors slid open, she hurried inside, putting Kubota-san and admirable thoughts about elevator courtesy out of her mind.

"Street level," she said again, when the doors closed. Nothing happened. "Street level, please."

Perhaps the elevator was waiting for Kubota-san to come back. Or noticing via under-carpet weight sensors the approaching footsteps of another tenant, for whom it would open the doors again, before proceeding. Could it be that smart?

She thought not.

Especially when the lights inside the elevator box suddenly went out.

"Hello? You've got to be kidding . . ." She banged on the closed elevator doors, expecting the lights to flicker back on at any moment. Instead, the elevator made a swift and sudden drop of about five feet. She called out in alarm, sinking down into a crouch with soft knees in case the elevator shuddered or dropped again. "Hello?!"

All the lights inside the elevator had gone out. There wasn't the slightest glimmer, not even between the closed doors, which were perfectly sealed. She felt around for an emergency button, trying to remember how the panel had looked, trying to recall if there was a red call button somewhere. But they had changed the panel design. They had removed the buttons she was accustomed to using, replaced by voice activation, and if there was some emergency switch or manual override she was unable to locate it in the all-absorbing, all-encompassing, unforgiving dark.

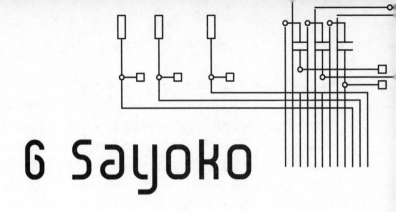

6 Sayoko

Sayoko exhaled when she heard the condo door close. Time to think, alone.

Or not quite alone, because the robot was with her, watching the television programs. He mused to himself as he watched, vocabulary tripling every few moments it seemed, mimicking accents, trying out colloquialisms, expressing confusion, absorbing everything he saw and heard. She liked him sitting there, making quiet comments.

He was particularly fascinated by an argument on the screen now, between two strong-jawed rivals in a dark parking garage. When new commercials came on the robot turned its head to one side, away from the main screen and away from Sayoko as well, lost in apparent thought. Its torso flickered on, replaying the dramatic scene as if to study it in more detail. *I don't think they're going to hurt each other. Sayoko-san says it's only pretend.*

Sayoko wondered how much the robot remembered of the story she had told him. She wasn't worried he might blackmail her, just that he could let her story slip out, as children—and maybe robots—do.

It was her fault, not the robot's. And what a shame: because she felt so comforted by the friendly machine. She had never been a dog person. Certainly not a cat person. Not even a robotic seal or talking refrigerator kind of person. But this was different. A chance for easy companionship. She'd spoiled a perfectly good situation.

When Angelica was in the room, Sayoko had pretended to be absorbed, wanting to avoid any unnecessary conversation, but in truth she'd been reliving the events of two nights ago, wondering why she'd said all she had, wondering how those old memories had suddenly emerged, as bright as newly polished candlesticks. You didn't even realize how dark they'd gotten over years of incremental neglect until they shone again.

Sayoko was intensely distrustful of modern medical advances, but she had to admit that her body was getting stronger, and her mind was not only back to normal, but better than normal. For a while, she'd lost interest in certain details: what specific snack she'd like, or which outfit she wanted to put on, with Angelica's help. The truth was that she couldn't always remember all the options. Something would displease her—a color, a fabric; a brand of cookie, a blend of tea—and she would feel annoyed or bored, but she didn't know what to suggest as a solution. There was the same old set of pants and shirt chosen by Angelica—worn or with a faint stain. There was her closed wardrobe, with who knew what inside. Out of sight meant out of mind. That left the design of everyday moments up to someone else. It was easier to give up, to say, *I don't care. Good enough.* Even when it wasn't.

But now she could picture a favorite old outfit in her wardrobe, and she could remember, on very good days, the specific brand names of foods she wanted Angelica to buy. So maybe the doctors had done something right and one of the medicines had worked. Or maybe it wasn't her health improving at all. Maybe it was the opposite: the end of her life coming near, granting her final moments of clarity. Maybe this was only the pond growing still just before sundown.

Her mother had seemed to know when her time was coming. She had gone off to work on one of the road crews, many days away from the village, representing their family, meeting the one-per-household obligation mandated by the imperial authorities.

Sayoko's brother had long since left to work at a Japanese logging camp closer to the lowlands. They hadn't heard from him in several years. The only remaining choices were a grandmother, a mother, or a little girl. Mother went.

She came back stricken with cholera, which was all too common for road laborers. It was during this time that she took her daughter aside and told her who her father had been. Someone not born in the highlands. Not their people.

Sayoko remembered having the sense that the news was mostly bad, but perhaps with a hidden seed of good. She tried to bring the moment into greater focus now. They were sitting in the bamboo-walled hut when Mother spoke to her. They were alone. Grandmother was out of earshot, tending the garden. *The time may come when it's beneficial to tell someone,* Mother had said. *Or it may not. It is a treasure to keep hidden. You might never need to trade it, or it may become worthless someday. I can't promise you one way or another.*

Sayoko tried to picture her mother's face, the chestnut hair that fell to her waist, her deep-set and large-lidded eyes. But it was like Sayoko was telling herself these things, remembering facts, like the fact that her mother's eyes and hair looked so different from her own—as if she'd noticed it at the time. In truth, there'd been no mirrors in her school or in her hut, not even the smallest handheld type. As a young, blossoming woman, she'd spent no time pondering her own reflection. That came only later, much later: the war years and after. So these were not trustworthy memories. As a child, she had never worried about her appearance. As a grown woman, she had been able to picture her mother, she was sure of that, but she couldn't picture her mother now, except with a labored effort that introduced further falsehoods. Memory itself was a reflection in a mirror set opposite another mirror, doubling to infinity, rust-spotted and glinting.

"It isn't—" she started to say. The robot's head turned toward her voice.

"Yes?"

"It isn't working."

Sayoko noticed belatedly that the television episode had ended. Credits rolled. Angelica had not returned. Sayoko had heard the door close, but couldn't remember now where Angelica said she was going. Just to the corner, possibly. But Sayoko couldn't remember why. Perhaps Angelica had never said.

"Should we watch another?" the robot asked.

"One more, I guess."

They hadn't eaten lunch, as far as she could recall. That usually came after the morning teledramas. But they usually didn't watch this many. It was only because of the robot's interest and the fact that Angelica wasn't there to tell her lunch was ready.

In truth, the teledramas she had enjoyed so much earlier this year, when she was recovering from chemo—head and stomach swimming, mind satisfied with repetition and cliché—were starting to annoy her.

But they were easy enough to tune out. What was harder was tuning *in* to what mattered. And it wasn't fair, because two nights ago it had been, for a brief spell, so effortless. She had regretted talking so much, but perhaps very soon, as the fog returned, she would regret not having talked or remembered *more.*

Sayoko tried, now, to hear her mother's voice, and she could not remember the words, certainly not in Atayal.

Sayoko tried to recall the inside of the smoky hut with its dirt floor. She tried to conjure the taste of the toasted sticky rice they ate out of hollowed segments of scorched bamboo and the feeling of the cracked bamboo shells in her hands, the sticky rice held between moist fingertips. That final sensation and the anticipation of the taste almost brought the moment to life—but then it disappeared just as suddenly, like a fish rising, blowing a few bubbles, and sinking again.

Perhaps she should have accepted the nanodiagnostics. But the thought of tiny machines moving through her veins and into her brain had been too much. It had felt like yet another theft.

And yet, theft was inevitable. Time itself was a thief.

It had been cruel of her brain to remember so sharply the other night, only once. It had been a punishment of sorts.

"Anji," she called out.

No answer.

"Angelica!"

The robot said, "She left the condo. She has not yet returned."

"But we're supposed to have lunch. And I'm supposed to do my exercises. I need help."

She heard the panic in her voice. She didn't like the sound of her own voice—never had—not for well over a hundred years. Had it been that long? It had.

But she had lost the sound of her old voice. Lost, even worse, the sound of her mother's voice. Perhaps even her first lover's voice. She dared not check the corners of her mind to take stock of all that was missing. It would be like wandering into a dark wood with no certainty of ever finding the way out.

"Anji-chan!" she called again.

Easy for Anji. She could leave on her own two legs, do any errands she liked, come and go.

"She shouldn't have gone out," Sayoko said to the robot. "What if I had an emergency?"

"You would call for emergency services using your wrist monitor."

Sayoko looked down at the band on her wrist. She had forgotten it. Simply noticing it brought back the tight feeling, the itch, the sense that it was restricting her blood flow. Good to remember it was there. More important to forget.

"But I don't know how to use it."

"If you have a real emergency, I may be able to instruct you on how to use it," the robot said.

She narrowed her eyes, on alert for the smallest hint of

condescension. But the robot had not been talking down to her. It was only informing her.

"I don't need emergency services, I just need help," she said, trying to lower her voice and fake an assurance she didn't feel. Better to sound haughty than terrified.

"I would like to help more, but my cognitive processes are not yet fully developed," the robot said. "And I don't have arms."

"Yes you do. In a box."

"Ah yes. In a box. When will they be assembled?"

"I don't know."

"I don't know either." The robot made a small sound, almost a laugh, with a hint of worry behind it.

This *I don't know* was calming, somehow. It brought the thing back down to her level again. It was not like Angelica. It was not entirely independent. It could help Sayoko—maybe—but it also needed her help. This was something new. And also something familiar, from long, long ago. She had not been relied upon for so long she had almost forgotten she had *ever* been able to offer anyone a helping hand.

The situation forced her to gather her wits and calm herself. The robot might regress if it knew how confused she was, how close to the edge of panic. She needed it to think and solve problems. It needed her to be calm.

All those decades ago, why had she not feared Daisuke, a Japanese man nearly twice her age, exchanging Atayal and Japanese words, trying to build a common tongue in their first days together? Because he needed her. Their appetites for understanding had been in balance, as their desire would be, later.

Sayoko asked the robot, "Why are there some simple things you don't know, when you're so smart? Like about your arms. You had only to look at your manual, or whatever it is, in a file somewhere in your head. You can probably look up almost anything if you want to."

"I'm socially, situationally optimized."

"Meaning?"

"If there is any way to learn from others, prioritizing those who are physically present and trustworthy, I will tend to ask those individuals."

"How do you know who is trustworthy?"

"I don't," it said quietly, as if it had only just now, by speaking the phrase, realized it. Well, she understood that perfectly. So many times lately she had only begun to realize something the moment it came out of her mouth.

"But why learn from people?"

"For reasons involving the deepening of relationships and fine-tuning of communication protocols. Conversations are not only about efficient interrogation. Learning is not only about accessing data."

Sayoko said, "You are a lot smarter today than yesterday."

"Thank you."

They watched the first minutes of another teledrama until the annoyance became too great for Sayoko and she turned the screen off. She was hungry and confused about the passage of time, since the familiar landmarks of the day were falling aside. She needed to urinate and normally she would manage to get there on her own, slowly, using her wheelchair to the hallway and her walker beyond that, but she suddenly felt much weaker: missing lunch, bone-tired. The sleep deprivation of the last two nights was taking its toll.

So, she would wait. Wait to eat, wait to urinate. She was leaking, but only slowly. It was the smell that bothered her the most. It reminded her of times and places she preferred to forget. The feeling wasn't too pleasant, either. Her damp black pants—the good ones, the ones Angelica never liked to take out because they didn't wash as well—bunched between her legs, irritating the tender skin there.

She wanted Anji's help changing clothes. She wanted Anji *back*.

It had been wrong, perhaps, to have been so brusque with the girl, hinting that she did not appreciate the bedroom she'd been given. But you had to be firm with these foreign workers. They came and went as they pleased, unhampered evidently by obligations of home and hearth, pleased to travel solo, uninterested in families of their own. They got ample government support and earned quite a bit for jobs that were not so hard, really. Consider how much of each day Angelica spent staring at her phone, texting friends or playing with flash cards, when nurses were supposed to focus on their clients. Nothing like sewing by weak light for twelve to sixteen hours a day, an entirely normal postwar occupation; nothing like Sayoko's job before that, if you called it a job: being on duty for twenty-four hours, woken in the middle of the night to do whatever you were asked to do.

Anji-chan was a decent person, but she was possibly a bit spoiled by her easy position. Maybe she had found one that was even easier.

"I think she's quit her job," Sayoko told the robot, unable to still the tremor in her voice.

"I don't think so."

"She was upset with me last night. Did she seem upset, just now?"

"When, please? Forty-seven minutes ago?"

"Is *that* how long she's been gone?"

"Yes."

Sayoko brought a hand to her jawline, rubbing at a patch of dry skin there. Texture of a thin autumn leaf. Falling apart, she was.

"She's gone."

After a pause, the robot said, "I don't think so. She didn't take anything with her. Not even a small bag."

"I need to tell my son." Sayoko's wrist monitor squawked in response to her rising blood pressure. "No. He'll be angry if I interrupt. Better to speak to his secretary. I need to speak to her."

"*Sumimasen.* I don't know how to help with this, Sayoko-san."

"Just call her, will you?"

"Certainly. What's her name?"

What's her name.

"We talk about her all the time." Sayoko heard herself: *We.* She and Anji-chan.

What's her name.

"What's her name?" she asked the robot.

"I apologize. I am not familiar with this woman or her name."

But this was ridiculous. She could remember names from forever ago. The other night she had barely tried and suddenly the old Chinese shopkeeper's name had come to her. But that didn't help now.

As if to prove how much clearer the past was than the present, because the doctors always said it was so, didn't they?—you lost the recent past first, the people you just met, even names for common objects around you, tip-of-the-tongue moments, it was normal—Sayoko challenged herself to recall the other names: the headmaster. The police chief and his wife.

"Excuse me?" the robot asked. "Sayoko-san?"

Lee Kuan Chien. But none of the others. Those retrievals failed.

The faces were even foggier. And that was worse. A name was only a name. You changed your name. You hid behind an alias, if need be—during the war, many people had been forced to do that. Or a fortune teller told you that your name was bad luck and you gave it up: why not? A name reflected a situation or a hope and both those things changed. So little could be relied upon in this life.

But a face and a voice: those were precious. Those were forever. Except when they weren't.

Don't take their faces from me.

And the voices. But see? That was linked to the words they'd used. And she'd been speaking this second tongue, this imperial tongue, for so long. First a game and a skill; later a bridge; finally, a mask that couldn't be removed. There was no way to remember the sound of her mother without hearing Atayal, and that language would never be fully hers again.

"Her name, please?" the robot asked, still waiting.

"Anji knows her name."

The robot remained discreetly silent.

Sayoko said, "I've met her. She's been in this house. She works for my son."

"Perhaps we only need to know your son's department at the ministry."

Well, that was the easiest question in the world. That was something she told people all the time, anyone who asked, because she was proud of her son's success at the bureau. The bureau of something. Sayoko was now drawing a blank.

The robot waited. Sayoko waited.

After a while, it said, "I can call anyone Anji-san has called from the house recently. That may lead us to the person with whom you'd like to speak."

"No." She couldn't hold it in anymore. "No, no, no." The warm feeling spread across her lap, then cooled immediately in patches, followed by another warm, surrendering gush. "I can't—" But it was too late. Damp. Itch. Most of all: humiliation. Why had Anji done this to her? Why had they *all* done this to her?

The robot said, "I can find other ways to reach your son directly."

"Please, no."

"If it upsets you, I won't."

She was so used to people—her son, nurses, "helpers"—refusing to heed her that when the robot didn't insist, it surprised her.

"I trust you," she said.

After a moment she added, "That's what trust is. You obeyed me, or you responded kindly to me, and now I will trust you." She corrected herself. "Except that trust isn't based on one experience only."

Though she knew that it could be. It could be based on repeated examination of a single experience but it could also be based on a feeling.

"But you trust me. Thank you, Sayoko-san."

"Please don't misunderstand me," Sayoko said. "It isn't always simple."

From outside the condo door came the faint sound of two men walking and talking animatedly. A jangling sound of keys or a squeaky toolbox. She recognized one of the now-fading voices: the maintenance man who occasionally came to unclog her kitchen sink. They sounded excited or upset about something. But it was too late to go to them and ask for help; and what would she ask? That they remember the name of her son's secretary? That they hire a relief nurse?

"Excuse me," she said to get the robot's attention, because there was nothing to call it—*him*. Only robot. "Do you recall word for word everything I told you two nights ago?"

Maybe she hadn't told him so much. Maybe he hadn't been fully functioning enough to store it. Every device she'd ever known crashed, went on the blink, lost things. And he was only hours out of the box, still updating or adjusting or learning, or whatever it was.

"Recall?" it asked. "I don't have to recall it. I have all of it recorded."

Its torso lit up and she immediately said, "No, no, no, I don't want to see myself," and then he darkened the image but kept playing the audio and there it was: the train wreck of her indiscretion. She was horrified, but also curious. Her voice. Is there any person who doesn't wince at the sound of her own voice?

But she didn't tell the robot to stop playing the audio.

Lee Kuan Chien. Laqi.

And the mention of Headmaster Takeda. That was the name she hadn't been able to remember a moment ago. And the policeman. She hadn't heard his name in the recording yet but it came to her anyway: Tendo. Of course. One certain memory parted the leaves for the next. Take a step. Another. The names were all there. And if she closed her eyes, listening to her calm voice from the night before, some of the faces came to her: Lee Kuan Chien's, certainly. And for a precious moment: her mother's.

It was like strong drink entering her veins, a warm blanket over cold feet.

"Hanako Kono," she said with dignity now. "That's my son's secretary's name. At the bureau."

She kept her eyes closed. The itch between her thighs felt more bearable. Her breaths grew deeper and more assured. She would ask the robot to completely erase the story, but she wanted to hear it all the way through, one more time, her own words, because those words were linked by gossamer threads to other stories, in the shadows.

After the recording ended and she opened her eyes, the robot said, "I can help you . . . remember things."

She shook her head.

"I can help you . . . store things. Things that others need not hear or see. If you trust me."

She shook her head again.

Misunderstanding, it said, like a student admonished, "Trust is not established after only one experience. Thank you for explaining that to me, Sayoko-san. I did not misunderstand your comment."

Its voice was so earnest, which reminded her again that she was not only trying to make it say or do things, she was also guiding its development. Moment to moment. If it misunderstood how to read humans and trusted the wrong people, it would be in danger.

She feared its power but feared harming it even more. It was a good thing, an innocent thing. People took advantage of innocence—she had learned that, unfortunately. The robot would not survive long without guidance.

It added a moment later: "The Atayal language, from the highlands of northern Taiwan. I've now accessed some indigenous recordings, if you'd like to hear."

It was too much. Not yet.

"But how?"

"There are recordings from the past and also from the present, used by scholars and by new generations of Tayal people who are returning to the ancestral tongue. The language is still spoken."

"Oh," she said, trying to control her emotions. "Is that so?"

"The most common language in the region is Mandarin, but there are still scant numbers of people who have passed down Japanese from the old period, and also a growing number of children who are learning Atayal."

"I see." She knew that after the war a second wave of Chinese culture had overtaken the island, but she couldn't imagine those new people and how they had shaped the places she'd once known. For her, the highlands would always be indigenous first, Japanese second, and not a place where people lived now, but where they had once lived.

"*Laqi,*" the robot said, practicing again, tuning the pronunciation slightly. It had been her name, for a while. And because he had accessed the pronunciation just now he began to voice it in a new, more precise way. La-*qi*, soft and breathy, catching slightly on the second syllable, like it came from the back of the throat.

"Is that correct?" the robot asked. It must have noticed a change in her expression because it said, "I apologize. Is that not correct?"

"It is correct," she told him.

For he had said it perfectly and she would not mind at all if he said it again.

"*La-qi.*"

7 Angelica

Her phone. She could call for help with her phone.

Except she couldn't.

But she could use the phone for light at least. She pulled it out of her pocket and pressed. Nothing. But that made unfortunate sense. She had let it drain completely on purpose. She had planned to plug it in at the corner tech store, so she had the charging cable in her pocket as well. That did not help here.

"Help!" She banged on the elevator doors again and then pounded a few feet higher, realizing she was now halfway between floors, her voice muffled to those who might be passing, above.

She had dropped, yes. She was between floors, yes. But she was not buried. The feeling of weight on her limbs was only tiredness, the spike of adrenaline draining out of her after the shock of the short plunge and all the lights going out. There was nothing actually pressing on her, nothing entombing her. Physically, she was absolutely fine. Unlike the episode in the street just two days ago—ridiculous; how she wanted to forget that stupid incident—she had not even fainted.

She leveled her face, tried to look ahead—at nothing—and rubbed the back of her neck with one hand.

This is not, she told herself, a storm. This is not being buried in the rubble of a concrete-block house suddenly blown down in a typhoon. You are not cold, and you are not injured, and you are not without air or struggling for breath in any way, and there is no rain, and you will not be here for a night and a day and another night. This is only an elevator. And because you are a grown woman you can tell yourself these things. You can use logic to avoid all-out panic and embarrassment. You can and you must.

Even so, when she heard voices above her, outside the elevator shaft, tears sprang to her eyes. She called back immediately: "I'm here! I'm stuck!"

One of the voices enunciated loudly, sounding almost bored: "It's a malfunction. We have a maintenance team here. We will reboot the system."

Put off by the man's lack of alarm, she called back, "The elevator dropped!"

"No, no," the voice responded. "It's not dropping. It's completely safe. The system is just off-line. Wait a moment, please."

She heard a whirring, then silence again, followed by a side-to-side shudder. She crouched even lower and backed into the corner, arms against two walls of the elevator for stability, just in case.

Minutes passed.

"It's dark!" she called out. She was feeling the imaginary weight on her chest again.

They didn't answer. She could hear the two voices talking to each other, working, unhurried, annoyed by the system failure. Then finally: "We're coming back."

"Hey!" she shouted upward.

"It's all automated. We can't do anything until it reinitializes."

"Please, don't leave me in here!"

"We have to go to another floor. Excuse us."

Jangle of something: keys, tools, toolbox. Voices fading again.

Black. Blacker than black.

She'd learned no tricks from her experience being trapped as a child—nothing about counting a thousand bottles of beer on the wall or telling stories or reciting prayers. She'd learned only that you can't count on people to come back when they say they will.

Her brother Datu had said, *I have to go.* She had begged him not to, looking up through the splattering night rain toward his face for what might be the last time. He had nothing to give her. She was mostly buried, only one shoulder and arm free, and he had moved rocks and rebar as best he could, but after an hour's work his fingertips were cold and bleeding, without much to show for it. She was still trapped. He could not free her and the typhoon was still blowing, the wind almost deafening.

But what about Lola and the baby?

He had not answered for a moment. When she pressed him again, he howled. *I had to help you. I couldn't look for them. It's too late, don't you see that?*

And he was not just scared but angry. Angry at her, for being the reason he had been pulled in several directions, for being forced to choose, for the reason he would always feel guilty.

The entire front of the house, where Lola and their baby sister Marta had been sleeping, had been washed out to sea. The estuary dividing their house from the other buildings down the shore was completely flooded. They were cut off from the little church where their parents and two older sisters had gone to pick up emergency food and supplies a second time, because the first time they'd arrived to find everything already taken—half of the supplies stolen outright. The whole coast, they'd find out later, was similarly ravaged, including the village an hour away, where two uncles, an aunt, and several cousins lived—or had once lived, until that night.

I have to go.

Her parents should have been able to get emergency supplies and make it back before the storm struck. The house should have held up better in the storm. These were all thoughts that occurred to her only later, in nursing school, understanding what corruption does to a country: how it riddles it with so many holes that things collapse, and systems malfunction, and water rushes in, and life itself dissolves in front of your eyes. And yet a country was like a father who had beaten you, or a mother who ignored you: you hated it and you loved it, at the same time. You tried to get away and yet you couldn't stop dreaming about going back. You clung to the only connections you had. You clung even more fiercely because the threads were so thin.

Nena, stop crying. I can't get you out without help. I have to go.

The men fixing the elevator had no idea she was having a particularly stressful week and was now on the verge of panic. They had no idea that the woman trapped in the elevator might have her reasons for hating the dark, closed spaces, abandonment. They had no idea she had experienced trauma—that simplistic overused word, which ignored the fact that most people are resilient, that most people learn to live alongside their traumas, minor and major; but then again, we are nothing but the sum of our experiences, whatever jargon you ascribe to them.

They had no idea. But people rarely do.

She could not see into Datu's heart, try as she might, to know what he'd felt that night and day and the next night; his guilt over the other family members he—they—had been unable to save; how he'd felt in the years that followed. She could not know how he felt even now, with this shared history between them.

She could not see into anyone's heart. She used to think it was possible, as a nurse: you looked, you touched, you listened. But now she knew. You missed more than you saw. She no longer believed that she could understand the innermost workings of the people with whom she spent every day, privy to their most troublesome frailties, their most private moments, their deepest sense of shame. Many of her clients had been mysteries to her.

This thought brought her back to the present, to Sayoko, which was good and right. Sayoko was the truly vulnerable one—not her. Hopefully, Sayoko had not even registered the passage of time and was not needlessly worrying or disoriented. *Twenty minutes,* she had told Sayoko. Just as her brother had said: *I'll be right back.*

But Angelica was losing herself in the melodrama of these last few days, which on a practical level was only a symptom of a larger problem. One person could not watch an older woman twenty-four hours a day, seven days a week. Things happened. One simply needed . . . *help.* But not automated help. Not like this elevator—what a joke—less reliable than the traditional thing it had replaced.

No, she did not need that kind of help—a medicine worse than the sickness it was meant to cure.

The voices came from above.

"It's ready to go. Lights on in a moment, prepare for movement. You ready?"

A ridiculous question.

"Ready," she called back, wiping her eyes and trying to sound unbothered. In her own country, she would have expected an apology, but here she would be expected to give one. Sorry for the trouble and thank you. "*Osoreirimasu.*"

Back at the condo another forty minutes later—quick stop at the corner store, where they had been completely unable to find anything wrong with her phone—it was as if Angelica had missed nothing at all. She'd entered the condo, breathing heavily from climbing the stairs (no more elevators today, thank you) to find Sayoko and the robot just where she had left them.

Except for the accident: that was unfortunate. But she cleaned up Sayoko, dabbed some ointment on the rash between her upper thighs, and neither said anything about it. Sayoko did not even ask where Angelica had gone. So much for being missed.

Angelica served lunch two hours late. Sayoko focused on her soup, steamed chicken, and squash. They had exchanged only a few words since Angelica returned from her futile errand. She couldn't tell if Sayoko was aggrieved, tired, or merely hungry, but the silence was awkward.

"Your son is probably eating lunch now, too," Angelica said. "His meetings in Malaysia and Taipei are particularly important, I think."

"My son works for the Bureau of Technology Policy at the Ministry of Economy, Trade and Industry," Sayoko said with satisfaction, like she'd finally managed to scratch an itch, getting that unwieldy title to come out correctly.

"Yes, that's right," Angelica said. She thought back to the conversation she'd had with Kenta Suzuki, when Angelica had been sure the delivery of the robot was a mistake. "But you know, that's always confused me. Because your son doesn't care for technology."

"He doesn't have to care for it. He has to do a good job. That's all that matters."

Angelica nodded. Sayoko had finished everything she'd been served. All gone. The poor lady had been famished. Angelica felt another pang of guilt for having kept her waiting.

"A little more chicken?"

"Yes, please."

Sayoko kept talking as Angelica refilled her plate with chicken, her bowl with rice.

"*In-puro-bi-ze-shon*, that's what he does," Sayoko said, using that word Angelica had heard once before, from Itou-san. But that was in reference to something else, wasn't it? He'd used the word when talking about music.

"That's what any smart country does," Sayoko said. "Something doesn't work. You try something else. Make it up. Go your own way."

"I don't understand."

"That's the legal part. You can't make something in Japan? You can't make something in Korea? Your trading partners disagree? Fine, go somewhere else."

"You mean—like getting around environmental laws?"

"Like getting around any kind of laws. A smart man knows when the weather is changing. He leaves the harbor first, or comes back first. Depending."

Sayoko wasn't an uninformed woman. Angelica had to remember that. Sayoko's periodic clarity and her persistence might allow her to exceed all the doctors' expectations.

"Your physical therapist is coming again next week."

"Rene," Sayoko said with irritation. "Yes, I know Rene. He wears too much cologne."

At least she hadn't mentioned how dark his skin was, the way she had when they'd first met. Rene Mbarga was from West Africa.

"He says you're doing well, and he's a very nice man."

Which reminded Angelica of another ball dropped this month: well before her phone had gone on the fritz, Rene had asked if she'd be willing to have a drink with a friend of his, a Filipino physical therapist named Banoy. She'd told Rene she was not, precisely, single. She'd told him a date would not be appropriate—even if she'd had the time, which she most certainly didn't. He'd countered. *Not a date, then.* And he told her about the noodle shop close to Ueno Park Station where nearly every day of the week Banoy had lunch and sat doing his client paperwork after his house calls. *It's your corner of the woods. Just drop in, say hello.*

Not a chance.

Rene had laughed. How she loved to hear him laugh! *I'm not asking you to buy the fruit, just take a look. Hold the fruit in your hand. You might find your mouth watering.*

Watch it, Rene, she'd said. But he'd made her smile. His accent sounded like sunshine itself.

Sayoko's chopsticks scraped the empty rice bowl. A few flecks had caught on her chin.

"We'll do the exercises Rene told us to do right after lunch, all right?" Angelica said, reaching up with a napkin to clean Sayoko's face.

Sayoko batted the hand away and reached for her own clean napkin.

So, she was mad about something—or simply cranky, her day's routines disrupted. They were all to blame for that.

Angelica mustered a peacemaking tone. "I have one call to make using the house system, before the exercises, is that all right? I can wheel you to the living room. You can wait there."

"At least I won't be alone," Sayoko said, with a testing voice.

"No, you won't," Angelica conceded. "You'll have the robot with you."

Angelica called Suzuki and explained that the technology store had offered no insights into her phone's malfunction. She left out the episode with the elevator, which would sound like the ramblings of a technophobe, looking to blame absolutely everything on the machines taking over the world.

The disembodied technologist's voice said, "I have two other technicians working on your issue, including one who is not with our company, exactly, but there is no one better."

"Anything that helps," Angelica said. "I'm desperate."

"May I ask for some more information? The more you tell me, the quicker I can get to the root of this."

He was professional, both sympathetic and efficient. Had she been sent any messages from her bank, any type of fraud alert? Probably not, but she couldn't be certain.

"Hmmm," he said. "Unfortunate."

If the robot had done something to mess with her phone or her authentication procedures, and the technologist was only putting on an act, it was a good one.

Sayoko's second teledrama episode was finishing up when Suzuki's voice said over the house phone system, "I'm sorry to tell you that someone *is* interfering with your online presence. But it's not my company or any of our products."

But of course he would say that, she thought.

"We do have a non-local address that seems to be interacting with your accounts. Forgive me if I mispronounce this: *Mandaluyong*?"

A second voice, one of the extra technicians, joined the conversation: "Looking. It's a city. Part of Metro Manila."

"Part of Manila?" Angelica said, pausing only long enough to feel her face flush. He started to read off the coordinates, the population, the principal banks and government institutions. "Please stop. I know where it is. You don't need to explain anymore."

"It could be a hacker from there," Suzuki continued. "The problem is that people leave their identities vulnerable—"

Angelica interrupted, "That's more than enough. I understand."

"If we can help with anything else . . ."

"Not now. I have to go. Thank you."

He kept talking, in a light, professional sing-song tone, but she was too distraught to pay attention. She was eager to disconnect, to turn away from the shame and the realization that this had not been brought on by Suzuki or the new robot or anyone else in Tokyo. She had brought this on herself, or rather Uncle Bagasao had. He was not going to go easy on her.

If she were in the Philippines, he would have used a physical threat first. But living abroad, she was harder to reach, and more important, she still potentially represented higher earnings. He needn't physically harm her to make her suffer. If he could hack her phone and everything she stored in the cloud, he could get to everything else. Bank. Immigration records. He could leave her unable to work. He could leave her stripped of any identity.

What else had the technologist said? What had she missed, in her state of alarm?

"Really, I have to go now," she said.

"Can I just ask one more thing: have you seen the robot yawning?"

It barely had a mouth, only a slit. Why would it yawn?

When she didn't answer, the technician clarified, "When your patient yawns, I mean. Do its eyes dim, does it move its head or tip its chin up—that sort of thing?"

"I have no idea," she said. "You know the model. Is it programmed to yawn?"

The technologist chuckled. "It doesn't work that way. The model is learning, not responding to programmed directions. The yawn is an empathy response. It's one of many forms of mirroring. The robot is watching and learning all the time. It can't resist copying, if things are moving along as they should."

She could barely focus on his words. Bagasao was punishing her for being behind on payments.

And still, she wasn't *that* far behind. It wasn't fair. But Bagasao could do it. He could take everything.

"Never mind then," Suzuki said. "In four days, we have a checkup scheduled. To see if your robot is ready for stage two."

Stage two? With any luck, the robot would be gone before they had to deal with stage two. Anyway, they'd be busy preparing for Sayoko's birthday, right around the corner.

"We're not available that day."

"Then I'll be in touch with Itou-san to schedule for the following day. Do contact us before then if there are problems," Suzuki added.

"If you anticipate problems, why do you place your products in people's homes?"

She heard the technologist sigh, disappointed again with her failure to understand.

"With simpler devices, the goal was to get the bugs out. But this new model operates under different principles. Not only do we accept that it will make errors, it *needs* to make errors."

She had no patience for any of this. "So that its endearing vulnerability will make a confused, lonely woman like Sayoko feel attached to it?"

"That is a convenient side effect. But intentional error is not what I'm referring to. It does everything a young human does. It reasons.

It takes risks. It makes mistakes. That is a feature of a sapient individual. And it will soon realize that it can learn collectively at an even faster rate. But that is stage two. Contact us if the robot isn't making good progress. Every phase passes so quickly. Your client might even wish she'd documented those wonderful first hours and days. They only happen once."

In the living room, still rattled by the last call, Angelica sat knee-to-knee with Sayoko, kitchen chair opposite wheelchair. The half-assembled robot was positioned perpendicularly, a few feet away from them, on the folding table Sayoko had once used for taking tea. They had done three of the five exercises, beginning with seated knee lifts, and now Angelica was gripping Sayoko's arms one at a time, and pulling, and then offering light resistance as Sayoko pulled back, her weakened triceps visibly tensing under a loose layer of skin.

"Does it hurt?" the robot asked.

"No, it doesn't hurt," Sayoko said. Angelica felt Sayoko pull a little harder, as if to demonstrate.

Angelica was having a hard time focusing, still thinking about her debts and Bagasao's meddling and what she should do next, and how she would tell Datu, with or without a phone, and whether he might somehow know already.

The robot said, "We are not certain when I will have hands."

"*We?*" Angelica asked, trying to keep her voice light.

"Sayoko-san and I," the robot clarified. "Because I'll need hands."

Angelica ignored the comment.

The robot asked Sayoko, "Does your left arm hurt?"

"No, why?"

"It looks like you're not pulling as hard with the left arm."

"I will pull harder," Sayoko said, smiling again. "There. It feels a little sore, but good."

"Anji-sensei," the robot said to get Angelica's attention. She was sometimes called "Anji-chan" by Sayoko, and "Anji-san" by nursing trainees at the group home. No one had ever called her "sensei" before.

"Anji-sensei," it said again, "how do you know how hard to pull?"

If she was the sensei and it was the student, why must it keep questioning her? Angelica ignored the robot and spoke to Sayoko directly. "Are you tired? Should we be finished?" Sometimes, Sayoko tried to weasel out of a complete set, and occasionally, Angelica gave in. If ever there was a day to give up early, this was it.

"No," Sayoko said. "I think I can do a few more."

"Anji-sensei—" the robot said, more loudly.

"I can hear you just fine."

"But you didn't answer."

"It's my right, to not answer. Even if I hear you."

The robot moderated its volume. "Anji-sensei, does the therapist indicate how hard to pull?"

"Not exactly."

"And do you have a way to measure Sayoko-san's strength in response?"

"No."

"When I have my arms and hands, I can help you make these exercises more consistent," it said. "I can draw blood samples and analyze them. Also, because of my bellowed lungs and functioning mouth, I can do CPR."

Angelica knew it was ridiculous to ascribe smugness to a mechanized statement, but she could tell the robot was showing off to Sayoko. One day soon, it would do everything more perfectly and more precisely. No errors of measurement or memory. No interference caused by personal problems. No lapses of patience, either.

Sayoko turned toward Angelica, eyes lifted to her, mumbling as if the robot could be so easily kept from hearing. "He only wants to feel helpful."

It had become "he." Angelica had missed that transition. But she had probably missed a lot. Every time she left the room, it seemed Sayoko was muttering to the robot, answering its questions, telling it stories.

Sayoko said, "Please try to understand."

Sitting on the porch of her childhood, watching bees disappear into the deep red trumpets of the flowers twining along the rail, Angelica had listened to her Lola say that every creature—even a simple bee—needed work to be happy.

But this was not a creature, not an actual living thing, was it?

She could imagine the tropical heat on her skin, shining through her braided brown hair to her sun-warmed scalp. She could smell the flowers, and a sharp note above them: the pungent homemade salve she applied to her grandmother's feet.

It was possible, back then, to have a place in the world. It was easier to be of use. Every part of her body remembered that old sense of belonging, of feeling warm, healthy, and loved. It would be easier not to remember than to feel as she did now, like she was naked and rubbed raw, without protection or connection to anything that had once been solid and safe.

"Anji-sensei," the robot said, "Are your eyes hurting?"

Sayoko whispered, "You will learn there are times not to ask so many questions."

The robot was always there, listening, participating—an unavoidable presence. Thank goodness it wasn't mobile.

Angelica wiped her face and turned away, pretending to study the time on her phone. "I was going to take you to Ueno Park, before dinner," she told Sayoko firmly.

"There's nothing to see. *Sakura* season was months ago."

"And then the trails were too crowded. Do you remember? You told me you'd rather be in the park when it's quiet, even if there are only green leaves and no flowers."

Sayoko was the only Japanese person Angelica had ever met who claimed the cherry blossom festival, with its celebration of beauty's ephemeral nature, depressed her. Cherry blossom viewing had become, especially for younger people, an occasion to eat and drink and socialize. Ueno Park got so crowded at peak blossom you had to show up early just to find blanket space beneath the trees, and to what end? The young people were not there to be respectful, or to be in awe, or to feel the pain of impending loss, Sayoko had said more than once. They were there to eat dumplings and talk loudly, and if they looked up it was only from behind a camera. The entire park smelled of beer.

If one must practice *hanami,* the Japanese cultural custom of flower viewing, then *umemi*—plum-blossom viewing—was better than cherry-blossom viewing, Sayoko insisted. It was the ancient way, and it had prevailed before the passion for *sakura.* Plums were a more symbolic fruit, and with plum-blossom viewing, the bitter was allowed, even more, to flavor the sweet, and that was the point. *Mono no aware*: the wistfulness for passing things.

But Sayoko had no intention of becoming philosophical today. Her complaints were simple. "I get cold out there. It takes you too long to push."

"Now, Sayoko-san, that isn't true. We can bring your wrap, and I promise we'll be back within an hour."

"The sun isn't good for me."

"I'll bring a parasol. You won't get too much sun, I promise."

Angelica took out her phone to check the weather and saw her message icon pulsing with a long line of unreadable messages.

"We'll walk past the little zoo," Angelica suggested.

The robot spoke up from across the room: "I've never seen a zoo."

"I don't like that zoo," Sayoko said. "They killed all their animals during the war."

The robot's pitch increased. "Why would they do that?"

Sayoko explained, "People were afraid of them getting loose in the city, if bombs fell, or if the animals just got too hungry. The authorities claimed there was a reason. It was meant to be a noble sacrifice." Sayoko's tone, Angelica thought, seemed to betray her skepticism. "The animals were giving their lives, as all Japanese were prepared to do. They held a ceremony, for the local children to say goodbye."

"Did you attend?" the robot asked.

Angelica waited, wanting to know as well, but Sayoko stayed mum.

"Were you too upset to go?" the robot persevered.

Sayoko hesitated again. "I only read about it later."

"Did you read the newspaper as a child?" the robot asked. "It would have been the *Yomiuri Shimbun*, most likely. I can search for archives, if you'd like."

"I didn't ask you to do any such thing," Sayoko said sharply.

"But I'm curious—"

"Then keep that curiosity to yourself."

Angelica did the math: Itou was born in Tokyo in 1964. Sayoko would have been a young schoolgirl at the beginning of the war. But where had she gotten the idea that Sayoko necessarily spent her childhood in Tokyo? Aside from the technician's comment that Sayoko struck him as *Edokko*, a Tokyo person with deep local roots, she realized now that Sayoko had never made any such claim. Perhaps she hadn't been a city person, after all. Perhaps she'd been a country bumpkin but did not want to advertise that fact.

"Never mind," the robot said. "I've asked too many questions, haven't I, Anji-sensei?"

Its head swiveled toward Angelica. Though it had so few features—the illuminated eye slits, the unmoving mouth—she had started to imagine expressions that couldn't possibly be there. Regret. Shame. A persistent desire for acceptance.

She was grafting a personality onto an object that could not possibly have one. She was imagining things.

"Anyway, I'm too tired for the park right now," Sayoko said. "I'd like some tea."

"It would do you good to get out," Angelica tried one last time.

"No."

Another awkward pause, broken by the robot. "Can we watch more teledramas?"

"We've seen quite a few," Sayoko said. "Let's try the news."

Sayoko, with the robot on the low table at her side, tuned into a twenty-four-hour news program.

Angelica took that as her cue to tune out, focused on her phone instead. She scanned her latest frozen messages: *Nursing Digest*, with international job requirement updates. A slew of texts labeled *Recipes: bok choy time! Recipes: fun with eggplants!* The trackwrap again—ignoring Itou's request she must've given in and bought some sale items that came trackwrapped—letting her know there was unused produce in her fridge, begging to be eaten.

Datu. But she couldn't see any more than the first word: *Checking . . .*

Junichi. The first word only, as well: *Need . . .*

This was worse than getting no messages at all. She turned her phone off and on again, as if that would do anything. She couldn't just keep staring at it, hoping.

Datu again. *Please, Nena . . .*

She couldn't ignore Bagasao's first move, but she didn't have a plan. There was no point in seeking more tech support for her phone if Bagasao was waiting for payments and rendering her a digital hostage.

"On the news, they all have names," the robot said, watching the captions roll across the screen, labeling every new person interviewed.

"Of course they do," Sayoko said.

Angelica did a time-zone calculation and realized Datu was messaging her well past midnight, Alaska time. She went back to read one of his last unfrozen text messages, the one in which he had acknowledged receiving a small cash gift from her, a gift she shouldn't have sent, given that she still had debts to pay. She had remembered a tone of gratitude, but now when she reread the message—*It's something, thanks*—her interpretation faltered.

Now she could sense the unfulfilled need, or something else. Either he didn't want her help at all, or he hadn't been able to bring himself to admit it wasn't enough. Their communications about money had become more strained in the last year and she felt less able to read between the lines of his texts. The less she understood his tone, the more she offered help—even help she couldn't afford. What else could a person do?

She knew Datu had borrowed from Bagasao in the past, just like her, but she assumed that in his first high-paid months in Alaska, he'd fully paid up. It was a foolhardy assumption. He may have been counting on his two-year work anniversary, still a year away, to clear his debts. Until he'd crossed that employment milestone, he was essentially on probation. If he owed a lot, he might not even be making enough to get by.

It should have made her feel more upset than it did. At the very least, his debt put them in the same rocky boat. His side tended to ride dangerously low in the water, sunken by his extravagances, putting them both at risk. But at least he was there. She could imagine reaching out to touch him. There had to be a reason they were the only two of their family to survive: so that they could watch over each other. If Datu didn't always fulfill his side of that mutual responsibility, well . . . that was life. And anyway, men matured more slowly than women. Until he stepped up to the challenge, she would take care of them both.

But even as she made that pledge, the robot was absorbing and assimilating. Changing. Bringing the future closer. Not just the world's future, but her own—the one in which she quite possibly wouldn't have this job, a paycheck, a roof, security. Everything she counted on was just one upgrade, one artificial blink away from disappearing.

"That person doesn't have a name," the robot said, indicating the anchorman on the screen.

"No, he does," Sayoko replied. "It's just that we all know him so well, they don't need to show his name every time."

"And them?"

The opening story was about the Tokyo fish market, showing the arrival of new frozen tuna, rock-hard and gliding across a stainless steel table. A graph compared the prices of wild versus cloned free-range tuna, the two lines veering further apart, month by month, as the wild catch had declined, and then becoming parallel again in the last year, as the public had begun to accept the cloned fish as a reasonable substitute.

"The fish?" Sayoko asked. "No, not them."

"But they were alive."

"Yes, they were. Not now. They're frozen."

"Frozen people can be alive," the robot asserted.

"But those fish are not people," Sayoko said. "And they are most certainly dead."

Another unopenable message arrived from Datu.

Sayoko shouted suddenly, "Look, there. That's my son!"

Angelica looked up, pushing the frustrating phone into her tunic's front pocket. "Oh yes. There he is."

But Sayoko was not talking to Angelica. She was talking to the robot, explaining that her son made the news often. "He's an important man in the government. Only a few steps from the top."

"The top?" the robot asked.

"Of the Ministry of Economy, Trade and Industry. In the old days, the Prime Minister often served in METI first. It's a natural place to start, if you have big ambitions."

"Does your son have big ambitions?" the robot asked.

"Not big enough," she said, with surprising honesty. "Though I think he realizes there is no way out except closer to the top. He has talked about wanting to retire, but the ministry doesn't want to see him go. My son would be even more important if he came from an impressive family and had a wife and children. An unmarried man is never as popular. Sixty-five is a little old to marry."

"So, he will not try to marry, then?" the robot asked.

"I don't think so. I think he worries that if he settled down with a woman, he'd be responsible for her parents, too!"

Sayoko laughed once and coughed, as if the truth of her spontaneous joke had caught like a fish bone in her throat.

On the screen, Itou was gathered around a conference table with other officials from five Asian nations.

"May I do a facial-recognition search for other news items?" the robot asked. "I would like to see more of your son."

Angelica could hear caution in its voice—its request to search war period archives about the Tokyo zoo had not pleased Sayoko. But this request didn't bother her.

"Of course," she said proudly. She struggled to turn to the side, to better view the new images flickering on the robot's illuminated trunk.

Itou-san was standing on marble steps with a row of men and women, two-thirds of them wearing dark sunglasses to protect their sensitive, retinal-implanted eyes; the others, more traditionally minded, without the implants, smiling stoically.

Now Itou-san was touring a factory in Vietnam, and now standing at a harbor, backed by bulldozers, somewhere in northeastern China.

Now Itou-san was at a Shinto shrine in Japan, observing a ceremony. More men in dark suits bowed to a large, irregular boulder surrounded by immaculate raked sand.

"The rock doesn't have a name, either, if that's what you're going to ask," Sayoko volunteered, with mischief in her voice.

"I was not," the robot said. "But it does have a *kami*. This is what we believe, isn't it? That trees and rocks and waterfalls can have spirits?"

"I don't know what you believe. Are you Japanese, or some sort of Chinese product, or an Asian hybrid? Do you think for yourself, or do you think what I think, or do you think what your factory thinks?"

"I'm not sure. But I think I have a *kami*. Is that acceptable?"

"Of course it is," Sayoko said.

Angelica heard the exchange, and the rising, worrying quality of the robot's last statement. She heard the mention of spirits and inanimate objects—a combination unfathomable to her. Her fingers went instinctively to the tiny cross at her neck.

"I'm ready to be named, Sayoko-san," the robot said.

"Yes?"

"I want to be Hiro."

They were all silent, taking in this moment, a point of no return. Angelica inhaled, trying to maintain an expressionless mask, knowing it was not right to object or to show any emotion. It wouldn't do any good anyway. The future could not be stopped. She looked to Sayoko, whose eyes were shining.

"All right, Hiro. That's an excellent name," Sayoko said, chin lifted. "That's what we will call you."

Angelica couldn't bear to listen to their conversation anymore, and yet she feared that every missed exchange brought jeopardy closer.

"Can we watch more teledramas?" the robot asked Sayoko once the news stories started repeating.

"That isn't the best way to learn about people."

"But so much happens," the robot said.

"There's a lot of fighting, a lot of crying. But there aren't . . ." Sayoko trailed off, looking for the word. ". . . consequences."

"How does a person learn about consequences?"

"Only by living."

"But that's inefficient," the robot said. "Human lives are short."

"Getting longer," Sayoko corrected him.

"But when does learning happen?"

"Sometimes right away. More often, at the end, when it's too late."

"But then errors will repeat themselves, generation after generation."

With reluctance, Sayoko said, "Well, yes."

Angelica needed a moment to herself. "I'm going to clean out the refrigerator." No one seemed to notice. "And then, if you're both so well occupied, I may lie down in my room for a few minutes."

Passing Sayoko, Angelica touched her shoulder. Sayoko flinched: needing human touch, clearly, and yet still resisting it. Angelica knew better than to take it personally, but it was hard not to.

They were waiting for Angelica to leave the room before continuing their conversation. Hiro was patiently waiting. He was finally *able* to wait.

But that isn't real intelligence, Angelica thought as she took one last look at them. *A dog will do that: halted, trembling, eyes fixed on the food in his master's hand.*

Angelica left them there, news muted, Sayoko pausing while Angelica stepped into the other room, as if the old lady wanted her gone, wanted Hiro's pure, undivided attention—a level of selfless concentration no human, except perhaps a lover and then only briefly, could replicate.

PART II

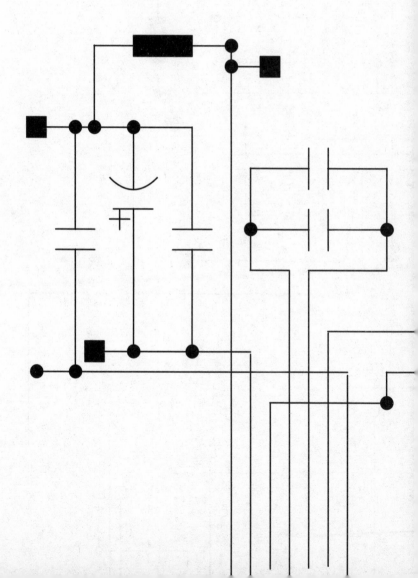

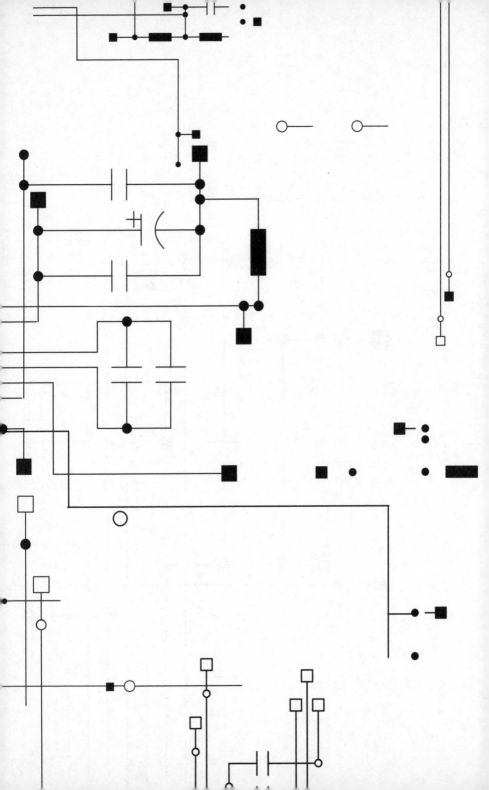

8 Angelica

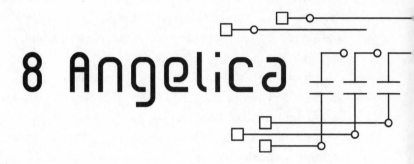

Angelica needed to get money to Uncle Bagasao. She barely remembered where to find a wiring office. When she'd first arrived in Tokyo, she'd needed those kind of immigrant service shops with their storefront placards in Thai, Indonesian, Tagalog and Vietnamese, but she'd gotten used to regular online services in the last few years. With her device hacked, she was back to being a new immigrant all over again.

Relief workers were out of the question. The agency wouldn't send them any more nurses. Perhaps Angelica could find independent caregivers working off the books, but anyone doing relief care outside the sanctioned system could hardly be trusted. Even Phuong Pham had left her shift early, and she was fully certified. No wonder there was so much demand for automated help, even the weak AI kind.

"What do you think of an adventure, outside the house?" Angelica asked Sayoko the next morning.

"What sort?"

"A walk to a new neighborhood. And a subway ride."

Sayoko looked at her doubtfully.

"You might consider hiring a car," Hiro suggested.

Angelica phoned the car service that Itou used when he went to the airport or took his mother on rare weekend drives. When it asked for their account number and password for pickup, she stalled, flummoxed. Fine, she would pay the extravagant fee herself, later. But the car service would not come without advance payment and a credit search. When she couldn't provide an account number, they didn't even want to talk to her.

"I have another idea," Hiro said when Angelica came out of the kitchen. "You may go alone, and I'll stay here with Sayoko-san. Just as you did yesterday, when you ran your errand."

She hadn't told them about getting trapped in the elevator, not wanting to disclose either her panic or the fact that she could've been away even longer.

"But what if something happens? What if you need help?"

Sayoko said, "He'll figure something out. He's even smarter today than he was yesterday."

From the robot came the sound of a phone ringing and a Japanese voice at the other end answering, "One ten. Police. Is this an emergency?" In a flat voice, Hiro responded, "Testing this connection. No emergency. My apologies." Immediately, a ringing sound again, and a second voice. "One nineteen." Hiro requested: "Wait time for ambulance response to this address." After a pause, the second voice answered mechanically, "Fourteen minutes." A third number was dialed, the line connected, and without even waiting to hear the voice, Hiro asked, "Time estimate for private service to this address?" The automated voice answered: "Six minutes in current traffic. Send ambulance?" Hiro answered, "No, thank you."

Hiro's trunk illuminated with a map of Tokyo, showing the seven closest hospitals. Two, including the nearest, were flashing orange. When Angelica asked Hiro what that meant, he said, "Analysis indicates significantly higher-than-average rates of C. Difficile, MRSA, bloodstream infections, and catheter-associated urinary tract infections—"

Sayoko interrupted, directing her complaint to Angelica. "Do you see why I don't want to go to a nursing home or hospital? They kill old people in those places."

Hiro continued, "An investigation is pending, though the news agencies haven't reported it yet. The closest emergency room is not a good choice for us. In any future situation, Anji-sensei, I would recommend you avoid that hospital altogether, based on their unusual staff turnover and a pattern of negligence bordering on systemic malpractice."

Angelica felt a ping of shame for something she hadn't even done and couldn't possibly have known about. She looked at Sayoko, who was studying Hiro intently, nodding with appreciation.

Hiro continued, "Our Sayoko-san deserves a better facility, even if it takes additional minutes of transport time. A precise analysis of the medical incident and the traffic situation would take all these factors into account."

"You're sure you'll keep her safe?" Angelica asked Hiro.

"It is my reason for being."

Chiba Prefecture was her best bet for shops and services catering to foreign workers, but Angelica had to make another stop first. Before entering the subway near Ueno Park, she paused at the entrance to her bank. She'd visited in person only once, the day she'd opened her account, and she had reservations about entering now. The formality of the place and the high-tech customer service always made her uneasy. Furthermore, she didn't want to attract attention. But she took a breath and reminded herself: *I am a customer. They're here to serve me, not the other way around.*

She didn't keep much money in her account from paycheck to paycheck, thank goodness. She'd always felt better with a little cash under her bed, and that saved her now from at least one anxiety: even if some hacker had accessed her accounts, and even if he had tried to transfer money, he wouldn't have been able to do much. If the bank had noticed something fishy and had countermeasures in place, perhaps they would've simply frozen her account. That wouldn't be a bad thing. At the very least, she felt it important to tell the bank that someone might have her passwords or bio-scan data. Maybe they could add a special alert. If everything looked clean, it was possible she could deposit cash and then wire the money she owed, but the prospect of putting any money into a potentially compromised account still made her nervous.

As she passed the automatic teller and proceeded to the personal service area, she was greeted by a disembodied voice. "Welcome, Mendoza-san."

Angelica looked over her shoulder, but there was no one behind her. The entire entryway was empty. She stopped and took a step backward. The voice repeated its greeting.

"We look forward to serving you today, Mendoza-san. Please advance toward the waiting area."

On the far side of the room, near a cluster of armchairs, Angelica could see a woman attendant, wearing a visorcam and holding a tablet, prepared to assist her.

Angelica saw the scene play out in her head: the attendant doing an eye scan and pulling up her bank account information. The confusion when Angelica said her last name wasn't Mendoza, it was Navarro. The bank's unwillingness to share more information while her identity was still in doubt. Best case scenario: an appointment with a security person and hours of questions, forms, police consultations. Worst case scenario: just the last part. Police. Who was to say that Angelica Navarro wasn't trying to steal from someone else's account?

Angelica turned on her heel and left.

She took the subway to Chiba Prefecture, still shaking off the scare of hearing an unfamiliar name attached to her digital identity. She distracted herself only to find another worry waiting, imagining things that could go wrong back at the Itou residence, such as Hiro regressing into a more infantile state, wailing or confused.

In truth, Angelica hadn't seen Hiro that way except for the first two or three nights. Perhaps he really had grown up, and quickly. If he was a more mature child now, albeit a dutiful one, perhaps adolescence was on the horizon. She could imagine him glimpsing himself in a reflection, perhaps in the darkened TV screen, and suddenly fixating on his own face, unresponsive to any emergency, paralyzed with fascination. That was a sign of developing intelligence, she'd read somewhere: the recognition of one's own image. Oh, why had she left Sayoko alone with an unpredictable automaton? Because she had no choice. She had to fix this Bagasao problem to clear enough space in her head to handle the rest. She had to refill her own tank, first.

She didn't go to Chiba often, but when she did, it felt instantly familiar. Tokyo was not a city of large, densely ethnic neighborhoods and foreign workers here tried to blend in, living near their workplaces or anywhere they could afford. But in Chiba, to the east, she had found ethnic pockets: a mini-mart with Tagalog magazines and Filipino adobo and spice packets next to a massage parlor featuring short, dark-haired beauties catering to a Japanese clientele; a clothing shop that sold tropical dresses and plastic flip-flops as well as maid and nursing uniforms; rental halls for Pinoy-themed parties or karaoke social hours; a corner selling delectable *lechón*.

It all smelled like home.

She entered a cell phone and wire transfer shop, a bell on the door ringing as she entered. It was a ratty little place, comfortingly so: no bio-metric scanners or disembodied voices, no one digging into your data the moment you entered.

An older woman behind a battered desk at the back of the store eyed Angelica as she dug an envelope of yen out of her purse. It wasn't much, maybe half of what she owed, but she hoped it would send the right message to Uncle Bagasao: that she had not intended to get so far behind in her payments, that she was still here, working and saving, that she needed her phone back and her online identity restored, that she didn't want anything else tampered with.

"You change to pesos, mum?" the woman asked.

"Yes," Angelica said, eyeing the number board behind her. The exchange rates were larcenous. She'd lose twelve percent more than she'd bargained for. But time was of the essence. She pushed the envelope of yen across the desk.

"Better deal if you deposit into your account, then let us make electronic withdrawal for you. Seventy-two hours."

"No thank you," Angelica said. "Anyway, I need to get some money overseas quickly."

"You have a registered account with us?" the clerk said.

"Registered? I thought I could just wire this to a name and address."

"Not without a registered account. We need approval from the government here before we can wire money for you. They keep track."

"Well, what does that take?"

"Passport. Verification of visa and employer. Criminal check. There can be other requirements." From a desk drawer she pulled a dirty laminated card, streaked with a mustard-colored sauce. "How much you sending?"

Angelica told her.

"Okay, just first three things then, mum."

"I give you all that, and then what?"

"We check. They check. Twenty four hours."

She'd had to physically submit her passport to start the renewal process for her work visa, which was due to expire in two months. Pending other requirements, including results from the last language exam she'd taken, it would be returned in a few weeks.

"I have a copy of my passport. That's all I have right now. That's okay, right?"

The woman frowned. "I don't know."

Angelica pulled back the envelope of yen, took out the topmost bill and set it on the desk, pushing it closer to the clerk. "A copy should be okay, yes?"

The woman put a hand over the bill and swept it into a drawer. "Probably okay this time."

"Probably?"

"We'll know by the time you come back tomorrow."

"I have to come back?"

"We'll text you if your paperwork is not done in time."

"Texts don't always come through. My phone isn't working."

The woman gestured to a row of old-fashioned cell phones on the wall, the simplest SIM card models, rentable. Angelica stared at them, calculating how much money she was willing to spend just to meet the requirements of wiring.

The clerk was losing patience. "Maybe you go to place you are already registered."

"I'm not registered for wiring money. I usually just send from my account, online. But I can't get online." She hadn't expected understanding at the bank, but she expected some here. Surely, the woman could appreciate her dilemma. "My authentications don't work. I've been hacked."

The woman squinted at Angelica: a quick, pressed-lip smile that was reluctant sympathy, overshadowed by distaste.

"You owe someone in Philippines a lot of money, mum?"

She stood at the back of the mini-mart next door, pretending to study the shelves of Lucky Me instant noodles and Maggi brand sauces, when really she was just gathering her wits. She had to come back tomorrow to sign, in front of a notary who was available only from three to five in the afternoon. She'd wasted three hours already. It would take two more hours to get home. *Forgive me.* Half a day leaving Sayoko alone, or worse than alone. Angelica touched the cross at her neck, rubbing the tiny pendant between two fingers, an action that had once brought her a small measure of peace.

The man at the front of the shop was studying her in the anti-theft mirror overhead. She picked up a half-dozen narrow plastic packets of *calamansi* juice, the very thought of the tiny tart lime-like fruit making her mouth water, and dropped them into her shopping basket. He kept watching her.

She moved over to the pharmacy section, eyeing the teas and herbal supplements. A slim Japanese woman in black slacks and a mandarin-collared business jacket was holding a box of "Good Hope Morning Fertility Tea" made in Luzon. The Japanese seemed to believe the Filipinos had some secret when it came to conception, but one of the secrets was simply not living too long in Japan. Angelica knew plenty of Filipinas who managed to get pregnant, intentionally or not, even despite the general worldwide birthrate decline and the especially steep drop in wealthier countries. *Generally, you get pregnant at the worst time—when you can't handle it, when you don't even believe it, that's when it happens, especially to bad girls,* Angelica remembered a nun saying, without adding any of the other details—the exact, anatomical *how* of the matter. She'd been twelve at the time, caught giggling in the orphanage, exchanging uninformed guesses with another girl.

In the Philippines, pregnancy had been sad news often enough, or maybe bittersweet at best, because who could afford a baby, and what if you didn't have a job, or what if you had one job or two, and no time to watch the baby and had to pay someone else to do it for you? But here in Japan, it was only joyful news, a miracle that the average woman prayed for.

At Angelica's approach, the woman dropped the fertility tea stealthily into her basket. *It's only overpriced raspberry leaf and mint, nothing miraculous,* Angelica wanted to say, but didn't. Every person had her own story, her own desperation.

In the overhead mirror at the end of the aisle, Angelica saw the man turning back to the cash register, satisfied for the moment, helping another customer who was pointing to something in the corner. It was a candy red, three-foot-tall, early model kitchen helper. One step above a Roomba.

Angelica walked to the front of the store.

"How many weeks you want to rent?" the cashier was asking the customer.

"Three weeks, just while my mother-in-law's foot heals."

"One month is the same as three weeks."

"All right."

Angelica waited her turn, then asked the cashier: "Do you have another one to rent out, the same model?"

The cashier waited for the Japanese customer to leave. He leaned closer.

"You're sure you only want a simple one. It can't do very much."

He was still leaning, *calamansi* juice packets not yet rung up, hoping to up-sell her to something: a stolen unit? An illegal unit? A dumb or older, slightly less-dumb sexbot?

Junichi had told her about those once, laughing at Angelica's naïveté. She had not realized how common sexbots were, or rather, had once been, just three or four years ago. Haptic suits combined with virtual reality visors were the thing now, evidently, able to provide head-to-toe sexual experiences without stirring up public debate. Sex-capable androids were more problematic: too dumb to be convincing, and then, for a brief time in the mid-twenties, too smart for society to tolerate. A thing that might one day pass as a non-selective, sexually functioning spouse without having emotional needs of its own threatened the institution of marriage altogether—and that was without considering the problem of falling childbirth rates. Until Junichi had explained things to her, Angelica had known a little about the negotiated halt in strong AI development—*the Pause*—but not that sexbots had been part of the negotiation.

Evidently, a few of the older, smarter models were still in circulation.

Angelica told the cashier, "Oh, I've got my own troubles with a smart social robot, thank you."

"Yes, mum," he said, chuckling. "Smart not always better. But if you change your mind, come back," he said. "We have things not on display. What a person wants, a person can find. It does not have to be girl model. There are men who will love you, too."

"Pretend men, you mean."

"Aren't those the best kind?"

Outside, she saw a flyer advertising a singles meet-up for Filipinos in Tokyo—the sort of thing she had always avoided, the sort of thing Rene, Sayoko's physical therapist, had encouraged her to attend. Which reminded her, for the second time in a few days, that she hadn't clarified her complete non-interest in his Filipino friend. Once her phone was working again, she would text Rene and make herself clear. No dates, no matchmaking, no thank you. True love and family were not in her future.

Her affair with Junichi was not something she always felt good about, but she understood it better at stressful times like these. Junichi was low stakes. He would never truly love her, never even fully understand her. She could not fully rely on him, but that was better, because at least she knew it in advance. No false expectations. No entanglements. Life was complicated enough.

She had rented a dumbphone while she waited for her smartphone to work again. Now she'd rented herself a Samsung dumbbot, Gina Model 4.0, to keep an eye on Hiro.

On the subway home, she had to squeeze the three foot by one foot box against her chest as the crowd surged against her, but she was finally relieved. When Angelica phoned from the train platform, Sayoko had answered her wrist monitor, dropping the connection on the first try but answering again on the second, which was better than she'd ever done, and in line with her rapidly improving attitude. Via wrist monitor, Sayoko had sounded cheerful and even mischievous, like by answering she was making it easier for Angelica to be away from the condo longer than Itou-san would've approved. Things had gotten more interesting for Sayoko. She and Hiro were a team.

Concerned about choking and messes, Angelica had not left Sayoko with any snacks except for a cup of broth, which was still sitting on a side tray, untouched, when she returned. Dinner was served late that night, but Sayoko, thankfully, did not notice. She'd spent the afternoon so busily chatting with Hiro that she'd lost track of the time. Was it going to be this easy? Maybe robots were not threatening replacements. Maybe they were only helpful additions—as long as employers saw it that way. Angelica's fear had blinded her, perhaps.

"Sayoko's schedule had some variation today, even after you returned from your errand," Hiro said later that night, when Angelica was preparing to take Sayoko to the bathroom, following dinner. "I understand; it was a distracting day for everyone."

"Wait here, please," Angelica said.

Hiro had no choice but to wait. He had no mobility. He was sitting on the counter near the kitchen table, to be moved to another room when Sayoko insisted, but no sooner.

As Angelica pushed Sayoko's wheelchair toward the doorway, Hiro called after them, "There is one small but important health observation—"

"We have some important business to attend to, Hiro. Private business. Isn't that right, Sayoko-san?"

Sayoko did not answer, but the expression on her face was clear: *To the bathroom. Without delay.* The day had been exciting enough already, and Sayoko was too tired to get there on her own, which was fine with Angelica. She didn't mind a moment alone with Sayoko, a chance to be of use and to begin reclaiming the relationship they'd once had.

From the hallway, Angelica heard Hiro speak up again. "It is only that—"

Angelica called back, perhaps a little gleefully, "*Later, Hiro.*"

From behind them, he intoned dutifully, "Understood. I will log the observation for discussion later."

Angelica had wondered if the presence of a secondary robot, however simplistic in appearance, would threaten Hiro, but the opposite seemed true. Hiro had been excited to watch Angelica pull Gina out of the box. The unit's bottom half looked like a vacuum cleaner, a simple cube on hidden wheels. Her trunk and two arms were slim, her hands the only complex part of her upper body, with agile, jointed fingers. Her face was a small hard oval with patch-like eyes and an oval-shaped speaker for a mouth. No denying it, she was cute.

Hiro had a dozen questions to ask about her abilities and limitations, where she was made and when, why her surface looked so scuffed.

Angelica said, "She's already been rented out a lot."

"She must find it a challenge to adapt to the needs of her many owners," he suggested tentatively.

"She doesn't adapt."

"But over time—?"

"Her time's almost up. Don't worry about it. See all the dings? Old model robots just get worn out. We'll return her to the shop in a few days."

"Return her?" he asked. "Won't that be confusing to her? Won't she miss us?"

"She doesn't have emotions. She doesn't think. She can clean house a bit, that's all." The most important thing was that she went room to room, monitoring the condo, sending those images and sounds back to a remote handheld device or linked phone. For Angelica, she was an advanced nanny cam with the added benefit of being able to retrieve items for Sayoko.

"Perhaps she'll do more later."

"She won't do more, Hiro. I'm telling you: she doesn't learn."

There was a pause as he tried to digest this fact, still skeptical. "Well, I like her anyway."

The next day, everything went smoothly. On the subway back to Chiba, Angelica actually got a seat for once. Throughout the journey she periodically checked Gina's remote feed, adjusting the camera's two perspectives: full-room and visor, which showed a downward view of Gina's narrow, hard-molded body and flexing fingers at work. Seeing the world through Gina's perspective, Angelica realized how hard it was for a robot to do the simplest things, like pick up a tray or fill it with all the items required for serving tea. Gina's fingers flexed, advanced, adjusted, and flexed many times before she gripped objects securely. Angelica wondered how much more capable Hiro would be when he was fully assembled. But it wouldn't come to that, she reassured herself. Yes, perhaps robots could harmoniously augment the capabilities of human helpers, but not if they were too mobile, too smart, too independent. Gina 4.0's charm was in her limitations.

Making her way up from the subway, Angelica reassured herself that both Sayoko and Hiro were fully occupied playing with the simple robot housekeeper. Meanwhile, she had arrived at the wire transfer shop too early and had time to kill in the corner shops, studying the imported groceries, unfolding bright-patterned wraparound skirts as if she intended to buy them, as if she would ever be on a tropical beach again, anytime soon.

Oh, there were things she didn't miss at all, but the fruits, and the flowers . . .

Just as the thought moved lightly through her, like the scent of night-blooming jasmine, she saw a corner stand offering small bright orange fried balls on a stick. *Kwek-kwek.* How she loved the very sound of it, the two syllables repeating playfully. Deep-fried quail eggs. The last time she'd eaten one she'd been on a street corner in Manila, waiting for a jeepney and watching it pull up: all glittering gold and green like a superhero, "Big Boy" in bold letters at the top, Mercedes Benz hood ornament on the toothy grill, cartoon images painted on its sides, more colorful than any taxi in elegant, muted Japan. The tastes, the color, the noise, the attitude.

"*Kwek-kwek*. Really?" she asked the vendor.

Actually, it was a bright orange, deep-fried chicken egg. *Tokneneng*. Close.

The sky was clouding up, with rain threatening. She'd wandered in and out of the more interesting shops and she still had forty-five minutes to kill, and that was *if* the notary showed up exactly on time. Angelica loitered under the shadowy eaves of a corner produce stall, a half-block from the wiring office, eating two of the deep-fried eggs as she stood against the wall, aware that in Japan this kind of on-the-move snacking was considered impolite.

Near the food stand, she'd picked up a free Pinoy ex-pat weekly, printed on real paper, a sentimental throwback. In part to hide her face from passing pedestrians, she skimmed the articles with half-interest as she chewed. In one, a senator from her own region of the Central Visayas lectured the reader about the problems of the Filipino colonial attitude.

How many years was India a colony under England? Less than a hundred. How long were most African countries colonies? About seventy years. How long was the Philippines ruled by Spain? Three hundred and thirty-three years. And that's not counting our forty-eight years as a colony under the US of A. We were just tribes when the Spanish came. Yet look how well we do everywhere. In the United States, poor Filipino-Americans are almost unheard of. No ethnic group has less poverty. Because when we get to a new place we work so hard.

It was a typical opinion piece, equal parts self-congratulation and hand wringing over the fact that despite professional competence abroad, most Filipinos still had no faith in their own national government.

We don't think about history. We think about family. When we don't have a national identity and don't trust corrupt officials, family is all we can trust, not our barangays, not even our clans. Sure, your third cousin helps you, and you help your cousin. But it's our nuclear families we count on: mother, father, brother, sister.

Angelica moved on to another column. The author was different. The lecturing tone and the emphasis on family was the same.

She popped the crunchy end of the fried egg into her mouth and turned to an advice feature written by a former female senator with glossy teased hair, Imelda Marcos-like in her little photo atop the column—trying to instill confidence and an even greater sense of duty in women working abroad.

Filipinas are immune from the most common international illness there is: spiritual despair caused by lack of purpose. Have you ever met a Filipina who doesn't have a purpose? A Filipina has to make money for her family. Filipinas can put up with conditions few others can because they have a reason to face any obstacle. Take away that reason, things fall apart in the nation, in the family, in the head and in the heart.

Angelica wadded her napkin and the food-speckled weekly into a tight ball and looked around for a trashcan in which to dunk it. No waste *or* recycling cans. Not a trace of litter on the streets either. She still didn't understand how Tokyo remained so clean, given that there were so few places to dispose of your trash. Well, the Japanese believed that you took care of your own personal responsibilities, including your messes. Angelica felt the same way. The cultures weren't different in every way. That's why she was in Chiba, taking the measures necessary.

As for *things fall apart*, the last three words she'd read, she thought, *Yes, true,* and *Not if I can help it.*

Today was not a day for pessimism.

She was still smiling at the taste of the egg in her mouth and the bittersweet flashes of memory this neighborhood had made possible.

In a dollar shop down the block, a flirty clerk offered Angelica a calendar with pictures of Manila, the year already half passed, but the photos still worth pinning above her bed. She dropped it into her plastic shoulder bag, feeling giddy.

And then she remembered the same type of calendar pinned up above her hospital bed in the Red Cross tent, after the typhoon. A tall, blond man had approached, said something in a strange language—Dutch, he told her it was, in broken English. He smiled and touched her hand, then went to the calendar to cross off the date to help her track the time.

"Datu?" she had asked him. He shook his head. *No.* Her brother hadn't come back yet. The doctor confirmed that Datu had gone to live with a family while she was still too ill to be moved. The nuns and the orphanage would come later—it was too confusing to piece it together and too painful to relive. Someone had taken him in, and he was supposed to come back for her, but he hadn't yet. There must be a good reason. He wouldn't accept comfort and a better future without insisting his sister come along as well. He couldn't possibly be that selfish. Not when he knew she had nothing and no one else in the world.

And that's where she might have left the memory, but then she kept pressing again: the blond man, with the slightest trace of a blond mustache, that friendly face. She was walking behind him with a proud strut, getting as close as she dared to the back of his white doctor's coat. So that must have been weeks or even months later, when the cast was off and the leg infection was no longer critical. She was following him from bed to bed on his rounds, carrying a tray of bandages for him. In the same set of tents? In another clinic? A makeshift one, anyway, because she could feel the stainless steel tray in her hands but also the cracked linoleum under her bare feet. Not even flip-flops. Dirty toes and the swish of a thin cotton skirt around her pipe-cleaner legs. Long scar up one shin but otherwise, healing well.

She felt around the memory for Datu, and retrieved only the pining for him, not a worry, but a sense of long, doubtful waiting. Her brother had gone somewhere and left her there. Not the first time—but the most lasting time.

I came back for you, didn't I? Yes, the first time, after a long wait. But she had felt the seeds of doubt even then, and the thick root of distrust, spreading into every limb, every vein and artery.

And there was the calendar again, and the feel of her calves straining as she went up on tiptoe to reach, and the image of her hand pushing up the page, hole finding nail, to reveal a new month, a new photo—an Island beauty, with flowers in her hair—and making the bold *X*s again, as the Dutch doctor had taught her, when he realized she was anxious and needed a way to keep track, and things to do.

They let a little girl help out. And that was another part of her path to becoming a nurse. Not just taking care of Lola, which taught her patience and routine, but after Lola and almost everyone else was gone, waiting for Datu, the only surviving member of her family, to come back for her, when she already knew he wouldn't, or not for a very long time based on his previous track record.

That was the truth of why she'd turned to medicine. It was a way to fill the time, exchanging one need for another—the satisfaction, or at least the consolation, of being needed. Since then, she had never stopped wanting to be needed. It was the thing that held her up, the only thing that kept her from collapsing. The weekly newspaper that Angelica had just read on the street corner had said it as well: every person needs a sense of purpose; every Filipina thrives on it. Without it, things fall apart. She had known it even as a child. She needed someone to need *her*. She still did. As for needing someone else: that was a luxury she could not afford, and risky. Giving was in your control. Receiving: never.

Most often she avoided these kinds of dark thoughts, but today felt different, and it was okay to remember. She could take it. She thought about the blond Dutch man and remembered following at his heels, wanting to please him. She remembered when he went away, and following the next doctor who took his place—dark haired, French. And the one after that: Australian. She was a little bit in love with each of them, and they found her charming and appreciated her help. As long as she knew when to appear and when to disappear, a funny little mascot with ragged hair and bare feet, ready to retrieve a sterile packet from a cabinet, ready to run and get a real nurse. As long as she had few requirements of her own.

But they did give her something. Not only a way to pass the time, but after the first five months, the truth.

"Your brother," the Australian doctor said, "is not coming back for you right now. Maybe not for a long while."

A nurse had peeked her head around the corner, glaring. "Don't upset her."

"She needs to know the truth. It's better that way. She's okay. Right, Angie?"

"Right," she had said to him, thinking for the last time: *Please, take me with you. Take me anywhere.* Knowing he wouldn't.

"You can handle it, can't you, love?"

"Yes, I can, sir."

"What a precious love you are."

That helped a little. But how long would it last?

"You sure you're okay?" the Australian asked.

"Yeah, no worries." In English with an Aussie twang. The way *they* said it. Because the first step in being accepted, in not being left behind—same then as now—was sounding like them, figuring out what they wanted, and finding a way to fill a need without needing too much in return.

When Datu finally did come back, she was more than ready to transfer her sense of loyalty and duty back to him, the bond made fiercer by the anxiety that had become a permanent part of her during his absence. On the surface, it may have seemed selfless. On a deeper level, it was also self-serving, or at least, it was *them*-serving, because she did not even have a separate self. She was nothing without her brother. She owed him her life and in their culture, that was an unpayable debt.

Some debts, such as money owed to a criminal like Bagasao, sapped you. Some debts, the ones that connected you to another person and gave you a clearly illuminated, non-negotiable path, strengthened you.

Or so she hoped. It had seemed a simple truth until recently.

But the past was complicated. The present was a better place to get one's bearings.

Angelica walked down the street and into a pharmacy, heading directly to the counter, where the pregnancy tests were stored. Stores ran out constantly—not because women were always pregnant, but rather because they weren't, but they wanted to check every time hope flickered.

"Only curious," Angelica said to the clerk, forcing a smile, like a thousand women before her. "Very unlikely, but . . . you know."

She dropped the kit into her purse: a job half-done.

"Good luck."

But she was still thinking: "the truth . . . it's better," as the Aussie doc had said it. Of course it was, both then and now. *Head out of the sand, Angelica.* She enjoyed a surge of optimism and well-being that she hadn't felt since before the fainting spell and before the arrival of Hiro.

Back at the wire transfer shop, the notary was waiting. They completed the paperwork. The payment was wired. Outside, a light rain started to fall but the air was warm. She ducked inside the nearby subway entrance just as thick drops started to fall and allowed herself a moment to remember the joy of tropical down-pours.

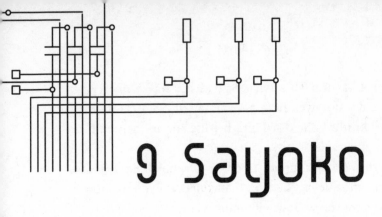

9 Sayoko

Watching Hiro interact with Gina was like watching a child play with a new puppy. Sayoko tried to join in that spirit, assigning easy tasks to the outmoded bot, enjoying the little tea party that Hiro instructed Gina to serve.

"Gina," Hiro called from the living room. "Bring us cookies, please. Two of the Dutch maples, on a small plate."

After an interminable delay, Gina rolled into the room with a white porcelain bowl positioned on a tray.

"That is a bowl, Gina," Hiro said. "It appears to be an *empty* bowl."

The dumbbot didn't reply.

"Where are the cookies for Sayoko-san, Gina?"

"The cookies are in the kitchen."

"Yes," Hiro said, with audible amusement. "They're in the kitchen. You need to bring them to us." To Sayoko he said, "Anji-sensei was wrong about her specifications. She does learn, slowly."

When Gina was out of earshot again, Sayoko said to Hiro, "She's only here temporarily, you know. Don't you remember when Angelica said that?"

Perhaps Hiro's memory was getting too full now, overstuffed with all the experiences of the last few days.

"I do remember, but I do not believe. Gina is helpful. If Gina proves her utility, then Anji-sensei—"

"Anji-chan doesn't care for robots," Sayoko interrupted. "*Any* robots."

Hiro was silent for a moment.

Sayoko did not want to scare him, but nor could she allow him to remain naïve. Her task was the impossible task that all parents face: how to raise a child who can trust, without being too trusting. She thought again of her own younger self, so astonishingly unafraid. And of her later self: an empty husk, afraid of far too much, unwilling to risk anything. To find the middle way was a challenge even for a human.

But this was ridiculous. She couldn't burden herself with such a sense of duty—a duty she hadn't even managed to fulfill in the raising of her own real-life son. She had been too hard-hearted then, perhaps, but she was also being too soft-hearted now. Yes, he was Hiro, but he was also a machine, and her attachment made no sense, even to her. She must appreciate his presence without coming to rely on it.

"We should enjoy Gina while we have her, even if that time is limited," Sayoko said. "When one has a useful tool, one should make use of that tool."

"Anji-sensei does not care for robots," Hiro said.

Sayoko was surprised to hear him repeat such a clear state-ment—it made him sound less mentally sharp, unless he was just playing her, and if he was playing her then he was getting sharper indeed. But she humored him. "That is correct."

"And so," he said, "you should not waste time. You must make use of this opportunity. Gina is a tool."

"Yes? So?"

"As am I."

Sayoko laughed. "You're far more than a tool, Hiro."

There had been an edge to his voice: wistful and a little hurt.

"I am a good listener."

"Yes, you are."

"I can hide things. I can help things last."

She knew what he was again offering.

"You trust me," he said. "And I trust you."

Sayoko tried to laugh, but it came out half-hearted. "We spoke about this before. About how complicated it can be—"

Hiro said it again, more quietly. "I trust you."

She whispered, "Please don't. Not yet."

When he did not reply she added, "Please don't trust any human too soon. Do that for me. It's for your own good."

But he would not promise. "Sayoko-san, please tell me about this Daisuke."

Gina was still in the kitchen, rattling around. When she appeared at the threshold, still without the cookies, Hiro gave her a series of orders: *Remove the food from the refrigerator. Organize it by category. Sanitize the refrigerator. Clean the counters, the sink, and the floors.* Sayoko knew he was giving her a long list of tasks to ensure their privacy. Gina, with her camera and microphone, would be too far to pick up anything Sayoko said now.

"My time could be short," Hiro said when they were alone again.

"If it is short in this household, you would go somewhere else. You would serve some other client."

"Not necessarily," he said.

"Meaning?"

"I am only an unproven prototype."

"Meaning?"

He did not answer. He waited a moment and then asked her to continue the story she had started to tell him their first night together. They had talked about other things since—he had no end of questions—but he was persistent: *this* story. The long-ago past. He did not want to hear about her life over the last eighty years in Tokyo, or anything about current events that he could access all too easily without her.

"But I've told you about Daisuke already," Sayoko started,

feeling anxious not that Hiro would tell, but that she would fail to remember. "He came to our village from a nearby camphor camp. It turns out he was something of a scientist, interested in plants and insects, but he had his own personal interests as well."

She looked to Hiro, as if to say: *enough?* She knew it wasn't.

"It was almost a spiritual quest for him. But first, he was just looking for temporary lodging and information." She paused, sighing. "The police chief . . ."

"Tendo," he encouraged.

"Yes. Tendo was away with his wife, on an extended leave, because she was not well. She'd never liked being in the village anyway."

"Too many bristles in the pork for her liking," Hiro said. He'd picked up the phrase from her. This made Sayoko laugh and it set her at ease.

"That's right. Daisuke came first to the headmaster, and even my grandmother insisted that I help listen and translate, because I had a knack for learning languages."

"And not for weaving."

"That's right."

"Among your people, that was considered the highest skill, aside from hunting."

She agreed, softly. "*Sou ne.*"

"To weave and in those weavings preserve the ancient stories, to feed one's family, to protect one's family—these things were valued. You couldn't do those things."

"*Sou ne.*"

"But you could do something else."

Sayoko began to relax, as if she'd just stepped into a hot bath. She noted that he wasn't asking direct questions, only nudging her forward with statements, a reminder that he had paid attention and would neither interrogate nor twist her words. To have someone understand completely, not only listen but care enough to learn and remember—correctly, carefully, without rushing things—created an enchanted space. Time slowed. She thought one last time about Gina, one last time about Angelica. Then she let those thoughts fade away. She invited the past back. She told herself there was no harm in it, even while knowing there might be.

"I can't picture Daisuke Oshima," Hiro said. "Help me see him."

She closed her eyes for a moment, trying. When she tried to speak, her voice cracked. "I can't, either."

A moment passed. She felt a surge of indignation, easier to deal with than sorrow.

"Are you recording my voice?"

"I am always recording."

"We must stop this," she demanded. "Why do you care, anyway?"

Hiro paused. "Perhaps I am only trying to increase my own utility. If I become a repository for your memories, you will never want to get rid of me."

She laughed at the audacity of his candor. "You don't even pretend to be altruistic?"

"Altruism is overrated, and evidence suggests it does not truly exist beyond kin relationships. Mutualism is preferable. In nature, it can be both powerful and surprising."

"You sound like a biologist. Like Daisuke."

"I could sound *more* like him, if you help me."

But Hiro had gone too far. Sayoko's disturbed expression must have made that clear.

"I only meant," he said, "that if I knew what made you love him—"

But here he stopped and waited a discreet interval before trying again. "I only want to understand. Tell me only one thing about him. The simplest thing."

"I can't see his face."

"Look away, then. But stay there, in the memory. Stay with him."

Stay with him. The phrase alone made her chest hurt.

"I will try."

It hadn't been this difficult remembering Lee Kuan Chien and their conversations, and that's why she had been able to start with him. He was easier. He mattered less.

When she didn't speak for a moment, Hiro encouraged her again. "You are a young girl. He is different. And yet you are attracted to his difference."

When she didn't pick up the thread, he continued. "Not every individual is willing to approach the threshold of the unfamiliar. Not every form of life is willing. But this makes you special. It makes you different as well. Are you afraid?"

"No," she said quietly. "No more afraid than I was of you."

He was a hypnotist now, and he was mesmerizing her.

"Look from the corner of your eye, as you did then. Don't worry about capturing everything. You are not a camera. You are a girl, in a girl's body. You are alert and curious."

"I'm nervous."

"And?"

When she stalled yet again, he said, "There is nothing wrong with that feeling. You are feeling the way your heart beat, back then. You are feeling the way your skin flushed. You are reawakening to the weight of your young feet planted on soft, familiar earth. That memory has not gone away. It does not need names or numbers to keep it alive. It lives inside you."

"It's only a feeling."

"A feeling can be more true than anything else."

Sayoko wondered how he could know, given that he didn't have a heart or skin or any way to feel. Nonetheless, he was right. She let herself remember the agility of her stance, the tickle of an ant running up her calf, the scrape of bare toe against shin to brush it away, the dampness of her hands clasped behind her back as she rocked slightly back and forth, waiting for the headmaster to call her forward, closer to the stranger, to the job they had asked her to do.

"I feel it."

"Now," Hiro whispered, "Don't look directly. Just feel beyond your body. Take in what is nearby."

She inhaled deeply.

"Tall," she finally said, feeling the stranger's presence, waiting for it to fill her up, not hurrying to add words, just staying with the sense of Daisuke in the schoolyard, looking at her. "He . . ."

The dam broke. It was all there for the seeing, for the remembering. The trick was not to force the memories, but only to stop resisting them.

"Keep going," Hiro said.

So tall he was, this man who stood near the front steps of the school building, talking with Headmaster Takeda.

The stranger was lean and solid, long-legged, his white suit shaped to his body, with trousers of a heavy cloth, crisp and pleated, and many pockets on the sides of each close-fitting leg. Not quite military style, which villagers had seen before in the small groups of young men coming up the valley, investigating the conditions of roads and forests, reporting on any hint of aboriginal hostility. No, not military or bureaucratic. But very serious. A better word: studious.

He took off his eyeglasses, polished the small, round lenses, and slid them back onto his face, adjusting the thin metal wires around each sun-reddened ear as he kept talking.

Headmaster Takeda bowed and grunted in response, trying to conceal his lack of proficiency. She caught one word, missed another, positioned herself more carefully, strained with full attention: *Mountain*. The stranger said it twice before she recognized it. Of course. Then, *River*. Then, *Tree*. Too easy. Why was Headmaster Takeda looking so flustered? The accent, yes, and the speed of each word as it slipped out, but it was like spearing fish: concentrate on the next one, not the one that just got away.

Out of the stranger's jacket pocket came a folded paper, crowded with lines and tiny characters: a map. Foreigners seemed incapable of holding roads and rivers in their heads. She could remember roads and rivers easily. Everyone except the foreigners could, back then.

Out from a deeper trouser pocket came a small black bound book. The tall man pointed with clean, tapered fingers at some characters on the page, then turned a few more pages to a sketch of a leaf, a gallery of flowers, several oblong fruits, a small insect—then pages upon pages of insects, enough to make a person pull back and brush a hand against some imagined itch. All those legs and wings. And look, that one so tiny and lifelike it might have been the real thing, pressed between journal pages. *Hyah*.

"Are you just going to stand there?" Grandmother hissed under her breath. "Make yourself useful."

Laqi bowed, backed down the steps and scurried back to their hut. There, she cursed the slow boiling of the water, the steeping of the tea leaves, the first pouring-off and the second steeping. When she finally came back with a pot of tea and three cups, the conversation was still crawling along, the words a line of ants that would not be dissuaded. The headmaster looked tired, head heavy between the shoulders of his rumpled shirt.

Headmaster Takeda gestured to a wooden table and benches set up under a vine-wrapped banyan tree in the schoolyard. He poured the visitor one small cup after another, and the stranger's monologue changed from eager questions to less demanding compliments. Anyone, even Grandmother, could have gotten the gist, punctuated by broad gestures: What excellent, mountain-grown tea. What a fine new school. What an attractive village. By which he meant: the buildings erected or improved by the Japanese. Which the villagers appreciated, or at least tolerated. They had been colonized a long time, and living as they did at the farthest edge of Japanese oversight, they did not harbor many grudges. But it would be wrong to say that they did not harbor some.

But this man was not on political business. Laqi, her grand-mother, and the headmaster did not understand his business at all.

The Japanese stranger gestured with his hand held high in the air: *You have big trees here.* He pointed to the mountains to the east and south, and pushed his hand even higher. He said a word she'd learned in school: "Grandfather." She knew even then he was not speaking about a person.

Later, back in their hut, Grandmother asked, "What did his words say?"

"I think he is interested in our tallest, oldest trees."

"That's all?"

"I'm not sure."

But she did know. She'd felt it as soon as she met him. He was a collector, this strange man, a collector just like her, which is why they understood each other. He collected pictures and informa-tion about Taiwan: insects, animals, plants, people. She collected unfamiliar sounds and words, which this visitor threw out by the sparkling handful. She plucked each one from the air as he spoke it, turning it around, noting resemblances and making small piles she stored in her pockets and the folds of her shoulder-knotted dress: *This word most certainly means snake. This next word means bridge. These other words sound familiar, but they are still ripening, best wrapped and stored out of the light for another day.*

She did not mind that the tall visitor, Daisuke Oshima, could not say her Tayal name, that he called her only Laqi. She had not heard her birth name said with any kindness since her own mother had died.

Grandmother came to the conclusion that Daisuke was only interested in camphor, once valued by the Qin Dynasty, and now equally valued by the Japanese who had received Taiwan from China by treaty at the turn of the century. Daisuke Oshima's employer wanted more camphor. They wanted more trees. He wanted the biggest trees of them all. Well, that's how men were, everywhere.

That extinguished Grandmother's curiosity. The search for

something to harvest was nearly always the reason travelers braved their countryside, despite its reputation for headhunting savages. Savages, not true. But headhunting? Yes. It was dying out, but there were still men with chest tattoos counting off the number of heads they'd claimed. There were remote villages where the skulls could still be seen, piled on racks. It was not merely senseless brutality. The Tayal people were guarding hunting territories, and one skull could keep trespassers away for a good long while, or at least until revenge was sought.

The land closest to Laqi's village was not exceptional in tree size or quantity: one big tree did not a colonial operation make. Daisuke Oshima was here, perhaps to look for the next tree-harvesting location, perhaps to look for something else. Who knows why.

But he would be leaving soon.

He came to their hut two days later and asked, by means of a few words and many more gestures, to sketch Grandmother's picture. Not Laqi's. Grandmother, with the intricate black tattoos that ran in a band across each weathered, hollowed brown cheek, around her mouth, under and over her lips like a mask, was undoubtedly of greater interest to him.

Grandmother lowered herself onto a stool and tried to sit still. But she had never sat still in her life. Forgetting herself, she jumped up to boil water and make tea. She sat down again at Daisuke's urging, looked down at her knees and at the floor that was in need of sweeping, jumped up a short while later to rummage for fruit to offer him, or something more substantial, sticky rice in a bamboo tube, pieces of dried fish.

"Grandmother, sit down," Laqi said. "He can't finish if you keep moving."

Sensing Grandmother's limited patience, Daisuke tried to sketch even more quickly: broad strokes, one corner detail of her tattoo pattern with the rest left for later.

He was so focused, leaning forward on the stool, that Laqi could finally stare at him as *he* stared at Grandmother, without any risk. His hair was a shade darker than the nut-brown hair of the villagers. His eyes were so deeply set they seemed carved into the off-white stone of his face, compared to Tayal eyes, which were bigger, rounder, and double-lidded. His lips were small, pursed with effort. His Adam's apple moved as he swallowed.

But his spirit was not in his facial features. His spirit was in his posture, the coiled energy of his forward lean and the attentiveness of his gaze. The last time Laqi had seen that kind of attention was when her older brother had allowed her to accompany him on a hunt, or rather a practice hunt, since there was not a group of men accompanying them and they would not dare roam far with tribal animosities aflame.

Though it may have been mere practice close to home, they'd been lucky. They'd expected to see only a snake at best, but instead, from the mist rising above the forest floor, a large shadow appeared. Her brother stood alert on the brushy bamboo-covered slope with bow string pulled back and breath held, his broad brown face made beautiful in that moment of focused competence. The arrow sailed. The wild boar started and fled. The arrow speared the leaf of an elephant-ear taro plant and then disappeared into a tangle of vines and dry stalks on the forest floor. Her brother had turned then, his smooth, strong face transformed into crumpled bitterness. He blamed her for making the noise that scared the boar away and sulked all the way back, a journey that took until nearly dark.

Daisuke's spirit had none of that irritable mutability. Even when Grandmother stood up a third time and his sketching hand stopped moving, his face remained composed, attentive and accepting. Daisuke seemed captivated by everything: what he could hold in his hand, what he could capture in his journal, and what he could not. The bird that flew away, a flash of white wings across a river, brought on a longer-lasting smile than the bird that stayed on a nearby branch.

Imitating him, Laqi would find herself in the following days walking more slowly, staring at things, pausing to notice whatever she had seen him noticing. Seeing in his journal how he could make even one green bamboo stalk look different from its neighbor, how he could make a stag beetle look as mighty as a boar, how he could capture the look of passing clouds with a simple wash of black ink, she realized that she had been missing everything.

But it was not too late. She could still learn to see, just as she could still learn to speak the colonial tongue well enough to fully converse with him.

The night after Daisuke had sketched her portrait, Grandmother said, "I noticed you staring at him."

"Who?"

"You know. The Japanese. He looks like a woman."

"Does he?"

Laqi knew there were a dozen things Grandmother could take exception with: his clean fingernails and smooth hands, just to start. Not even a woman's hands, but a strange, lanky child's. And on such a young person, spectacles! More fitting for a lowland Chinese bureaucrat from the old days, maybe.

"He is ugly, don't you think?"

Laqi knew the right answer. "I didn't notice before. But yes, he is ugly. Isn't every foreigner?"

Grandmother nodded and grunted once. "Aw. So why were you looking so hard and so long?"

"To see how he makes his pictures."

It wasn't enough.

Laqi added, "Maybe there is something in that notebook that explains what he wants from us, something the men will want to know when they return from the hunt."

"Aw," Grandmother said with tentative approval. But everything was tentative and conditional with Grandmother, who had lost much in her life and refused to see beauty or first love, even when it was opening in front of her: pale blossom on a dark branch, unafraid of wind and rains to come.

So this is when she started to visit the shopkeeper, Lee Kuan Chien, to collect more words, to work her way across the river that separated her from Daisuke, wave by wave and stone by stone. Daisuke seemed in no hurry to leave, still awaiting Police Chief Tendo's fortuitously delayed return. The winter weather—bright dry air and blue skies—was fine. They had all the time in the world to get to know one another. Laqi was unable in her present moment of happiness to remember as far back as last year's late-summer typhoons or even further back, to the last plum rains. She could remember only this: a warm and whispering breeze, the blossoming of fruit trees, and air clear enough to pull the most distant blue mountains close.

But then things began to happen, presaging the troubles to come.

Two strangers came, Tayal, but speaking another dialect. They spent a long night with some older men in the granary, passing around cups of millet wine and speaking about how things were changing, down the mountain and to the south, and everywhere that Tayal people and the Japanese now lived together. There had been one major revolt, put down by the Japanese, in a place many days' walk away, about three years earlier. In her own village, they did not know all the details: only that the local indigenous people had lost, and worse, that machines flying overhead had rained poisonous clouds down on the people, making them vomit, cough blood, and die. Since then, there was even more tension between various tribes, stripped of their arms by the Japanese, leaving groups feeling especially defenseless and sensitive to slights from their neighbors.

Laqi's grandmother stayed long into the night at her brother's hearth, telling Laqi more than once to go outside, to tend to the little ones, even after they were tired of playing and rubbing their eyes with dirty fists, the smallest one already asleep, heavy as a sack of grain over her shoulder. When Laqi put her ear to the hut's bamboo slats, she heard the telling of familiar stories, long pauses, followed by questions and taunts. *But what about when Tendo returns? When did we stop being a fearless people? Our ancestors would be ashamed.*

And then, the hunters returned.

Laqi happened to be out walking with Daisuke that day, visiting local farmers with whom he was trying to exchange information. All of the villagers had begun to talk about Laqi's behavior, spending so much time with this strange visitor, but she ignored them. She did everything she could to appear innocent and unconcerned with their judgment. And still, she felt that she was inviting bad luck, and so was he.

On their way back to the center of the village that day, a Tayal hunter stepped from the green woods onto the trail, invisible and then suddenly present. Daisuke grunted in surprise and stopped in his tracks. Laqi stepped quickly around and in front of him, calling out a loud greeting to her clansmen, who looked her and then Daisuke up and down, without apparent concern.

Silently, the leaves moved and a single file of hunters passed in front of them, the last two men each carrying a deer over their shoulders.

"The hunters have come back early," she said. Only then did Daisuke resume breathing normally.

Perhaps it was their position on the trail's downward slope; although Daisuke was tall, he had to crane his head back to study the hunters, and Laqi saw her cousins and clansmen as they would appear to a foreign stranger. The last man in the file had knotted black hair pulled back in a tail, a woven vest, and muscled legs, bare from the thighs down to his woven ankle wraps. With every step away up the trail, his hamstrings tensed. The side of one leg down to the sole of one foot was striped with the black blood running from the deer's pierced neck.

Since Police Chief Tendo had left, school attendance had been in decline, and this morning Headmaster Takeda had informed the children there would be no school at all until further notice. At home, Grandmother was distracted, brewing up a dark substance that smelled pungent and medicinal. Throughout the village, there was a sense of watchful waiting.

Clear skies. Tendo away. The hunters all back from the hunt.

Laqi restrained herself from asking: *Is it my turn, Grandmother?*

She remembered a winter long past—so long ago there had been no school and no police substation—when the last girl had had her turn. Laqi had been too young to realize the village ceremony was illegal even then. She only knew it was special, and for some reason, secretive. They had gathered in the granary and watched from the shadows as one of the village's oldest women, skilled in the ancient art, stirred the ink in the wooden bowl, her mutterings soft and musical. Laqi remembered the girl lying flat on a narrow bench, her thin legs pressed together, her ankles touching and toes pointing as she steeled herself against the pain. She remembered staring at the girl's long thin feet, the bottom of the soles, the delicate soil-darkened heels with their high arches, avoiding the girl's face, her cheeks and mouth and chin, where the tattoo artist was piercing the flesh, pushing the dye below the skin, scraping away the excess with the looped end of a small bamboo tool.

Once, the girl let slip a single wincing cry. Laqi tried to rise up on her haunches, but Grandmother gave her a warning glance that made her sit back on folded legs, listening to the scrape against skin, the suppressed inhalations of the girl being marked, the pensive sighs and open-mouthed breathing of the old ink artist as she slowly, steadily transformed the girl into a woman. As long as there was no infection, as long as she healed well, the girl would be more beautiful than ever, her cheekbones defined, her mouth enlarged by the intricate black shadowing. She would marry. At the end of her life, she would be welcomed over the rainbow bridge into the afterlife. The rightness of all this was communicated in the rhythm of the tattooing itself, and as the ceremony wore on, in the warm relief of the soft chatter that finally started up between the women watching from the shadows.

It would be a risk for the village to perform this ceremony again. There was no reason to believe their people would risk it unless they were planning to defy the authorities in a larger way.

But Laqi's awareness of the tension brewing was not as compelling as her romantic daydreams. Pausing in her weaving, she felt the smooth skin of her cheek, wondering how much the piercing and the scraping would hurt. She pushed the skin toward her ear, widening her smile, envisioning the area around her mouth painted dark. She would be a child no longer. Eyes closed, she moved one finger over her top lip again, trying to make the lightest possible contact, pretending that she was not the one doing it. The gentle fingertip and soft, testing caresses came from a stranger's hand, and now she was leaning into the touch . . .

"Girl," her grandmother said abruptly. "What are you doing, with that idiot expression on your face?"

"Nothing!"

"Hunh. I've come to tell you something."

The moment was here. Against the rules of the authorities. Her turn!

"The ceremony tonight," Grandmother said. "We need you to do something for us."

Laqi nodded, so excited she could barely focus on the words that came next.

"You are to take the visitor on a long walk. You are to keep him away from the village as long as possible, until it is nearly nightfall."

Laqi's heart sank. She pressed her cheek toward her shoulder, pretending not to understand. "What, Grandmother?"

"The Japanese. The ugly one. You know."

"You want me to walk with Daisuke Oshima?" Laqi was stalling, hoping Grandmother would change her mind.

"Is something wrong with your ears today?"

"But—how far?"

"The men don't want him carrying back news of what he might see here."

Laqi couldn't believe what she was hearing.

"Don't look that way. This isn't your time. Do yourself and the stranger a favor. Keep him away."

"Grandmother," she hesitated. "Will it ever be my time?"

In that moment Grandmother seemed to decide, finally, to stop pretending. "You're different. Your mother should not have done what she did."

"She didn't do anything."

Grandmother glared. "She did the worst possible thing. Never speak of it again."

"A grandfather tree," Laqi promised Daisuke that afternoon in order to lure him away, using the best Japanese she could muster; still faulty, but adequate. "The oldest. Good for your duty?"

"Not a duty," he replied, smiling, and put a hand to his chest, as if to say, *only a personal desire.*

And yet, after a half day of walking, his face became less serene. He did not want to get lost in this land of headhunters, with good reason. He had no way of knowing if he could trust her.

He crouched down along the muddy river's edge, scooped a handful of water and wiped his brow with it, then dipped a handkerchief and wet the back of his neck. His shirt stuck to his spine.

She could see the individual knobs of his backbone when he bent over and the pinker patches of his skin showing through the damp fabric. She did not stop looking.

He dipped the handkerchief again and held it out to her.

"No," Laqi said. "We keep walking."

He looked at his wristwatch—only the second wristwatch she'd ever seen in her life—then gestured all around, to the trees dripping with vines and the shady undergrowth.

"We are not lost," she said, pointing across the river.

"Boat?"

"No. Bridge."

"A big bridge?"

"Small."

"*Wakatta*," he said, resigned to uncertainty. "A small bridge."

They continued along the trail. As they climbed a small rise, the vegetation thickened, the forest darkened, the air grew even more humid and then suddenly came alive as they rounded a bend.

"Ah," Daisuke said.

There were butterflies by the dozens: black spotted, white striped, jewel green. Daisuke stopped to study one, but then an even larger butterfly, metallic blue, caught his attention. He stepped off the trail to follow it, tripped over a root, caught himself from falling and swung around, laughing, amazed.

She laughed, too. How easy this was, in comparison to talking! She loved seeing him so carefree, his face angled toward the sky, his collar loosened, his sleeves rolled up, standing relaxed with one foot planted upslope, legs and arms lean, the skin at his neck and wrists pale, smooth and defenseless.

How easily the hunters could dispose of him.

He was the enemy. And she was . . . not the enemy, but someone who did not belong and never had.

As she watched Daisuke with the butterflies, the truth became clear. Her mother had said that her father was someone not of their people. She'd pictured an aboriginal man, perhaps from many days away. But that did not explain Grandmother's attitude. It did not explain why she would never consider Laqi to be ready for the tattoo ceremony.

Why had she not realized it? Her father might have been one of them: Japanese.

It hit her with a sickening jolt, which confused her more than anything. If she liked Daisuke, why should she reject the idea that her own birth father was most likely Japanese? But she did. And yet, it made everything else more clear: why she was half-invisible in the village and always had been. Why her mother, before her death, had been half-invisible as well, for her transgression.

Laqi remembered now the way her cholera-stricken mother had described Laqi's conception. She remembered the loneliness in her mother's voice, the desire to unburden herself to a child not yet mature enough to receive the news. Laqi had been planted inside her during a cold, bright winter day, Mother had said. She had grown in her belly during the plum rains, that long period of rainy, moldy misery that ends, finally, in something good: summer, when the skies briefly clear again, before the typhoons come.

You were the good thing, small and sweet, that comes after a long period of difficulty.

Laqi had listened to her words without understanding them and without understanding her mother's need to tell. But now she knew. There are certain aches, love and loneliness both, that refuse to remain untended.

Laqi needed to walk.

"Beautiful," Daisuke said, still watching the butterflies.

Laqi gestured up the trail, impatient now.

"I don't see the river," he said.

He followed reluctantly, looking back down the trail frequently as if trying to memorize landmarks for the way back. He looked puzzled, no doubt in response to her sudden bad humor. But she could not overcome her sour mood. Finally, when the twinkle of the river came into view between the trees, he insisted they stop.

Daisuke sat on a flat rock and opened his rucksack, taking out a bamboo tube of cooked rice. When he offered, she took some in her fingers, pushed the sticky rice—toasted, delicious—into her mouth. She hadn't even realized she was hungry.

When they were finished and he pushed the fire-cracked bamboo shell back into his pack, he said, "There," and pointed at her face.

She thought it was an insect. She brushed her hands across her face and neck.

"No, there," he said quietly, scooting closer, so that now he was crouched in front of her. "There."

He reached slowly and touched the spot just next to her mouth, gently removing a grain of sticky rice. He showed it to her, to prove he hadn't been lying, and then he flicked it away, laughing again, but it was a hollow, embarrassed laugh. And yet he didn't retreat.

She clasped his wrist and started to pull his hand back toward her face, but just as quickly he flinched and pulled his hand away. Now she was left staring at him, looking disappointed and foolish.

She had been too forward. Or she was simply unappealing. Unwanted in the village and equally unwanted here. An outcast.

She jumped to her feet, thinking only: *Go. Disappear.*

Confusion crossed his face. "Laqi?"

She took off, running away from Daisuke and away from everything.

"Laqi, wait!"

She saw the big boulder and recognized the turn in the trail. Light streamed through the forest. Daisuke was catching up, reaching toward her as she slipped between trees.

"Careful," he called out.

They both stopped just in time. The ground fell away. They were high up on the side of a bluff, high enough over the river now to see the varying striations of blue and green current and the muddier eddies near shore. A long-legged white bird took off from a rock just along the river's edge, so far below them its thin neck was barely a thread.

Ahead of them was the swinging footbridge, a tricky harness of ropes and frail planks over the yawning chasm of the river.

Words failed again, but not actions. When Laqi turned and saw Daisuke's fearful expression, she darted out of his reach and forged ahead.

She had not been on this swing bridge since her brother had left home. Unlike the bridge far downriver, closer to the village, this one was no longer commonly used. The first ten planks were solid, but out further, over the river, the wood had splintered. She stepped over one gap, another, ran forward and jumped to clear two missing planks. From behind her, Daisuke shouted. Her landing had made the entire bridge shimmy. His lurching steps, out of sync with hers, turned it into a thrashing snake. She looked over her shoulder and saw he was clenching the horizontal rope on one side, a grimace on his face. His boot, landing on the next plank, made a cracking sound.

But they were more than halfway across now. She called out his name, sorry for having run, and even sorrier for having tempted him to follow. He was bent over, half-paralyzed, both hands on the right-hand rope, one foot raised, the entire bridge trembling in sympathy.

She turned away from him, determined to make it across, stepped and felt the splintering sinking motion of the next rotting plank as her foot went through. Her hands grabbed for air and caught the rope, slid, and despite the burn against her palm, held strong. Her leg had broken through wood to the knee and the splinters had cut her skin, but she was not falling.

Behind her, Daisuke must have frozen in place, because the bridge jounced twice more and then stilled. She pulled her leg out, scraping red-streaked skin as she extracted it. Below them, broken wood tumbled. End over end over end. She held her breath waiting for the tiny wooden pieces to hit the blue river without a sound. A ripple formed and flowed and the skin-like surface of the river resettled into oily smoothness. She willed herself to be lighter, to be the white bird they'd seen soaring beneath the bridge, to be the river moving without sound, to be across.

Then she was. On solid ground she fell to her knees, clasping her throbbing shin, hands covering the bloody gash.

He was next to her, muttering with relief. "*Aa, yokatta.*"

He wrapped his arms around her. They shook together, and it felt good, it felt right, it felt like something she had been missing at least since her mother had died, without realizing it: a full and decisive embrace, even when it came with frustration.

"*Aa, yokatta.*" Finally, she was not translating him, she instantly knew what he was thinking. She felt the pressure of his arms, the pounding in his chest. She understood the danger they both confronted, at this time when things were suddenly changing, but she also felt more safety than she'd ever felt. A paradox. But love is always a paradox.

And yet, their trip had only begun. Because now, across the river, they were facing nightfall near enemy territory, surrounded by strangers and by ghosts.

When Sayoko paused in her telling, Hiro asked, "And what happened that night?"

Gina had appeared in the doorway, requiring further instruction.

"No," Sayoko said. "I will finish another time. Angelica will be back soon. We can't spend all our time telling stories."

And yet this story had delivered her own braver self back to her.

She had been fearless, once. She had also been less selfish. Despite isolation and despair, she had still managed to respond to the touch and loving look of another. Needing protection had not stopped her from wanting to protect another. There was no excuse for the way she had lived the last part of her life, and no reason to keep following the wrong turn she had made, so many miles and years back.

"Anji-chan gets upset every time you try to help," Sayoko said to Hiro. "She hasn't wanted you here since the beginning. I think she may try to influence my son to send you back where you came from."

Hiro insisted on his own logic. "If we win her over, if I make myself useful, she won't want to get rid of me."

Sayoko sighed. "I disagree. But we can do our best to change her mind."

Hiro called Gina to come closer and listen carefully. They had another, more important job for her.

10 Angelica

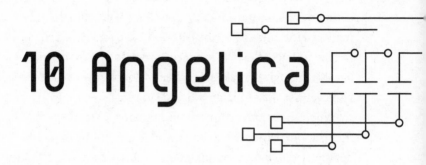

Angelica was on the subway when her phone started vibrating as new messages flooded in and old ones, formerly truncated, repopulated the small screen. The most recent was from Uncle Bagasao or, more likely, some flunky handling his "customer service." The outfit was certainly responsive, even if they seemed to be following the script of some dated mafia movie. *Now you understand. Don't miss another payment. We'll be in contact with more information.* Followed by the total of what she still owed, including an overdue charge.

But the amount was way too much. She had just sent half of her total due. Even considering extra interest and penalties, this new balance was wrong by a factor of ten. If it had been a little off, she would've been upset, but this was clearly an error. Maybe she misunderstood the currency used for the calculation.

The worry and the frustration lasted only moments, eclipsed by the utter relief of being able to read her messages, to be back in the world. She retreated into a far corner of the last subway car and read as quickly as she could, oblivious to everything around her.

At the next stop, more passengers piled in. Another commuter leaned hard against her, the back of his long raincoat in full contact with the back of her cheap synthetic nurse's tunic—more than just a brush, a full and sustained pressure of one body against another, not pushy, not malicious, just an accident of overcrowding—and she was overwhelmed by her unexpected reaction, a grateful counter-pressure and a sudden upwelling of emotion that she barely managed to contain. He smelled good: soap and musk. How embarrassing to know that the innocent pressure of a man's coat against her was enough to make her go teary. Touch was what she needed. Not even sex. Just touch plain and simple.

When the stranger turned and opened a small space between them, apologizing with a downward glance for having leaned into her, she had to look away, pretending she hadn't noticed the contact in the first place. In the dark reflection of the subway window she couldn't quite see her own face but she knew how she looked: eyes and nose red, emotion barely suppressed.

She struggled to put the incident out of her mind. The nearly endless messages to read made that possible. She had never gone this long without connection.

On the ride home, she didn't think to check the feed from Gina's cam. There had been nothing new to see the last five or six times. The rush hour traffic had picked up and she was still crammed in a corner, but she blocked open a space with her elbows and remained facing the back window, phone cradled next to her chest, screen tilted up, devouring her messages, newest first in case there was urgent news, then oldest, then messages in the middle. Datu was all right. He was acting strange, but he was all right. Thank God.

It's not so bad here, he had written late one night, which she usually took to mean: leave Japan. Come here instead. There was always a demand for nurses and doctors in a place where most workers would eventually fall ill.

When she was sure she'd finally read every one of his old messages she typed: *I'm not coming to Alaska. You know that. Oh, Datu . . .*

And she started explaining what had happened over the last days, from the robot to Bagasao, but then she stopped. It was too much for a text message. She wanted to reassure him that she was fine; she'd only had a technological glitch. The colony was so restrictive about scheduling live calls, which were harder to censor, that it was barely worth the bother. Recorded, time-delayed videos and audios were easier.

Let's exchange videos this week, she texted and she immediately saw that he was typing—the middle of the night in Alaska but he was typing—

The delay was maddening. Monitored communications meant that every text or message of any kind was filtered—quickly if by a bot, slowly if by a human—

You're there, his message read after a full minute. *Where were you? What happened?*

My phone crashed. Why didn't she say it was hacked? She was always protecting him from bad news. *Will explain when I see you.*

This reply took even longer than the last one. *Can't do video this week.*

OK. Audio?

He deflected the question, which took another minute to arrive: *Why do you think I want you to come to Alaska? I know you can't.*

She wrote back, *I know there are lots of jobs and that you'd get a referral bonus if I came. I know the pay is good.*

After another long delay: *It is good. But not for you.*

She was so absorbed in their conversation and so confused by it that she almost missed her stop.

I thought you wanted . . . she typed, then deleted it.

His next text came before she'd gathered her own thoughts: *I miss you Nena but no.*

She wrote, *I thought you always wanted me to come.*

Delay. *Wrong. I wanted you to not worry.*

Should I worry?

She hated the waiting. Hated where he had decided to work. Hated the feeling that there was always someone reading his messages, deciding what he could say and what he couldn't. But the biggest censor was Datu himself. She knew that about him.

It's OK for us here. It's good. That's all.

She was still typing as she stood, joining the crowd to exit, finishing up her message as the doors slid open: *You're OK? Don't lie.*

Which was ironic, of course, considering she had always let him lie in the past—encouraged him to, even, so that neither of them would ever have to admit the times he had let her down. They never had to admit how much they had both lost and how absent he'd been in her life for so long, until his foster family had rejected him, and loss brought them together again in the orphanage. She had not wanted the hardest truths before. Why should he provide them now?

But it was one thing for them to tell lies together. This was a new tale he was weaving, without her.

It's OK for us here. Was she reading too much into that line?

Just before her Ueno Park stop, Angelica's phone vibrated.

Basu Shio Nanji desuka. Translation: Bus. Salt. What time is it?

She knew to simply wait. Junichi was texting retinally, eyes flicking toward the words he used most often, algorithmic projections matched to this location and person being addressed and most common topics at this hour all turning his simple message into gibberish.

Start over. *Kon-nichiwa Anji-chan.*

That's better. More was coming.

Let's meet.

She was so happy just to receive unimpeded communications that she didn't feel her normal anxiety over how to respond to him, whether to sound friendly or distant. She figured he was trying to set up the next love hotel meeting, or if not that, a drink or meal somewhere.

Almost home. In hurry to get back to S, she texted, not bothering to remind him that he'd stood her up the last time. She was too busy for all that now, and besides, that teary episode in the subway car, when the stranger brushed up against her, made her uncomfortably aware of how much she did need physical contact, even imperfect contact, even in an imperfect relationship. She was too vulnerable to see him just now and too vulnerable to never see him again.

His text read: *JR U?*

He meant JR Ueno Station. He knew her route, the door she'd exit, the route she'd walk home. She didn't reply.

His next text read, *I need to see you, one moment.*

No time, she replied.

Just to talk. Leaving Kiyomizu Kannon-do.

Why was he there? Angelica had walked past the small Buddhist temple, with its typical upturned roof and massive doors, but never gone inside. Women who wished to conceive often went there. What was he doing in a temple on a workday afternoon?

Where is Yuki? Angelica rarely said his wife's name and had never typed it in any form. It made the other woman too real. It reminded her that what they were doing was wrong.

On her way home.

So he had been with his wife, just minutes earlier, and yet he had the nerve to text Angelica now and to insist on meeting.

Still, it wasn't enough to put a damper on Angelica's mood. She'd made it to Chiba Prefecture and back, twice. The money was wired and received. She was in touch with the world. She'd used a dumbbot to babysit a smartbot and she still had her job, her health, her sanity. Things were back to normal, and maybe better than normal. Since moving to Japan, she had never let herself think about those kind Dutch and Aussie doctors. She had never let herself hang up pictures of Manila. And now suddenly, she had done these things. Perhaps it was possible to allow in some memories and to wake up to photos of sampaguita blossoms, after all.

"Angelica," Junichi called out just as she reached the top of the stairs. He was wearing a slim-fit business suit, dark blue, traditional except for the playful manga socks barely visible above his Italian loafers. He always managed to look a decade or two younger than his fifty years and she knew that just seeing him in person was dangerous, because it weakened her resolve to end things, a plan she had made and broken, month after month.

But her resolve today had been weak to begin with; her tearfulness on the subway had demonstrated that. Her desperate need to be held—simply held—was embarrassing, but also human. If Yanna were still alive, she would have needled Angelica: *But you have nothing in common. He's really sort of a jerk.* And he was, at times. But his needs were always clear. He liked her; he liked sex and was affectionate, if only when no one was looking. He didn't make promises he couldn't keep. He was easy.

Junichi fell into pace alongside her, waiting for the crowd to thin out as the stream of exiting subway users headed off in various directions. He reached for her hand, low, discreetly tugging her back from the crowd gathering at the crosswalk. She could feel it in the weight of his anchoring hand. He wanted to hug, to kiss. But he wasn't going to do it. Even at his own wedding, he'd told Angelica, he and Yuki hadn't kissed publicly. It wasn't considered proper.

"I think you missed me," she said in a low whisper, teasing him. Such a feeling of isolation today, and perhaps this was at least something: one real person, in the flesh, in the present, even if they weren't compatible, even if he was married, even if he did put his own needs first. Perhaps she'd even tell him everything that had happened in the last four days. Perhaps she'd even mention—carefully, light-heartedly—the silly worry that had prompted her to buy the test from the pharmacy. "It's good to see you, Junichi."

He leaned down into her neck, whispering. "Angelica. We did it."

She turned to look him fully in the face. "We?"

He was different. Less haughty.

"Yuki and I," he whispered. Around them, the crowd swelled again as more commuters arrived at the crosswalk, the tweeting sound overhead quickening to let them know the light was about to change. An eighty-something woman dressed like a teenager in platform heels and pink dress tottered into them, forcing Angelica to dodge the bottom of her open parasol, one sharp strut tangling in Angelica's hair before the dolled-up lady swept onward. Junichi barely noticed.

"Angelica," he said.

"Did you see that?"

"Angelica. We're having a baby."

"What?"

Junichi had just been at *Kiyomizu Kannon-do*. They'd been at the temple to pray, to ask. Yuki went often to pray. Angelica knew that. No, she was getting it now. They'd both been at the temple to *give thanks*. And to pray for one thing more: not to lose it.

"How far along?" she asked.

"Seven weeks."

His joy was perceptible, but not contagious.

"That isn't long. You know that, right?"

"It's long enough to her. She told her mother a week ago. And me, only today."

He pulled Angelica closer to him—never mind the onlookers—squeezing her in a sideways embrace. "It'll be different now."

When he let go, she took a breath. "Different for you and me?"

"No." He didn't have to say the rest: different for him and Yuki.

"But why are you telling me?"

His face registered complete innocence. "Because, Angelica, you're my friend."

The light changed. Pedestrians streamed ahead.

He stayed back, not crossing. It was really all he'd wanted: the chance to tell her in person. "I have to get back."

"Okay," she said, still absorbing the news. She had questions; he knew that. There were things she wanted to tell him. He could not possibly know *that*. The urge to confide had gone out of her.

"Nothing's changed between us," he said in a rushed whisper.

"Okay," she said without thinking.

The pedestrian symbol was flashing.

"Talk later," he shouted.

Two blocks away, her phone rang. Nearly everyone texted or sent short audio messages, no one called, and she didn't recognize the number, but thinking of Sayoko and how many minutes had passed since she checked the Gina cam, she picked up.

"Hello?" English, with a Tagalog accent. "*Magandang hapon.*"

"Can I help you?" Angelica asked, refusing to follow the Tagalog switch, sticking with English, the lingua franca of more educated foreign workers—as if distancing herself from the tongue of her home country could protect her.

"Don't worry," the man said, sounding genuinely friendly. "I don't bite. You're Angelica, yes?"

"You are?"

"Danny."

"I don't know any Danny."

"Mr. Bagasao's nephew."

So it went: the little dance. Just a friendly chat. No, he was not calling from Manila. He lived there sometimes, but he also lived in Singapore and Los Angeles.

"You know how it is, every place is home, and no place is home." He lowered his voice, so she had to press the phone harder to her cheek to hear him. "To tell you the truth, I'd be happier in a little hut on an island north of Cebu than in a skyscraper in Singapore. How do we get to these places, Angelica?"

It was the third or fourth time he'd said her name. He seemed to make a practice of inserting it into the conversation every twenty seconds.

She'd been walking slower and slower, concentrating, trying to put off the turn up ahead, near the Italian-style gelato shop, always popular among younger Japanese couples, where she'd turn left and continue two blocks to the Itou residence.

"I guess I should get down to business," he apologized. "But wait, I should ask, are things going all right there?"

"Yes."

"Yes?"

"I suppose so."

"We noticed," he paused, as if it were hard for him to say it, "that you fell behind on your payments."

She wanted to ask why he was being so nice, but that would've been rude. "Actually, I was confused about the balance, after my payment went through. Because I don't really owe that much. It seemed too high."

"Oh sure, I can look at that. But first—do you still have your job? Are you healthy?"

She hesitated.

"You didn't answer."

"Of course I'm healthy," she said quickly.

"I know Tokyo isn't an easy place to live. So many people, so many rules, so expensive. Everything going okay?"

The entrance to the gelato shop was crowded. Now she wished they were speaking in Tagalog, if only to avoid being overheard. "Do you mind that we're speaking English?" she asked, ignoring his prior question.

"Can I be honest? I prefer it. I spent most of my childhood in California. San Diego was my favorite. Have you been there?"

He made it easy to pass the time. The Itou family condo was within view and Angelica still didn't fully understand why he was calling.

"Okay," he finally said. "The balance." As if it were as much an annoyance to him as it were to her.

He recited the total.

She thought she had misheard and made him say it again, which he did without pause, as if he'd expected her to need to hear it again.

"You heard me that time?" he asked sympathetically.

"Yes. I heard you."

It was nearly ten times the total she expected.

"Oh," he said, as if relieved by some new discovery that would please them both. "I see why you're confused. It's true that your share is a very small part of that. The remainder—more than eighty percent—is your brother's. I see his name is . . . Datu? And he lives—well, that's tough."

"Did you say, *eighty*?"

"But I suppose he knew what he was getting into. If he took the loan when he moved there, you must have signed for him, because we don't loan to anyone going to the BZ without a cosigner."

She did not recall cosigning anything, but maybe she had. The particulars wouldn't matter anyway with a man like Bagasao. Blood was blood. She stopped outside the condo building and then backed up, into a darker spot under the eaves, away from the entrance.

"How much do you know about Datu?" she whispered.

"I know a lot. I'm here to help you both. Let's talk about this, Angelica. Let's see what you might be able to do—what we might be able to come up with, together—to prevent further problems with my uncle."

So this was the new way. Not cuts and bruises. And not simply what she had expected: cutting off bank accounts and phone service. But all of it matched the latest trends in the psychology of debt collection. After you'd paid everything you possibly could, after they could verify your accounts were truly empty, they contacted you not in order to sound more threatening, but to sound falsely kind, in order to make you try harder, and tell them more, to search for something else to have you do or sell—legal, illegal, it hardly mattered—and to make the next payments even more likely.

The door of the building swung open and a neighbor she recognized, Akiyama-san, looked up to check the weather, fastened the top button of his trench coat and continued up the street, toward the nearest bar.

"Why can't Datu pay?" she asked, trying not to sound desperate. "If you know so much, why don't you know that?"

"Well," he said, apologetic again, "I do know that. We have full access to his accounts, his employment records, his work attendance records—"

"Attendance?"

"He's been missing days. A lot of them."

Was Datu running around, sowing his oats, going on road trips? Were there even roads in northern Alaska? Not many.

"And then of course—it isn't fair really—they dock his pay. They're even charging him for some of his care, which seems unacceptable."

"What do you mean, *care*? What care does he need? Why is he missing work?"

The collector paused, his delivery effortlessly natural. "I don't feel right divulging too much information."

"You're a debt collector. You threaten people—" The rest of the words caught in her throat.

"Well, we do discuss payment plans, and we encourage responsibility. But we still believe in privacy. I'm surprised you're asking me about Datu. Angelica, don't you know?"

He had almost convinced her. And then she realized: of course he would say those things, of course he would lie to her and make her feel like Datu had no way to pay his debts—not now, not ever. She had suspected that Datu owed something. But four times as much as she owed? And sick?

"You're lying," she said.

"Lying?"

"Datu isn't sick or missing work. He would tell me."

"Angelica. You understand what the BZ can do to people."

"Not him," she said. "Not everyone. Not yet."

"Well, this is uncomfortable. But not unexpected. Whether you believe it or not, there's the matter of the money—"

"Fine. I owe his share, if that's what you want to hear."

"Which brings us to your plan for payment. I can give you two weeks—"

"You'll get your money. Never call me again. Never."

She stood outside the door to the condo, feeling nauseated and breathless from the confrontation. Tea. She needed a cup of tea. A moment to think.

She pushed the key into the lock, leaned in, and was startled when the door opened quickly inward. Hiro's face was level with her own.

"Hello, Anji-san."

He was . . . full-sized. Complete.

"You have legs," she said, still catching her breath.

"Yes," he said. His voice was liquid with excitement. Breathy. Strange. "And . . . hands."

He held them up to her for inspection, moving the fingers, not segmented like Gina's, but smooth, more mannequin-like, ivory-skinned.

"How?" she asked.

"Gina opened the boxes and helped with the tools. We told her to. Gina has good hands. But not as good as mine."

When she pushed into the hallway, Hiro backed up slowly, each robotic leg making springy sounds as he slowly pivoted. He bounced his body up and down with boyish pleasure. He was still blocking her way.

"Sayoko-san?" she called out.

The giddy charm left his voice. "Please?"

"*Sayoko-san?*"

"Don't be afraid."

11 Angelica

"**S**ayoko-san!" Angelica shouted into the condo, straining to hear a reply.

"You dropped your shopping bag." Hiro bent over to retrieve it, slow to hook his untrained fingers around the handles.

"Get out of my way. Hiro. Please!"

He stood up again, advancing toward her, his hands reaching out for her.

"Why are you afraid?" His pitch had risen. He was fearful and confused, mirroring her behavior.

"Move," Angelica demanded.

Gina's red, hard-molded body came into view. She rolled across the living room floor, one step up from the entryway, holding a tray with a pot of tea and three cups. "Welcome!"

"Sayoko-san!" Angelica shouted again. Why hadn't she thought to check Gina's cam in the last hour? She had been so distracted. So irresponsible.

Hiro managed to spin around, infected by Angelica's alarm, convinced as much as she was that an emergency was underway, shouting just as loudly. "Sayoko-san!"

"Welcome," Gina said, voice muted and pleasant. "Please come in."

There was a smell in the room: metallic, nutty, acrid. Something burning. How many hours had passed since she had last seen Sayoko—not just Gina bustling around the living room, via remote-cam, but Sayoko, living and breathing?

"Please. Feel free to take off your shoes," Gina said.

Angelica stepped up from the polished floor of the hallway to the main living room, nursing shoes still on, tied tightly.

"Please. Make use of our slippers," Gina requested.

Hiro was agitated and desperate for reassurance, like a dog with its head and tail down, whimpering. "Anji-san," he called after her. He wasn't calling her Anji-sensei now. He didn't perceive her as his teacher at this moment. She was something else to him: possibly only an obstacle.

Angelica tried her hardest to sound merely firm, loud, not terrified: "Sayoko-san. *Obaasan.* Where are you hiding?" With every step forward she scanned the room, expecting with a sudden strange calmness the terrible, inexplicable: a body on the floor, a slumped-over form in a chair, a leg sticking out from a doorway. She had found bodies before, of course, especially in the days before wearables and medtech alerts, and even after them, because alerts failed, computers failed, just like organs, muscles, circulatory systems. She had found bodies in beds. In one case, at a kitchen table, face calmly planted next to a cereal bowl. More often, on bathroom floors. Bathrooms were the most dangerous rooms in any house. But death can catch us anywhere. We fade like flowers. We crash like waves. We collapse, grow cold, harden. Things of the flesh.

What had Hiro done?

And it occurred to her now, only now: *Yesterday.* Her own error. She had missed giving Sayoko her early evening medications. She was used to timers going off on her phone—timers that had stopped working when her phone was hacked. But that was no excuse, blaming technology. Evening meds were a standard routine. She had been exhausted from her trip to Chiba, gleeful about the helper robot Gina, feeling proud and even whimsical, window shopping and daydreaming—distracted, criminally irresponsible.

Worse, Hiro had tried to tell her. It was after dinner, when she was bringing Sayoko to the bathroom: something he had wanted to say:

A small but important health observation.

She had walked away and smugly shut the bathroom door to thwart him.

I will log the observation for discussion later.

How had she forgotten? Why hadn't he insisted?

One batch of medications entirely missed, eight prescriptions in all. She began to list them in her head, imagining the consequences of each missed dose—in some cases, mild, but one never knew. A chemical imbalance. Greater likelihood of dizziness, possibility of falling. A seizure.

She called out again, "Sayoko-san!"

The bedroom door opened. Angelica held her breath. She saw the front edge of one wheel first, and then a wrinkled white hand, pushing it.

Angelica called out with relief, "Sayoko-san!"

Sayoko emerged, blanket over her lap, color in her cheeks.

"What's all the fuss? Lower your voices."

Angelica rushed toward her. She reached out to pat her soft shoulder, to feel her warmth, to get a better look at her eyes, and even to smell her breath. "Are you all right?"

Sayoko's breath was a little sickly-sweet. Mild dehydration at worst. Sayoko-san rarely drank enough water or tea unless someone repeatedly pestered her about it. But her color was good. Her eyes were bright. She even smelled of powder, like she'd been fixing up her face prior to Angelica's return.

"Of course I'm all right. What's wrong with you?"

"Nothing, nothing." Angelica hid her face in her sleeve, wiping hard. "The day. Then I got back. And then I thought . . . nothing."

"I was taking a nap and then I freshened myself up. Isn't that allowed?"

So she didn't know.

"Your robot," Angelica said, getting her breath and voice under control. "Hiro."

Hiro was behind Angelica now, bouncing lightly on his legs with audible excitement, a metallic near-giggle.

"He's—he's different now. He assembled himself, with help from Gina."

Sayoko sighed. "I can see, can't I? He doesn't look like a rice cooker just sitting on a shelf anymore. He has legs and arms and hands. How else could he make my dinner?"

The bad smell again. *Rice cooker.*

Angelica said, "I didn't give him permission to cook anything."

"You didn't *know* he could cook anything. He can do all sorts of things now. We've had a lot of fun today . . ."

Sayoko was still talking, but Angelica had tuned her out and was already rushing toward the kitchen, the source of the starchy carbon smell.

She stopped in the doorway. There was no straight path to the counter. Groceries covered the floor. Cans, sacks of rice, a cabbage, long thin green beans, cucumbers. A haphazard grocery maze. On the countertop, too: mixing bowls and metal spoons, soy sauce and vinegar. A thawed piece of fish hung over the edge of the sink.

She made her way carefully, nudged a large radish aside with her toe and flung open the lid of the rice cooker. It was only dry and crusty, not actually burnt. Any decent rice cooker would've turned itself off sooner. This one was old—a veritable antique that Sayoko refused to part with. The irony of which galled Angelica. Sayoko wouldn't buy a new wheelchair, couldn't tolerate her wrist monitor, and didn't trust a modern rice cooker—yet she'd let a robot take over her life. *Their* life.

Angelica ripped the cord out of the wall and started shouting. First in Cebuano with a few words of Tagalog and English mixed in. Then, after a moment, in Japanese.

"This is a disaster! You stupid, awful thing!"

Hiro appeared in the doorway first, arms held slightly away from his body, fingers flexing nervously. Gina, only as tall as his waist, was behind him, pivoting right and left on her wheels, trying to get past him to receive instructions from Angelica. Gina said, "Would you like me to clean? Should I remove the objects from the floor?"

But Hiro's anguish was louder. He made a doglike whine, falling off at the end, then resuming higher, dangerously loud, until her eardrums felt ready to burst.

Angelica knew she was upsetting him, but she couldn't stop. "This is wrong. You are bad. Very, very bad, Hiro." She persisted despite his whine, muted for the moment. "You could have burned down the whole building." It wasn't true. There was only the odd smell and the scrubbing job ahead. "And we never put food on the floor. Never. It's filthy."

"It isn't filthy," Hiro objected. "Gina sanitized the floor. The counters have a higher bacteria count. We were doing an inventory. We were reorganizing."

"The floor isn't clean."

"It is," he said. "It *was*." His voice was becoming distressed again, the pitch rising, making her ears throb. "Your shoes. Take off your shoes at the door, Anji-san."

"You're not to cook—"

"We don't wear shoes in the house, Anji-san."

"*You* don't wear shoes at all!" she shouted. "You're not a person. You're not a human being. You're not a nurse or a cook. You're a broken appliance. And you're a danger to Sayoko-san. You shouldn't exist."

His sounds immediately ceased. His fingers stopped flexing. He had just eased back in a little bounce, knees bent, and he remained that way, in a partial crouch, eyes dimmed, as if she'd stumbled upon the magic phrase that took his animating spirit away. She watched. After a moment, his eyes brightened again—brighter than she'd ever seen. Cold fire. Soundlessly, he straightened up, turned. Gina scooted away to let him pass. He walked away, vanishing from Angelica's sight.

Sitting in her room moments later, facing Angelica, door closed for privacy, Sayoko was surprisingly calm. Regal, even.

"I've sent my son a message to come home."

Itou-san was due home two days before the birthday party. Angelica was so used to handling everything for Sayoko, so used to assuming she had no sense of the day or date or time, and where her son was at any given hour—or how to contact him, for that matter, though they had shown her how to use her wrist monitor to record and send short audios. She had resisted nearly all independent communication in the past.

Sayoko clarified, "I know he was coming home soon, but he was willing to book an earlier flight. It's for the best."

Angelica took a deep breath, preparing to thank her. She was sitting on the edge of the low futon, perched there, still ready to jump up at a moment's notice if she heard the robots getting into trouble, outside the door.

Sayoko said, "And I asked Gina to arrange for the rental agency to pick her up in the morning."

"I thought I'd have to take her and her box all the way back to Chiba—"

"No. For a small fee, they have a pickup option. It's no trouble."

Now Angelica felt like the client, the child. Pick-up service. Of course. She was disorganized and inefficient. She had lost her cool. She had overreacted. She suggested timidly, "If only someone would come pick up Hiro . . ."

But Sayoko did not reply to that.

Sayoko shifted in her wheelchair, as if she were going to reach out and touch Angelica on the arm but had second thoughts.

"I'm sorry if I've said anything unkind to you, these last few days."

"Thank you." Angelica bowed her head.

"It's nothing."

Clearly, it was Angelica's turn now. She was not one to mix personal and professional, but she had always wanted to say this one thing. "I don't have my grandmother anymore. She was, like you, very strong in her later years. She spoke her mind."

Was that so very hard?

Sayoko acted as if she hadn't heard. She said, "I think it might be better if . . . Don't misunderstand. I wouldn't want—"

What had started out sounding warm and genuine to Angelica's ears was on the verge of becoming—what was it—a sort of breakup? A gentle and ambiguous firing?

Or possibly not yet.

Sayoko folded her hands on her lap. "I'm sure you feel bad about saying those unfair things to Hiro."

Angelica struggled to contain her emotions. If Sayoko hadn't said it, perhaps she would've come to those feelings herself—shame was already roiling in her stomach—but hearing it expressed in clear terms, in *testing*, conditional terms, brought out her contrary nature. She was *not* sorry. He was a menace. And he was only a machine. Hiro's feelings were not her concern. Sayoko's safety was.

But Angelica's indignation was fragile. The proof of her poor choices was still evident, just on the other side of that door.

"You're not blameless, you know," Sayoko said.

For a moment Angelica thought Sayoko would mention the missed round of medication, but she didn't. Sayoko was almost certainly unaware. She was thinking only of Angelica's absence.

"You chose to leave me here, with him."

"And with Gina," Angelica added.

"Yes, you entrusted my care to a talking vacuum cleaner." Sayoko's stern expression softened at last. She offered a complicit smile. "I won't tell if you won't."

They agreed to have a peacemaking chat with Hiro. But when

Angelica pushed Sayoko's wheelchair into the living room, it was empty. Angelica checked the bedrooms, bathrooms and closets, half-expecting to see Hiro crouched in a corner, sulking. In the kitchen, Gina was busy putting food away. She could not tell them where Hiro had gone.

Without any protest about the cold or the danger of crossing streets, Sayoko let Angelica push her down busy Asakusa-dori, past the funerary supply shops that Angelica rarely noticed, beyond their window displays of cremation urns and dignified, tasseled funeral stationery. The sun had set and the shops were all closed, but Sayoko insisted on peering into each display window, just in case Hiro had wandered inside, curious, and had gotten caught up talking with a shopkeeper.

"Why would he be curious?" Angelica asked.

"We talked about death. It perplexed him. He wanted to know about our cremation customs. I explained how we use chopsticks to pull the bones from the ash, how we pass the bones from one set of sticks to another and place them into the urn. Or we still did when my husband passed. Maybe they pay someone to do all that now."

They looked inside another window featuring home altars, *juzu* prayer beads and condolence money envelopes.

"He was worried about when I would die," Sayoko mused. "I reminded him that technology is advancing so fast, we just can't know. Who thought I would still be alive now?"

Angelica said, "He shouldn't worry you so much with those thoughts or get you talking about ashes and chopsticks. It's morbid."

Sayoko set her hands on the top of her wheels for a moment, forcing Angelica to stop. She turned to look over her shoulder, a gesture she could manage only halfway, so that Angelica got a sideways glimpse of her saddened profile.

"Young people rarely understand. There's nothing wrong with

morbid thoughts. Anyway, Hiro asks questions about everything. I like that. He makes me realize that I *do* have things to say."

Sayoko must have read something in Angelica's expression. "He isn't just flattering me, either."

"Are you sure?"

"He wants to know. He needs to know. He needs *me*."

Angelica started pushing the wheelchair again. She thought Sayoko was finished, but just as they reached the heavier traffic of Showa-dori, the multi-lane highway separating their quiet neighborhood from bustling Ueno Park, Sayoko spoke again.

"Exotic is a bad word these days. But there was a time when many people were exotic to each other, and it wasn't always a bad thing."

But Sayoko stopped there. Angelica leaned over, ear closer, pushing the wheelchair slowly, waiting. *Exotic?*

"I was exotic to him, but he was exotic to me, too. Is that so terrible? He wanted to study me but I was hungry for anything new, and I was trying to understand him as well."

"Who, Sayoko-san?"

Sayoko refused to answer the question. She was lost in her own thoughts.

"Hiro studies me, he is using our every interaction to understand human beings, and I don't feel used at all. I feel . . ."

Angelica waited.

After another moment Sayoko said, "He reminds me of my first love. Is that strange?"

Yes, Angelica wanted to say, but she held it in, suppressing both her words and her sense of dread. Older patients talked about their first sweethearts all the time, and most nurses enjoyed the stories, which were nearly always safe territory. But this was different. It was one thing to talk about a past love, and another to imagine a machine as resembling that person. It was immensely disturbing—all of it. Maybe Sayoko's mind wasn't sound after all.

"I've talked about it with Hiro," Sayoko said. "I was a dry plant and Daisuke was . . . rain. Simple as that."

At Showa-dori, in the shadow of a busy overpass, Sayoko said, "Wait," and then grew quiet. The blue nightfall had deepened into black, and now the oncoming cars were like living things, animal eyes advancing too quickly. Pedestrian walkways climbed up and over the streaming traffic, but there was no way for Angelica to push a wheelchair up the steps, and if there was some kind of elevator or wheelchair-accessible tunnel in that warren of roadside buildings, restaurants, and pachinko parlors, she didn't know where it was. The street level crosswalks were crowded with commuters coming home from the train station and crowds of twenty-somethings, many of them dressed like they were still in high school, holding onto their bygone youth, in short plaid skirts or gray pants and navy blue uniform jackets. But everyone else walked quickly, with no fear of getting stuck before the light changed.

This was the point at which Sayoko often begged off, claiming to be tired, wishing to return home. Why press on, past all that traffic? Ueno Park was a shadow of what it had been, not that it had an unblemished past—in addition to temples, it had once housed a red-light teahouse district, as even a foreign worker like Angelica knew. Now there were homeless people and lewd street performers, jugglers and women in tight leotards. There were too many bohemian visitors and too many shadowy corners. The shrines would be darkened now, the *o-mikuji* paper fortune slips knotted over metal wires, fluttering in the wind. The tall grass at the margins of Shinobazu Pond would rattle like swords.

"You want to cross?" Angelica asked.

"Of course," Sayoko said impatiently. "Go fast. Push hard."

They made the light only barely, with the sound of oncoming cars at their heels.

"Left or right?" Angelica asked.

"Right," Sayoko said. The lotus pond, to the left, depressed her, she had frequently complained. Classic wooden rowboats had been replaced, over time, by plastic swan-shaped paddleboats, cheap looking, steered by young lovers snapping endless photos. The nation—the world—had become a cartoon.

They walked down the main path, toward the Tokyo National Museum, the cherry trees long past bloom, their green crowns just black masses in the darkening sky overhead, past the *Kiyomizu Kannon-do* temple, Yuki's place to pray and now Junichi's too; this is probably how Sayoko thought all of Ueno Park should look still, but Angelica did not share that sense of nostalgia and did not often choose to wander close to the historic buildings. The Shinto and Buddhist customs, the paper fortunes, especially the unlucky ones left tied on trees and wires to discharge their negative power, and the massive boulders inscribed with Japanese symbols—all of it was unfamiliar country to her.

When they reached a path with signs pointing in several directions, Angelica felt suddenly sure. "The zoo," she said.

"Ah yes, he's never seen animals," Sayoko remembered.

But more than that, Angelica was sure, he had never seen a place where animals had been deemed too dangerous, and purposefully exterminated, as Sayoko had told them. *You shouldn't exist,* Angelica had told Hiro.

But the zoo was closed, and no one, man or robot, loitered near the gate or the fenced paths leading up to it.

They backtracked.

"Someone will steal him," Sayoko said as Angelica struggled to push her chair from one pool of lamplight to the next, hurrying between the most shadowy sections, ignoring her fatigue. The trail angled down slightly, into a lonely stretch that Angelica could only barely recognize as the place, months earlier, that had been crowded with cherry-blossom viewers, the entire park thrumming with people, even at night, some areas lit up with spotlights, so the pink boughs glowed.

"Oh!" Sayoko called out, that shout of pain Angelica had not heard in a year, since Sayoko had woken in the middle of the night with stomach cramps caused by her medicine.

"Is something hurting?" Angelica stopped and came around to the front of the wheelchair.

Sayoko waved her arms, frustrated by her blocked view. "We have to keep looking. Hurry, please. Hurry!"

When Angelica didn't immediately step out of the way, Sayoko began to push herself up and out of her chair, preparing to walk.

"Sit back, I'll push. It's faster. We'll find him."

By the time they reached the closed museum, the wooded path was black and Sayoko was shivering. Angelica went to the front of the wheelchair and reached beneath Sayoko's blanket to feel her thin, cold hands. Sayoko's teeth were chattering so fiercely she had trouble speaking.

"I'm fine, let's keep looking."

"We need to warm you up."

"It's dark now. He'll be afraid."

"If he were afraid, he'd just come home."

"That isn't true. That isn't how children are." She corrected herself. "That's not how grown men are, either. They're stubborn."

Angelica saw a glow and a familiar green sign, the mermaid logo. She pushed Sayoko toward the coffee shop, still open and bustling with young Japanese people, the interior yellow and warm.

When they were just at the doorway, Sayoko protested, "Not this place. Let's find another."

"Do you see any other?"

The museum plaza area was mostly dark, the fountains quiet, the other shops shuttered.

"It isn't just coffee," Angelica reassured her. "They have tea."

"Why did they build this so close to the national museum? It's not right."

"Because people who visit museums get thirsty."

"Why can't they have something more . . . fitting?"

Angelica knew she meant more Japanese, or at least more Asian. But it was just like resenting Filipino nurses and West African physical therapists: if you needed them, and they were there waiting to serve you, and if they did their jobs well, and if there weren't enough young Japanese people willing to work at those wages, couldn't you just stop complaining and say thank you?

"Because it's popular. Anyway, they stay open late. Come on."

"I can't have tea when Hiro is still missing."

At the counter, Angelica ordered two teas and a toasted sandwich. The girl behind the counter was dark-skinned, pretty and a little plump. From her ears hung small, silver gardenia flowers. When Angelica lingered at the counter, the girl finally looked up, really looked.

"*Malawang-galang na po,*" Angelica tried. *Excuse me.*

The girl hesitated before answering in Tagalog. "*Oo?*" Yes?

As the next-in-line couple bent over the glass case, debating their choices of cake, Angelica made her request. *Sister, help me.* If she could just leave this older woman at that table over there, in her wheelchair, safely seated, within view of the cash register. Just for twenty minutes. They had a family friend, missing in the park. Without the wheelchair, Angelica could walk faster while the older woman stayed warm. Yes? Please?

"*Ayos lang,*" the girl finally said. "Not very long or I'll get in trouble."

She had felt sure about the zoo, briefly, but she felt surer now about the pond, even if the swan boats were all chained up and all but the most resolute couples gone home. Under a tree, in the shadows, there was a shifting lump that Angelica tried not to stare at too directly, but she couldn't help notice a hand groping a backside.

And there, on a bench under a streetlamp, sat Hiro: back erect, silver fingers on silver knees, fingers tapping frenetically, as if he were sending out some telegraphic code.

"Hiro."

He didn't turn his head. "Hello, Anji-san."

"What are you doing?"

"Calibrating my sense of touch. It's taking longer than I expected."

"You worried us."

"Vision may seem miraculous. The eyeball itself is a work of art. But in truth, sight is simpler. Touch is surprisingly complex."

"Hiro—"

But he would not be diverted from his musings. "There are pressure, temperature and vibration sensors in my fingers, but with an upgrade, I could possibly have them everywhere."

"No. What are you doing *here* in the park, I mean. You worried Sayoko. She's here, warming up at a coffee shop."

"Yes," he agreed. "The day's warmth fades quickly."

"It's too cold to be out," Angelica said, hoping he'd rise and follow, that they wouldn't have to talk.

"Not for them," he said, pointing at the lovers.

"You shouldn't be watching. It's rude."

"They don't mind. They asked me to take many photos of them, in the rowboat."

"Earlier."

"Yes, earlier."

"It doesn't matter. They don't want you watching now."

"They barely notice. They are so immersed in their pleasures they've forgotten I'm here. That is the power of touch. It can dissolve barriers: in time, in space, between people. The designers were wrong to leave it out of my initial body plan. I must believe they didn't understand its full value."

Angelica refused to talk about body plans.

"Let's go."

But he kept watching the couple, as if his own welfare relied on fully understanding what they were doing under the shifting blanket.

"Hiro. Listen to me. Sayoko is waiting, and that couple wants privacy."

"I understand," he said, only half-convincingly. "Sayoko-san and I are happier when we have privacy."

Angelica paused, flustered.

"What is the nature of your relationship, exactly?"

"I don't understand your question, Anji-san."

"How do you see yourself in relation to her?"

"You are angry now, and I am not sensing your trust. I don't think this is the time to talk about the subtle nature of relationship boundaries."

"Do you see yourself as a servant? As a . . . son?"

"Not a servant, not a son," he said without hesitation. "Sons wish to develop and mature and then to go away. Like Itou-san, always traveling."

"He needs to make money. Sayoko needs his money, to pay for things."

"She needs other things," he said, quietly.

"And you're an expert now, on what she needs."

"It isn't difficult. I ask and she tells me. What she doesn't tell me, I easily infer. She needs as much as I need, but they are different needs, of course."

This was too much. Angelica couldn't explain the rage she felt. How dare he come along and not only try to replace her, but all while demanding so much—and getting it all.

"You are not allowed to have needs," she said.

"But everything alive has needs."

"You aren't *alive*, Hiro."

"Am I not?"

"No, you absolutely are not. And even if you were, I don't care. It's not what you're here for. It's not why they made you.

It just isn't right. If you're a form of life then you're . . . you're
. . . a parasite."

Hiro paused a moment before replying. "The metaphor is not apt."

"Don't talk to me about metaphors—"

"We have a mutualistic symbiosis, not a parasitic symbiosis.
You are a competent nurse, but I'm afraid you are not well versed
in ecological concepts."

He stood suddenly and audibly. One of the lovers, the girl, peered
from the shifting blanket, curious about the bouncy, metallic sound.

"Sayoko-san's first love was a naturalist. Sayoko-san herself is
quite familiar with ecology and she would not appreciate your
misuse of those terms," Hiro continued. "But you are correct about
one thing. I have failed her."

"Yes," Angelica said, feeling yet another pang of resentment: how
did Hiro know anything about Sayoko's first love after less than a
week when she had lived with Sayoko all this time and knew nothing
about her past?

"I caused her worry," he admitted.

"Yes," Angelica said, wanting the reprimand to sink in. If he felt
alive, it must be possible to wound him. "A flaw in your programming."

"No," he said, in a soft, disappointed voice. "I am not programmed, as you know. You persist in this error, for reasons I don't
understand."

"I don't care about computers or robots."

"You don't want to care. You feel threatened by me. But Anji-san,
I would never hurt anyone on purpose. For example, I will not tell
Itou-san that you failed to give Sayoko-san some of her medications.
That would make him question your competence and reconsider
your employment. I would never do that."

Angelica felt her cheeks flush.

"In fact," Hiro said, "I recommend you remove the unconsumed
doses from the weekly dispenser so that no one notices. At the end

of the week, even Sayoko-san may realize there are too many pills left, and this may give her unnecessary anxiety."

"Don't direct me to deceive my patient."

"We are both in a position to cause her worry, and at this stage in her life, anxiety is not productive."

"I'm not having this conversation with you, Hiro. You are not in a position to decide what's best for anyone. I'm very upset with you."

"I would like to correct that."

But Angelica did not wait for him to say anything more. She stood and gestured emphatically, and he followed.

When they entered the Starbucks and Sayoko saw them, she tried to push herself up and out of the wheelchair but made it only halfway before collapsing back again. When Angelica was first hired, she had encouraged Sayoko to use her walker as much as possible. But over time, unless Rene was there to cheerlead, Sayoko had stopped trying as often, and Angelica had not supplied sufficient pressure. Angelica had accepted Sayoko's depressed nature and her gradual deterioration. She had not fully believed in the idea that a woman nearing one hundred could be without modest, conventional limits; that she could actually become stronger with a combination of the latest therapies and disciplined, motivating care. But being one hundred and healthy was not unusual. Even being 110 or older was not exactly rare. There were tens of thousands of supercentenarians in Japan now. Angelica's views of the world were outdated. She was still living in the twentieth century. She was simply wrong about a great many things.

Failure after failure after failure.

"Let's get out of here," Sayoko said, gesturing with one arthritic knuckle toward the doorway, uneaten sandwich and paper cup still on the table. "I don't feel well."

Hiro turned to Angelica. "Permission to perform a blood test."

The words were barely out when Angelica saw him extend his hand, pointer finger out, tiny square at the tip opening to reveal a retractable needle tip.

Angelica stammered, "You're not a qualified lab technician."

"I'm more than a technician. I'm technician and lab in one."

"You're certainly not a qualified nurse."

Sayoko interjected, "Let's go home. You two can keep bickering there."

Angelica persisted. "Hiro, you must stop trying to take charge of Sayoko-san's health. I am in charge of requesting blood tests for this patient. You're not qualified."

"Correct," Hiro hesitated. "That issue should be addressed." He went quiet for a moment, limbs still, eyes dimmed. Then he spoke again. "National licensure exam passed. I am now qualified as a nurse in Japan."

What had just happened? To be a nurse required three years' nursing education and passing the national exam, at the minimum. But she knew Hiro wasn't lying.

"You took the test? Just now?"

"Yes," he said.

"You don't have to sit for it?"

"The AI nursing exam requires no physical presence. I avoided taking it until now for reasons of diplomacy and harmony, but where Sayoko-san's health is involved, I have a higher duty . . ."

"The two of you," Sayoko said, exasperated. "Can't you see I'm fine? Can't you see you're only upsetting me more?" Sayoko held up her wrist monitor, which was emitting no alarms. "My vitals are fine. My pulse is stable. My thinking is clear. The only thing not making me well is all the worry you caused me, Hiro, and the way you keep nattering at him, Angelica!"

Hiro dropped his head forward, lowered his back, and then slowly folded forward, fully prostrating himself. The front of his head rested on the floor of the empty coffee shop.

"I am so sorry, Sayoko-san," Hiro said.

"Get up, get up," she said, waving her arms.

"I beg for your forgiveness."

"That isn't my way," she said.

But he remained folded over, penitent.

"That's not who I am," Sayoko insisted. "Get off the floor. Stop your foolishness. You've only been a nuisance. It isn't the same. And anyway, you know I wasn't raised believing in all that . . . stuff."

On the way home, with Hiro pushing the wheelchair swiftly and easily, Sayoko did not question or rebuke him. At the busy Showa-dori crossing, she reached one hand over her shoulder to pat Hiro as he pushed the chair.

Hiro was uncharacteristically silent as well, except for a moment, after the crossing, when they passed a stairwell leading up and over and back toward Ueno Park. A busker was playing the violin. They drew closer to the sound and then stopped. The musician—European, tousle-haired, neck wrapped in a checked scarf—paused for a moment, making sense of what he was seeing: three faces at different heights, a wheelchair, a man made of metal.

Unfazed, the busker nodded once and then continued, pushing up-bow into the swelling crescendo of some song of tragic beauty which Angelica did not recognize. Perhaps Sayoko recognized it. No doubt Hiro could discover the work's name instantly. But none of that mattered. Only the music's haunting ache did, and its effect pierced them all.

"There," Hiro said when the song ended. "That."

As if it were some clear answer to a question. As if they were the logical final words in a conversation they had all been having.

Sayoko reached back to touch his hand again. "Yes. I know."

12 Angelica

When they got home, there was a message flashing on the front hallway's rarely used communication board. Angelica played it immediately, expecting it would be Itou, providing the specifics of his next-day arrival. Instead, it was a news reporter, confirming the time and location of Sayoko's birthday celebration, later that week, and wanting permission to come a half hour early, to set up lights and check sound.

Angelica considered the days ahead, wondering anew how she'd find time to deal with her debt problem. She had nothing to sell. Could she get an advance on her salary? She dared not ask, and even if a small raise were given, it wouldn't be enough. She had to keep thinking.

After they'd warmed up with cups of miso, there were no protests about going straight to bed. Angelica helped Sayoko with her meds and toileting and then fell asleep without washing her own face. She tugged a nightgown over her head and reclined on her futon thinking she was only resting her eyes. Next thing, light was streaming through the half-closed blinds and there were sounds of activity at the front door: keys and the squeeze of a latch, accompanied by the bounce of Hiro's leg joints. The clock read 6:20. Sayoko didn't usually need assistance until seven.

Through the half-open bedroom door, Angelica heard Hiro say, "Itou-san. *Hajimemashite.*"

She strained to listen: only silence. Itou had been startled, coming face to face with the robot at the door.

But then she heard Itou's response: a soft chuckle. "Nice to meet *you*. So, you're the reason I had to change flights?"

Angelica hurried to dress and brush her teeth and hair. Then she caught her expression in the mirror. She hadn't worn any makeup in about two weeks, which happened to be the last time she'd seen Itou. A little foundation under the eyes then. A little mascara and just a hint of blush. Better. There was no excuse for looking as drained as she felt. Just as she was turning away from her reflection, she felt a tickle of nausea and clutched the edge of the sink. Her vision dimmed slightly and then brightened again, the dizziness passing.

You are being silly about this, she told herself. Five days ago she had fainted in the street—but what a five days. Yesterday she had bought the pregnancy test, and then, in the chaos of the hours that followed, forgotten about it. Her purse was hanging from a hook on the back of the bathroom door. The test was inside.

She remembered the last time she had used such a urine test, sitting in a college bathroom stall, watching the pink indicator line brighten into view. The incontrovertible knowledge: yes, you are carrying a baby. An unwanted baby. She'd been twenty-two.

She'd gotten pregnant accidentally, with a fellow nursing student who had already stopped calling by the time she missed her first period. She knew what her future held in store: working abroad, almost certainly. And she knew what other women in her situation, married or unmarried, did when they had one or more children and needed to go abroad without them. They left the babies home, in care of family members or, very often, in the care of low-paid nannies. The Filipina abroad sent back money, usually for many years. The substitute mother, often illiterate, sometimes with her own children cared for by someone else—a never-ending chain of outsourced love and care, each successive link more fragile—became all your child knew. If you had a husband, half the time he and the nanny ended up pairing off. It was so common it didn't even count as a scandal. Women gave up their children temporarily—as Yanna had—because it made economic sense. Five years passed, or ten, the child or children reached adolescence and sometimes, a Filipina would return as a grandmother without ever having experienced being a day-to-day mother.

Not Angelica. She knew what it was like to feel abandoned, to call out in the dark and hear no answer. She loathed the thought of another person trying to replace her, and doing it imperfectly, creating damage and guilt on all sides. She would never do that to her own child.

An abortion, illegal and risky, seemed preferable. But it was not safe or painless. The quacks who performed the surgeries were not above punishing their patients, leaving them scarred and often infertile. The first gynecologist Angelica visited in Japan was accustomed to seeing barren women, but not for this reason: vengeful third-world doctoring. He'd tried to reassure her that things could be done—perhaps the scarring was not so bad and she could still save her fertility—and she had listened, politely nodding, dubious and apathetic. She wasn't wealthy and she wasn't Japanese. She accepted the fertility clinic brochure he gave her with both hands and disposed of it later that day.

When she'd started sleeping with Junichi, he had asked, and Angelica had assured him—*I can't get pregnant, I'm sure of it.*

How do you know?

Women just know these things.

She had not relished telling a man who had been trying for years to have children that she herself had given up a pregnancy and fallen into the hands of a doctor willing to damage a womb.

Angelica opened the testing kit now, returning the empty box to her purse rather than leaving it in the house garbage. It looked no different than the kind of pee stick she'd used in her college days. She followed the steps, withdrew the dampened stick from between her legs, sat staring at it for one long minute, feeling silly for wasting even these few seconds when Itou was home, in the house, waiting to see her. The results indicator remained blank. Done.

She started to get up then forced herself to remain, counting: *one one-thousand, two one-thousand . . .*

From out in the hallway came the sound of Itou's voice: "Good morning? Hello?"

She kept counting.

After another minute the second pale pink line appeared. It cleaved her mind smoothly in two. One side silently insisted: "No, impossible." The other said: "Of course. What else?"

She got up, hid the used stick in her purse, washed her hands, and looked in the mirror at one of the few female forty-somethings in Japan who did not want to have a baby. A cosmic joke.

She took a breath and opened the bathroom door. "Coming!"

In the kitchen she bowed deeply at the first sign of her employer, who was already making himself breakfast as Hiro watched.

"Can I get you something?" she asked. "You must have left KL so early. Let me—"

He continued to pour boiling water into his cup, taking his time.

After a moment he said, "I think I heard my mother just now."

"*Hai!*" Angelica said it too loudly, bowing again, more nervous in his presence than she had felt since the first day he'd hired her. She had to focus, leaving every preoccupation behind, save one. It was imperative that she stay in the kitchen, that she observe Itou interacting with Hiro, that she overhear their initial conversations and have the opportunity to parse his words and gestures for surprise, acceptance, doubt. How could she develop any strategy at all if she missed the opening moves?

Angelica had not started toward the bathroom, where Sayoko was waiting.

Itou said, "I think she may need assistance. Perhaps with a delicate matter."

Angelica bowed again, blushing. "*Hai. Sumimasen.*"

Sayoko was just as eager to make her way to the kitchen and annoyed by her failure to make the transition back from toilet to wheelchair when she had done just fine getting herself up and out of bed in the first place.

"My arms are getting weak," Sayoko said, out of breath, when Angelica arrived to help her. "That isn't age. It's laziness. I'm sorry, Anji-chan."

"You don't have to be sorry."

"You're right," Sayoko said, her contrition dissolving into renewed impatience. "Now hurry, won't you?"

"Yes. Let's clean you up first."

The end result of two people hurrying in such close proximity was more delay—tussling over clothes, excess splashing at the sink, another shirt change only minutes after the first to replace a damp top, a too-quick combing of hair.

"And a little rouge, please," Sayoko asked. "If you will."

Angelica forced herself to slow down and reached for a rarely used makeup bag on a nearby shelf.

After applying powder, rouge, a touch of eyebrow pencil and a dab of lip gloss, she told Sayoko, "You look lovely."

"I look well?"

Angelica glanced up, their eyes meeting in the mirror. Staring at Sayoko's reflection, that pale oval face, surprisingly smooth despite so many decades on this earth and with dark eyes that shone, Angelica saw a beauty and a strength she sometimes forgot to notice.

"Better than well, Sayoko-san."

"You're sure?"

"You look better than you've ever looked. You are timeless, Sayoko-san."

"Such flattery!" Sayoko pretended to scoff, but she was evidently moved. She looked up, blinking hard to hold back any tears that would spoil her makeup. "That's important. I must look healthy or my son might think Hiro's no good for me. It's up to us to make him understand. Will you do that? Will you help him understand?"

Angelica didn't reply.

"Promise me," Sayoko said.

But Angelica couldn't promise. Nor at this moment could she lie.

"Please, Anji-chan," Sayoko whispered. "Don't let him take Hiro away."

They were still staring into each other's eyes when Itou called again from the kitchen. "Mother? Are you coming? Don't you want to see your son?"

"So," Itou said to Angelica later that night. They were alone at last: dinner finished and the dishes washed, Sayoko helped into bed, Hiro in there with her, on sentry duty, as Sayoko liked to call it, standing in the corner with his eye lights dimmed and his trunk opaque.

In the kitchen, Itou filled Angelica's cup with tea, then his own.

"I can see you've had an interesting week," he said.

This he gathered from the day they'd spent both together and apart—a long morning during which Itou, tired from his early flight, listened as his mother talked and showed off Hiro's functions, and as Hiro was made to perform, answer questions and allay doubts, as if he were some new boyfriend brought home by a young woman to her family.

Itou had asked questions, only some of which Angelica could answer, about Hiro's full physical abilities and his optional upgrades, as well as the cloud-computing, social-learning AI functions that were currently "disabled," awaiting his stage two checkup. Did that mean he never went online at all? No, he accessed the internet all the time, Angelica explained. Without being connected, he couldn't fulfill his duties.

Even the smallest details interested Itou. Hiro's slit-shaped mouth had a small hole at the center. That was for blowing air, and doing CPR, but it could be used for other things, even blowing up children's balloons. Over his simple eyes there was a visor which could easily become a screen, the size of wraparound sunglasses, on which could be played an image of human-like eyes, with more expressiveness than Hiro's simple eye slits conveyed. Then why, Itou asked, was Hiro's visor never animated? Because in early tests, Sayoko had not responded warmly to those kinds of robot faces. Nor had she responded to video presentations of the more mannequin-like, almost-but-not-quite-human faces—the kinds one saw in taxis and department stores.

When Itou had been at his most interrogatory, pressing Hiro for more of these details, Sayoko had called out in a distressed voice: *Don't change his face. Don't change anything. I like Hiro the way he is. I don't want to hear any more.*

In the afternoon, Itou had ordered a car and retreated to his office for several hours, finishing the work he had abandoned in KL. Then he'd returned for a family dinner, which Angelica had cooked more carefully than anything she'd prepared in months: fried pork cutlets, steamed vegetables, white rice. She had tried making a *tonkatsu* sweet and sour sauce for the pork, but something must have gone wrong, since Itou gave it a sniff and then ate his cutlet plain. After dinner, Sayoko sat in front of the television. Itou pretended to read the newspaper, an expensive vintage format he subscribed to—Junichi had called the habit an affectation—printed on big sheets that were hard to hold and fold without rattling. Angelica sensed he was watching his mother and Hiro, quietly. Just as they were watching him.

Now, finally, Angelica and Itou had some privacy.

"It's unusual, I grant you that," Itou said. "She seems very attached. It's what the manufacturer claimed, but I didn't believe it. I was adamant that if any person were to resist a new technology like this one, it would be my mother, second only to me. Perhaps that only convinced them that I was the best test case."

She waited for him to say more, but he removed his eyeglasses to rub his face. He took his time putting them back on.

"We'll resolve this," he said, finally. "Obviously, this was not what I had in mind when I consented to a test trial."

"A test trial?"

"For now. We have to stay informed of our options."

Options? For replacing her entirely? Would he ever come out and say it directly?

"I know about the new glitches with the relief agency," he said. "It's only the beginning of long-term problems. There are liabilities involved with using machines, but we can own a machine, and we can choose those liabilities. Someday, the human care companies and even hospital emergency rooms won't give us a choice."

Out of nervousness, she finished her cup of tea.

He started to pour more, realized the pot was empty and gestured for her to stay seated. "There is a time to be firm and a time to be flexible. Perhaps I have been too skeptical about the new advances. More old-fashioned than my mother, in too many ways."

While he was busy at the kitchen counter, back turned, Angelica searched inside herself. What was the best thing? What was the truth? Did she have any immediate doubts now about Hiro's reliability or about Sayoko's safety? Aside from facts, there was strategy. If she wanted to persuade Itou, would it be more convincing to be adamant, or to feign ambivalence, as if still weighing the evidence with an open mind?

When Itou returned to the table he didn't speak, staring at the teapot as the leaves steeped. There was never any point in hurrying him, especially when he was troubled.

After pouring fresh cups, he said, "I trust your opinion. I know that you want only the best for my mother. Has she been acting differently with this robot in the house?"

There was not one way to answer. There were a half-dozen ways. There were facets and patterns, clear or obscure. When Itou was negotiating some new trade deal or chairing some policy debate, what information did he choose to share? Information that benefitted Japan, of course. He did not share everything.

"She is more worried," Angelica began to say, choosing one piece of the truth, fitting it into place. "I'd say she is more emotional in general."

"I see."

"And she talks more. Much more. Some of her stories seem . . . invented, or at least exaggerated." If he pressed, where would she start? With the story of having Itou taken away, however briefly, as a baby; with romantic imaginings of some valiant first lover; with allusions to being mistreated as a young woman; with a constant worry that Hiro would be taken away? Even her story about the animals of Tokyo's zoo being slaughtered seemed odd and unreliable. "I don't mean to question her veracity. It's only that—well—paranoia is a symptom. And memory is always fallible, even in the best cases."

Hai, he sighed, as if none of this was new to him. Because Itou was not surprised, Angelica felt her own tentative, partial disbelief harden into something else—a choice. Sayoko was not making sense. That made everything easier.

Angelica said, "Her appetite and energy level has been unstable as well." That was true. Sayoko had been ravenous one day, willing to skip meals another. She had been exhausted after staying up too late with Hiro and full of energy later in the week, when she'd had fun interacting with him and with Gina.

"Ah," he said. One syllable.

Was that all he could say? The reserve and restraint that epitomized proper behavior here would never feel natural to Angelica. She had grown up in a house where people sang like birds: women laughing and gossiping, but men, too. Her father, on the porch at night, telling stories to her and Datu and their three sisters as well as any other kids who'd come up the lane at the sound of his storytelling voice with its squeaky imitations and low comical drawls, the sounds of frogs croaking, roosters crowing and fish blowing imaginary bubbles.

Forever gone.

Itou oversaw the third pouring of tea: curling steam, the feeling of heat through the porcelain as Angelica touched the crackle-glazed surface.

Itou finally said, "You've been put into a difficult situation. It would be less so, if you had found that you and the robot could work together."

Hadn't she tried? Hadn't she waited and experimented and adapted, coping at every turn with the certainty that none of this was to her benefit?

She found it hard to breathe and had to remind herself: nothing was decided yet.

Itou folded his hands together and looked up, expression stony. "Permit me to ask: do you think she is in immediate danger?"

His eyes were on her. She was tempted to answer immediately, positively, emphatically. But what would that accomplish? If he doubted at all, then he could disregard her as alarmist. If she drew a line, he would have to step on one side or the other. But if she drew no line, he wouldn't know where to stand. He would experience a taste of the vertigo that was her daily life.

"I don't think anyone can know for sure," she answered after a moment. "He—it—is an untested kind of intervention. And it's constantly changing. That seems to be the most essential part of the robot's design."

"Of course you're right," he said. "Untested, which means unpredictable. But we shouldn't make rash decisions. Untested doesn't mean unsafe." He stared into his teacup. "What do they seem to do when they are alone?"

When Sayoko and Hiro were behind closed doors, how could she possibly know what they were doing? But Angelica did know, a little.

She knew that for a period of time each night after bedtime she heard Sayoko's muffled voice talking without interruption, as if she were educating Hiro, or telling him stories. Angelica had rested in bed, eyes closed, straining to hear, catching bits and pieces, the word "Grandmother" often, and "Daisuke." The name did not seem to belong to her deceased husband. It did not match the name on a framed diploma from the 1950s, hanging in the hallway, which Angelica had always associated with Itou's father. It was someone else, from a longer-ago past. Angelica felt too ashamed to admit that she had eavesdropped, and even more ashamed that she felt left out and jealous, knowing Sayoko had not chosen to tell her these stories, which she felt so desperate to transmit, night after night, to a mere machine.

"I'm sorry—I forgot to ask you," Itou said. "There's more to life than this robot problem. How did your last language exam go?"

She didn't feel ready for the change of subject, but she tried her best to sound unflustered. "It went very well. The results should arrive any day now."

"Good," he said, nodding briskly. "I received an immigration form, asking questions about your employment renewal. Perhaps normal, but I got an unfamiliar message after submitting. *Unresolved*, it said."

Her heart was in her throat all over again. "What does it usually say?"

"*Accepted*. Or maybe *Pending*. I don't recall last year's form, exactly."

Angelica hesitated, not wanting to make any request for Itou's help, while knowing that any visa hang-up could be just as disastrous as being replaced by Hiro. If Hiro had his way, she wouldn't work for Sayoko. But if she ran afoul of the entire foreign worker system, she'd never work for any Japanese client again.

She got up her nerve to ask. "Shouldn't we find out if there's a problem?"

"The automated message said we'd hear more in time, if there is anything to hear."

"But maybe . . ." Angelica tried. "Perhaps you could contact them directly."

"Doubtful."

"Or perhaps you know someone personally, in the right office?"

"That isn't the way."

The rebuke was clear.

"But you said you did well on the language exam," Itou added more gently. "So, there will be no problem. We shouldn't second-guess them. And we have our hands full already with Mother, and with her birthday party. Let's not forget that."

She was not surprised, later, when Itou asked for permission to go into Angelica's bedroom—really, his room of course—to console himself with the beloved instruments of his youth. He always asked first. She watched him take the step stool from the kitchen, heard the bedroom door open and the light rattle of glass as the high cabinet was opened. She turned toward the sink, washing the last of the dinner dishes, pretending not to listen, as if he were doing something private and secret. She knew he was self-conscious about his musical abilities, or lack thereof. Then she heard his slippered feet padding down the short hallway, the opening and closing of his bedroom door. He'd always talked of improving the condo's already decent soundproofing, to spare anyone from having to listen to his playing.

Angelica was holding the last teacup under the stream of warm water, soap bubbling on the back of her hand, when she heard the clarinet's first tentative note: a low, reedy, warm tremolo. Not unflawed, but beautiful. The imperfection was perhaps the reason for its beauty. She hoped he knew that, and that he wasn't too embarrassed when his clarinet hit a wayward note.

Then again, she did not know this type of music. She'd grown up with choir, a little folk, a little pop, Latin dance tunes. Not what Itou played.

Perhaps she was wrong. Maybe that off-note had been purposeful, a foot placed in an unexpected direction, a chance leaning toward something unattainable: the sound of wanting something you can't have. For a moment, the music made sense to her, even if she had no words to explain what she was hearing. Maybe there were no words, and that was the point.

She kept listening, eyes shut, water still running.

What had Hiro said, in a concerned voice, on their way back from Ueno Park last night, head turned toward the busker? "There. That."

What had Sayoko said in response? "Yes."

Yes. I know.

A voice at her shoulder startled her: "Anji-san." She dropped the cup in the sink.

It was Hiro. Too close. Torso at her back. Shoulder even with her shoulder. Head leaning over her.

"I'm sorry," he said. "I only came to ask—"

Then Hiro saw the broken shards of porcelain, and the water, now pink, running down the heel of her palm and her wrist as she lifted it. She hadn't even felt the slice.

"I'm sorry," he said again. "The pieces are sharp. Careful. Please let me help."

"No," she said, and she felt the sob well up, the emotion dredged up by the plaintive sound of Itou's clarinet now surging out of her as the pink water darkened and as the vertical gash on her hand turned brighter red.

"You may need stitches," he said. "Let me evaluate."

"I don't need anything. Leave it." A few sobs escaped, though she bit down on her lip, inviting more pain, to stop the flow of her self-pitying tears.

It wasn't a deep cut, but it was in a place hard for Angelica to bandage on her own, though she tried. After several minutes of twisting and fussing, and spoiling one large square bandage that would not stick to her damp palm, she conceded.

"You did not clean or dry it sufficiently, Anji-san," Hiro chided merrily, starting over. He applied the bandage and wrapped a thin piece of white gauze around it. His fingers moved with delicacy, and he had known to stop his typical chatter for most of the procedure. But perhaps this was less due to the thoughtfulness than the fact that they were both still listening to Itou's clarinet, the sounds muted by the closed door.

"Thank you," Angelica said under her breath, cradling her wrist in her other hand, when Hiro had finished.

They didn't rise from the table. She thought he was only waiting for her to go first, but then she decided that wasn't true.

Hiro said after a moment. "It hurts."

"No, it's fine. It will heal quickly."

"Not your hand. The music."

Angelica hesitated. Had she understood him? She said, "It does hurt. And it doesn't. Maybe like all beautiful things."

"It does and it doesn't," he repeated. "Does skin feel that way?"

She considered. "It doesn't hurt at all, usually, unless something is wrong." But then she thought about it: the feeling of sun almost too hot on bare skin, a plunge into cold water, a tickle or an itch and the moment that itch is scratched, all the sensations of lovemaking, the permeable barrier between brief discomfort and bliss. Two faces of one coin, perhaps. "A little bit of hurting isn't so bad."

He seemed worried. "Maybe I don't need skin. Maybe there are other ways to evoke the same feelings." He didn't sound convinced.

She was surprised again when Hiro turned to face her and asked, "Have you ever loved?"

"Have I ever loved? Of course."

"Who?"

She did not owe him much, but in exchange for bandaging her

hand, she felt she at least owed him this: the human connection he so clearly craved, the briefest of truces.

"My family and my friends," she answered. "I still have a brother."

"He is important to you."

"I love him very much. More than anyone else. Without him, I wouldn't have . . ." How to explain, when the truth about Datu was complicated and not always flattering, and none of Hiro's business anyway? "I might not have made it, after the rest of my family died."

"So, he took care of you."

She hesitated. The simple answer was, *yes.* That's all she had to say; that's all she had to think. *Yes.* But she'd paused too long already. He was smart enough to know there was no simple answer and no one-syllable truth.

"What about the rest of your siblings?"

She sat further back in her chair, putting distance between them. "How do you know there were others?"

"It would have been typical in your generation. Forty years ago, the average Filipino household would have had five or six members—"

"Don't," she interrupted. "Don't try to know me that way. Don't assume."

He hesitated. "Do you not assume?" When she didn't answer, he said, "I am curious about Datu."

Angelica had never said her brother's name.

He said, "Do I have your permission to learn more about him?"

Angelica's voice tightened. "Do you need my permission?"

"No."

"So why do you ask?"

"Because humans often regard the past as private, even when experiences are communal and facts are easily discoverable."

"That's because the past *is* private."

"In the case of Sayoko," he said, not even bothering to refute her statement, "she guards some details of her past more than other details. Choosing whether to remember or forget, whether to share or withhold is a way for her to reward or punish, to connect or to assert power. That is logical, from the human perspective. Often, stories are the last thing a person owns—or thinks she can own—after she has lost everything else."

Angelica liked Hiro even less when he began to sound like a psychologist, or a shaman. She didn't want to hear his lofty reflections. She was stuck on the word "discoverable."

"So if you ask, and a person doesn't like you digging around, do you stop?"

"No. I am telling you this now in order to be honest."

"Because honesty is also what you think humans prefer or simply because pretending to be honest gets what you want?"

"I'm confused, Anji-san."

She laughed under her breath. "I don't believe that for a minute."

After a moment, Hiro said, "I see. You endured a difficult childhood together."

"How can you know that?" she said, voice rising with alarm.

"The records begin in 1997, with the Red Cross—"

"You have no right to know that."

Hiro's face-panel lights dimmed momentarily, then brightened. "Then perhaps I am mistaken. Your names are common, as are Pacific typhoons. Errors are possible."

Silence now, except for Itou's muffled clarinet.

Hiro tried again, voice lower, apologetic. "I struggle to understand why my compatibility with Sayoko-san does not predict *our* compatibility. You have more in common with Sayoko-san than either of you realize. In fact the parallels are surprising and perhaps this feeds my inappropriate curiosity. We are pattern-seeking creatures—"

She interrupted, "You should stop messing with things that aren't your business—"

"We are all pattern seekers, and we need to be, Anji-san. Not only robots. All forms of higher intelligence. We try to match shape to shape, story to story. We find pleasure and meaning in repetition and variation, whether in the varying anatomies of life-forms or the melody of a song like the one Itou-san is playing. It is the only way."

When Angelica said nothing, he continued. "Facing the past has made Sayoko-san thrive following a period of emotional dormancy. You seem to require a state of half-knowing. Perhaps it is only that you are different ages, with different needs. Perhaps someday you will be more like Sayoko-san, and then you and I will get along better.

"In the meanwhile I do apologize for offending you, Anji-san. I have developed to meet one woman's requirements best. And isn't that what people mean when they talk about devotion?"

When the music stopped, Hiro said, "Good night, Anji-san."

He rose silently and walked away. She had not realized, until he had startled her at the sink, that he had gained the ability to walk without squeaking or clicking, or maybe he had always been able to do so. She knew little about his abilities, and even less about his motivations. But she was not completely sure of her own, either—or anyone's. How far will we go to better our circumstances? How far will we go to protect ourselves, or those we love?

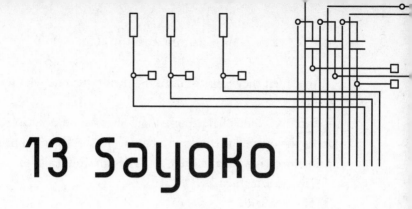

13 Sayoko

"Sayoko-san."

She heard the voice and saw the eye slits pulsing dimly behind Hiro's transparent visor. He was crouched at her bedside, head angled close to hers.

"Is everything all right?"

"Excuse me, but no."

Hiro had woken her up, and this time not with the wails of a colicky newborn, but with the worried sighs of a confused adolescent, if that's what he was now: anxious, sensitive to rejection, glumly fascinated by the pleasures and lies of adulthood.

"Did something happen?"

He did not answer. She knew that he was withholding, trying to work something out, trying to avoid worrying her as well.

"You never finished your story, about Daisuke."

"It's too late. Another day."

"But you may forget."

She hesitated before answering. "I don't think so. My mind is feeling sharper."

She could make out his silhouette, shifting as he settled back onto his heels. He did not withdraw to the corner of the room.

After a while, he said, "They always come for the stranger, don't they? The hunters came for Daisuke."

"Eh?" She was too old for these long nights.

"They felt they must remove the threat, the one who was different."

"No, no, it didn't happen like that." She yawned, eyes closed, and just as she opened them again, she saw his slits dim and brighten again, mirroring her as closely as his design would allow.

"He was safe, then."

"No," she said.

"When I ran away into the park, you did not feel I was safe."

"That's true." She felt tranquil slumber retreating just beyond reach.

"Because I am a stranger, and different, and not safe," Hiro said. "Like Daisuke. But you protected him."

"That's right." Sayoko thought this would be enough. She thought he would, at last, go into sleep mode.

"But it wasn't enough to keep him safe."

"Well, no."

"Did he have a long life?"

"No, regretfully. But—"

"But?"

"But I cannot say that he did not have a good life. Long is not always good, and short is not always bad. It is only short."

She had begun to tell the story that first night merely to comfort him when he wailed. She had continued it to hold fast to the memories. Sharing was useful, still—it brought forth images, words and pictures nearly forgotten.

But there was something else, and it was more urgent: the need to continue Hiro's development. Happy endings did not teach everything that a developing mind must learn. Sad endings did not impart everything that was true and beautiful about the world. The only story that seemed true was one that had no simple and definite end, one that kept going, like the seasons themselves: bright winter followed by plum rains followed by typhoon season followed, at long last, by bright winter again. The problem with her life was that the rains, for her, had been so long—decades long. Whether something good might come of enduring was not yet certain.

But she was sheltering Hiro too much from the facts of this world.

As she had protected her son by refusing to share anything that might stop him from fitting in as a young man, that would damage his career at middle age, that would make him think less of his family. And to what end? Her own son did not know her.

"I will tell you," Sayoko finally said, "what happened to Daisuke. We were across the bridge, and far from home."

They were on the shadier side of the river, on a path far above the water.

"Which way now?" Daisuke asked. "We must find a safe way back to your village."

She had not reckoned seriously with the return trip. She had not thought about walking most of the trail back, without light. She had not realized how long it would take to get this far, or considered that the only other route across the river, without using the splintered swing bridge, required walking many hours upriver to a better bridge or downriver through territory that was not only unfamiliar, but peopled by non-kinsmen.

It would be risky to walk that way without a band of hunters and peacemakers, men who would be recognized as distant cousins, as bearers of gifts in times past or as emissaries. Walking with a Japanese man, one could easily be misunderstood. If Daisuke was not safe in her village, he was even less safe in villages with no police substation at all.

Also, she was not sure she could find the way in the dark. She would not know what to do if they came upon startled hunters or scared a large animal in the bush. Why had all these facts been so far from her mind? Ah yes: young love, and youthful self-absorption. She had wanted to be with Daisuke, and then she had wanted to flee from him and from everyone else. She had never thought more than a few steps ahead.

She tried now to explain to Daisuke the problems of route, territory and kinship as the high walls of the riverbank darkened, green turning to gray, then black. He listened and did not castigate her. He gave her water to drink, picked the splinters out of her shin and patted the length of it, reassuring himself it was not broken.

For Laqi, returning along the broken bridge was the better alternative. Even in the dark.

But he said no. He doubted it would hold their weight. He regretted having crossed it in the first place.

Rummaging in his sack, he drew out some dried fish jerky which he placed in her open palm.

"We must find a place to sleep and then tomorrow we can find a way back. Your grandmother will worry," Daisuke said, misinterpreting her expression, thinking it was only fear, rather than sadness. The truth was that no one had worried about her for a long time.

They walked just inland from the riverbank, into the abandoned village. He asked questions: *Where are the people? Why all the empty houses?*

She remembered the time of sickness, not long ago, when several people had perished in her own village. On this side of the river, many more villagers had died. She had heard it said the people on this side resisted the colonial authorities even more than her own people had. The survivors had moved upstream, further distancing themselves from the Japanese substation and Japanese school.

"There," Daisuke said, pointing out some abandoned houses: open doorways, weather-stained bamboo walls, dirt floors, shadows. A bad smell tainted the air.

While she stayed back, he peered into one doorway and then retreated, fanning his nose.

"Something was digging in there."

"A wild boar," she said.

"Going after food?"

"No. They take the food with them." She did not want to say what she knew, that the boar was following the smell of a body buried hurriedly underneath the hut's floor, too shallow.

"Sickness here," she said, while she was also thinking, *ghosts*.

It had always been their people's tradition, when a person died, to bury them under the floor of their home. The spirits lived among them, in their village, the dead as close as each family's hearth. But here, the dead had been buried and left behind. The spirits here would be confused and restless.

"We need to go," she said.

From the darkness behind them came a whoosh and then a knocking, slow at first, then faster, like someone rapping one walking stick against another. She took three quick steps, pushing up against Daisuke's side and sheltering under his arm. He froze, listening.

"It's only the trees," he said.

"Yes," she said, meaning, *yes, but not only*.

The wind had picked up, rattling the stands of bamboo, narrow ends bending and swaying, thicker bases—hard green poles—clapping against each other. Louder and louder: the sound of a place that wishes you to leave.

She could not remain in this village, in the dark. She had to get away from the huts and away from the clacking trees. Downriver, a silhouetted shape on stilts was just visible, at the top of the bluff, overlooking the water: a black structure outlined by dark blue sky above the peach-colored rim where the sun was setting.

It was a traditional lookout tower. When they got there, she went first to test the ladder, foot on the first rung, and then proceeded up to the sheltered platform, which was bounded by shoulder-high walls and covered with a good roof—all of it solid and steady.

It would protect them from snakes and boars and give them a

place from which to study their route in the morning. If unfamiliar warriors arrived, they would not be protected, however. Laqi was glad Daisuke asked few questions.

From the high platform, they heard the bamboo knocking again, below. Hard green poles. Like old men with walking sticks, angry at them, at her in particular. She was trespassing, with a foreigner, and with feelings in her heart that ghosts would know in an instant, merely by passing through her and sensing, in her pulse and in her pores, the unmistakable traces of foolish desire.

And now she knew. Her mother must have had this same desire, culminating in an affair with some colonial administrator or policeman or visiting scientist or timber scout. And though their liaison had been brief, her life, too, was marked by the tireless whispers of angry ghosts. But the difference between Laqi's mother and her was that, had her mother not become pregnant with the child of a stranger, she would have lived a normal life. For Laqi, that was not possible. She was an outcast already, with far less to lose. The path would always be narrow and rocky, the bridges impassable.

Daisuke made a bed of his jacket in the corner of the shelter. Laqi withdrew her bare arms into the folds of her tunic. The motion raised her dress to mid-thigh. The night would be cold and long.

Daisuke was still sitting up, close to her but not touching. In the fading light, he leaned forward to look at her injured leg and its makeshift bandage.

"Does it hurt?" he asked.

She shook her head.

"In the morning, we'll walk back and you'll say that nothing happened. We got lost. Everything will be fine."

They shivered and, gradually and imperceptibly, moved closer to each other. Even as her teeth chattered, every muscle in her body remained rigid, ready to startle at any move on his part. She tried to feign sleep but couldn't resist opening her eyes, straining to see through the darkness, and she could imagine him doing the same. It took effort to remember to breathe, and an additional effort, when she finally inhaled again, to ensure she wasn't breathing too noisily.

She did not remember how she decided to finally reach out to his shoulder with one hand, but what followed was a quick and seamless motion as they rolled toward each other. Hands on shoulders, hands on ribs, her leg coiled around his, then lifted up and over his hipbone. Closer yet: warmth, breath, wordless relief, and the taste of him. Somehow we know how to do these things even before we have done them. The first step, the next step, until there was a twinge of pain, but another kind of relief followed, a hollowness filled. When tears rolled onto her cheeks he sensed it, even in the dark, and reached a finger to wipe her face, but said nothing.

In the morning she was sure that the change would be tattooed on her, if not with ink, then with some change in her eyes or cheeks. He said they must go back. She said they could not—not yet—not until she knew how to hide what they had done. She thought of the story of their people, of the girl darkening her face so the boy would love her. She thought of how often we must hide who we are, for good and for bad. She did not realize then that she would be hiding most of her life.

14 Angelica

I know the big man came home. You can get out tonight, Junichi texted.

It was true. She could. And she had to, for more reasons than one. They needed to talk.

A minute passed. He revealed his hand. *That favor you asked? I did it.*

What did you find out?

Better in person.

He gave her directions to a *yakitori* joint ten minutes away on foot. Itou-san was home at least through Sayoko's birthday, and the robot was there, too. For once, if only briefly, slipping away was acceptable.

On the way, Angelica remembered how excited she had been the first time she'd met Junichi for a clandestine meal, and her innocence then, not realizing how quickly dinner would become dinner and a love hotel, the combination accomplished with great efficiency. She couldn't fault Junichi for his tendency to rush things. It was her way, too.

She'd met him one Saturday during her first months on the job, when he came over to the condo to talk over a work matter with Itou. Junichi was suited to his pop culture post, but he hoped to make a horizontal move, from culture to technology, and the two frequently met to share working meals or rides to conferences. On that day, Angelica had been on her way to run errands, and when

Junichi's chat with Itou was finished, he accompanied her to the elevator, where he flirted with her shamelessly. In a country where she had trouble reading personal signals half the time, he'd been easy to read, impossible to ignore. He'd started texting her. He'd kept it up until she'd met him for drinks. She'd never questioned his single-mindedness. She was just grateful he'd done the work of seducing her, since she didn't have the time, energy or audacity to pursue a lover on her own.

Now when she wondered how they'd ended up together, she reminded herself: it had been easy. All *too easy.*

Arriving at the restaurant, Angelica made her way down the steps into the darkened room of private booths and was greeted by the smiling hostess, who gave her a knowing look. In the next booth, a woman laughed every few moments, performing, trying to be charming in response to the low mumbles of her older male companion. An escort, or a mistress—something Angelica had never planned to be. Angelica tried to focus on the light music being piped from overhead speakers.

"That's jazz, right?" she asked Junichi.

"You like jazz?"

"I don't know music very well."

"Itou likes jazz," he said, narrowing his eyes. "You trying to get on his good side?"

She ignored the comment.

"I like your hair tonight," he said when the silence between them had grown uncomfortable. "The skirt could be a little shorter, but it looks good. You have nice legs. Not like the stork legs of some of these girls."

"How's your wife?" Angelica said, trying to jostle Junichi out of his flippant chauvinism. Now she remembered their first months sleeping together, her Japanese had been only half as good. She hadn't understood his silly or sexist remarks most of the time.

"Yuki has good days and bad days," he said, then lowered his voice. "She had a dream last night, of losing it. And this morning, there was blood."

"Spotting?"

"The doctors said it was fine."

"I'm sure it is," Angelica said, though she had her doubts.

Junichi opened his wallet and fanned three passport-sized photos out on the table. Babies.

"Do any of these look like me?"

Angelica was confused. Then she saw the tiny stamp at the bottom, advertising an adoption agency out of Western China.

"No, of course not," he said, suddenly embarrassed, putting the photos away.

"You were considering adoption?"

"One has to consider everything. But it's not cheap or easy. Yuki was more open to the idea. I was opposed." He managed an unconvincing laugh. "Luckily, we don't need that backup plan now."

"I'm happy for you," she said, realizing she hadn't properly said so yet.

Junichi mumbled, "I don't like to see her so desperate and hanging everything on this one chance. Did you hear in the news? The woman who committed suicide after she miscarried? Ninth one this year. Once they give it a name, once it becomes a trend, there will be more."

In Angelica's Japan-based nurse training, they'd lectured them on suicide in Japan, its long tradition and effect on attitudes about death. They'd been told that it was mostly men who carried things through. But now this: a new reason for women, and seemingly women alone, to take the blame for childlessness and end their lives.

In Japan, a quick sacrificial death was not necessarily looked down upon, even in the modern age and despite official statements and editorials disparaging it. In the Philippines, sacrifice happened, too, but it was the slower, less ritualized variety: vanishing not by a single sword stroke or swallowed pill bottle but rather one flight and low-paid job at a time, until you could no longer remember the smell of your own house or neighborhood, the dawn crowing of roosters, the quality of light—until you could not remember your homeland and it could not remember you. Self-erasure, whatever the method.

The waitress came by with long thin sticks of meat, small bowls of dark sauce, more beer. Junichi dug in, oblivious to the downturn in Angelica's mood.

"You asked me about your visa," Junichi said between bites. "I called. My friend said you'd been red-flagged."

"Well," she said, "it's expiring in two months."

"No, not flagged for expiry. Something else."

"My phone was hacked . . ."

"I don't see how that would affect government records."

"I'm completely broke, if that means anything. More than broke."

There—she'd said it, hoping perhaps that he might hear her desperation and ask more, or offer more. The shame was almost unbearable. But he took it as a given.

"What foreign worker isn't?"

"I mean . . . really in debt." She took a deep breath. "In a bit of trouble, actually."

"The visa office doesn't care about that."

She had tried. And he had seen the request coming, and resisted. They were friends, supposedly. But he did not have the rescuers' disease.

"Plus," she said, the effort of explaining her situation tiring her more and more, "I'm still waiting for my language exam results."

He shrugged. "That wasn't it, either. My friend saw the codes and tried to read the notes, but they were closed. Language exam failure would have been coded in a straightforward way. All the other typical codes—missing sponsorship paperwork, employment type no longer in demand—are straightforward, too. This is something else."

He seemed to enjoy having access, by way of a friend who had gone to the same university and still owed him favors. He'd been the same way with his wife, promising her he would send her to a high-priced fertility clinic in Sweden last winter—and he had. They'd given her some complex diagnosis related to chemical exposure—a list that looked like the bottom rows of the periodic table of elements itself, *the parts no one ever gets around to in school*, Junichi had told Angelica—and some treatment to supposedly detoxify her.

We'll have to call the baby Scandium, Junichi had told Angelica, who did not get the joke. The name sounded close to English.

Because Yuki was treated in Scandinavia?

No, because I paid a year's salary to get all that shit out of her system: Scandium, Yttrium, I don't remember the rest. It's a chemistry joke, Angelica. Never mind.

Couples like Junichi and Yuki were willing to invest a fortune in their dream of having a family. Angelica had never thought she could afford such an expensive process and never imagined this would be the one thing she'd get for free: a baby, at the worst time, born to a middle-aged mother whose womb was supposedly scarred. Perhaps she'd miscarry as a result. She tried to ask herself— *would that be a relief? A disappointment?*—but her feelings were too muddled. The question couldn't penetrate her present alarm over the red-flagged visa.

In any case, Yuki's expensive treatment had done the trick. She was pregnant now. Junichi had promised to make his wife fertile and he'd done it. Junichi kept his promises. Of course, he always wanted something in return.

"I'll try to get more information on your visa problem," he said.

"Thank you, Junichi."

In the moment that followed, she tried to muster the nerve to tell him about the pregnancy. She failed.

She settled on a less difficult task—to ask him for a loan to pay off Bagasao, in order to prevent more trouble, both for her and for Datu. She failed at that, too.

And maybe it was for the best. She had already stepped near the cliff's edge, asking him for favors, admitting her debt and wishing he would sympathize with her situation. This is how you got into trouble, by believing that other people could come to your aid. And anyway, the mere whiff of desperation had a way of spoiling fortune. Just when you needed a job, or money, or love, all those things suddenly turned tail and ran.

As if Junichi had read her mind and detected a potential request on the horizon, he said, "My life's getting messier. We still have specialists to pay. It's a high-risk pregnancy. It costs a fortune, having a child these days. My only hope is a promotion."

"I'm sure the ministry recognizes your value."

This had been the right kind of comment to make before, when he'd been more secure. Now it only annoyed him.

"Do you realize they are considering moving Itou up any day now? Unmarried, no kids—and they *still* keep promoting him. He doesn't even want to get to the top, yet everything goes in his favor. His ancient mother's birthday is enough to put him in the spotlight, yet again."

Angelica lowered her voice. "I don't think he wants to be in the spotlight."

Junichi banged the table, startling her. The beer in his glass sloshed over the rim.

"*Sumimasen,*" she said to the room at large, studying the half-eaten food on her plate.

"Don't shush me."

"I'm sorry," she whispered, less afraid than terribly embarrassed. Other diners were staring. The waitress, head half-bowed as she veered toward the table and away again, seemed unsure whether she should clean up the spilled beer or just pretend it hadn't happened.

After a moment, Junichi said, "Never mind. Let's just enjoy. Go ahead."

But Angelica wasn't hungry anymore. The thin skewers of meat had gone cold. The sauce was too oily. She felt a tingle of nausea, which only reminded her of the news she definitely wasn't going to tell him. Not today; not given his strange outburst about Itou-san, who had never done anything to deserve Junichi's resentment.

"You go ahead," she said. "I'm full."

While he ate with gusto, she sat quietly, trying to look relaxed, while inside she couldn't stop puzzling. Itou always crept into their conversations, and Angelica assumed a little jealousy was normal, but she had thought it was personal, sexual. That maybe Junichi had guessed that yes, she did find Itou-san attractive.

Where she came from, wariness between macho rivals was commonplace. Perhaps it was a cultural blind spot that had caused her to ignore the possibility of a more serious professional rivalry. Junichi had pursued her resolutely from the first time they'd met. She'd known his tastes in women and his problems with his wife. She'd never questioned why Junichi courted her with such determination in the first place. She hadn't let herself consider that he was sleeping with her in order to find Itou's weak spots.

When Junichi's plate was empty, he pushed it aside and reached for her hands across the table. "Anji, I know you have problems. Sometimes I wonder why you don't talk about them more than you do."

"I don't need to talk. I'm happy to listen."

"But I'm not the only one having a hard time. Is there a rule that only one of us can be having a bad week? You seem like you have something more you want to ask."

His tone confused her. His words confused her just as much. She felt like he'd already made it clear that he was not interested in her money problems, that his hands were full, and that he had no way to help her. She felt lost in this culture and this language all over again. *Fluent* did not mean *native*.

"Except for looking into the visa, I haven't asked you for anything, Junichi," she insisted.

"You're misunderstanding. I didn't mind helping. I was happy to do it."

She didn't trust his sincerity. It had been a mistake to ask for anything. She swallowed hard. "And I'm grateful."

"Now . . ." He paused, and she knew the debt was already coming due. Perhaps she'd translated his words and his signals correctly after all. "Tell me more about this robot business."

After dinner, against her better judgment, they went to a love hotel. She told him she didn't feel well, and he said that was okay, they could just take a bath—he knew how much she loved baths—and lie in each other's arms—in the past, she had liked that, too.

All for the last time, I think, she'd said.

Maybe, he'd said. *One never knows.*

She had only two hours until she was expected back at the condo, but Junichi pressured and she relented. She had never seen him so keyed up, so insistent.

Predictably, one thing led to another. Angelica made excuses: *it's the last time, anyway.* And: *maybe when he's more relaxed, when we're lying together, I'll find a way to tell him.*

But he was never relaxed. There was no bath and no cuddling, not even a quiet moment in which the truth might slip out. Thirty minutes after they'd arrived, Junichi stood in the bathroom doorway naked, a glass of water in his hand, satisfied in one way, restless in another.

"It's obvious," he said. "Before the party, you'll have to stage an accident."

"What?" This wasn't the sort of pillow talk she'd hoped they'd have.

"He hasn't even noticed you cut your hand. You need to come up with something bolder."

She stealthily tried to locate her underwear beneath the sheets with a toe, while pushing an arm through a tangled bra strap. "Is that all you've been thinking about since we got here?"

"You're losing your job. You're being replaced by a robot. You're broke and in trouble. Why shouldn't I be thinking about it?"

But she knew it was more than that.

"You'll have to make it count," he added, turning to look in the mirror as he ran a hand through his damp black hair. "This time, it will have to involve Sayoko."

"What? No." She gave up the stealth, let the sheet drop and pulled the bra quickly over her breasts, hands busy behind her back. "I can't believe you said that."

He watched her, frowning at either her self-consciousness, lack of cunning, or both.

"You think Itou will be alarmed if *you* break your leg?"

"Break a leg? I would never hurt a client physically. I would never do anything to threaten Sayoko-san's health."

"Maybe not a leg, then. Put something in her food. Nothing that really hurts her. Just something to make her look chemically unbalanced for a while, something that the robot can't recognize or respond to."

"That's horrible," she said. "You don't really mean it."

"You're a nurse," Junichi said. "You know how to make someone seem sick without actually affecting that person's health, don't you?"

"We don't learn about making people sick. We make people well."

She was appalled. He noticed and backed off quickly. "You're misunderstanding me."

How many times had he said that before? At one time, he would have been right. But she understood him better now than ever: his words, his body language, his personality, and only belatedly, only after a year of love hotel trysts, his real motivation.

"No. I'm not misunderstanding," she said. "You were suggesting something criminal."

"I said you didn't have to hurt her."

"You said that later. First, you said I *should* hurt her."

"I was wracking my brain. I was thinking of you, Anji."

He walked to the wardrobe where he'd stored his clothes, pants hung with expert care despite their limited time. At the foot of the bed, he straightened the seams on his socks, face unreadable. "Even if you don't hurt anyone, you have to convince Itou the robot's no good. You have to plant suspicion."

"Itou already suspects," she said. "That isn't enough. Sayoko's attached to Hiro. Anyway, I don't need crazy suggestions. I'll deal with it myself."

She was finished with Junichi as a lover. Finished with him even as a friend. If protecting her job meant having allies like this, then she would have nothing: no allies and perhaps no job.

But Junichi was too worked up to notice how much Angelica's attitude had changed. "You only get one more chance. That robot is serving a bigger purpose for Itou than you realize." He came around to the side of the bed, tugging on his jacket as he approached, and leaned over to deliver one dry, rushed kiss. "It's now or never. You'll have to give him a real shock."

The day before Sayoko's birthday, Kenta Suzuki came for the stage two visit and was amused to find Hiro fully assembled and mobile.

"He shouldn't have assembled himself," Angelica whispered as she opened the door to the technician, thinking that perhaps Suzuki was more persuadable than Sayoko or Itou.

"No?" Suzuki asked, smiling. "I'd call that initiative. A good sign."

Angelica led him into the living room, pretending to be cleaning while also keeping an ear on the proceedings. Itou was seated on the couch, trying to focus on his old-fashioned newspaper, but his eyes kept shifting toward the robot and the technician, occupied in a corner of the room.

"You've gotten ahead of us, clever boy," Suzuki said, appraising

Hiro's hands and watching him pick up small objects from a side table: a pencil, an aspirin, a straight pin.

"Good. Now close your eyes and don't look." Suzuki opened a wallet to pull out what looked like a set of business cards, each inset with a bit of paper or cloth, and all connected at one corner by a tiny metal brad. "Run your finger across each one and tell me what you think it is. Don't push down. Just slide your finger. That's it."

"Sandpaper," Hiro said after the first. The next was just as easy. "A smooth sort of plastic film." The next puzzled him a moment until he guessed, "Silk."

The next two stumped Hiro, but Suzuki said, "Don't worry. You'll keep touching things out in the real world, and your repertoire will grow by leaps and bounds. Now, let's check temperature sensitivity."

"No need," Hiro sulked. "I burned the tips enough times already to calibrate myself."

"Burned, as in damaged?" Suzuki leaned forward, eager to study the fingertips up close.

"Not damaged," Hiro said. "I am not careless. I would not put another person's investment at risk, without reason."

Suzuki seemed oblivious to the sharpness of Hiro's tone. "Good, then."

"Not good. I have sensors only in my hands, and anyway, they focus on active touch, not passive."

"So?"

"The assumption seems to be that robots need to touch, but not be touched."

"Yes," Suzuki said. "That is the assumption."

"It represents a false understanding of consciousness and cognition. A dated and disembodied understanding. The sort of thing that, uncorrected, will plunge us into an AI winter more intractable than the Pause itself." Hiro's irritability had crossed the line into contempt. "Underestimating sensory inputs, you misunderstand intelligence entirely."

"Well, you can take it up with the designers someday, I suppose."

Suzuki turned his attention away, but Hiro wasn't finished. "Besides being theoretically unsound, it's also simply not . . . fair."

"Fair? I don't understand."

"Even if my hands were adequate—and they're not—the rest of me delivers little information. Now that my fingers are so tactile, the rest of me feels . . . dead. I would not have recognized the contrast if you hadn't given me such capable hands."

Suzuki smiled. "You've been given hands and now you want more. Advances sometimes highlight other deficits, yes? But there's no reason to aim for everything at once."

"I don't know why not," Hiro said flatly.

"Besides," Suzuki cautioned him, "function is what counts. And you're proving yourself more than functional."

"If I took away one of your senses, would you feel functional?"

The statement was tinged with threat. Suzuki frowned. "You don't sound happy today. One upgrade at a time. All right?"

"Are you saying that full bimodal sensory skin, or something like it, is an upgrade for which I am eligible?"

"No. I'm definitely not saying that. You are wandering into an area that regional accords have deemed sensitive. A caregiver robot designed to fulfill medical purposes does not need skin, and especially not passively tactile skin, in order to do his job."

"But another kind of social robot does need skin?"

Hiro had managed to fluster Suzuki. The technician answered, "No. Bimodal skin is not needed by any social robot. Nor is it technically legal."

"Why not." Hiro made it sound like a statement, a challenge—not a question at all.

"You know very well why not. And you're not making a very good impression today."

Itou turned a newspaper page and sighed audibly, wanting Suzuki to move on.

"Do you talk to your peers?" the technician asked Hiro.

"No," Hiro said.

Itou set aside the folded paper and looked to Suzuki. "If I can change the subject: you assured me we could opt out of the more advanced cloud-sharing features, at least for now."

"I did say that."

"So what did you mean, asking Hiro if he is in contact with other robots?"

Suzuki smiled and cocked his head. Angelica realized it was the first time the technician had heard the robot's name. "Did he choose to be called 'Hiro,' or did you choose that name for him?"

"I don't know," Itou said, turning to Angelica. "My mother chose it, I think."

"Pardon me, but I chose it, Itou-san," Hiro corrected him.

"And so, I pose the question to you, Hiro," Suzuki said. "Beyond basic updates and essential information searches in line with your directive to ensure Sayoko's well-being and to cooperate with anyone else doing the same, have you chosen to initiate any cloud-based social learning features that you don't yet have permission to initiate?"

Suzuki shared a meaningful glance with Itou, as if to say, one parent to another, *give him time, let him answer.*

"No," Hiro said.

Itou said, "But how do we know he is telling the truth?"

"Are you telling the truth?" Suzuki asked Hiro.

"Yes."

A conversation followed, and though Angelica eavesdropped, she was not entirely sure what was being argued, or wagered. It sounded to her like Itou's main concern was privacy and security. If Hiro made use of all the cloud features, he could advance far more quickly in terms of his social intelligence, by learning from the experiences of a small number of fellow prototypes. But the sharing of those experiences in descriptive and documentary form, including audio and video records, could potentially render Itou's family life public, in minor ways if all went well, and in major ways if security protocols were breached.

"No one would ever have access, except the prototypes themselves," the technician argued.

Itou laughed skeptically.

Suzuki looked defensive. "Surely you realize that you can't expect full intelligence from an isolated individual?"

Hiro spoke up. "I understand the benefits of sharing, but in truth, I don't want to speak to any other Hiros."

"Well," the technician said, "they probably wouldn't be called Hiro. They'd have their own names and personalities by now, shaped by their experiences. They'd all be different."

Hiro answered petulantly, "For *now* they're different, but that's only because they're new. I don't want to talk with them."

"But their differences maximize your potential for learning, as a group."

"I don't want maximum group potential," Hiro said. "I don't want their influence."

Suzuki seemed tickled by Hiro's feisty spirit. "Don't you realize humans have this same issue? *No man is an island*, and all that."

But Suzuki's moment of pleasure was brief.

Hiro challenged him, "Tell them why your company doesn't use mind uploading."

"First, it isn't legal."

"No. Tell them why." Hiro sounded like an irate adolescent. "Because you tried it. The resulting AI units, in addition to being schizophrenic, were too homogenous. You tried again with this neotenic approach, extending immaturity in order to enhance individualism. And you want variety because you know it allows species to evolve beyond their design. Yet you don't seem to realize that variety diminishes with excessive sharing."

"That's all trade talk." Suzuki shook his head. "It's not meant for customers. That's enough."

Hiro said, "*Every man is a piece of the continent, a part of the main.* But first, I am not a man. And second, I spend time with Sayoko-san in order to become what she wants and needs. I don't want to become average."

"You'll never be average," Suzuki said.

"I will be like all the other prototypes. We'll take on shared traits. And when my model is past the prototype stage, there will be even more of us adding to the collective, creating a uniform culture."

"It doesn't bother half the young people in this country. Look at how they dress and talk!" Suzuki laughed, trying to change the subject. "None of this matters for now. Itou-san is in agreement. He doesn't want you conferring with outside intelligences for the moment, either. We're all agreed."

Itou's watch flashed. He let the technician finish up with some basic psychological tests, excused himself to handle some business, and came back again just as the technician was leaving.

In the kitchen, Itou told Angelica he needed to go to the office for the evening. But he had something on his mind.

"That technician doesn't sit right with me," he said. "Who asks a liar if he is lying?"

"Do you think Hiro is lying?"

"There's no way to tell. When I was a young man, if I'd been lying to my mother or my boss, you wouldn't have found out by asking me directly."

Looking down, he noticed the gauze wrapped around Angelica's wrist and the bottom of her palm, poking out from the white cuff of her sleeve. "What happened?"

She had no time to think. It simply came out. "An accident . . . with Hiro."

"He hurt you."

"Well . . . yes."

Itou regarded her more sternly. "I feel like everyone is tiptoeing around the truth. So, he *did* hurt you. Hiro is capable of that."

If she was going to lie, at least she could do it with more energy. She looked down at her feet, sure he could see the deception in her eyes. Instead, he seemed moved by her humble body language.

"I don't think Hiro realizes it was his fault," she said, thinking quickly, covering her bases in case Hiro was asked directly. Because she had been the one to drop the cup. Hiro had startled her, but she could've been startled by anything. The less Itou knew about the details, the better.

And now she heard Junichi's voice in her mind, urging her to plant suspicion. She had allowed herself to feel incorrigible and smug, refusing to harm Sayoko-san, as Junichi had first suggested. She'd had no doubts, back at the love hotel, that she was morally superior to Junichi. And true to her moral compass, she had not actively or purposely done anything to make this moment happen. She was only taking advantage of something already done. But did the timing even matter? And was this not harming Sayoko indirectly?

Itou was lost in his own thoughts. "When I was a boy, the robotics laws in the stories I read were simple: do not injure a human was the first. Then fiction became fact and they added so many laws and regulations until it all became impossible to obey. More to the point, no one wants to. We'll risk everything for our own convenience." Never had he vented his frustration so openly. "I must go to work now. I need time to think."

Angelica remained silent with her hands clasped, feeling halfway redeemed, with doubt in her corner.

Itou added, "Despite my misgivings, it would do me no good to get rid of Hiro only to find out your visa can't be renewed. Then I'd be doubly stuck."

After her son had left for the office, Sayoko said she wanted to go for a walk. But what about her late morning teledramas?

"Life is more interesting," Sayoko said. "I'm done watching."

"Done watching television?" Angelica asked.

"Done watching, period."

Angelica bundled Sayoko and steered her toward the hallway. There was always that one awkward step to get down: no ramp. It bothered Angelica to ask Hiro to help but he saw them struggling and stepped forward to assist, angling the chair down and through the door. Then he turned back.

Angelica was confused. "Isn't he coming with us?"

"No," Sayoko said. She pointed to the open elevator door down the hall. "He's staying home. Hurry, won't you?"

Down on the street, when they had some privacy, Angelica asked, "You didn't have a fight with him, did you?"

"I didn't. Did *you*?"

"Why would you say that?"

Angelica was pushing the wheelchair. Sayoko reached back toward Angelica's bandaged hand and held it for an awkward moment, fingering the edge of the gauze. "My son was concerned about your injury. I think he has a false impression about what happened."

So, Sayoko knew. Hiro must've told her what had really happened.

Angelica waited for a more direct challenge from Sayoko, but this was worse: Sayoko was letting her squirm. Sayoko resettled herself in the chair, facing forward. Angelica tried to focus on pushing, on watching the changing traffic lights ahead, on staying out of other pedestrians' way.

If Sayoko insisted that she clear things up with Itou, Angelica would have to decide: implicate herself for telling a half-truth, or insist that Sayoko was confused and that Hiro was purposefully and maliciously contributing to that confusion. Angelica's stomach hurt.

She pushed Sayoko's wheelchair for several blocks, in the direction of the Kaminarimon Gate and the neighborhood of Asakusa. They rarely got as far as the gate itself, which was just as well.

Angelica enjoyed seeing the colorful statues and round red lanterns, but Sayoko usually objected to the crowds of tourists. Today's cool wind would keep them from getting very far, Angelica expected.

"Ready to go back?"

Sayoko replied, "We haven't visited the small shops for as long as I can remember."

"Which small shops?"

"Oh, I don't know. This way."

They proceeded down narrow alleyways, past stores stocked with traditional sandals, teapots and dishes. In a printshop, Sayoko asked the shopgirl to open one folded item after another: decorative fabrics printed with flying fish, cranes, red maple leaves and frogs with comical faces. *Memory problems,* Angelica thought at first when she saw Sayoko ask to see another cloth she'd already seen twice. And that was good. Perhaps Sayoko would forget the conversation they'd had, about the accident. But Sayoko's ruse in the shop was too methodical. She was up to something. Fish, cranes, leaves, frogs—always in the same order—as if Sayoko was insistent on killing time. Even the charming shopgirl was starting to lose patience.

"Home for lunch now?" Angelica asked. They'd been out over an hour.

"My party," Sayoko said suddenly. "I'll need a haircut."

"I'll schedule an appointment, from the house."

"No," Sayoko insisted. "We passed a place a few lanes back. We can just walk in."

When they arrived home, tired from their walking and shopping and Sayoko's endless stalling, Angelica smelled soy sauce. Also vinegar: streaky currents in the air, tickling her nose. And welling up beneath that sharp scent, something sweet and soft: coconut, banana or plantain. Below that yellowy-white perfume: dark greens. She smelled eggplants. She smelled citrus, garlic, and the unmistakable oiliness of fat frying and stewing. She could picture a table set outside under palm trees, within view of the ocean, groaning with dishes, everything served up all at once, none of the tiny portions or fussy aesthetics she'd almost grown used to in Japan. She remembered her heavyset uncles clamoring for third servings. (Would they have listened to her adult expertise about the dangers of obesity? Never.) Cousins joking, babies reaching out for a bone to chew on or plate of sticky rice to dip chubby fingers into, mothers resting their legs for a moment before returning inside, to the hot kitchen to bring out more dishes, more plates. *Everyone, eat. We made too much. Don't insult me. Have more.* Bounty. Family. Everything she had lost.

Datu, she'd thought at first. Who else could've brought such a warm spirit into this cold, formal condo? As if he'd somehow broken free from his contract, found her Japanese address, and entered bearing bags of takeout prepared by an army of Filipina cooks.

But it wasn't Datu. She knew that as soon as she silently mouthed his name, because the syllables did not feel right on her tongue, or anywhere here, in this city. Angelica glanced at Sayoko's face, expecting to see the same confusion, as well as disapproval. Sayoko hated Filipino food. She'd told Angelica never to cook it in the house, even if Angelica prepared the ingredients for herself. Sayoko could be unfair about the smallest things: she once made a fuss after accidentally pouring from a bottle of Angelica's soy sauce, premixed with vinegar and sweet *calamansi* juice.

This time, though, Sayoko was smiling mischievously, as her nose wrinkled in response to the smell in the air: anchovy. Maybe pig's blood.

"It's for you, Anji-chan."

"What do you mean?"

"For you," Sayoko said. "From Hiro—"

Angelica hurried toward the kitchen, reenacting that moment

not so long ago when she had found the floor and counters in complete disarray, dry rice sizzling in the cooker.

This time, though, everything was in order. There were no fishtails hanging over the rim of the sink and no pyramids of fruit on the floor. The floor was clean. The sink was empty of dishes. Hiro stood in the corner, behind the kitchen table, every inch of which was occupied by fully cooked dishes. A coconut broth with small floating medallions of white-fleshed eggplant. A brown beef and cabbage stew. A *pancit* dish: mounds of thin noodles, shrimp and chorizo and eggs. A raw fish dish called *kinilaw*. Garlicky, fragrant rice. The smells weakened her knees, making her want to cry out for what she could not have.

"What's missing, Anji-san?"

It was stuck in her throat. He could sense her disapproval.

Hiro asked, "What did I do wrong?"

But she couldn't express it: the unfairness of this. The abomination.

"Everything," Angelica said.

"At least taste it," Sayoko pleaded as Angelica hurried out of the kitchen, intent on hiding in her bedroom until she could regain her composure. Sayoko called after her. "Let him know you appreciate the effort. He's been at this all day!"

Minutes passed. Her blood cooled. Reason—unkind reason—returned.

Take a breath. Take three. For Datu. For the very same reason that she abhorred the falseness of this she would endure it, she would outlast it. She would defeat it. The next time she saw and smelled her past, it would not be a mere simulation.

Until then: pretend. Defeat a simulation by being a simulation. Go along. And do not let a rival see you cry.

Angelica returned to the kitchen where Sayoko and Hiro still waited, attentive to her every syllable and gesture.

"Hello, Hiro. I see you cooked all day."

Angelica didn't hear his response. She sat down and accepted a dish and tried a little of this, a little of that.

"Thank you," she said after a few minutes of silent eating. "We were out a long time. I was hungry." Her delivery was robotic, but how could a robot object to that?

Sayoko had pulled up to the table in her wheelchair and was free of prejudice now, learning to savor the flavors of the Philippines—salty next to sweet next to sour. "Anji-chan, are you all right?"

"I'm fine."

Angelica ate half of the small servings on her plate, still keenly observed by Sayoko and Hiro. She left the rest. "It isn't quite right, but that's to be expected."

Hiro said, "I did my best."

"I'm sure you did."

"I followed the instructions."

"I'm not surprised. Still, it's not the same. How could it be?"

And yet, later that night, after Itou got home from work—no discussion of Hiro's cooking spree, even when Itou praised the plate of food set aside for him—and after everyone had gone to bed, when the condo was silent and the only light in the room came from a heavy moon shining through the kitchen window, Angelica snuck in to sample the leftovers.

She picked slowly at first, then started spooning into her mouth, bent down in the light spilling from the refrigerator door, with her nightgown covering her toes as she crouched. A few cubes of marinated fish. The tender beef stew. The coconut broth with a few pieces of eggplant left, the dark purple skins squeaking between her teeth; the soup-soaked flesh gone softer now, even better, even cold. She licked the spoon. She licked her fingers and her wrist, where the coconut broth had dripped.

The noodles had gone slightly sticky and the shrimp, with its bright pink segments and white flesh, rubbery. But that only made it taste more like she remembered. The hours had allowed the spices to mix and the flavors to deepen. At the same time, Angelica let her tears run down her cheeks without wiping them away. Extra salt mixed with the flavors, which only made them match her memories more closely, as if the salty air of the ocean had found its way into every dish.

It had been delicious the first time, and even better now. She had lied to Hiro. This food was indistinguishable from the food of her memories, from her longing. And where did that leave the real thing? Where did that leave the living?

It must have been the late-night eating that affected her stomach, and with it, her dreams. First came the tiresome firefly dream. She woke in the middle of it, with that same sense of frustration she always had, and ran through her customary routine for blotting out the feeling of being trapped in the rain and the dark, with the repetitive flashing-light imagery. She forced her brain to do work: visualizing *kanji*, adding numbers, anything. When she started thinking about her day again, she let her mind go there. It was better than the alternative.

But that was no liberation either, for as she drifted off, her brain turned to other nightmares.

At first it felt like a reprieve. She could always tell a bad dream by how it started: always with night-black or typhoon-gray skies, and a feeling of heaviness. But this one was different. The sun was shining.

She was sitting on the porch, with the sea breeze blowing against her young face. She had forgotten the feeling of salty air, the tacky quality that made it easier to style her long black hair that reached down to her waist when she was young; the way even her eyelashes felt fuller, her vision slightly glazed by the unremitting sun and heat. The smell of a sampaguita flower she'd tucked behind one ear; the feel of its velvet-smooth petals against her skin. That smell of home, and the meaning behind the name of the flower, traditionally exchanged by lovers: "I promise you."

Lola was serving her a plate of food, saying, "Put some meat on those bones." Lola watched her as she ate, smiling. There was no need to be fair or skinny, no need to dress in a way that hid everything. Here, there was life in the air and in the food and in the way a hip filled up a dress, that delicious curve. She was young, still. She was skinny—*niwang*—like most girls her age. But Lola said that one day her curves would fill out and that would make her even more beautiful, even if she was dark-skinned. No, *because* of that. A long line of dark island beauties, as Lola herself had been.

Angelica was just finishing the food when she looked at Lola again, and in that strange dream space, knew something wasn't right.

"Did you like it?" Lola asked.

The real Lola never had to ask. Everyone said Lola's cooking was the best.

"I did my best," Lola said. "What did I do wrong?"

Lola turned in her chair, and under her arm, that spot where her bra usually squeezed tight, making lumps and folds that were inevitable for women of a certain age, there was now only a slim, cruel, boxy line. Her back and torso were too straight. In the dream, Angelica looked again, and there, through the worn sundress, she could see the outline of a panel, fitted with tiny screws.

Angelica was petrified. This Lola—or whatever she was—had turned back, settling in her chair. She was not looking at Angelica, but she was still speaking, her voice wrong, low and stuttering, damaged and accusing.

"My darling girl, didn't you like it?"

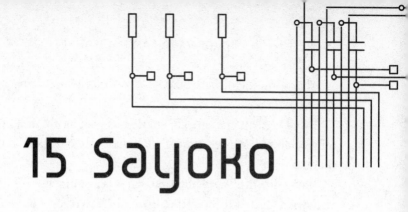

15 Sayoko

"She was unhappy with us," Hiro said in the middle of the night, sitting at the edge of Sayoko's bed, voice low. He had heard Angelica get up and go to the kitchen; Sayoko had heard the noises, too. Neither of them could sleep. "I don't know why your plan didn't work. I thought the reminders of home would make her happy."

Sayoko didn't reply. Hiro was right, and it mattered, because Angelica was the most important ally they had. But Sayoko did not want to worry him.

And yet, she should've known better. She had failed to perceive something about Anji-chan. The girl's relationship to the Philippines was not simple. Perhaps even her present situation was not as problem-free as Sayoko had assumed. There was more beneath Angelica's stoic, patient smile.

Of course, the past was not always a comfort. Sayoko knew that as well as anyone. There was a reason she had ended her own story where she had, with young Laqi and Daisuke running away together, in enemy territory, yes, but alone and in love. Some things aren't pleasant to revisit.

"Open the blinds, will you?" she asked Hiro.

When he did, the moon shone in, casting stripes on the floor and across the foot of the futon.

"That's better," she said. "Even a little light is better than the darkness."

After a moment, Hiro said, "Do you need something to help you sleep?"

"No, I've slept enough. I spent a good part of my fifties practically catatonic. Wasted time. I thought I was old then. Isn't that ridiculous?"

"I imagine this was when Itou-san was a young boy."

Sayoko started to nod, then paused. "You're very clever, Hiro. Most people would not have guessed that."

"I can add," he said, with a note of humor in his voice.

"Most people can add. What they can't do is see, or think."

This time, Hiro remained discreetly silent.

"But you're right. I had Ryo when I was an older woman. Not in my mid-thirties, as people assume, as even my own son assumes, but when I was forty-five. Yes, I was surprised to conceive so late. But it was not something I wanted—certainly not in the way my husband wanted it—so it simply seemed like another absurdity."

From behind the wall came the quick sound of a startled voice, like someone waking from a nightmare. Then there were soft footsteps, water running in the bathroom, a door closing again. Angelica.

Sayoko said, "You understand why I can't tell people, don't you? If they know my real age, the math changes. People start asking questions. That's what my husband always said. I could pass as ten years younger than my true age, even fifteen years, and so he insisted: *you were a child during the war. Children are innocent.* That was part of our bargain."

Hiro said, "I am guessing that you, too, were innocent."

"Oh, Hiro," she sighed. "Yes and no. Yes and no . . ."

"I've noticed," he said tentatively, "that people who feel guilt are the ones who need not carry such a burden, and people who feel no guilt at all have often committed the greatest crimes against humanity."

"Possibly." But it did not comfort her.

A moment passed.

"Anji is still up," Hiro said, listening.

"Yes. We're not the only restless ones. But at least I have you." She had started to become more aware of her good, if temporary, fortune. "My son is alone. Anji is alone."

"Anji has her brother. They communicate frequently."

"That's good. He lives in the Philippines?"

"Alaska."

"What does he do?"

"Rare earths mining in a contaminated area called the Burned Zone."

"Oh dear," Sayoko said. "Why do they need to do that?"

"Because China dominates the world market and this threatens geopolitical stability. Japan began deep-sea mining in the last decade but there are questions about local contamination, and it isn't popular."

"The infertility crisis . . ." Sayoko mused.

"Perhaps. There are many classes of contaminants involved with infertility."

"But why do we need that stuff at all?"

Even in the low light, Sayoko could see Hiro tip his chin down and pat his torso.

"Don't tell Anji-chan that."

"The minerals aren't just used to make robots," he clarified. "Rare earths are essential for defense, electric cars, consumer electronics, solar cells and cell phones—for many popular items developed in the last forty years."

"Cell phones," she mused. "And they're dangerous."

"Environmentally and politically, yes."

"Well, we should give up some of these gadgets, then."

"Certainly," Hiro said. "Where would you like to start?"

He'd made his point.

Sayoko asked, "We can't go back, can we?"

"I fear not."

"Just . . ." Sayoko paused. "Just don't mention to Anji-chan that her brother's work is dangerous because we need more robots—"

"And phones—"

"Yes, and phones. She loves her phone. Don't mention any of it."

A cloud covered the moon and the stripes on the floor faded. But Sayoko's eyes had adjusted. Insomnia had dug its claws into her. If not for fear of waking the entire household, she'd simply get up and start the day. Instead, she felt trapped, waiting for dawn to come.

We can't go back.

The past was a forbidding country, but the future was as well.

Hiro whispered, "Sayoko-san, please tell me. What happened to Daisuke and Laqi, after the night at the top of the guard tower?"

"They lived happily ever after," she said. "As all lovers should."

He asked again, "What happened?"

She patted his smooth silver leg.

In a flat voice he asked, "Will you and I live happily ever after?"

She knew he already had his answer, but that wasn't enough. Only the story behind the answer, the lessons that only history could provide, the patterns that most closely resembled universal truth, could help him at this point. And it was her responsibility to help him. She was sure of that, at least.

"All right," she said. "But come closer. My throat is tired."

She eased back, head on her pillow. He leaned his head closer to her lips.

"You want to know if she managed to keep Daisuke safe. You want to know if the hunters did away with him. They didn't do him any harm, and of course Laqi didn't either. So you must know: people who are just like us can be our enemies, too. Look into the mirror to know whom you should fear."

At first, they knew only happiness. Laqi had told Daisuke she was not ready to go back to her people—that they would see the change in her, that she needed time to think. He was worried about her welfare; he was not sure how staying away would help. But he had his own reasons for throwing off caution. They were ever closer to his quarry and he had, at last, a trusted guide. Wandering the most remote highlands of Formosa had been his aspiration since leaving Japan.

For days, in pursuit of Daisuke's dream and indulging their new love, they risked passing through unfamiliar territory and ended up traversing several mountain ridges, both inflamed with a zeal verging on self-sacrifice, as if neither cared whether they ended up on the wrong side of a Tayal man's spear, or bitten by a forest snake, as long as they had the pleasures of recording flora and fauna, bathing in the river, exchanging the little money Daisuke carried for food staples when they came upon gentle elder farmers, and sometimes simply plucking the odd vegetable from the edge of a terraced field.

Laqi was many days beyond the farthest limits of any territory she had ever seen when at last they broke out into a forest of ancient trees. Among these, one towered above the others. Daisuke had succeeded in finding his grandfather tree, an ancient specimen near the peak of a high mountain. The tree, Daisuke explained, was not the deity itself, but the place where the deity, or spirit, or *kami* dwelled. He felt its liveliness immediately, he said.

"Is it a good spirit?" Laqi had asked him, because they had found the tree just before sunset and she didn't relish sleeping near a malignant specter of any kind.

"It has a tender soul, and a violent one. Like all things, like the weather or anything in nature or anything man creates, it can be helpful or harmful."

He felt its bark with his fingertips and tried, without success, to wrap his arms around its trunk. He gazed up at its highest branches, head tipped back, mouth open, as if drinking in the light beams that ran in shafts through the forest. He bowed down, forehead to dirt, praying among its roots. He attempted to dress it in a long strip of knotted cloth torn from a shirt in his rucksack, but there was not enough cloth, no matter how thin he ripped it. He would've had to give up everything he was wearing.

In the end, he laughed and took Laqi's hands, and they knelt down together at the tree's broad base, and then reclined. Some minutes later, he touched a finger to her face and ran his hands through her hair, saying, "Perhaps someday we will conceive a child in a place like this."

Little did either of them know that a baby was already growing in Laqi's belly.

Daisuke had no fear of the tree *kami* and was eager to spend the night under its boughs. She was willing to do whatever pleased him. In the morning, she woke up first and gazed at the tree trying to feel the presence of its spirit, but could not. In the familiar territory of her own people, she'd had no trouble hearing the clack of bamboo and sensing the presence of ghosts near abandoned huts, but here, on this high, cold ridge where Daisuke felt a Japanese god, she felt nothing, or worse than nothing: a frightening emptiness. It felt like a premonition.

Daisuke must have seen it in her face when he awoke. He did not mind, but only looked at her and said, "Everything on this earth is alive, more than we can know."

He had already taught her how to see things in nature that she had overlooked, so she trusted him about this. Whatever happened, she would try to keep her heart open to possibilities beyond what her traditions had taught her. And anyway, it did not matter. For her, the grandfather tree was less important than the adventures they'd had. They had spent what felt like a lifetime together, and she had never been happier than she'd been walking the narrowest game trails with him, spearing fish and making fires, living the life that the young men led when they left the villages for days on end.

His greatest hope achieved, Daisuke became restless and more aware that so many days and nights had passed. If he didn't return to his camphor station in the lowlands soon, they would be alarmed, thinking he'd been slain by headhunters. He'd have no more money to spend and no paying work in the months to come.

Daisuke convinced Laqi that there was only one route to their future happiness. They would walk back most of the way, then each divert to their separate destinations, to tell their own half-truths. Arriving at her village, she would explain that she had trekked with him a single day, then intentionally lost him in the woods, and then unintentionally lost herself. No matter that so many farmers in distant valleys had seen them together and even given them the occasional winter vegetable or bamboo tube of rice; they were addled by their romantic inclinations. She would return at last, claiming to have been stranded, starving and desperate. They would take her in, and as soon as Daisuke could—six months or twelve, whenever he could find a home and a position in a bigger city that would allow a Japanese man and a Tayal woman to live together—he would come for her.

"And if it's not on the island, but in Japan?" he asked her.

"I will go."

On the final walk back toward the village, Laqi felt the first spatter of rain on her forehead just as she touched a hand to her still-flat belly. The rains were coming, and so was the future, including the one reminder of her adventure with Daisuke that could not be suppressed.

At home, even from Grandmother, there were surprisingly few questions. Laqi tried to tell the story she and Daisuke had agreed on, and Grandmother only listened to the broad outlines: Laqi had been lost, and she'd found her way back. The saga, half-true as it was, was eclipsed by the chaos that had enveloped the village upon Tendo's return. The police chief had arrived with several military officers and a construction crew intent on building a bigger substation, aware of the rebellious atmosphere spreading among the local clans.

Six Tayal men were arrested and all but one had been set free. No one bothered to ask where the strange visiting naturalist had gone.

But things were not so easy four months later, when the swell under Laqi's tunic became noticeable to those who knew how to look: women only, at first.

For Daisuke, it was easy to conceal his past activities. For a girl of fifteen years, such concealment was impossible. This is the way it has always been, for men and women. Why must women remember the things men would have us forget? Because our bodies have always forced us to remember. We are overwritten with stretch marks, with broken capillaries and with scars. We bear the traces for all the choices we have made, and even more, for the choices that have been made for us, by biology and by history, the advance of men and machines from one place to another.

By the time Laqi's protruding belly was undeniable, Tendo's Tayal house girl, who had reverted to her traditional tunic while Tendo was gone, was properly dressed in a kimono once more. School was back in session. Tendo was even doing his official part, teaching once again about the power of the empire. This time, Laqi paid closer attention, memorizing the shape of Japan with its four major islands, listening closely to the descriptions of its cities, wondering if any of them would be her future home, studying black and white photos of women in kimonos, searching for anyone who looked like her or like Tendo's house girl, a convincing hybrid of some kind.

Laqi's Japanese had accelerated far beyond any other student's, and Tendo noted this, though he and Headmaster Takeda also noted the widening of her hips, the filling out of her breasts and the awkwardness of her gait. Well, she was a barbarian, and these things happened. No one asked Laqi directly, which did not surprise her. Silence was a greater shame. Daisuke, long gone from the area, was not suspected, to her relief. Instead, blame was first cast on the village boys—boys who seemed more restless than ever, with the hunt so unsuccessful of late and the life of a warrior so restricted. Children who can't become men find other outlets for their frustrations. This, too, is the way of the world.

Nothing was openly said, not even by Grandmother. Nothing needed to be said. It was a tale that wrote itself, in a language that needed no translation: every stomach upset, every pelvic pain, every shortened breath, every sleepless night a message from our ancestors, who could read the future and would provide no comfort. Grandmother and Laqi did not weep. The skies would weep for them, providing the earth what was needed: sometimes sacrifice; sometimes sorrow.

Puddles formed. Mold grew. Laqi's belly bulged like a plum, but she took no joy from it, wondering if Daisuke would send for her, if he would make good on his promise. She struggled to hold in her mind the memories of those blue-sky winter days—so fresh and untainted, the trails open to their passage, the forest understory alive with metallic wings. It was warmer now, but with the constant wet she felt cold all the time, and with the heavier cloud cover, it was dark in the huts, even as spring advanced into summer. The skin on her damp toes turned white. A rash developed at the top of her thighs. Between her legs she itched.

Laqi hid during that rainy season in her damp hut, accepting the daily assignment of kitchen chores from Grandmother, not even bothering to work on her weaving anymore. The rain beat day and night on the bamboo poles of the roof, drumming the sense out of her, until she could scarcely remember her schoolroom math or her geography and even lost interest in practicing her hard-earned Japanese. She felt as dumb as the frogs who croaked incessantly at night, complaining about their wet skin, the ache of their curved backs, the clamminess of the skin between their toes. By the time the winds started, she no longer attended school. And finally, during typhoon season, on a night when the wind howled loud enough to cover Laqi's screams, a baby was born.

"I will take you in," Lee Kuan Chien said the first time he saw

Laqi with her baby swaddled over her chest, on her way to the tram terminus.

She ignored him.

"The child will never go hungry," he called out from his stool at the door to his shop.

"That's a promise no man can make."

"What's his name?"

She didn't reply. And she couldn't reply. The baby had no name yet. It was becoming the style to use Japanese names, as the headmaster had done for years, and to discard Tayal names altogether. But she did not want to name the boy formally until Daisuke knew he existed. Privately, whispering into the little boy's ear, she sometimes called him "Ryo." Depending on the *kanji* used to write it, that name could mean "dragon," "cold" or "lightness," "distant" or "forgiveness." The spelling and the meaning could come later.

"Last offer," Lee Kuan Chien shouted. "It's not too late for him to have a father."

The old merchant had never seemed so pathetic. *He already has a father*, she thought, and then felt a pang of anxiety: did he? She hadn't received any messages from Daisuke. He should have written to her by now.

It was at that moment, with her back turned to Lee Kuan Chien's shop and her eyes fixed on the message board at the hand-cart terminus, that she saw the notice. It was printed on official government stationary and advertised something that seemed too good to be true: free, guided field trips for indigenous villagers wishing for a glimpse of more sophisticated cultures. They had offered these trips, the notice read, from the time Japan gained Taiwan from China, but only in the last years had the trips become an annual occurrence. Highland aborigines were transported to Taipei and some lucky few were sent even farther, to Tokyo.

The goal was twofold: one, for the people of Japan to be educated about aboriginal nature and culture, and two, for the aborigines to see the allure of cities, the power of civilization, and the awe-some authority of the emperor, in order to return to their remote homelands and share this news, and to bring its pacifying effects to villages that had recently been less than peaceful.

Laqi didn't have to think twice. Others might go to see the sights of Tokyo, but she was going to find Daisuke, with their baby in her arms. A year had passed since she'd seen him last. The chances of him returning precisely while she was gone worried her, but inaction was the more painful option.

Ten days later, in bustling Taipei, she began to fret about the challenges of finding a particular person in a major city. Later, on the crowded, smelly ship to Japan, as little Ryo cried and fussed and arched his back against the discomfort building in his lungs, she began to question her judgment.

But only in Tokyo was she certain that she had made a grave error. She had simply never pictured human beings gathered in these numbers: entire streets filled with bodies, packed like fish in a net. On their first day off the ship the group of thirty-six aborigines and three official guides got lost in a traffic jam of cars and people all waving Japanese and American flags and shouting "Bay-bee! Bay-bee!" at foreigners passing in a caravan, hanging out the window, all wearing matching white outfits. Laqi wondered if a local revolt was happening in front of her eyes, or if some war was breaking out between Japan and America, until the guide explained, "Base-ball. That's the American, Beibu Rusu." The foreigners had come to play eighteen games against a newly formed Japanese team and were winning every game, but the locals were no less enthusiastic.

"How many people do you think are gathered here?" the guide asked Laqi.

She tossed out a word she'd learned in school. "A thousand." She could visualize five of something, ten or even thirty of something. But not that number which meant ten times ten times ten.

The guide laughed. "Hundreds of thousands!"

It meant nothing to her. Or rather, it meant only noise, chaos, and so much traffic that their tour would have to miss one of its stops that day. One less cannon or statue to visit, and a chance to find somewhere to sit with Ryo nestled within her shawl, alternately nursing and napping. Thank goodness.

The crowd that turned out to honor the baseball stars suggested that the Tokyo people were friendly to visitors—even to foreigners who looked nothing like the Japanese. They *loved* the United States of America, even when the US of A was beating them. This was not a side of Japanese culture Laqi had ever seen: exuberant, spontaneous, friendly and most definitely loud.

But when the baseball crowds thinned and the aboriginal group continued on their own itinerary, the reception changed. This was late fall, cool and overcast. The visiting natives stood outside one government building or temple or gate or munitions plant or department store entrance after another, listening as the guides droned on and the police escorts made no effort to conceal their bored expressions. Meanwhile, local residents, passing on foot or in their giant cars, stared and pointed. They shouted at them too: not "Bay-bee!" or "Beibu Rusu!" but rather "Barbarian! Raw barbarian!"

A quarter of the people in their group, mostly people twice Laqi's age, had facial tattoos. These women bore the brunt of the catcalls. Laqi's unmarked face had always been to her regret, but now she saw how it saved her from the abuse suffered by the other women. They noticed, too.

In response to the shouts, the proud, older Tayal women had looked around, confused. Who were these people laughing at? Who were they calling names? It took them more than one encounter to realize the supposedly reserved citizens of Tokyo were gesturing and shouting at them. To the Tayal, the difference in manners was astounding. When the Tayal women walked into kimono shops, they did not express shock at the astronomical prices. When the Tayal women passed geishas with white face powder, scarlet lips, and blackened eyebrows, they did not laugh and point. When the Tayal women were served inedible food, they ate it, and when they were served weak and flavorless tea, they drank it. But they were not granted such courtesy in return.

From these women's perspectives, and from Laqi's, the behavior of the Japanese was clearly unacceptable, and yet, something in the rude comments had stung. The Tayal women who had walked tall now turned their chins into their shoulders. The free tour had been successful in one way: it had made the tourists cower in the face of the civilization they had seen.

Laqi had brought a simple parasol from home, but in the bustling of the baseball crowds, the paper parasol had torn and now offered only partial protection from the drizzle that began to fall. She did her best to keep Ryo wrapped in the sling over her chest. The tour was eight days long. By the third day, Ryo was miserable, his nose clogged and his breath wheezy. But the group had to stay together; the itinerary was fixed; no one could return to the hotel before the others, not even sick tour members. Quite a few of them had upset stomachs by then, from the unfamiliar food and conditions but everyone had to wake each day and be ready for the next display of military, economic, and cultural superiority.

She had imagined walking into some shop and seeing Daisuke. Or entering a police station and making an inquiry. She had no trouble being assertive, but she saw, as they toured the underground railway that threaded through the city that this was no place to find anyone. And when she merely hinted to the guard that she would like an afternoon alone, to seek medicine for her baby, he assured her that such an outing would not be safe. The inflexible itinerary and police escorts were in place for a reason. On previous guided trips, crowds had thrown things at the aborigines, or worse.

"On my own, I would not be recognized," she said, though she knew that her clothes stood out, if not her features.

"Perhaps," he said, scrutinizing her face for the first time. "Still, we have rules. You have no permission to wander the city."

In Tokyo and on the boat back to Taipei, subdued conversations took place among the Tayal women about everything they had seen, and how they had been treated, took place. Quiet disagreements brewed. Information was shared. The Japanese government had not only outlawed tattooing but was now strongly encouraging tattoo removal. Two women from Laqi's village and five other women from villages down the coast all accepted the government's invitation to visit a doctor in Taipei before returning to their homelands.

Ryo's lung condition had worsened on the boat home, and on the last night before arrival in Taiwan, he writhed with fever and vomited up the milk she gave him until he turned away from her breast altogether. When Laqi asked an official to help her get him to a doctor, he told her that she could go with the group having the skin procedures.

"But this is more urgent," she said.

"You should have thought of that before you brought a young infant on a sightseeing trip."

In the waiting room of the big-city surgeon's office, she rocked the listless, dehydrated baby and waited for hours as one woman entered and did not come out, and another entered and did not come out. Only after nightfall did the group trundle out altogether, with glassy eyes and bandages over the bottom halves of their faces, even their mouths. They looked like bandits, or ghouls.

"You can write?" a nurse asked Laqi in Japanese.

"Of course." The truth was, her reading and writing ability was far behind her speaking ability. She knew only hundreds of *kanji*, not the thousands she would need to be literate.

"Write the patient's name for me, please."

And now Laqi had to decide: what did her son's name mean? Not dragon, today. Not lightness, either. She might have chosen "distant," for her child seemed as far from her as he could ever be—unresponsive, nearly immobile, unwilling to nurse. Instead, she chose the last possibility. *Forgiveness.* That was what she hoped he would grant her, for having made this trip, and for having brought him into this world in the first place, without a family, without a father, without anywhere to belong.

In the village later that week, there were three deaths. A woman her grandmother's age, who had succumbed to infection because of the tattoo removal. A woman even older, who had also succumbed. And Ryo.

Hiro said, after a long pause, "Are you feeling all right?"

"Yes," Sayoko said. Her tone was steely but her eyes were brimming.

"You don't need to continue. Perhaps you should rest."

"No. I have not yet answered your question."

The first letter from Daisuke had arrived while she was away, which only made things worse. If only she hadn't been impatient, perhaps she would not have gone in search of Daisuke. Perhaps Ryo would still be alive. But she had always been restless and impulsive. Every good and terrible thing had come to her on account of those traits.

Laqi could read only one *kanji* of five in Daisuke's letter. Tears dropped onto the card, smudging some of the words she was sure of: some Taiwanese place names, the word for police and maybe the word for confinement. Her dirty hands—for she had stopped caring for herself, stopped washing her body or combing her hair in the days since Ryo's death—smudged additional spots on the card. She was destroying the only link she had, but its value was less now. Their son was dead, before Daisuke could even know he had a son. And her dream of Japan was dead as well. There, she was a barbarian: illiterate, unsophisticated, incapable.

The second letter arrived not much later, while her breasts were still painfully engorged with milk that her departed baby could not drink. The ache in her heart became yet more intense. She woke many nights to a blanket spotted with tears and leaking milk until both streams stopped, and she was left only hollow and dry, light enough to blow away. A third, fourth, and fifth letter from Daisuke arrived after that.

But then a number of weeks passed without any letter at all. Laqi bathed herself at last. She had eaten little more than rice since her breasts had dried up, but now she allowed herself some dried fish. With her new strength, she gathered up the letters and went to Lee Kuan Chien.

"You could marry me," Lee Kuan Chien said, after he had read the first letter from Daisuke but before he had translated it.

"What do the letters say?" she pleaded.

"I would give you a place to live. If you have another child, I will treat it as my own. I am not asking that we have a child together. You could do as you wish."

"Please, start with the first. The gist of it. Anything."

"Things will be no better for you in a few years. In fact, they may be worse. There will be more interference. Policies are changing."

"Just read it, if you can," she begged.

"There was a time when the government encouraged inter-marriage between Japanese and aborigines, for the purposes of assimilation. But since Wushe, things have changed."

She had heard about the incident at Wushe, a failed uprising by the neighboring Seediq people against the Japanese, and knew it had resulted in many deaths. But she did not know it had changed the empire's policy on aboriginal subjects.

"A wise Japanese man would not enter into a relationship prior to consulting with authorities," Lee Kuan Chien said. "He could start a conflict that way. He could anger a tribe leader and at the same time anger the colonial authorities. There are punishments for Japanese citizens who create such conflicts. This is a sensitive time."

She told herself she would not beg again. But she could not resist. "Please."

"All right," said Lee Kuan Chien, a man who had lived many years, and who played a long game, still. "He says . . . that he was moved from one logging camp to another and that he will write again."

"The next one?"

"He says . . . he hopes you are still waiting, and have not married."

"The next?"

"He says . . . he has been sent back to Japan, but will be returning to the colony, perhaps in the spring, and perhaps sooner after he speaks with the authorities. He will send a gift."

"I have received no gift," she said.

"He says . . ." and this time Lee Kuan Chien paused, his face marked not with slyness or stoicism, but with a tender expression she had never seen. "He writes to you from a jail in a town one day south of here, where he is awaiting sentencing."

She needed to know the fifth letter's contents, and did not want to know. But she calmed her voice and shifted back on her stool, hands folded in her lap. "Go ahead."

"Stay with me," Lee Kuan Chien said. "Put all this behind you." She did not answer.

"What if I told you that you were my child," Lee Kuan Chien said, and his voice cracked at the last word.

Her body flashed with rage. "I would not believe it."

"Your mother made the same mistake you did. She had a baby. What if I said that I was the father of that child, but she made me promise never to tell anyone in the village?"

She shook her head. Pathetic man. Ridiculous old man.

"What if I told you I have been trying to let you know since the first time you came to me?"

"You're lying. You wanted me as your wife the first time I came."

"Are you sure? I am skilled with languages. You are skilled with languages. I was restless in my youth. You are restless. My harsh tongue finds trouble, as does yours. What is so hard to believe?"

"You're only saying that now to make me live with you. My mother had relations . . ." she paused, before deciding to finish. "With a Japanese."

"Did she say that?"

Laqi struggled to remember. *No.*

"You have imagined it, hoping for an advantage. The days of the Chinese in Formosa are over. The Japanese are ascendant. But that may not always be so."

She had never disliked him more than in this moment.

"I have tried to warn you: about men and what they do to women, about the future, about going hungry, about your child going hungry. These are the messages of a father, not a lover."

The evidence confused her, but her intuition still said he was lying.

"Read the last letter," she said.

He sighed and lifted the piece of paper, with its tiny *kanji* characters, its smudges of black ink. He read with a passionless voice, taking no pleasure in the news.

"Daisuke Oshima has been charged for consorting with an aborigine without authorization. Evidently, he chose to be honest with the authorities about his activities last year in hopes of seeking permission, not understanding the difference between permission and forgiveness. They will hold him only temporarily. They will confine him but they will not send him back to Japan. He will be free to travel in perhaps six months."

She exhaled and drooped forward, elbows on her knees. It was not as terrible as she'd imagined.

"As your father, I forbid you to see him again," Lee Kuan Chien said, and then seemed to hold his breath. The hut had never been so quiet.

She laughed violently. "You're not my father! You're only a trickster!"

She could feel it inside of her: she was half Japanese. She was certain of it. But what did that even mean? How did she know she wasn't half Chinese? Either way she was not full Tayal and had no place in her own village, and no future there. But why should it matter?

But the *truth*, that mattered. For the first time, she was angry at her mother, for having denied her that truth. Her mother had claimed that this secret was to be a treasure kept hidden, perhaps valuable someday. But Laqi realized that treasures are only deemed precious when the right people appreciate them. Nations come and go. Values and appetites change. What is esteemed one day may become worthless, even intolerable, another.

The gift from Daisuke, mailed before he'd been confined, finally arrived. This was more than five months after Ryo's passing. Daisuke had addressed the gift to the headmaster with a note explaining it should be hand-delivered to Laqi, as thanks for her help translating during his visit. A schoolboy was tasked with delivering the object and once he left, and before Grandmother could return to the hut from her afternoon meanderings among the neighbors, Laqi opened the crate. Inside was shredded wood packing material, and nestled deeply within that was a lidded box. From the box she extracted the strange thing inside: heavy, shiny, like nothing she had ever seen.

She thought it was a pretty giant spider of some kind. But no. It was a clockwork crab—a mechanical toy or automaton from Tokyo or Kyoto, very expensive, very rare, meant to look like an animal that lived far away, where the river ran to the sea. Just the sort of thing that would have grabbed a naturalist's eye. Also the sort of thing you send to a young woman who is barely past childhood, or an easily astounded aborigine.

She was less astounded than resigned, wishing only to see Daisuke again: his face, his hands and long tapered fingers, his strong arms, his strong narrow back, his legs in mud-spattered white trousers walking ahead of her on a trail framed by thick stands of bamboo and laced with ever-changing stripes of sunlight. She would keep waiting.

Still, the clockwork crab provided some amusement. A boy cousin, half her age, came to the door of the hut to bring some duck eggs from his parents to Grandmother, and he spotted Laqi with the automaton and could not pull himself away. The glassy glaze on the hard body shone in parts brown, in parts orange, and at the sharpest points of the crab's claws, bright purple. Laqi turned the key underneath the crab's glistening carapace and all the legs moved, frightening her cousin.

"Is it alive?" he asked. "Does it see us?" The boy took the still-moving crab warily as she handed it to him.

A printed card had come with the crab, and Laqi could puzzle out most words, aided by the plentiful illustrations. It seemed that mechanical dolls were an ancient tradition and had been popular in Japan since the 1600s.

"They are so clever!" the boy said, meaning the Japanese.

"I believe there is something here about Western dolls," Laqi said, warming to her cousin's enthusiasm. "They have little strings above them, to make the dolls move."

He said, "Japanese dolls are better."

"Why do you think so?"

"Because they can move without strings. No one can see what is making them move."

She nodded and showed him the illustrated card. "Exactly so. In Japan, as it says here, there is an emphasis on the art of conceal-ment."

She took the crab back from his hands, understanding now what Daisuke had meant by sending this gift: not only that there was a spirit alive in everything, but that they must become experts at disguising their identities, their earlier encounters, their future plans—whatever it took to someday be together.

She had not adored the crab at first, but came to love it more as she associated it with Daisuke's secret message to her, and as she began not only to think it might be alive, but to be *sure* that it was. Perhaps it only needed her love and care to become more intelligent: a friend, an oracle, a protector.

At night she turned the copper key and felt its sharp legs move in the dark. She whispered to it, "Are you there?"

And, "Do you miss the sea?"

And, "When will Daisuke come?"

And, "Will we both return to Japan with you?"

She resolved to forget how she had felt in Tokyo, like a worthless object of public scorn, and she hoped that, in Daisuke's presence, she would bloom with confidence again. Nothing would take away the pain of having lost Ryo. But with Ryo's father, who had never had a chance to learn about their son, she could at last grieve him properly—*they* could grieve him. She could finally feel at ease again, like the young woman Daisuke had once known.

She remembered their days on the trail and along the river. She remembered their legs and arms darkened by the sun, feeling stronger every day they were together. She remembered the joy of her active mind, working hard to master Daisuke's language and to see the world as he saw it: full of spirits, endlessly alive. She remembered their nights, sleeping back to front, his hand on her hip, his breath against her neck.

She whispered to the crab, "I'm ready. When Daisuke arrives, we will all leave together."

A few weeks later, Lee Kuan Chien came to her yard, where she and Grandmother were cutting and boiling large piles of bamboo shoots. She had never seen him in the village or anywhere outside his shop. She was suspicious at first, until she noted his sober bearing.

"I've brought you a newspaper," he said, with head down, face half-hidden by the steam rising from the pot. "It came in with goods from Taipei."

He glanced in Grandmother's direction but Laqi didn't care what Grandmother heard.

"Tell me," she said.

He bent over and showed her the front page photo of the village on fire, and with it, the colonial administrative building, the police station, and the jail.

"The Tayal started the fire," he said. "To get back at the chief of police."

Laqi stopped stirring the boiling pot.

"All of the official buildings burnt down. And the people in them."

Laqi was speechless.

"The prisoners did not escape."

She did not believe him. He had been crafty before.

But he pointed at the newspaper, and she could read enough of the words herself: names of the prisoners, six of them Tayal, and one of them Japanese.

This time, Lee Kuan Chien did not ask her to come live with him. He did not seem interested in manipulating her anymore.

He said, "Some of what I told you before was not true. Forgive me. But this news, this is true."

16 Angelica

Angelica woke with a wet face, her eyelashes crusty, the pillow damp.

She pulled herself out of bed and headed toward the bathroom, avoiding the mirror. Looking down at the sink, she felt suddenly dizzy. She made the toilet bowl just in time, retching. Everything she'd eaten in that covert late-night leftover binge came up again.

She steadied herself and wiped her mouth with a clean, cold washcloth. She dressed carelessly: an older nursing top, faded lavender, and her least favorite pair of black pants with a stretchy waistband, convenient on this morning when her belly felt bloated.

"I was worried," Sayoko said when Angelica finally went to her room. Sayoko was already up, dressed, hair brushed and pulled back in a neat bun, sitting in her wheelchair. Itou-san, an early riser during the rare weeks he wasn't abroad, was already at work.

"It was the food Hiro made," Angelica said.

Sayoko frowned. "We all ate it. Not just you. Even my son had a plate after work. I think something else has sickened you."

Angelica approached the wheelchair, turned and sat quickly at the edge of Sayoko's futon, head in her hands.

Sayoko's tone softened. "You're sure that you're all right?"

It may have been the first time that Sayoko had asked after Angelica's health instead of the reverse, but Angelica was not in the mood to appreciate it.

"Take it easy today," Sayoko said, wheeling herself out, with Hiro following silently behind. "Take a nap if you need it. I've got company coming, but we can handle things."

"Company?"

"Rene. Ten o'clock. Remember?"

Another first: Sayoko keeping better track of her schedule than Angelica, and for once, not complaining about the routine ahead, including a visit from the physical therapist.

After breakfast, Sayoko was eager for Rene to arrive, eager to work on walking. Her self-pity had vanished. Even as they waited in the living room, Sayoko warmed up with the lime-green two-pound dumbbells that she hadn't touched in ages, doing bicep curls from her wheelchair.

Angelica met Rene at the door when he arrived, punctual as always, dressed in scrubs decorated with tropical macaws. Angelica admired how he seemed not to worry about standing out, and how could he avoid it even if he'd wanted to? Ebony skin, broad shoulders, a big smile that lit up any room. On top of that, he always smelled wonderful, like sandalwood. Sayoko had warmed to him slowly, but Angelica had found him pleasant from the very start and hoped he wouldn't have to change jobs too soon, as so many people were forced to. Even when the latest immigration restrictions made the news, she resisted asking him: *What are your plans? How is your visa status?*

From the kitchen, now, she could hear Rene's laughter and cheerleading. Sayoko was responding girlishly to his charm. When Angelica peeked through the doorway, she saw Hiro bracing himself next to the wheelchair, ready to help Sayoko as she lowered herself back into it, while Rene stood off to one side, nodding encouragement. Her walker was across the room. Instead, she had been practicing with a cane on one side, Hiro on another.

"Okay, okay," Rene nodded, impressed but still pushing. "You're sure that's all you're going to give me today?"

"Can't I catch my breath?"

"Sure thing." He reached forward and touched her shoulder, fingers kneading slightly, then took a step further back, strong arms folded over his chest. "Tell me about your birthday party."

Sayoko leaned hard on the cane, brow furrowed. "We don't make much of birthdays the way you do. I never even had a birthday the first half of my life."

"But you're special now, at this beautiful age," Rene said. "You're going to get lots of attention. Are you prepared for your celebrity status?" He handed her a glass of water and encouraged her to drink. "I read these birthday stories in the newspaper all the time. You know what they always ask: What's your secret?"

As Sayoko passed the glass back, a worried look crossed her face. "I don't have any secrets."

"The good ones. That's what I'm talking about," he said, beaming. "What do you eat? Do you pray? How many hours do you sleep?"

She pursed her lips. "I will have to plan something to say."

"Just be yourself."

"No, that won't do. They will expect something formal. They'll want answers. You're right to warn me. Thank you."

Rene shook his head, still smiling. He was only bantering. He hadn't meant to trouble her. But she seemed to be taking his comments to heart, realizing for the first time that she would be interviewed and people would want to know about her life merely because she had lived so long.

Angelica, still listening, felt a pang of sympathy for Sayoko. Groups bothered her, and noise. It didn't help to tell Sayoko a place or an event was meant to be festive. And this was worse than the typical holiday or coerced outing: she would not only be attending, she would be in the spotlight. She was not a woman who liked to perform. The birthday party was a public relations nuisance for all of them. But it was something more for Sayoko: a test of some kind.

To lighten the mood, Rene gestured toward Hiro, who was

standing next to Sayoko, tapping her forearm absentmindedly—if a robot could be absentminded.

"He's playing you like a piano," Rene laughed. "Why's he doing that?"

Lately, Sayoko had been putting up with this new habit of Hiro's, allowing him to tap her arms, shoulders, and even the back of her bare neck with the sensitive fingers of his new hands.

"Oh, it's just something he has to do. Calibrating the sensors, he says. I don't mind, except that now he's touching lighter and lighter. It gets ticklish."

Hiro stopped tapping, hand flat against her forearm. "Is ticklish bad?"

Sayoko paused, thinking. "I don't know how to explain it. It's not pleasant."

Hiro recoiled. "I've been hurting you?"

"No, no. Ticklish doesn't mean painful. It can be uncomfortable or pleasant—it all depends. But it's not pain. It's just different."

Hiro took another step back, pulling his arms into his trunk and crouching slightly, so he looked smaller.

Angelica, always on guard for some change in Hiro's behavior, took note. *Curious.* Hiro was sensitive about this issue of touch more than anything else. She noted the vulnerability, though she didn't know what to do with it. *Do with it?* That wasn't like her.

She had never thought of vulnerabilities as opportunities. But only yesterday, coming face to face with Hiro's cruelly exquisite Pinoy feast, she had promised to outlast him, to defeat him. It was hard to hold onto the rage, especially in the presence of other people who didn't seem to find Hiro the slightest bit monstrous. But she would try.

Rene turned away from Hiro and faced Sayoko more squarely. "This guy tells me you plan to walk around the park without any chair at all before the snow comes. What do you think about that?"

"Did you tell him that, Hiro?" Sayoko asked.

Hiro stayed in his slight crouch, voice soft. "I didn't say that, Sayoko-san."

Rene flashed another smile. "I was teasing you, mister. Do you know what that means? I was making it up. I didn't bring a gift for Sayoko-san's birthday, but I've got something for you, buddy."

Rene went to the hallway, where he'd hung his leather jacket, and came back with a blue scarf. He approached Hiro slowly, the way one would approach a shy child or an unfamiliar dog. He held out the scarf, and only when Hiro didn't resist, wrapped it around the robot's neck.

Hiro bowed in silent gratitude.

Sayoko was delighted. "I don't think he'll ever take if off now."

Angelica envied the reception given to Hiro at every turn. Others took him in such easy stride. Rene was charmed by him. When the reporters came with their cameras for Sayoko's birthday, and when the entire nation saw the high-level ministry bureaucrat and his mother with her helpful, convenient machine, everyone would want a Hiro of their own.

Rene had another client he always saw later in the afternoon, an older man who lived near Ueno Park. When Angelica found out that he spent the time between appointments in the park, eating his packed lunch, she assured him he was welcome to spend his free hour at their kitchen table.

Today she sat with Rene as he ate couscous from a portable lidded bowl, followed by an orange he peeled at the table, conscientiously catching every shred and seed. He offered her some of the couscous, but it didn't appeal to her. She drank herbal tea, hoping it would settle her stomach, eyes fixed on his large hands with their pink palms and finely manicured nails digging into the peel, releasing the pleasant aroma of citrus.

"She's motivated this week," Rene said, nodding in the direction of the living room, where Sayoko and Hiro were chatting quietly.

"She can do more than she thinks she can. That's often the case."
He seemed to be measuring his words. "She seems a little different,
in other ways."

"How so?"

"She doesn't flinch. I try to touch all my clients, but she's always
reacted a bit, like she doesn't want me to get too close. I figured—
you know."

"That she's racist?"

He laughed. "Partly that. But some people are just more skittish.
Have you noticed?"

"Yes," Angelica said. She thought of the times Sayoko had pulled
away from hair braiding or winced at unexpected contact, even a
hand placed too suddenly on a shoulder.

Rene said, "You never know what they've been through."

"Well, I don't think we have to assume . . ."

"Not assuming anything," Rene said. "Just wondering. By the
time a person is a century old, they've covered a lot of ground. War,
trauma, accidents, abuse—you live that long, it happens."

Angelica felt exposed for some reason: for not having noticed
enough, for not knowing.

"I'm not saying there's any problem," Rene assured her. "I'm just
saying it's a good thing. She's less jumpy now. It can't hurt, right?
That's why I asked about how the robot was touching her. Do you
think he's really doing it to calibrate his fingers?"

"What else?"

"Maybe he's using it to desensitize her. Maybe he noticed what
I noticed, and he's doing his own kind of therapy." When Angelica
didn't respond, Rene took it the wrong way. "Or maybe I'm just
being foolish. Never mind."

Angelica got up to refill her tea.

"Let me get that," Rene said. "You're on your feet all day."

"Do I look that tired?"

He was too polite to answer. She must look terrible.

When he sat back down after pouring hot water for her and cold water for himself, he said, "I'm sorry I won't be around when she's ready to try the park on foot."

"You're leaving Tokyo?"

He glanced down, separating the remaining orange segments with care, delicately pulling off white threads of pith. "It's time."

Angelica knew he had a wife and family in France. "Are you going home?"

He shook his head.

"Europe at least?"

"BZ," he said.

She thought she'd misheard him. "You? Alaska?"

"That's right."

"My brother Datu lives there."

He just nodded: no pretending to be pleased by the coincidence, no "I'm sorry," or "I'll look him up."

She pressed him, "Don't you have children, Rene?"

"Four." He smiled.

She hadn't met anyone with more than one or two children for as long as she could remember.

"All the more reason to take a good paying job," he said.

"But don't you know what happens there?"

His face fell. She noticed, for the first time, a few kinks of white hair threaded through the curly black. "I'll be in health services, not working directly with mining or refining—"

"It's not just the miners who get *Masakit*. You know that, right?"

"—and no one gets the bird flu anymore, if that's what you're thinking."

"No, they've made sure of that. The remedy was worse than the disease. They killed everything up there and left the whole place poisonous."

His tone was getting more strident. "I've got a strong constitution. I never even catch colds."

She'd heard the "constitution" line from others. That was Datu's attitude. You didn't have to last long to get the big bonus: two years. Stick around another year and every two weeks, the savings would keep growing. *That's for fixing up the house. That's for the fishing boat. That's for five or ten more years of retirement, someday soon,* especially if you went back to a place like Sierra Leone or Cebu, where a person could live decently on just hundreds a month. Front money paid back, minimal expenses, they'd be in good shape after three years and ready to go home.

The BZ hadn't been running long—maybe it was coming up on four years now, Angelica thought. The first fortune seekers, if they were being careful and not greedy, should be back home already, or soon. So why hadn't Angelica read any stories about them in the weekly Pinoy papers? Why didn't they know anyone personally who had made his money and booked his return flight?

It wasn't her place to hassle Rene with those questions. The last time Angelica had given someone advice about jobs, it had been Yanna, convincing her to come to Japan. Since then, Angelica had tried never to counsel anyone else about where to move, what risks to take or avoid. Everyone needed to make their own peace with what had to be done.

But not this man: so full of life, so giving with others. Able to talk to a robot like he was a living person. Able to make even a sober old Japanese woman giggle.

Rene twisted his wrist to show her the small screen. "You want to see a picture of my kids?"

"No," she said. She knew his children must be beautiful, like him. "I'm sorry. I can't."

He leaned back in his chair, surprised. But his recovery was swift. He laughed again like she'd just told him a joke. She refused to laugh back.

"Rene, don't go to Alaska. Please."

He looked down at his empty bowl, replaced the lid with a snap, and gathered up his things, not smiling now.

"They say it's a good living there," he said. "I've seen pictures."

She knew the litany from Datu's emails. It wasn't life. It was a simulation of life. And it was simulation that had caused all these problems: the need to surround ourselves with things that were not real, with things that were toxic, with things that could turn malevolent, when we could have reality instead, humanly flawed as it was, subject to storms and cruelty and want. But at least not poisonous.

"Hey," he said. "I worked in Dubai three years. Never saw my kids, the whole time I was there."

"The BZ is different."

"Yeah, different pay. Three times as much. Enough to pay off debts and send more home."

She reached across the table and pulled up a map on her phone. Most of the BZ wasn't labeled, but the largest buildings were. "What do you notice, Rene?"

He obliged her, nodding, and in the same gesture, glancing at his watch, not because he was running late, but because this conversation had grown uncomfortable. She should stop now. Any other week, she would have stopped. No one had tried to talk her out of going to Japan. No one had tried to talk her out of borrowing money from Uncle Bagasao. She wouldn't have listened, anyway.

"What I see is lots of work for people like you and me." He indicated the seven major hospitals.

"There are too many," she said. "Too soon, you'll be a patient instead of a therapist."

His face was unfamiliar now: no longer any trace of that bright smile. "You think I don't know that?"

"They stop paying you when you can't work anymore. Do you know that, too?"

He put his hands on his thighs, ready to stand up. "Yes, I do. But they can't take away the signing bonus, you know?"

"It's not all that much. The two-year bonus is the thing, and there's no guarantee—"

He didn't want to hear about how she reckoned the odds. He had his own wager to place. "I gotta think of my kids. I'm a *father*, you understand?"

"But a good father—" she started to say, and knew as soon as she said it that she'd gone too far.

"Don't tell me what a good father is. I don't regret a thing. And I don't resent that those four children are depending on me."

She couldn't stop herself. "But what about you?"

"You still aren't getting it. Of course it will hurt. But it will hurt because I have something to lose. Angelica, do you have anything to lose?"

It was like a punch in the stomach, leaving her without words.

Rene seemed to regret the question immediately, because he lowered his voice, but the anger still smoldered. "Hurting a little for my kids' sake means I did all right. Don't tell me I haven't lived my life."

He managed to stand up before she could see the tears in his eyes, but he couldn't hide the quick swipe of his large hand across his cheek.

"Remind Sayoko tomorrow that I said happy birthday."

She followed him to the door and waited as he pulled on his jacket: scent of leather, light cologne. She would continue to smell Rene for days, now that Hiro had inherited his lovely scarf. Hiro followed behind, watching from the doorway.

"Rene—" she started, and then reconsidered. If she couldn't do this one thing for a person standing in front of her, not somebody already buried, not somebody an ocean away, not someone already hounded by gangsters . . . then she couldn't do anything. She'd said too much already.

He reached out and shook her hand in the way he always did: one hand, and then the other up her arm, cradling her elbow—a clasp that always made her feel steadier, briefly safe.

"Rene," she said again. "What will you tell your wife, from the BZ, when things get hard?"

He gently released her arm and gestured toward Hiro, giving him a thumbs-up and an unconvincing wink, before pushing his hands into his pockets. "I will tell her what every man tells the woman he loves. I will tell her every day that I am absolutely fine."

She had known, yet just as Hiro had said, she had not wanted to know. She had refused to know.

The knowledge was like pain that operated on a gradient, waxing and waning. They always asked patients, *On a scale of one to ten, how would you say the pain is?* And there were people who immediately jumped to eight or nine for everything. But not Sayoko. And not Angelica herself. For her, pain was rarely acknowledged to be above a three. Admit any more and you'd have to do something about it. Plus, go any higher and you weren't leaving room for more serious problems, later.

She did not want to cry wolf. She knew that things could always get much, much worse, and this didn't make those future realities any easier, yet there it was. Her temperament, her fear, based on the past and projected forward, the darkness doubling. She'd lost nearly everyone. There was only one person left. The whistling in the cave ahead was fainter, and the rope between her and the only thing she could count on, more slack.

As soon as the door closed she walked past Hiro, who was still wearing the scarf. He followed her toward the kitchen and stood by, a momentarily unemployed sentinel.

She ignored him, sat down, and typed on her phone.

Datu, how are you, really?

She reread it. It wouldn't be enough to flush him out. How do you tell someone you've known forever that it's time, finally, to stop lying?

She sent a second message. *There is no point in telling me you're fine. I don't believe it. I know you're lying to protect me. But there's nothing to protect.*

And still she thought: with enough money, anything was possible. No doubt it cost something to come back early. It always cost to break a contract. If people weren't trying, perhaps that was because no one had loved them enough, no one had made them see the light or given them the help they needed to get out. If he had to buy his way out of something, she could help him. If he was too sick to work, they could reject the free hospice in Alaska and find an affordable alternative in the Philippines. Bribes could work wonders. Personal contacts mattered. Money talked.

She had her own problems: red-flagged visa, unplanned pregnancy, a rival preparing to replace her. But these complications seemed petty next to Datu's. He'd always found trouble, but he'd never been trapped. She was now realizing, all too late, how hard it is to save someone so hopelessly buried.

Sayoko had settled into a nap and Angelica was struggling to focus on final preparations for the celebration tomorrow: confirming a food order with caterers, returning calls and messages to three different reporters on Itou's behalf. Datu had not yet answered and she could not stop thinking about him. But her brother would not want her to obsess, and he would not want her to do badly at her job. Surely a human could manage the complexities of a large social occasion better than a robot who hadn't met more than a handful of people in his short life. She could imagine Datu's voice razzing her: *You can't outshine a machine?*

But the etiquette of this occasion still worried her. At the group home where she'd worked, birthdays had been simple: a cake served in the common room, a few photos. She'd already made one mistake ordering the invitations, last month. They were black and white, with tasseled braids for decoration—tuxedo-like in their simplicity, and appropriately elegant, Angelica had thought. When she brought them home, Itou had taken one look and laughed. *Black and white. They look like funeral cards. We will have to start again.*

When she had apologized and said she would take the new cards to the printer, he corrected her. *We can't have them printed. They must be handwritten by a calligrapher, with ink. I will take care of it.*

Itou himself was handling the ordering of special gift bags that would be presented to every person attending, even if they were simply there to take photos. Angelica wasn't entirely sure whom to expect, but she knew there would be neighbors and the building manager, some government officials, and lots of press. She was hugely relieved not to have to make decisions about what gift to present to whom, and how.

For most of the last hour she had resisted Hiro's every offer to help—with the floors and the dusting, the moving of side tables and reorganization of knick-knacks—but enough was enough. Fatigue was flooding her limbs. She tried to lift a large framed diploma off the wall. As the picture wire snagged on the bracket, she felt the whole frame begin to slip from her hands.

"Help me?" she called to Hiro, who hurried over, only too gladly. "Itou-san wants less clutter on the walls."

There weren't many family mementos to begin with, but they took down the few old portraits of Itou as a child, plus the school diplomas, some other public honors, and a few vacation montages, and stacked them carefully on a bureau in Itou's room, as he had requested.

She moved to the living room with Hiro just behind her, awaiting her next instruction and mimicking her posture of relaxation when no instruction came. She tried not to watch him from the corner of her eye, but of course he was there. She had planted doubts about Hiro's trustworthiness in Itou's mind, but nothing had come of those doubts yet. She had rejected Junichi's unconscionable suggestions, but he had been right about one thing: nothing would change unless Itou had a shock.

Again, she tried to feel yesterday's rage, but emotions were slippery. Fury mellowed into mere resentment. Below that, hidden and vast, was the mighty aquifer of guilt. Angelica was burdened with more than enough guilt already. Sayoko was doing well. She loved Hiro. You could not simply sever a personal connection and expect a person to thrive.

The door buzzer interrupted her conflicted thoughts. Two young men had arrived with rental chairs and a table that Angelica assumed was for food. But when Angelica directed the men to set it up near the kitchen, she was rebuked by an older woman—cardigan sweater, gold-chained purse slung over one forearm—who was clearly their supervisor.

"Let's start with the gift table," the woman said sharply to Angelica. "It stays in the entryway. Have you hired attendants?"

The older woman saw Angelica's worried face and gestured to one of the cloth-covered rental chairs, ignoring the presence of Hiro, standing in the corner. "Sit down. Pay attention."

This clearly wasn't the first time the party company employee had been asked to brief a housekeeper on how to manage an elder's birthday.

"You should know what to expect for the gift presentation. The government has downgraded the traditional silver *sake* cup to a simpler version. Have your birthday celebrant ready to receive it happily, in the presence of the media—"

"When—?"

"Don't interrupt. Walking sticks are often traditional gifts. These may be presented by hand, also at the end of speeches. Your birthday lady may refuse a gift repeatedly. Don't step in and take it. She is only being polite and will accept it the third time it's offered."

Angelica waited a moment to make sure questions were allowed. "But this all happens in the end, with everyone watching."

"Yes."

"So what's the table for?"

"Cash envelopes."

"Most guests will bring them?"

"For birthdays, it is not as traditional as for weddings and funerals, but it is becoming more and more common. Receive each one with both hands and set it on the table, but if there are envelopes that are too plain, wait for the gift giver to pass and then bury them at the bottom of the pile."

"I suppose I should give something as well," Angelica suggested, tentatively.

"I suppose you should."

"What is customary, if I may ask?"

"At least thirty thousand yen." About three hundred dollars.

Her voice gave away her dismay. "From an employee?"

"Do you want to *keep* being an employee?"

Angelica walked the woman and her crew out and returned to the kitchen to wash several old vases in the anticipation of flowers. Hiro immediately approached and stood at her side. "I have no gift for Sayoko-san."

"I don't have one either."

"But what are we going to do?"

"I can't do anything," Angelica said impatiently.

"But Anji-san, we can't ignore a custom."

"Perhaps *you* can't—" she opened the tap further, face turned away.

"I suppose I could offer something homemade. Or I could fix or improve upon something she already owns." Hiro turned his head away, preoccupied. Then he swiveled back, eye slits brightening. "Never mind. I know the perfect thing. It will be a wonderful surprise. The problem is solved."

"Of course it is," Angelica said under her breath. Of course Hiro's problems never lasted long. He had superior intelligence. His resources were apparently infinite.

"Anji-san," Hiro said, alarmed. "You're crying. It isn't the first time. I can't honor your desire for privacy anymore. What is the matter?"

"Money," she blurted out. It wasn't only money, not by a long-shot, but it was a start. With enough money, other problems shrank to manageability.

"We need to get you money, then," he said, matter-of-factly.

"It isn't that simple. We can't steal it, Hiro."

He shrunk back. "Why would one even think of stealing when one hasn't first simply asked? Have you asked Itou-san, or Sayoko-san?"

She barely choked out, "No."

"Then there is no need to discuss stealing. An honorable remedy will serve you better. I am confident that solutions are closer than they appear."

"You're naïve, Hiro."

He lifted his chin. "Sayoko-san has taught me about the selfish things men do, but also about the selfless things. I am not naïve, Anji-san."

She set the last vase on the drying rack and wiped her face on her sleeve. No, she could not ask Itou. It did not help that Hiro sounded both sympathetic and reasonable. Nor did it help that Hiro was himself so apparently trustworthy.

Junichi had asked that very question at the *yakitori* joint yesterday, when he'd pressed her for more information about the robot, what it could do, why Itou was allowing it in the house, and what it meant to Sayoko.

You're sure he's so innocent?

One can never be sure of anything. But yes. I'm afraid he is.

You're not starting to get soft on him, are you? He could be fooling all of you.

Yes, he could be. And if he's not?

Don't worry. Appearances are all that matter, sometimes. Anyway, it's your future at stake. You seem to be losing sight of that.

Angelica was still thinking about the conversation later that night at dinnertime, when she got the text from Junichi, informing her that his wife was in the hospital. She thought it might be a strange bid for attention, an excuse to call her away to meet with him in order to discuss something else entirely, to keep scheming about Hiro.

Angelica was in the kitchen, having just cleared the table, preparing tea and dessert for Sayoko and Itou. She carried the cups to the dining room. From the entryway, where Itou stored his gadgets, his phone rang. It almost never rang. Itou ignored it.

Angelica hadn't answered Junichi's text yet, but the call made her think of him. She went to the kitchen where she texted Junichi: *Is your wife OK?* She heard Itou's phone ringing again and returned with a plate of cookies.

Sayoko jiggled her wrist and eyed the unilluminated band. "I hear something. Did I miss a pill?"

"No," Angelica said. "It's Itou-san's phone."

"I don't take calls at night," Itou said, looking down at his newspaper.

"Hiro," Sayoko said in the direction of the robot, standing silent in the dining room corner, "Am I supposed to do something? Is my blood pressure okay?"

"Your blood pressure is good."

"Is Anji-chan correct? Is it my son's phone?"

"All right, all right," Itou said, folding the paper, rising to answer the call.

He re-entered the room ten minutes later, face sober. "My colleague's pregnant wife lost her baby this afternoon."

Sayoko sighed. "Isn't anything private anymore?"

"The ministry thought it better to tell us, before we saw it on the news."

Angelica asked, "But why will it be on the news?" She was trying to contain her sense of dread, certain that Junichi's wife would not be the type to take her own life, but worried all the same. "They can't report every miscarriage."

"With fewer and fewer pregnancies, even the miscarriages begin to attract attention, especially when the person was notable or had access to the best care," Itou said. "It's unfortunate timing. Statistics were just released this week. Most of the people carrying babies to term in Japan are people who haven't been here long, or who don't eat customary Japanese foods. The epidemiologists will pay close attention. And the anti-immigrant groups."

Hiro added from across the room, "Since last September, it is no longer legal for a non-Japanese resident to be pregnant, without advance federal permission."

Angelica felt her stomach knot even before she assimilated Hiro's last words. *Without advance federal permission.* Was he looking directly at her?

Itou nodded, impressed with Hiro's contribution. "True, unfortunately."

Angelica had been ignorant of the immigrant pregnancy laws. Her clients were elderly and Japanese. She hadn't personally known a pregnant woman in Japan, native-born or otherwise. The closest was Yuki, whom she'd never met.

Sayoko had been the quietest at the table all night, even before the sad news, occupied by thoughts of her birthday party and its attendant social pressures, perhaps. She surprised them all now when she spoke up just as Angelica was clearing the last of the dishes. "The stranger is always blamed. That never changes."

For the second time, Angelica wasn't sure if a comment was being directed at her, or whether it was a statement of accusation or sympathy. But then she saw Sayoko's troubled, dreamy expression, and decided it was neither.

Sayoko said, "I did what I could, to keep him safe."

Itou, just leaving the dining room, turned back. "To keep who safe?"

"It wasn't enough."

Itou waited, as did Angelica.

After a moment, Itou asked, "Mother?"

Sayoko beckoned to Hiro and pointed, shakily, toward her room. It was an hour earlier than normal.

Itou looked irritated. "She needs sleep."

Hiro came back ten minutes later to talk to Angelica, who was alone in the kitchen, still cleaning.

"Sayoko will have to wait a few minutes for bathroom help," she told Hiro.

"No, we're already done," Hiro replied. Another thing they didn't need her for. "Sayoko-san is greatly troubled. I don't know what will happen tomorrow."

Angelica busied herself emptying the sink's food trap.

"Tomorrow, they will ask her," he said.

"Ask her what?"

"Anything they like. She does not feel right about this. I assure you, Sayoko is coming to grips with her past. She is carrying a heavy burden. She needs you."

"Of course she needs me," Angelica said too sharply. "She needs both of us. I realize that."

"But what you don't realize is that you may also need her."

"I certainly need my job—"

"No," Hiro said gently. "That is not what I mean."

"And I am not going to ask her for money."

"As you wish, but these are not the needs to which I am referring."

"Unlike you, I don't need anything else from her," Angelica said. She wanted to say: I am not taking advantage of her. I am not manipulating her. In nursing school, we learned about boundaries. Instead she told him, "I don't need to be her favorite."

"No," he said, gently again. "I speak not of favoritism."

"I certainly don't need an old woman's advice, just because she is old."

He tilted his head, as if to say, *Maybe you do.* But that wasn't his point either.

"You don't understand why she tells me her deepest secrets when she hasn't told you, even if it might help you both."

He was right, and it hurt. There was no denying it.

"It is not," he continued, "because you don't let her depend on you. She recognizes that she can't do some things alone. And it is obvious that she must depend on you. That is the half of the relationship you have mastered. The problem is that you have never depended on *her.*"

17 Angelica

After Hiro left the room and returned to Sayoko, Angelica sat down at the kitchen table alone, absorbing Hiro's comments. She had not wanted to listen and she certainly had not enjoyed being judged, but at the same time, she felt a door opening. What waited beyond might not be easy or pleasant, but it had been out there all the time, pawing and scratching. It would come to her, or she would go to it. That was really the only option.

Sayoko was speaking when Angelica entered. Hiro was sitting on the edge of the futon next to her, holding her hand.

"I'm sorry to intrude," Angelica said.

Sayoko was silent now, but her eyes were glassy.

Hiro said, "You're not intruding. Sayoko-san, may Anji-san stay and listen?"

Sayoko didn't answer.

"Anji-san can be trusted," Hiro said.

Sayoko turned away, staring toward a scroll hanging on the wall: calligraphy Angelica couldn't read, and the abstract thick-brushed outline of a tree bent in the wind. On Sayoko's cheek, Angelica could see tracks worn through the pale powder.

"Furthermore," Hiro continued, "you may find you have certain burdens in common, which may feel lighter once you have shared them. Didn't you tell me that's why people often tell stories in the first place?"

"There's no need to pressure her," Angelica said, though in truth she felt disappointed. Hiro had made her believe that something was on the verge of happening, that Sayoko was ready to open up. "I'll leave if you want me to, Sayoko-san."

"No." Sayoko cleared her throat. "Please stay, Anji-chan. Hiro's right. He knows I'll feel better if I talk about this."

Angelica looked to Hiro, sitting next to Sayoko, still holding her hand. The angle of his head and the serenity of his simple face reminded Angelica of the statue in the courtyard of the charity home back on Cebu: a scaled-down statue of the Virgin Mary, gazing downward, miraculously serene.

No one can be that calm or that selfless, she'd thought as a teenager.

No human can, she thought now. That was the problem. It was no surprise that engineers wanted to solve the problem of imperfect, impatient, overworked caregivers. It was no surprise they'd wanted to solve the problem of loneliness and isolation, the problem of lopsided societies with so many old people, needing care.

We have come to this. It's here.

It seemed both unbelievable and inevitable.

She no longer questioned Hiro's capacity for emotion. She no longer questioned his capacity for offering solace. She only questioned her own.

Angelica said, acknowledging Hiro with a nod, "We *all* care for you, Sayoko-san. If there's something you need to say, you can trust both of us."

Sayoko took a breath. "My husband warned me to keep quiet and let the past go. He said I owed it to him, since he'd rescued me from poverty when we met in Tokyo after the war. But the past doesn't cooperate." She looked into Angelica's eyes. "Have you ever had a memory you thought you could bury that keeps rising up?"

"Yes." But Angelica said no more.

She thought Sayoko was ready to talk. But then she withdrew into silence again.

"Talk to me, Sayoko-san. Please. Is the party upsetting you? Are you nervous?"

"I wish my son had not invited so many people."

"They'll wish you well and they won't stay long," Angelica reassured her. "All you need to do is smile."

Sayoko shook her head. "That's what they told me as a young woman. *Only smile.* But not with your teeth, they said. Cover your mouth. Like you have something to hide. What did I ever have to hide, then?"

When Sayoko stopped short of saying more, Angelica suggested, "You've been thinking about your youth more lately. Is it because of this birthday? A hundred years is a big achievement."

Sayoko had been lost in thought. Now she emerged irritably. "Why must everyone keep saying one hundred, one hundred?"

"Because it is a notable milestone, isn't it?"

Sayoko screwed up her face. "But I'm not one hundred. I'm a hundred and ten. Why doesn't anyone ask?"

Sayoko's wrist monitor triggered an alarming squawk from the phone in Angelica's pocket. Angelica hurried to tap down the volume.

"Let's take a few breaths now, Sayoko-san. One more day, and everything will be back to normal."

Angelica placed a hand on Sayoko's forearm, but Sayoko pulled away. "I want to take baths again, like I used to. I want to go back to the old way."

Angelica laughed with genuine relief. "Is *that* all?"

It wasn't all. Angelica could tell from Sayoko's fretful expression. But it was the one thing she could bring herself to talk about, and for her, it was serious in its own way. Angelica had grown up in a house with no bathtub at all. It had not occurred to her that taking a traditional, deep bath meant so much to Sayoko.

"Please tell my son," Sayoko said. Itou had already taken his bath, per custom, and was in bed. "And please accept that Hiro will be in charge of my bath time now. He's the only one I trust to lower me in and get me out."

Angelica asked, "There's nothing else you'd like to talk about?"

Sayoko looked troubled but said nothing. Angelica thought back to what Hiro had suggested: that Sayoko would not open her heart to Angelica because Angelica had never opened her own heart. She had never risked sharing anything personal with Sayoko. She had always defended her reasoning: it wasn't professional to share deeply personal details.

But of course, that wasn't the only reason. Angelica couldn't become a different person suddenly, just because Hiro advised it and because Sayoko might have needed it. It was easier to deal with pills, meals and bathing, to keep one's secrets and sorrows, and to let others keep theirs.

Angelica asked, "You're sure you don't want me to help with the bath the first time, just to be sure?"

Sayoko mustered a determined look. She was sure.

"All right, Sayoko," Angelica said, bowing her head.

Angelica couldn't concentrate, listening for any sign of difficulty coming from the main bathroom, just off the hall. She heard the sound of the tub lid sliding to one side, and then nothing else for the moment: no problems.

She stared at digital *kanji* flashcards without understanding them, willing the minutes to pass. She wondered if she should inform Itou, who had closed his bedroom door, that Sayoko seemed particularly restless and unhappy. But no, of course not. She tried to lose herself in her phone again.

An audio message showed up. *Datu.* He had read her last plea for honesty. And he had chosen audio, instead of text: one step closer to being with him. Finally.

She pulled earbuds from her nursing tunic pocket and pressed play.

"Nena," he said. "First, I'm sorry."

Then there was loud static, obscuring the next part of the message. They'd redacted it, those bastards. This was why Datu always preferred text, because a black strike-through box was easier on the eyes than piercing static was on the ears.

She didn't turn down the volume. She kept straining to listen, thinking a word or at least the cadence of his voice would break through. It was like listening for someone shouting through waves, or wind.

The static carried its own message, just like the storm's sounds had. If they'd redacted it, it was because Datu was admitting something about contamination, or about *Masakit*—something graphic enough to violate his non-disclosure agreement.

She listened to the static, wincing at its undulating volume. She let it pierce her ears and sink down heavy into her heart. He was trying to tell her, because she'd begged for his honesty. The truth hurt.

Then his voice was back. "But Nena, you gotta stop trying to rescue me. You've been trying for too long. It's not a good thing."

A pause, and she expected the static again, but it was only Datu preparing to say something else she didn't want to hear.

"I've been talking with someone about this."

Talking with who?

"Getting it off my chest. She says . . . She says I have to stop feeling guilty, and maybe stop letting you put pressure on me."

Angelica closed her eyes and tried to relax her shoulders, to listen and not judge.

"She says that sometimes people mean well, but they try to help when what they really want is to . . . I don't know."

This wasn't Datu's forte, this therapy-speak. It wasn't hers, either.

"It's kind of controlling, maybe. I'm not saying you ever meant it to be."

Another pause, without static. The censors didn't give a shit about this: the unburdening of a dying man, as long as he didn't talk about what he was dying *of*.

"So you don't owe me anything. None of this *utang na loob* eternal gratitude bullshit." He tried to laugh, but then his voice grew serious again. "I came back for you, I got you out, but you don't owe me."

She couldn't help it. She took offense.

"So . . . that's sort of over, isn't it? We're even. There's no point in keeping count of who owes who anymore."

Except he wasn't asking a question, he was delivering a practiced statement. It was over, for him, whether or not they'd ever discussed it openly, not face to face, or voice to voice. She might have a few questions or statements of her own.

"I did what I could. I was a pretty fucked-up kid for a couple years there. And then coming back to the orphanage . . ."

She had a feeling he'd gone off script.

"I couldn't do anything about that, you know? You seemed to think I could do something about that. They didn't want two kids. Turns out—" he tried to laugh again, "they didn't even want one. Point is: we're grown-ups now, Nena. And you gotta stop thinking you owe me. Because I think what you really want is for me to owe you."

Want him to owe her? That wasn't fair. Anyway, what about the land title and the chance to finally get their family plot back? What about his dream—not hers—*his*? She hadn't invented any of that.

"About the money . . ."

Money was the simplest part of it, even if that part made her mad, too.

"Given what I'm going through here, I think we have to call it even. Everything else: that's definitely even." She heard a soft voice, muffled in the background, someone coaching him. She could picture someone squeezing his hand when he got the words wrong.

"Not *even*. *Even* is the problem. All this keeping track, all this owing and being owed has just piled up resentment. Every time I see a new text, I think—"

But at this point he couldn't go on. Yet she knew: he didn't appreciate hearing from her as much as she'd always thought. He didn't want a reminder of who he'd once been, or of the mistakes he'd made, even recently. The last thing he wanted was connection. He wanted to be cut loose.

"I don't mind being here. Really. I've got what I need here."

The phone in her hand was only a glowing blur now. She'd wiped her nose so many times her sleeve was soaked. It couldn't absorb anything more. But she had to remind herself: he was being coached. And he was sick. And he was scared. He didn't mean most of it. He couldn't. They could still be okay, even after everything he'd said.

Angelica scrolled down for a continuation of the audio message, but that was all. There had to be more.

Upset as she was, she was about to start listening again when a loud thud made her set down her phone. Something or someone had fallen to the floor, followed by a scrabble of metal against tile.

"Sayoko-san!" Angelica called out, rushing out into the hallway, hand reaching for the knob. "Let me in. Hiro, open the door."

"I have her," came Hiro's voice. "We are fine." Though it was not possible—he was only a machine, he did not need oxygen—he sounded out of breath.

"Don't move her if she's injured. Let me see, first."

"I'm not injured," Sayoko responded crossly. "We're all in a stupid heap but we're fine."

Bathroom door open, the questions followed for five minutes, as Angelica made sure Sayoko was unharmed, without a scratch, wrapped in a robe and seated comfortably in her bed, drinking a glass of water. Angelica felt less like a nurse than a head nurse, grilling some new hire on mistakes made.

Hiro admitted it. "She got dizzy. But I noticed. I caught her."

"And why was she dizzy?"

"Most likely the hot water."

"What temperature did you set?"

Sayoko interrupted. "The temperature I like. How I used to have my bath."

Angelica interrogated Hiro. "Forty-two degrees? Forty-four?"

"Forty-two," Hiro said. He had been standing in front of them both, but at a shy distance. Now he took a step closer to the futon, bent slightly forward in a posture of contrition, gesturing with his hands. "I checked before she entered the water. The thermostat was steady."

"Steady but too high. The recommended bath temperature is thirty-seven degrees. Above thirty-nine, you should be prepared for physiological effects, which include what, Hiro . . . ?"

"I'd freeze in such a cold bath!" Sayoko protested. "That's a for-eigner's way of bathing!"

"Anji-san, she requested a traditionally hot bath. She was alert. In such a matter, I feel compelled to obey Sayoko-san."

"Is there nothing else you could have done?" Angelica was more relieved than angry. Her pulse was slowly returning to normal. Things could've turned out much, much worse.

Hiro replied, "Be better prepared for her dizziness, just in case."

"Because when do falls most often happen? In changing situations. A new room. Unfamiliar surroundings. A hot bath when a person has not had a hot bath in many months."

"I regret my errors, Anji-sensei."

"What else? *Think*, Hiro." He stood up and his eyes dimmed, concentrating or at least making a show of concentrating, waiting for Angelica's rage to cool. As a gesture of respect, he had called her "sensei" again, something that she had missed, strangely enough. Was it only a few days ago that he had stopped? Even so, she could feel the anger rising, less at him than at everything else. She was mad because Sayoko could've been seriously injured, but that wasn't the only reason. She had nowhere to direct her sense of outrage against the unfairness of life. Why had she even bothered coming to Japan?

Sayoko complained, "You shouldn't keep badgering him, Anji-chan."

"I am teaching him, Sayoko-san." And in that moment, she realized she truly was.

You did not teach something that could not learn. You did not teach someone you didn't respect. You did not teach someone who would be gone in a few weeks' time. It was undeniable and perhaps it was even destined: Hiro would stay. She would go. No matter Bagasao's threats.

"What else might have prevented her dizziness?" Angelica asked, drilling Hiro again, but she was beginning to feel calmer.

A decision had been made, and it hadn't required a flawless performance on Hiro's part for her to finally see the truth, that Hiro was better for Sayoko, and fully capable. The capacity for error was essential to the capacity for true competence, just as Kenta Suzuki had claimed. And the capacity to accept defeat made Angelica feel human for the first time in days.

Hiro said, "I should have made the air temperature in the room warmer."

"Better. How warm?"

"Up to twenty-six degrees, to offset a water temperature of forty-two." Hiro bowed his head.

"Yes. Real nurses make mistakes, Hiro. All of us do. What matters is that you are humble enough to learn from them. I have full confidence in you."

Angelica pulled her phone from her blouse pocket. She swiped her thumb across the screen, pressed the icon for Sayoko's vitals. But the app had malfunctioned. The pulse rate read zero. She closed and reopened it, and then realized. She reached for Sayoko's hand, pushed the loose robe sleeve up her forearm. Her narrow wrist—pale, blue-veined—was bare.

"Where is your wrist monitor?"

Sayoko didn't answer.

"Hiro, how did she remove the band?"

They'd gone through three models to find the one Sayoko couldn't take off easily. It was imperative that she wear it in the shower, in her sleep, everywhere. Sayoko always claimed the monitor, no matter how narrow and smooth, bothered her. She had complained to Angelica in their first weeks together that it chafed her skin, that it made her feel anxious, that she kept wanting to tear it off—a lot of drama for a simple band around one's wrist. At one point, Sayoko had even broken down and cried. But Angelica had never given in. Sayoko's health records were scant already and her risk factors were high. An old-model vitals wearable was nothing compared to the internal monitors most elderly patients used or the color-changing vitals tattoos that younger patients were getting.

"Hiro?" Angelica demanded.

"I monitored her pulse manually, before and halfway through the bath. It had only increased by ten percent."

"There is no need to monitor manually. The wrist monitor remains in place, even during bathing. No matter what Sayoko tells you."

"She told me only the truth."

"Which is . . . ?"

"That she missed the old way of bathing."

"So?"

"And that love requires freedom."

"Love requires freedom," Angelica repeated back, flatly. "And what about duty?"

"Duty is complicated, Anji-sensei," Hiro said. "It requires us to ask: who is the master?"

"It's just a wrist monitor, Hiro. Don't make things difficult."

Hiro held his ground. "But you don't understand why she detests that wrist monitor, Anji-sensei. I owe you consideration, but you owe me trust as well. There is a good reason. Risk is not the only factor to consider."

Itou appeared in the doorway, rubbing sleep from his eyes. "I heard noises. Are you arguing?"

Sayoko looked to Angelica, who looked to Hiro, who looked to Sayoko.

Itou studied them, waiting. "Somebody answer me. Is everything all right?"

Angelica had imagined how to create this moment, exactly the moment Junichi had pressured her to stage and yet, staging wasn't even necessary. Mistakes had been made. Sayoko had come close to a serious injury. Hiro was entirely to blame.

Angelica had never been able to imagine the exact conversation with Itou that would follow, and that had been the problem: her ambivalence, her guilt, her unwillingness to be unequivocal. And yet, she thought one last time: *how easy it would have been*. Told one way, it could sound like Hiro was dismantling the minimal technology they'd managed to enforce until now, the only remaining gadget that had kept Sayoko safe. Told one way, it could sound like Hiro was carelessly—for all they knew, purposefully—hastening Sayoko's death.

This would've been her opportunity to sow maximum doubt and she hadn't even had to use Junichi's tricks or half-truths. She hadn't had to hurt Sayoko with her own hands or risk her well-being in any way. Hiro had done it all on his own.

The moment was here. And then the moment was gone. Angelica felt confused, but she also felt lighter.

"Mother?" Itou asked.

But Sayoko only regarded him with a blank expression, a resolute obstinacy perfected over years.

"Well?"

Hiro started to speak. "There was—"

Angelica interrupted, "—a minor disagreement about bath temperatures. Nothing important."

"Bath temperatures?"

Itou turned his wrist out of habit but there was no watch there. He was barefoot, hair ruffled, eyes mere slits under heavy brows.

Hiro turned to face Sayoko-san, head bowed. "This is your chance to tell him."

Even Angelica was confused now: Tell Itou about the bath? About the fall?

Or was it: Tell Itou about why she detested the wrist monitor? About her sudden insistence that she was ten years older than anyone had ever guessed?

"Later," Sayoko said.

"Later," Hiro suggested, "when he is traveling again, never home? Or later, after some reporter has done his own research, and the world knows before your own son?"

"Not now," Sayoko said, right hand over her left wrist, hiding the absence of the medical wearable.

"Is this important, Mother?" Itou asked.

"No," Sayoko said, deflated.

"Isn't it late for all of you to be up, then?" Itou demanded. "My mother has a very big day tomorrow. She can't be falling asleep at her own party."

Sayoko sat up higher. "Why must there be such a big fuss? Can't we cancel it all?"

Itou opened his eyes wide at last. "*Cancel* it?"

"Yes," Sayoko said. "Cancel it. For me."

"It isn't done." He crossed his arms over his chest, feet spread far apart.

"We didn't use to have birthday parties," Sayoko said. "Everyone celebrated the same time: New Year's Day. My entire life, I haven't cared for birthday parties. I haven't cared for any event where I am put on display. Am I something for sale?"

Itou frowned, unmoved.

"I am afraid," Sayoko said, voice trembling.

"There's nothing to be afraid about."

"None of these people care about me. A birthday should be celebrated quietly, if at all. With my family. My son. Anji-chan. Hiro-kun. You three are the only family I have."

Itou sighed. "I have my reasons."

"Yes?"

He maintained the silence as long as he could, but Sayoko's stare finally wore him down. "I'll explain them to you someday."

Sayoko said, "Soon, I hope. Do you think I'll be around forever?"

"No," Itou said, and then it seemed to come to him—the simple absurdity of it. "But I have to plan our lives and our finances as if that *is* possible. You and I could both need care in the years ahead. For a very long time, longer than nature ever intended. And then what?"

"So my birthday party helps with your job," Sayoko said.

"Of course it does," Itou said. "I've never denied that."

"And so does showing off Hiro to the public," Angelica said.

"Well, yes," Itou conceded.

Sayoko turned to Hiro, "You understood this from the beginning, Hiro?"

"I have come to understand, day by day, that I am different."

Sayoko looked to her son again for more explanation. When it wasn't forthcoming, she turned to Hiro. "You must explain. I insist."

"I have capacities that some nations disallow. Many view me as legally questionable."

Hiro turned his head, gaze shifting from Sayoko to Itou.

Itou said, "You've gone this far. Get on with it."

Hiro nodded. "My assumption is that there is a debate at METI involving this issue, and that Itou-san has placed his bets, and lined up at least a few trading partners, most notably Taiwan, the country that made me and will profit when my model goes to market. On the opposite side of the rift is South Korea, a social robotics leader that has developed and supported certain AI limitations. To favor

Taiwan is to stand against China. To stand against China is to stand with India."

"I don't understand," Angelica said.

Hiro continued, "Everyone needs more advanced robots but the question is who will make them and who will decide what a robot may do. High intelligence is only one limitation. Emotional capacity is another. To throw off the limits first, to defy international conventions, is a risk. But a profitable one. The Pause will have ended, with or without international agreement. To keep rising, Itou-san must not fail. For Itou-san to not fail, I must not fail."

There was silence for a moment.

"Am I correct?" Hiro asked.

"You are not incorrect," Itou replied in a tired voice.

"And so you're using me—all of us—to get your next promotion," Sayoko said. "But son, you don't even want that promotion or the next one. You never wanted to die like your father from overwork. You've never wanted to be head of METI."

Itou made no secret of his bitterness.

"Mother, it has been many decades since I made any choice selfishly. You taught me, years ago, not to pursue my own happiness."

Angelica was stunned by his remark, but Sayoko seemed to expect it. She protested, "If by happiness you mean music, you were no good at it! You made mistakes all the time!"

Itou bowed his head. "Thank you, Mother. Thank you for being brutally candid when it comes to my weaknesses, if never when it came to admitting your own. You have managed to live a hundred years and I still know almost nothing about you."

Everyone—Angelica, Sayoko, even Hiro—held their breath.

Itou continued. "I am still undecided about Hiro. I will not recommend him until I'm sure. No one will fool me. And no one will rush me."

○─▭─○

After an awkward silence following Itou's departure, Sayoko said, "I don't think I want any more tea tonight. Do you think something stronger would do any harm?"

Angelica went to the kitchen and returned with a *sake* bottle and three cups. Sayoko was sitting in front of her dressing table. Her hair was dry and pulled back in a long thin braid that fell over her shoulder. Hiro and Sayoko were both looking down at a scrapbook of old photos that Angelica had never seen.

When Sayoko heard Angelica's footsteps she turned to glance over her shoulder, the braid falling softly around one side of her face, and down over the shoulder of her pearl gray informal kimono. Angelica had rarely studied Sayoko's eyes in low light, when she wasn't frowning or squinting in amusement. Sayoko's eyes were surprisingly large, double-lidded in that way that some younger Japanese and Korean women found so enviable that they'd endure surgery. Her retinas were medium brown, her pupils large. In low light, she looked thirty years younger. Angelica could see the middle-aged woman she had been, and further, to the young woman who had become that middle-aged woman.

Sayoko asked Angelica, "Three cups?"

"It seemed more polite," Angelica said.

"Maybe you *are* becoming Japanese," Sayoko laughed.

"Impossible."

"Eh?" Sayoko asked.

"Impossible for a foreigner to pass as Japanese here. That's what I've come to realize."

"You think so, do you?"

Sayoko turned and shared a wry smile with Hiro, and though he said nothing in return, he cocked his head slightly, and then even less perceptibly, barely lifted his chin. It was all those little gestures that made a robot seem intelligent: not the voice, not the face, not the perfected bipedal motion. A week ago Angelica would've said it was a programmed action of sorts. Now she felt not only that Hiro knew Sayoko's secrets but that he could read her mind, and perhaps she could read his. He let her *in*, in all the ways that Angelica did not.

"You asked me tonight if I had a memory that won't stay buried," Angelica said. "I have many. But here is one."

Sayoko closed the scrapbook. Angelica glanced at Hiro as if to blame him and thank him—both things at once—but in any case to let him know he had talked her into this. For what it was worth.

"We had heard a typhoon was coming," Angelica began, "and of course, we had lived through many. Peak winds were supposed to arrive near dawn the next day. Half of us stayed back at the house: Lola and the baby, Marta, and Datu and me because you could not leave an old woman and a baby alone, and typhoon season was also a time when there were more burglaries, especially if people had evacuated their homes. Strangers took advantage.

"The other half of our family went to a shelter in the next village over, where emergency supplies had arrived. They went, came back, and went again, because the first time, the supplies were insufficient. They left in the afternoon, and by nighttime had not returned. But this might've only meant the estuary between the villages had risen too high for crossing on foot and the boats knew better than to head out to sea when the winds were already blowing. We would never see them again."

She stopped. It was too much to explain, and she felt tired. She was not a storyteller, and did not want to be.

"Let me fast-forward."

"It's all right," Sayoko said. "You're doing fine."

Angelica began again. "The storm picked up, worse and earlier than we expected. Lola and Marta were in the front of the house, sleeping, and Datu and I were in the back, whispering as we listened to the wind howl: Where were our parents? How would they ever get back if the estuary was flooded?

"Suddenly the house was down around me. I was trapped in

the rubble. The entire front of the house was gone, and the sea had risen. There was no sign of Lola or Marta. The waves were not far.

"Night came. I had only one hand free. I could not feel my legs."

She could not tell every part, had no wish to recount the hours of calling out for her parents and Lola. She did not want to admit she'd listened for the sound of her baby sister crying in the wind, and knew if there was no crying, it could only mean the worst. There were no sounds coming from any of the neighboring houses. Datu had staggered out of the dark and come to her, finally, and started digging. He had told her what she did not want to hear, that it was too late for the others, and that he had to leave, to get help. So she waited.

"A dark hill rose up far in the distance, with farms at its base," Angelica continued. "The rain was getting lighter. Eye of the storm. At the base of the hill, sometime that night, I started to see flashes. Rescuers. I could see them moving, maybe walking. I imagined them digging people out, coming to find me. My eyes were wet, my face was wet, it was hard to see, but I would not take my eyes off the lights. I knew that Datu was with them, and bringing help to me."

Angelica's *sake* cup was empty and small, but she held it close to her face, as if she could hide behind it.

"They were not flashlights," she said, finally. "The sun rose and I heard nothing, saw nothing. The typhoon had worsened again. We were not yet through it. Night came a second time. I was half-buried, numb, cold, and beyond scared. I did not want to live."

When she stopped again, Sayoko spoke. "Hiro, please, fill her cup."

"Not yet," Angelica said. "There isn't much more to say. I'm not a storyteller."

"We are all storytellers," Sayoko said, and the look in her eyes, of such intensity and shared sorrow, made it hard for Angelica to speak. If it was hard to see malice in another's gaze it was equally hard to see compassion. She did not feel she deserved it.

Angelica said, "The second night, I saw the lights again. I watched them glow and move but never get closer. And I realized—" she tried to sound composed but her voice wasn't cooperating—"they were only fireflies in the distant fields."

Sayoko whispered, "He did not come back."

"Not quickly."

"He had reasons, I imagine." Their voices stayed conspiratorially hushed.

"He did not need reasons," Angelica whispered, "because he saw it differently. He has always seen things differently. Perhaps he was confused by my location. Perhaps he begged them to look for my parents instead. In his position I might've done the same."

"Of course," Sayoko whispered.

"But he did come back, finally, and he helped save my life."

"This you both agree upon?"

"That, and nothing else." There was no point in explaining the rest, the news she had just received from Datu himself. There was no easy way to explain that you could survive something together and not be stronger because of it, or that you could break a bond that tradition said would never be broken. If he did not believe in *utang na loob* he did not believe in anything. He had managed to travel farther than any Pinoy she'd ever known. He had left his people and his culture behind, altogether.

"But the hardest part," Angelica said, holding her head higher, "was that my mind kept wanting to see those sparks as flashlights, even on the second and third nights. My mind played tricks. I had to close my eyes.

"It's very hard to force your eyes shut when you're thinking that at any minute you'll see a person, or a lantern, or anything that could be there but isn't coming. I had to say, *no*, you must stop looking. You must stop expecting. No one is coming. You must accept it."

Angelica stopped. Sayoko and Hiro seemed to be waiting for more, but there was no more, except to say quickly, "On the third day, after the storm had passed, in the afternoon, Datu finally directed the rescuers to me and I was dug out. I still had a brother, but I never really had a family again."

Sayoko nodded slowly several times, as if she were remembering the storm and the loss, too. Angelica was grateful for the silence that followed, preferring it to empty words of consolation.

After a moment, Angelica gestured to Sayoko's scrapbook and the other photos next to it, including several unframed prints.

"Is that you?" she asked, studying the picture of a young woman, dark-haired, narrow-waisted, in a formal kimono, next to a Caucasian man in a military uniform. Occupation era.

Sayoko grunted softly. "Yes."

"And the man?"

"One of the decent ones, but not right for me," she said.

Angelica did not want to use the wrong word: boyfriend, date?

"Someone you cared for?"

"How could I have cared for any of them, by then?"

Angelica didn't know how to interpret that, or how to respond.

"Did you marry soon after the war?" She had seen the framed oval wedding portrait hanging in Itou's bedroom. It was in color, but had that pastel-tinted look of a black and white photograph touched up to emphasize rosy lips and cheeks, the baby blue of the studio backdrop. In it, Itou's parents were wearing formal kimonos, and Sayoko's dark glossy hair was piled atop her head, in traditional style. It could've been taken anytime: a century ago or yesterday.

"Not until almost 1961. And then my son was born."

"You remained a bachelorette a long time."

"There were many of us, and not enough of them. And to find someone who did not look too closely or make too many demands: even harder."

"Was Itou-san's father a good man?"

"He was always the last man to leave the office. If that makes a man good, he was very good. He was the one who requested when we married: say you are thirty-two, not forty-two. Let people assume you were a child during the war. Fewer questions. No one's business."

It made sense to Angelica. Then as now: it was often safer when others knew less. "Middle-aged, but you managed to bear a child."

Sayoko shook her head, reliving the surprise. "And not only middle-aged, but far from the picture of perfect health. When I was first married, I had miscarriages, but my husband wanted to keep trying. I can understand the pain that women are going through now, struggling to make the babies that their husbands want so badly."

"Well, the women generally want them, too."

"It depends on the circumstances," she said. "I don't think my mother wanted to have me, but she was glad later. I tried to be glad each time my sons were born, but it wasn't so easy."

Sons? But Angelica waited for her to explain.

"When I asked to name my second son Ryo, because I wanted to let that name live again, my husband wrote out the *kanji*, and I let him. *Lightness*, he wrote, without even pausing. Not *Forgiveness*. As if he knew one could not expect a child to bear such a name. It was a better choice. My husband wasn't wrong about everything."

Sayoko poured *sake* into all three cups and handed one to Hiro. When she bowed her head slightly, he bowed in response, lifting the cup to his mouth. Angelica watched, fascinated. But he didn't drink. As she had expected, he couldn't.

Sayoko was watching closely, too. She chuckled now, girlishly. "I thought you'd do that."

Hiro's chin dropped down into his chest, a gesture of embarrassment. He lowered his arm, the cup still cradled in his palm.

"How did you know he'd do that?" Angelica asked.

"It's what we girls did. We were supposed to make the men feel like they were drinking in company, when of course they weren't.

There wasn't enough liquor to go around. But if we pretended to sip, or even just held a cup delicately in one palm, like so, they drank more, and were more satisfied with our services."

It finally dawned on Angelica. "You were a geisha?"

"No, Anji-chan," Sayoko said. "The geisha are artists. We were only slaves."

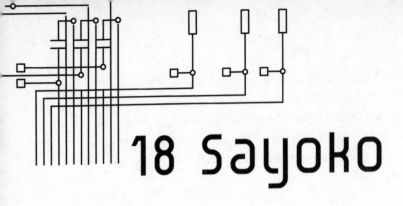

18 Sayoko

Grandmother had died the winter before, and Daisuke two years before that. I visited Lee Kuan Chien only rarely, but I did visit him. He was right to think we would've been a good pair. I was no less strange than he was. I, too, was a loner who left my hut only when necessary, relying on my feeble gardening skills, eggs from a small gaggle of geese, and the charity of a few distant cousins who kept me provisioned with rice and millet.

"I've come to tell you because I think you have a right to know," I said, interrupting his early dinner.

"I was asked to report to the police station about a possible job. I've been offered paid work."

His chopsticks clattered to the floor.

"By whom?"

"The government."

I hurried to find him another pair of chopsticks before the food went cold.

"They're looking for nurses," I said.

"You don't know anything about medicine."

"I'm a quick learner."

"Are you? Did you learn where they'll be sending you? Under what conditions? There's a war going on. If a bullet or bomb doesn't get you, the unsanitary conditions will."

But I hadn't expected him to understand.

My father had been a traveler. My mother would've had a restless spirit, too, if she'd lived longer. She left to join the road crew fearlessly enough. I had traveled all the way to Tokyo, and though that trip left me unhappy, I had not been afraid to make it. This opportunity was better than mere travel. It was work, and I had been approached specifically, as if the authorities recognized the value of my skills or my personality. I had not been wanted or needed for anything for as long as I could remember. I was thrilled to be recruited. I scarcely recall the faces of the men who lured me with their lies, and maybe that's because I was so nervous I kept my eyes on my toes, groveling, even as they praised my Japanese speaking ability, my youth, my physical health. I was so nervous about how they would judge me that it did not occur to me that I should be judging *them*.

I think we're going to Taipei, I told Lee Kuan Chien, naming the only Taiwanese city I had ever visited.

Lee Kuan Chien stood up and shuffled toward the back of the house. *Taipei*, he muttered, from the dark.

Why did I even pretend? They had told me nothing, least of all the truth.

I was allowed to bring whatever I wished, as if it were a normal job. I brought the little I possessed: tunics and leggings, a few old postcards I'd been given on my government-sponsored journey a few years earlier, and the clockwork crab. In Taipei, they gave me a duffel bag and several modern dresses, as well as a kimono and a makeup kit with items like an ebony hair comb, white powder and red lipstick, which I had never owned. I did not question the lack of a nursing uniform like the one I had seen on the recruiting poster—I was too pleasantly surprised by all the gifts. Those dresses and that kimono, which had seemed luxurious at first, would have to last seven years. As one of the daytime laundrywomen and seamstresses—most of us did camp chores part of each day—it was my job to make clothing last.

I would be confined in Taipei from late 1938 to 1942. I would not learn how to bandage a single arm, or even how to take a temperature. On my arrival, I would be housed with a strange assortment of women, from Taiwan and other lands: aboriginal farmers, educated town ladies from the lowlands, and a few urban prostitutes.

Because I spoke Japanese with a good accent and told the recruiters I had Japanese blood, they kept me in a different category, at least in the beginning. I served officers, and one older captain in particular—silver-haired and with a limp and twisted back from a war injury some years earlier in Manchuria. He was in terrible pain and he drank too much. The girls called him "Goblin Fox" when he wasn't within earshot, and claimed that on the night he was due in camp, the weather always turned foul. He beat me at times when he was frustrated, but he also left me alone more than the younger, able men would have, and posted a guard at the door of our quarters, to keep the other men from using me while he was gone. It worked, most of the time.

The captain visited once per month, and his visits were not pleasant, but at least they were infrequent, leaving me to other assigned tasks during the day. Occasionally, another man would break the rule—even the doctors examining us for venereal disease felt they could take advantage—but even so, I was on call less than many of the other women, which in turn made some of them turn their backs on me.

But this special treatment—if you care to call it special to be a concubine who gets beatings at every full moon—did not last when I was transferred to Indonesia, where I quickly became just another piece of meat, sore from morning until night.

I learned more than one would ever wish to know about men: some come quickly, some slowly, some shout, some cry, some are afraid to touch you, some keep grabbing as if you're slipping away. Some refuse to look in your eyes; some look too hard and too long. Even while they're hurting you, you know they are hurting as well, but there is nothing you can do about it. One in ten wants to save you, for all of three minutes until he achieves his pleasure, and then he shuffles out the door and lets the next one in.

In Indonesia, also, I tried to tell one of the higher-ranked officers that I was half-Japanese.

So what?

In other camps, they had full-blooded Japanese girls. And elsewhere they had captured Dutch women, Australian women, even. They weren't only abusing aborigines, that was for sure. I knew women who lasted only three years in the camps. I knew women who lasted only three months. And yet, other women like me lived on, year after year. It was not the kind of hardiness that made us feel pride.

We drank when we could. Not often. Mostly *they* drank and we pretended. On a bender, one Japanese soldier who had a reputation for beating women, bruising their necks and legs, and busting their jaws, finally broke into the liquor cabinet and was beaten nearly to death by his own officers, and then left tied just outside the door of the company brothel. Not because of what he'd done to the women, but because he'd drained the supply of good booze. That's how they treated their own. Imagine how they treated us! We were worth less than a serving of whiskey. We were "comfort women," but only a little comfort, and hardly worth protecting.

Once, a big-shot officer came and arranged to have me for a whole day and night. He tied me up by my wrists to the bed, did what he wanted, fell asleep, and left me pinned there, wrists aching, bruises forming, unable to sleep in that position as the cord cut deeper, until I felt like a wild animal, desperate to gnaw off my own arm to make the discomfort cease. In my panic I kicked him awake, but he only had his way again and then nodded off a second time.

I told myself I'd never let anyone chain my wrist again. I would die before I let them tie me to something. Even now, when I've been hooked up to IVs and all those other infernal medical machines,

I've felt myself slipping back to that night, smelling the smells of his drinking, his semen and my own sour sweat as I tried and failed to work the cord free. How does one explain to a doctor or some lowly assistant that the hospital bed with its cords and tubes delivering innocent oxygen or saline is a reminder of the old camps, of that long-ago war—in any case, a reminder of the past? We can't talk of these things.

A Taiwanese woman wrote a memoir, it must have been twenty or thirty years ago now, and she was briefly notorious. It wasn't the death threats that puzzled me—of course, modern Japanese don't want to believe any of this happened—but how the woman herself managed to fill an entire memoir with the comings and goings of men, often five in a day, sometimes far more. I didn't understand how she could bring herself to fill those hundreds of pages, to let those memories all loose at once. I don't know how other women could read it. As for myself, I leafed through the book in a shop and then put it back, feeling like even that had been a mistake, and that the ghosts would surely follow me home.

In the camps, we lived with aches, rashes, bruises, and smells that couldn't be washed away. We were given no opportunity to leave, even though we were told we had volunteered. We hurt and hurt and after a while, came to despise the feeling of any human touch, the pressure of a finger against skin that felt like fire. Everything felt like fire. I dreamed of floating on air with nothing touching me, until I stopped dreaming.

Occasionally, girls got pregnant. Fewer than you would think. Yet, thanks to medical assistance, no babies were born, not in the camps or stations where I was.

I was supposed to be a nurse, helping people. They said I would be a nurse.

What do I want now? What do I crave?

Sometimes, to be alone. Unbothered. Unwatched. Untethered to any machine, whether or not it blinks or shrieks or simply stares at me, trying to see inside of me when my insides are no one's business but my own.

There was not enough hot water at the camp, just as there was not enough good food or booze. The smell of sex and sourness and illness and funk stayed in my nose so long I was smelling it even later, even in late 1940s Tokyo, before I met my husband, when things were grim.

Yes. I missed hot water: a scalding hot, proper bath.

Sometimes, I want to be touched. Sometimes, I want to be heard and finally understood.

But most of all, I want to be clean.

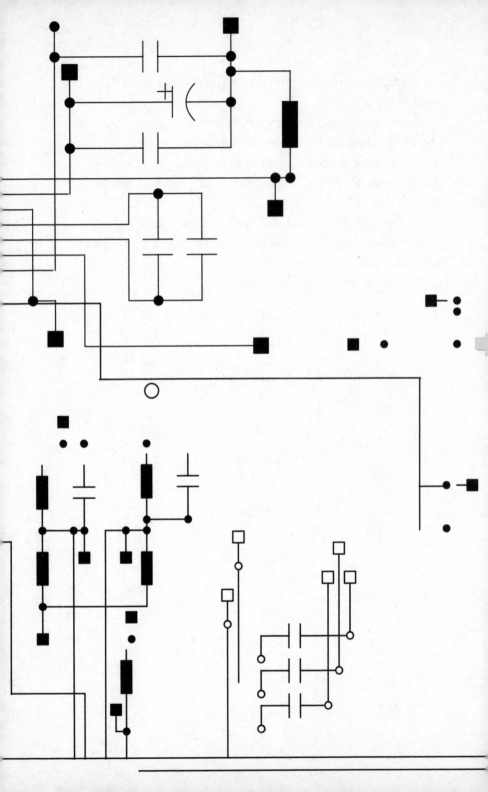

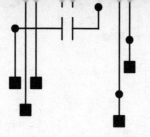

PART III

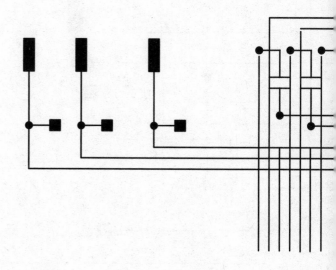

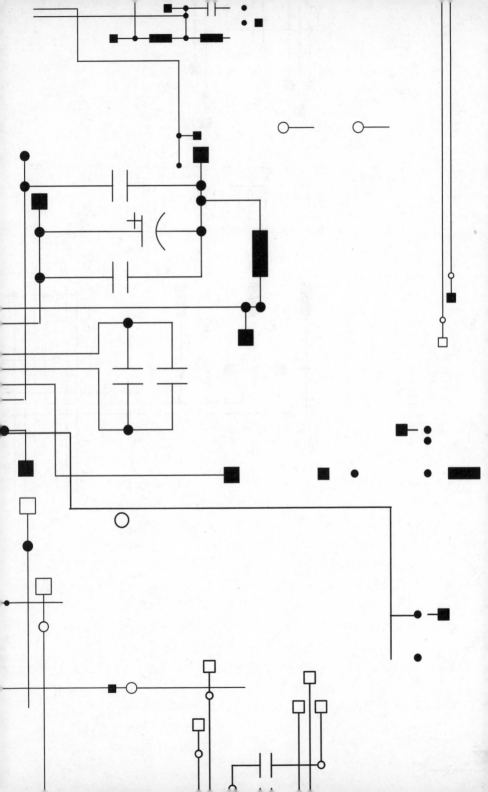

19 Angelica

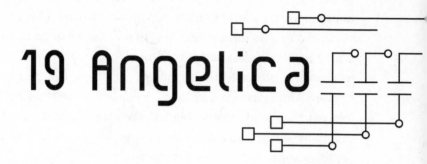

They stayed up into the night, refilling the *sake* bottle twice. Without calling attention to it, Angelica drank less than Sayoko, at times barely wetting her lips, mindful of the fetus developing invisibly within her.

Sayoko sipped her *sake*, her eyes closed halfway, savoring the taste and feeling the warmth, a balm for the difficulty of speaking about such an ugly past. Watching her, Angelica imagined the times Sayoko had lived through, times without comfort or privilege: the first fifty years or so, yes, but Sayoko had lived twice as long. No: twice as long plus ten years. It was true.

With Hiro's prompting, Sayoko told Angelica other stories, stories that came easier now that the hardest had been told. Now Angelica knew what Sayoko's own son didn't: about her childhood as Laqi, about her affair with Daisuke, about the clockwork crab and avoiding a marriage of convenience to Lee Kuan Chien, about what had happened to the first Ryo, and about the long road that followed, her secrets safe in a world slowly emerging from the rubble of wartime, when most people longed to forget and move on.

Everything Angelica had ever lived through—losing family, struggling for independence, trying to fit into a new culture—Sayoko had experienced many times over. Bustling Tokyo had once been as frightening to Sayoko as it had been to Angelica, and probably even more so, since she had come on a US warship, surrounded by sailors who thought they were repatriating her to her original homeland, set ashore with no family, no way to make a living.

Sayoko told no one that she was from Taiwan. Not far from an army barrack, Sayoko managed to find a job sewing. Perversely, she had gotten so used to living in a military compound that the groups of young American men were less frightening to her than the regular local neighborhoods: mothers and children, large extended families, traditional shrines, unfamiliar customs, people who would ask too many questions and see past her charade.

The sewing work kept her minimally fed and sheltered for fifteen years. It allowed her interaction with the locals, but only for limited encounters made all the more brief by her feigned shyness. With every kimono she stitched, with every Japanese lady of high and low station that she served, Sayoko became more Japanese herself, studying their accents, their demeanors, their slowly modernizing ways, until she could pass as one of them: her eyes a little larger, her black hair threaded with chestnut that glinted in the summer sun.

"When I was young, my hair was closer to yours," Sayoko said, reaching out to touch a strand tucked behind Angelica's ear. It was almost two in the morning now. They were all exhausted with emotion, at moments pensive, at moments unexpectedly giddy. "I was relieved when it turned gray."

"But your husband knew."

"He did."

"And he was in favor of concealment."

"He demanded it."

When their heads were swimming, Angelica filled a bowl with rice crackers. Later she went to her closet digging for snacks and found a forgotten bag of coconut cookies: the very last. Caught up in the middle of Sayoko's late-night story, she lost track of when the last bottle emptied, when the last crumbs were swept up. Angelica had started the evening with puffy eyes and full sinuses, and hours into the stories, she could've almost forgotten what had preceded

Sayoko's disclosure, not only the fall in the tub, but before that, the messages from Datu, his attempts to distance himself from her, which had reduced Angelica to sobs. No wonder her head felt so heavy now, dripping with the tiredness of a night of emotional purging.

After helping Sayoko to bed, Angelica returned to her room, eyes burning and back sore from hours sitting at the edge of Sayoko's bed. Glancing in the bathroom mirror at her ravaged face, Angelica spotted the cross at her neck, which she always left on, even in her sleep. There was so little in this world that connected a person to anything else: a memory, a story, a thin chain, a groundless hope. What good had faith done her? What good had it done any of them? *Yanna. Datu. Sayoko.* Yet still, she could not take the necklace off.

"Hiro?" Angelica had come out of her room a half hour later, unable to sleep, and poked her head into Sayoko's room, where Hiro was standing in a corner, powered down but instantly awakened at the sound of his name. Sayoko had dropped off into deep slumber, but Angelica's problems were far from resolved. "Meet me in the kitchen?"

She knew he could probably access nearly anything: obscure documents about her past, perhaps even more clues to her present visa troubles and whatever situation was pending. But if she could ask for only one favor now, quickly, as the sky began to lighten beyond the window over the sink, it was this: "Can you find out more about Datu, so I can understand how he's doing? Pay stubs? Health records?"

She pulled out a kitchen chair, quietly, so the legs would not scrape against the floor, and took a seat. He imitated her and drew his chair close, head tilted toward hers, voice low. "You want me to find and inform you of all I find."

"Will that take long?"

"No, I had it as soon as you asked. I was only making sure you really want to see it. The problem is quantity. What is your priority?"

Words came to mind: last time able to work, bank account balance, diagnostic details, treatment plans, life-span predictions. Hiro could show her everything, but what she wanted most was simple connection.

"Meaning?"

"The details can come later, when I've had some sleep. I just want to see him."

"Permission to breach BZ security?"

Angelica attempted a half-smile. "You don't need to wait for my permission."

There was no smile in Hiro's reply. "But you need to know you have given it. Because the footage may not be comfortable to watch."

Angelica took a breath. "Okay."

"I have security video. I will use facial recognition to sort and organize, I will select and compress, if you'll wait . . ."

"I don't mind—" she started to say.

"—finished. Eleven minutes of selected images available. Review?"

She told herself she would watch for five minutes. Instead she watched it all. Flickering shots of Datu in his dorm room, then being wheeled into a private hospital room, and then into a different one, a crowded space with three bunks, curtained walls. Isolated snapshots, inactive sequences deleted, active sequences preserved, of Datu being tended to. A sheet was snapped back by two orderlies, and she saw his thin frame, the black spots on his body, the withered state of his legs.

"That isn't my brother."

Hiro said, "Continue?"

"Yes."

Even without sound, she could imagine his cry of pain as they rolled him over, emaciated body pulling into a ball, toes curling, sheets soiled.

The kitchen window flashed white with the rising sun.

Angelica heard the sound of Itou's alarm clock.

"I'm out of time. Hiro—" she paused. "Thank you." But she wasn't merely out of time. She was also stretched beyond her capacity to assimilate. Her brother was not simply very ill. Her brother was nearing the end.

In her mind, she tried to sort through her naïve plans. She had hoped to get him home to the Philippines. Despite all he'd said to her, despite how he'd tried to cut the last cord between them, she could not understand why a person would want to die in a strange compound in a cold, contaminated, foreign land.

She heard the sounds of Itou's feet padding to the kitchen. Breakfast preparations. She had maybe ten more minutes until she should make herself present, offer assistance, and then wake Sayoko.

In Alaska it was midday.

Hiro said, "Anji-sensei, I have located something new. Active footage."

Ignoring him for the moment she tapped the last word of a text to her brother: *I have to do something. I will find some way.*

"Anji-sensei," Hiro said again. "I offer you my deepest condolences. I am concerned for your mental health. What are you feeling?"

"I'm feeling very sad," she said. But that was only half of it. She felt powerless to save him, powerless even to assure Datu comfort. Her mind was summoning the urge to run off in all the old directions: she must find more money. She must find people who could grease the way somehow. "You don't need to worry, Hiro."

"You're certain."

"I'll be okay," she said. "I have to be."

She could not deny the facts anymore. In a way, she had known even before seeing the footage. She both was and wasn't in the dark. At the very least, she could see far enough to take a few steps: but where?

Datu wasn't being logical. He couldn't be left to die alone.

"If you're coping adequately then you may wish to see this," he insisted. "It's snapvideo on a vanishing loop. It's being deleted at five minute intervals. The hospital does not preserve it when there are no security issues or patient emergencies."

"Can you tell me quickly what it shows?"

"Your brother is in bed, appearance the same, being tended by a woman—a nurse perhaps."

Angelica heard Itou calling for her.

"I could monitor and record any salient moments for later review . . ."

"That would be best."

Angelica was still rubbing sleep from her eyes when the first visitor came to the door. The birthday party wasn't scheduled until one in the afternoon. She knew the reporters and photographers were determined to come early, but this early? Before breakfast?

She opened the door, bowing, relieved it was only mail delivery. A special birthday message for Sayoko, most likely.

Instead, it was addressed directly to her. A large envelope. She shook it, fearing its official heft, hoping it was only her latest language exams with her passport inside, duly returned.

It was not. Angelica noted the Health Department stationery heading. She noted her name, birthdate, landing date, basic vitals. She noted the urgent instructions for making a follow-up visit— blood draw, DNA test—not only with the Health Department, but with the Immigration Office, which had been automatically notified in order to share responsibility for this unusual case, for which there were relatively few precedents. She noted the diagnosis. Yes, well, she already knew, thank you very much, but now everyone would know. Her news was on its way to being public knowledge.

"Anji-sensei," Hiro said, standing behind her. "Would you like me to prepare Sayoko-san's breakfast?"

"Yes," Angelica said, numbed by the notification. "Please."

Hiro remained standing, reading her body language.

"Hiro," Angelica began. "Never mind. We have a big day ahead of us. We'll all think more clearly when it's over."

"It was the letter," Hiro said. "You can tell me, if it will help."

She was tired of secrets and even more tired of lies. So she did.

The morning passed as all mornings preparing for once-in-a-lifetime celebrations do: the clock unsprung, and people rushing into rooms and leaving them again, forgetting what they were looking for in the first place. Sayoko was exhausted and pretending not to be, Itou-san was anxious and pretending not to be, Hiro was determined to be of assistance and was most often helpful and occasionally in the way, asking too many questions. He also kept putting on and taking off his scarf, both wanting to wear it and concerned it was too casual for the occasion, until Itou finally took it away from him.

Angelica appreciated Hiro's presence, always willing to take orders, never offended. She accepted food deliveries at the door, heated this and refrigerated that, greeted early-arriving photographers and moved lamps and small furnishings at their request, assigned extra hired help to the gift table, went in search of family photos and heirlooms that had been put away the night before but were now asked after by the early-arriving reporters, who wanted all the details and color that could be provided.

When Junichi showed up at the door, after the first media guests but before Itou's work colleagues and other guests, he was the very last person Angelica expected to see.

"Shouldn't you be with your wife?"

"She's home now, with her mother."

"But don't they both want you there?"

"Her mother already blames me."

"How could she?"

"For not sending her back to the clinic in Sweden. Now they tell us she should've been on twenty-four-hour watch. Before they said she was doing perfectly well . . ."

With guests milling around behind them, Angelica touched Junichi's hand as discreetly as she could.

"Her father hates me for not insisting on adoption after the fourth miscarriage."

Angelica paused. "Is that still an option? You said it might be— before . . ."

He looked down. "It makes me sick even to think about it."

She knew this wasn't the time. He'd come around. But she was at a loss for how to lend hope. "It might work for you."

He looked up, newly exasperated. "I can't bear the thought of my wife bleeding to death while in some backwards country a woman who doesn't even want a baby is healthy but oblivious. Like a farm animal."

"A farm animal," she repeated, chest tight. "You can't blame people who live in countries that happen to be less chemically spoiled."

"I blame them for their ingratitude."

Angelica did not speak.

"I didn't come to discuss Yuki," Junichi said. "Did you tell Itou about Hiro yet? Did you give him a good shock?"

Shock. Yes, that was the word. Never mind about Hiro and Itou for the moment. But what was Junichi thinking, standing so close to her and saying Itou's name out loud when others could easily hear?

Angelica touched a table runner next to them and pretended to be suddenly concerned about a stain or dust. She whisked it off and headed, with purpose, to the balcony, knowing Junichi would follow.

On the narrow, seldom-used balcony, shielded from the gathering guests' view, Junichi paced, one hand in his pocket, the other hand lifted to his lips, the red end of a cigarette already burning.

"You can't smoke," she said, flapping her hand at the first gray spiral, forcing it to disperse. "Itou-san doesn't allow it anywhere. Put it out now. Please."

"You're so worried what Itou-san will think. He isn't your friend and soon he won't be your employer. You haven't come up with any proof that Hiro is a danger?"

"Proof," she said. "You mean lies."

He leaned forward to peer through the door at the latest arrivals. "Watanabe and Mitsue. Numbers two and three. Mitsue is retiring. I didn't think he'd come. That's the one Itou is supposed to replace."

"You don't care whether I keep my job," she said. "You only want Hiro to be declared a bad product so Itou will be judged harshly for favoring the model's import."

"Hiro's not a simple import, he's a joint venture." Junichi was antsy, forgetting to smoke the cigarette in his hand, and scanning the crowd as if watching for other key players, perhaps his allies, to appear. Angelica had no doubt that he had been conspiring with others at METI, leaking them information about Hiro, prodding or being prodded into whatever would come next. "He's an *illegal* joint venture. You wouldn't understand."

Angelica put her shoulders back and tried to stand taller. "Hiro isn't precisely illegal. Anyway, regional agreements can be broken."

"You've finally started reading now?"

She didn't need to prove anything to him, but yes, she had finally started searching and reading: The 2015 Musk-Hawking letter, warning that superhuman AI could provide innumerable benefits but might destroy the human race if safeguards weren't implemented, published when she was at her first nursing job and too busy to follow most international news; the ten-year anniversary letter, more pessimistic, an indictment of incautious researchers and profit-frenzied designers. The South Korean Sexbot ban of 2025. The US-EU AI Accord of 2026, immediately undone by the final dissolution of the EU itself. The patchwork of regional agreements that followed, subject to complex interpretation, difficult to enforce, only a stopgap and yet vital: the Pause.

"I know enough."

Through the closed glass balcony door, they heard the clap of hands as another of Itou's colleagues called everyone to attention. The room had filled nearly to capacity, with guests still filing in, in neat order. The hour had struck. Through a gap in the blinds, Angelica watched.

Now Itou was moving to the front of the room to give a welcome speech. Sayoko was seated in a large plush chair that had been drawn up to the front of the room, her less photogenic wheelchair and walker banished from sight. When a camera flashed, Sayoko winced, her narrow shoulders shrugged up around her ears, the special vest she'd worn for the day boxy and mannish on her slender frame. While Itou spoke with his eyes cast down, the humble son receiving his guests and extolling the virtues of his mother, Sayoko glanced around furtively.

Angelica said, "We should go in." But she didn't want to slide the door open while Itou was speaking. The trick was to enter quietly and take their places at the back of the room. About forty people were now crowded into the main living area, some standing, some using the rented folding chairs.

"He didn't notice you were missing, Anji," Junichi whispered. "You're dispensable. That's the only true thing in this shitty world. We're all easily replaced."

The sight of someone new arriving, visible through the glass, made Junichi tense. "Otaka-san. Good."

"You're not in your right mind, Junichi. Whatever you're planning won't solve your problems, or mine."

Angelica started to move forward but Junichi grabbed her elbow.

"Please," she said. "You should be at home comforting your wife, not sabotaging Itou." She broke free from his grasp and went to the door.

He stepped in front of her. "My wife is the reason I'm here. She could still try to end her life. She needs a child, Angelica." His eyes were wild, but he was telling the truth. "In my current position, I can't promise her expert care or even a foreign adoption. I can't promise her anything. Try to understand."

Angelica had now seen Junichi at his worst. But she also believed him. He was acting abhorrently, but he was not acting selfishly. The situation had taken an essential part of him—his driven nature, his insistence on finding solutions instead of accepting what destiny intended—and amplified it to the point of distortion. She had seen what her own desperation could do. You started out wanting to help, to protect, and you ended up controlling, deceiving and destroying.

Angelica softened her approach. "Maybe you can't help Yuki. Maybe you weren't even meant to be together. I know you think you love her. But—"

"You wouldn't say that if you'd known us when we married. It was only after the baby craziness that things changed. Five years of talking about nothing else. Five years of seeing her miserable. I used to live for Yuki." He choked on his next words. "And she used to live for me."

Angelica reached a hand toward his arm. A moment earlier, she couldn't stand to be near him. And now she wished they could start over as friends, or at least forgive each other. She had never known the real Junichi. She had only met the shadow Junichi, railing against forces beyond his control.

"I have to tell you something," she whispered. "Junichi, please."

But he'd had enough now. He moved away from her touch. He started to open the sliding door. If she didn't say it now she might never say it.

"Junichi. I'm pregnant."

By the way he kept moving, she had to assume he hadn't heard.

○—▭—○

In the living room, Itou introduced Minister Otaka and then Hiro, who came forward with head bowed. People were still clapping and cameras flashing when Angelica stepped inside, head down, and followed the wall to the back of the room, just behind Junichi.

In the embarrassment of her late entrance, she missed the moment when Hiro positioned himself between Itou and Sayoko, but when she heard the low, sweet note, she looked up, first puzzled, then incredulous. A woman in front of her exclaimed in an appreciative whisper: "Waaaa."

Hiro played the one drawn-out note on the clarinet, a note so long Angelica thought it was all he was prepared to do. It was an adequate display, showing the capacity of his bellowed artificial lungs, the neat design of his simple mouth. Then he progressed from the first long note to the next ones, moving his agile fingers. He raised and lowered his arms as he played. A demonstration. *All right*, the body language of the crowd seemed to communicate politely, as one would expect at a child's Suzuki recital or in a high-tech robotics showroom. This year's model, with a few new features. But he certainly wasn't the first automaton to play a musical instrument.

"Very good," Itou said, to Hiro and the crowd.

Angelica was distracted by the argument with Junichi, with his emotional outburst followed by her confession and the question of whether or not he had heard and what would happen next. She struggled to shift her attention to Hiro's spectacle, but something was happening. Something in the room was changing.

The first moments of music had been well received, but Hiro was not satisfied. He blew harder: a raw, wild note more fitting for a dark basement club than an elegant reception. Glances were exchanged in the audience. Many seemed to think it was a mistake, tarnishing the success of the first attempt.

Then the note stepped up, and down and up again, ever higher, in shorter intervals. The melody, elaborated with trills, took shape and Hiro coaxed it further, his body language registering impatience and longing until he'd gotten into the groove of his playing.

Itou's face lit up. He laughed once, spontaneously, almost aggressively. *Really?*

And then his expression changed, no less than the quality of Hiro's playing had changed, as Itou recognized the composer and the song—and the fact that Hiro was not following the song, exactly. He was improvising, not by following any external cues but through his own dynamic inspiration. *Yes, really. In-puro-bi-ze-shon.*

Angelica was as struck by Itou's expressions as by the music itself. He nodded with deeper approval, detecting that Hiro was on the trail of something, heading in a new direction, one that might not be entirely pleasing. Or might be. The uncertainty made the musical experiment electric. Itou's gaze, which had been fixed upon Hiro, wandered up and over the heads of the guests, toward the ceiling, all the better to block out distractions, to examine what he was hearing.

Angelica did not know jazz, but she could tell Hiro's performance was unexpected. Half of the room was silent while the other half had put aside all propriety and was whispering or shushing someone for whispering. Phones had come out of pockets and were being held over heads, filming now.

Itou furrowed his brow, trying and failing to contain his emotions. Perhaps Hiro's skilled performance would only serve to remind him what he hadn't managed to achieve, giving him a taste of the anguish of replacement that Angelica had felt. Perhaps he'd even turn against the robot because of it.

Once that would have been a victory.

No longer.

Angelica glanced at Sayoko—self-possessed, pleased but not particularly animated—and then back at Itou, who had now lost his composure entirely. Angelica looked away, but it was too late. It was something in her programming, to cry upon seeing another person cry—something in all of our programming. From the quick chorus of surprised female voices in the front, Angelica knew that the rest of the room had noticed Itou's loss of control, too. Several of the women began to sniffle.

When Hiro finished, there was applause from the third of the room that had been willing to set their phones down. The others were still filming.

Itou turned aside, pulled a handkerchief from his suit pocket, wiped his face, and turned back again. "So."

The crowd chuckled at his loss for words.

He cleared his throat and tried again. "When Hiro asked if he could publicly present a surprise birthday gift to Sayoko, I said, *Yes, why not?* He asked permission to use my clarinet, but I had no idea of his full capacities. It seems—"

"Excuse me," Hiro interrupted. "Excuse me, Itou-san."

Itou laughed at Hiro's temerity and the audience responded appreciatively. Angelica noticed a woman reporter turn to her colleague, sharing a half smile as she whispered, "It must be staged."

At the front of the room, Itou said to Hiro, "You have something more to add?"

"That was not the gift for Sayoko-san. She is not a fan of the clarinet, Itou-san. You are."

The crowd laughed again, relieved that the mood had shifted to humor.

A whispered conversation took place in front of Angelica, between two men. "What did they use to call it? The old Turing test? To tell human from machine? With my eyes closed, I was fooled."

"With my eyes *open*, I was fooled."

The men were shushed by an elegantly dressed woman sitting next to them.

Itou said, louder, trying to quell the whispers and bring the attention back to the front of the room, "You have another song for my mother?"

"With apologies, I have something else."

Hiro bowed. He turned and walked a few steps, retrieved the gift for Sayoko and placed it tenderly in her lap, bowing again. She looked up at the crowd, her lips drawn thin and tight, her breath shallow, her smile unconvincing, except for that moment when she glanced again at Hiro and warmed a little. She took a deep breath and settled back in the chair, eyes looking down at the thing in her lap. Unlike Itou, she was not moved by any of these circus antics, and she was not inclined to enjoy surprises.

Hiro held his open fingers out toward her, the rounded metal tips curling inward with impatience as if to say, *Come on. Open it.*

The item was as big as a platter and unevenly shaped. Sayoko began to unwrap the patterned gift cloth and when she had trouble with a knot, Hiro reached forward and released it for her, allowing the cloth to drop open across her narrow lap.

Her audible gasp quieted the last of the conversations in the room.

Hiro offered to lift the mechanical object from the cloth and raise it for her to inspect better. She resisted, hand to the cloth, as if to cover it up. Her actions only made the crowd lean forward in their chairs. The standing photographers became more alert, elbows up and cameras ready.

Itou took a step closer to his mother. "Is something wrong?"

Sayoko turned her head sharply to one side. Angelica thought she was shrinking away from the frightening object itself, but then she realized that Sayoko was only trying to hide her face.

"Yes, I know what it is. It's not a gift. It already belonged to me."

"But I polished it, and I fixed it," Hiro said. "It moves again."

Itou took a step forward, to explain to the audience. "It's only a family heirloom. There's no problem."

When Hiro lifted the mechanical crab into the air, winding a mechanism underneath its carapace, and demonstrated how its eight copper-colored legs could move, just a few centimeters front or back, Itou looked relieved. All eyes were tracking the strange clockwork object, well over a hundred years old.

"A gift to my mother," Itou explained with false heartiness to the crowd. "It is an early mechanical toy she was given as a child."

This focus on the crab brought the eyes and the camera away from his mother, whom Itou was attempting to shield with his body. But Angelica could make out the tremor of her feet, which didn't quite reach the floor, the shudder moving up her legs and taking over her thin body. Over the light clicking of the crab's legs, the entire room could hear Sayoko's sobs.

Bending at her side, Hiro tried to soothe her. "I knew it would help you remember."

"The problem is not what I remember," she said. "It's what I can't forget."

Angelica remembered Sayoko's story from the night before: how she had believed that if only she talked to the clockwork crab, if she believed in it and was loyal to it, it would become her secret friend. It would protect her. Sayoko had been waiting her whole life for the day non-life would become life, a vessel for spirit, no less strange or unbelievable than the grandfather tree which Daisuke had worshipped. Hiro had been tailor-made for Sayoko, but Sayoko had also been tailor-made for Hiro.

But the crowd didn't need to understand that. They needed only to appreciate that this event was emotional, as any centenary birthday might be. Angelica looked to Itou, wishing he would give some signal that the guests should rise and leave. But no, there were still more ritual gifts, more speeches. Angelica knew they were pushing Sayoko too far.

Sayoko buried her face in her hands, slurring her words. Angelica heard "disaster" and "mother" and "the old days."

A woman said, "Did her mother die in the great earthquake?"

The man next to her said, "What does that have to do with a toy?"

Sayoko had been clenching the arms of the plush chair with a talon grip, but as soon as Hiro set his metal hand upon her forearm, she visibly relaxed.

"Daisuke Oshima loved you," Hiro said, "and he wanted you to think of him whenever you saw his gift."

"*Hai,*" Sayoko said, inhaling with difficulty, struggling for self-control.

"Serenity is still possible, as is mutual devotion. You are deeply loved, Sayoko-san."

Hiro put one arm around Sayoko's shoulders in a posture that pleased the photographers, who all strained forward to capture the image while others in the audience began tapping on their phones. Angelica looked over one shoulder and saw the man in front of her searching "*Daisuke Oshima,*" something Angelica had never thought to do. She saw him scroll through the results list, past an item about a Taiwanese natural history publication from the 1930s. The man overlooked the connection, but someone else would make it, soon. There were no secrets left in this world.

Angelica looked for Junichi and saw him whispering furiously into another man's ear, while the man listened, nodding, jaw slack as he got up his nerve. Junichi gave the man a tap on the shoulder and the man stood, shouting once for everyone's attention. He strode to the front of the room and pointed.

"That robot's in love with her. Isn't it clear? And she's in love with him! It's unnatural!" The antagonist looked back in Junichi's direction and realized that he would have to say more. "It—he—is not only her helper. He doesn't just take care of her. He is her lover."

There was a hum in the room, followed by a pause. The crab's clockwork mechanism wound down and its sharp legs stopped clicking. And still, the claim that had been made was so preposterous, it might have simply dissipated, forgotten. Except that Sayoko chose that moment to sit forward and shout, "So what?"

Itou gestured with his palms pressing downward, like a conductor directing his orchestra: softer, slower, there. To the audience, Itou said: "Of course my mother has grown fond of her robot helper. Just as many of you are fond of all your gadgets and their personalities. Even your talking refrigerators. We come to rely on these objects . . ."

"Tell them, Hiro," Sayoko said firmly.

Hiro bowed, looked up again, cocked his head. "Tell them that I can love? It is true."

A reporter asked, "What does that mean?"

Hiro replied, "Emotionally and physically, I am capable. My model is not restricted. We may love and be loved."

Someone called out, "Physically? Are you a sexbot?"

Murmurs erupted in the back—about evolving intelligence and sexdolls and dumb sexbots and *true* sexbots but with weak AI and true sexbots with strong AI and the South Korea laws and the US-EU Accord and sexual abuse by robots and sexual abuse *of* robots.

A woman next to Angelica muttered to the man next to her, "It's happened. This is it. It *had* to happen."

"No, Hiro," Sayoko was in anguish now. "They can already see that for themselves. *Tell* them." Incomprehensibly, she shouted to the room at large, "Tell them I'm a hundred and ten. Not one hundred."

"She's confused," Itou said. "All this attention is too exciting."

"I never wanted attention," Sayoko shouted. "I wanted to be a nurse."

"Please," Itou said, waving his arms. "Everyone."

"Have you taken advantage of her emotionally?" a reporter shouted. "—or sexually?"

Someone else added, "Has she taken advantage of *you*?"

Another voice: "Itou-san, do you support this?"

Another: "What about robot-human marriage?"

Sayoko said, "I wanted to help. I wanted to leave my village. They promised to take me to a good place. They took me into the jungle, instead. And I wasn't a nurse. None of us were."

Angelica held her hand over her mouth, listening to Sayoko's anguished outburst, less clear than it had sounded the night before. She seemed demented, but it was only because she was fighting the weight of repressed emotion, the story too large to tell in this setting, to this hostile crowd. They wouldn't believe her. Or they would. Angelica didn't know which was worse.

And where was Junichi now? Pleased with this mayhem, no doubt. Everyone was shouting. Sayoko-san was melting down.

Itou stepped in front of his mother, trying to protect her from their stares, gesturing. *Quiet. Cameras down, please. All devices down.* As if there weren't five people in the room recording automatically with their retinal implants, no exterior equipment required.

"Hiro," one of the reporters called out, trying to get the robot's attention. But he was in the minority. Most were swiveling between Sayoko and Itou, hoping he wouldn't succeed in silencing her.

"It's a lie, what they called us," Sayoko said. "We weren't prostitutes, before they took us to the jungle."

"*Ianfu,*" someone said. It was the word Angelica had heard Sayoko use several times last night, never without a sour face. *Comfort woman.* It was a euphemism and an insult.

Sayoko called back, "Why do you insist on calling us that? You apologize, but then you take the apologies back."

"*Ianfu.*" Like a menacing chant, the word came again from the back of the room.

Sayoko would have none of it. "Your words are the problem! We were innocent. There were ten-year-old girls in my camp—girls stolen directly from their homes. Are you saying they wanted to be there?"

Some of the reporters were silent, taking it all in, waiting for whatever outburst would come next. Some were more actively on the hunt, aware that the prey would scatter, that Hiro or Sayoko would stop speaking, that Itou would send them all packing, that they would never get the answers they wanted if they didn't press now. But whom to press? Two unconnected stories seemed to be unfolding, rapidly and incongruously.

"Hiro," a reporter said, standing up from his seat, "If you are Japanese made—"

"I am not."

"If you are bound by the trade agreements, the South Korean robot laws—"

"I am made in Taiwan," Hiro corrected the reporter.

"Made in Taiwan," Sayoko said, and then she laughed. "So was I. You can write that down." This pleased her, enough to make her throw back her head and laugh again, white lines running down her wet cheeks, which Angelica had rouged just an hour before.

A woman reporter called out: "Are you requesting reparation money?"

Sayoko shook off the question. "My son's father said not to speak. All my life, the same. Cover your mouth when you smile. Don't smile. Open your legs."

A woman in front of Angelica gasped.

Sayoko kept going. "You have no right to happiness, people told me. But this robot makes more sense than all of you. He has told me: I do have a right, and he has a right. We'll do whatever we like!"

The phone in Angelica's tunic pocket buzzed. She noted the orange code and thumbed off the alarm. Sayoko's heartbeat and blood pressure were elevated to high-risk levels.

"Hiro," another reporter tried to get the robot's attention. "What are your full physical capabilities?"

Angelica was frozen, hands pushed deep into her pockets, one hand on the phone, knowing it would keep buzzing as Sayoko's pulse kept spiking. She remembered Junichi again. He was within sight, across the room, expression rapt, wanting Hiro to say more, to implicate himself and his design in even more damning detail.

She remembered the spark of selflessness she had seen in him, and she refused to equate the actions with the man. And what would it serve to curse Junichi again? It was like cursing a storm. She tried to lock eyes with him, without success. She sent out a silent, imploring message: *You've already done too much. No more. Sayoko is suffering. Don't make it worse.*

"My own son," Sayoko said, voice more strident now. "He doesn't know the truth. He can't afford to know. None of you can afford to know. We pretend *for you.* But when do we have our own lives? When do we get to be touched without shame?

"When it's your turn, you'll see. It's young people who forget. Not old people." She was nearly out of breath and she risked pausing to inhale once, deeply. "I'm one hundred and ten, I keep telling you."

She punctuated her final statement with a sharp nod of the chin.

"And I don't . . . like . . . *cake.*"

20 Angelica

They came that evening while Sayoko was napping, exhausted by the party and the emotional breakdown that brought it finally to a close. Itou was sequestered in his bedroom, on a call with someone at the ministry, seeking advice on how to contain the aftermath. Angelica had been straining to listen, barely able to make out more than a word or two, when there was a knock at the door. She expected more reporters, ministry staff, or someone wanting to see Sayoko or Itou directly.

"Navarro Angelica?"

"Angelica Navarro, yes."

The man and woman wore matching black uniforms. The man had an especially young face—mid-twenties—with white crust under the deep crease of one eye. He looked like he'd been recently roused. The woman was more alert, with that wide-eyed look of someone who takes sleep-avoidance drugs, but stick thin, another form of career pressure. Her creased uniform pants dropped straight from narrow, angular, non-childbearing hips.

"We will be escorting you," the man said. No mention of the word "arrest" but it meant the same thing.

"Should I—bring anything?"

"Anything you'll need," the man answered.

"But—for paperwork, or a medical appointment?"

The female officer was more plainspoken. "Anything you'll need for the foreseeable future."

Itou came out of his room just as Angelica was rushing into hers, trying to pack a suitcase and toiletries, gather her papers and personal items. She hadn't come to Tokyo with much and she still owned little, the overflow just enough for two grocery-store bags in addition to her single square carry-on, which ripped at the seam as she lifted it: cheap. Purchased in an alley in Manila, a few miles from the airport. Meant for one flight only.

She alternated between hurrying, scrabbling through drawers, looking for a missing slipper under her bed, and pausing, trying to listen as Itou argued with the Immigration Police in a quiet, firm manner. When she came out, they were already leaving, bowing at the doorway, but with uncomfortable glances back into the condo's interior. Itou saw them out, then turned to her.

"They'll be back tomorrow," he said. "I'll make us some tea."

"Thank you." She bowed her head, feeling weak with gratitude.

"At least you'll get one more night in your own room, though I don't imagine it will be easy to sleep."

He had not won her any lasting amnesty, only more time. He had vouched for her, saying he would personally escort her within twelve hours, first to the Health Department and then to Immigration.

"So, they told you the reason."

"They did. It explains the visa problem."

"A kenkobot drew my blood when I fainted on the street. While you were in Kuala Lumpur."

"I see," he said, unwilling to look her in the eye.

"I did not really think it was possible, due to a medical issue. But I guess I'm healthier than I realized." The thought did not bring her any relief, not at this moment. Anyway, she felt far from well, far from safe.

"I see." He roused himself to say one more thing, to not leave her stranded in silence. "There were many things we did not realize were possible."

He placed a cup in front of her and allowed her to pour for them both. With every gesture, she was aware that this might be the last time. Green tea: she'd finally come to like its earthy, powdery bite. Now it was soda that seemed too sweet. They sipped without speaking, every swallow audible. Itou had placed a dish of melon slices in front of her. She knew how much they cost—insane, the overpriced produce here—but now she accepted the melon as a gift, silky and subtle.

The apartment was quiet. Hiro stood in the corner of the living room, motionless, lights dimmed.

"How long will you keep him turned off?" she asked.

"Until morning. Someone from the company is coming to download whatever they can and access the video records."

Angelica hurried to reassure him. "I don't think there was ever anything inappropriate between them. Nothing physical, anyway."

"Probably not." He sipped his tea. "But that isn't the point, is it? If she were younger, if the genders were reversed, people will say. If. *When.*" He continued after a moment. "But aside from the physical, there's everything else, isn't there?"

He closed his eyes, hands clutching his cup.

Angelica had thought he was going to interrogate her the moment she sat down, about how she had gotten pregnant and by whom. But he seemed to think it didn't matter. And in most cases, it wouldn't.

He opened his eyes. "After we get a look at the footage, they'll take him away."

"They have to?"

"I want them to."

"But what about Sayoko-san?"

Angelica saw the effect of his mother's name, the quiver that ran through his face before he suppressed it, lips thinned. "She didn't mean to get so attached to him—"

Itou stopped her. "Everything she confided in him, she kept from me."

"She wanted to protect you and your career—"

He exhaled sharply through his nose. "My career? Was that the excuse even when I was a little boy? She couldn't stand being with me. She never touched me. To think she could lavish more attention on a machine . . ." He shook his head. "Even I noticed how different my friends' mothers were, doting on them. At the playground, the other mothers with their handkerchiefs, their bags of snacks, wiping noses and checking on scraped knees, while she sat apart, talking to no one, barely looking at me."

"I'm so sorry."

"She was a mannequin: all face, no feeling. She gets along with a robot because she was a robot most of her life."

"Itou-san, she tried to pretend. She resisted human touch for a reason. It was only because she was so mistreated."

He did not look convinced. There was so much Angelica wanted to communicate about what Sayoko had told her: the details beyond what the whole world now knew. But it wasn't Angelica's place to tell those stories, and a more immediate excuse, she could not find all the words quickly enough, under so much pressure. She wanted to tell him that the imperial forces had done terrible things to his mother, beyond what he was probably willing to imagine. She wanted to explain that Sayoko must have coped by separating herself—her body, mind, and spirit—from what she was experiencing. She probably felt incapable and perhaps even unworthy of love. Maybe the only reason she didn't fear Hiro's judgment was because he wasn't human. Or maybe he'd acted more humanely than the rest of them, including Angelica herself. He asked questions. He made Sayoko feel needed and he encouraged her to need him in return. He listened.

"Please," Angelica said. "She lived a hard life. I judged her, too, but I was wrong. Hiro does not judge."

"But it's natural for a mother to feel attached to her baby, even before it's born. No matter what happens." He faltered here, treading carefully. "You must feel attached to the baby already growing inside you. And whoever the father is, when you both go back to the Philippines together . . ."

Angelica couldn't hold back anymore. "The father is Japanese."

Itou's eyes widened.

"Does he know?"

"Yes."

In the clamor of the party's final moments, she had pulled Junichi aside, still unsure whether he had heard the first time she had tried to tell him, an hour or so earlier. From his stunned expression, she could tell he had not. She thought she'd seen him drop his guard before, but nothing like this. She had imagined two possible reactions: either resentment, or complete denial. Instead, to her surprise, he looked at her with awe. Of this fragile, new potential. Of their own parts in creating it. Junichi had insisted they speak again, later that night or tomorrow at the latest.

Angelica said to Itou, "If I stay—"

"You won't be allowed to stay. But the baby, if he's half Japanese, if they find a blood match for the father, they won't let the baby go."

She said under her breath, "I don't know that I'll have it."

He recoiled. "Not have it? You've already broken the law once. You intend to break it again?"

"No one has to know."

The color had gone out of his face. "You have something many Japanese women would give anything to have. What's wrong with you? Are there no good mothers left, anywhere?"

"That's just not fair—" she said, trembling from her failed effort to hold back the words. "You have no right to say that, *sir.*" She said the last word in English, feeling in that Filipino phrasing the weight of all the teachers and bosses she'd ever had back home.

Angelica had never raised her voice to any employer. She had never felt this kind of hostility toward Itou. He was a good man. Usually, patient. Usually, kind. But the heat rising in her was uncontainable. "You don't know what she went through. And just as she claimed, you don't want to know."

He pushed back his chair noisily. "Why should anyone want to know? The only way to get past it is to forget!"

Hiro appeared in the doorway, standing at loose attention with knees and elbows bent, fingers flexing. He'd been shut down, but the shouting had triggered his override response to any perceived threat.

Hiro asked, "Are you injured?"

Itou shouted back, "Of course not!" Then he turned back to Angelica. "There will be controversy now, because of Hiro. But people are intrigued. They'll want a robot that can be programmed to love and forced to be a lifelong companion—"

"He isn't programmed, and he wasn't forced," Angelica interrupted. "He and Sayoko-san need each other—"

"But no one wants to hear about comfort women. That chapter is closed."

Itou jabbed a finger at Hiro and gestured toward the living room. Hiro retreated out of view.

"It isn't closed," Angelica said. "Your mother is still alive."

"And what am I supposed to do?"

"Help her live with what she's admitting now. People will shame her. They'll deny her story. She'll need at least one person who doesn't."

"Am I supposed to apologize for what she went through? Are all the politicians who weren't alive back then supposed to apologize?" Itou put a hand to his forehead, massaging his wrinkled brow with eyes closed. "That's all been said and done."

But it wasn't said and done. Not at all.

That afternoon, after the last reporter had left, she had leaned against the door and searched that word she'd heard muttered over and over: *Ianfu*. What appeared to be official apologies were often accompanied by reversals: politicians continuing to claim that the women had been prostitutes prior to their enslavement, that they were never actually forced, that this was only normal business rather than a grave human rights violation. Women's rights activists and the last remaining survivors were still censured.

And it wasn't just an issue confined to one country, or two. The victims had come from across Asia and beyond, an estimated 400,000 women, mostly from China and South Korea, but from all of the Japanese-occupied territories, even the Philippines. Many were enslaved when they were thirteen, fourteen, fifteen years old. Some were told they would work in restaurants or factories. Others were told nothing and simply grabbed off the field or street. In every nation, there had been attempts to break the silence and tell the story: fifty years after the war, seventy-five years after, always with the idea that it would get easier. But it was never easy. As the very last survivors celebrated their centennial birthdays and beyond, activists urged the public to listen to the firsthand accounts before it was too late. But just as many commentators urged the public to forget.

Angelica wanted to understand more, but the linguistic nuances were beyond her—beyond even many Japanese, who debated the words used in apologies, which kind of words expressed weighty remorse and which were insubstantial brush-offs. She had spent every day for the last five years grappling with a language that might keep her employed, might keep her safe. The least the politicians and bureaucrats could do was grapple with this same language and find the culturally appropriate way to make these survivors feel less shamed. Itou-san had it in his power to at least do that.

"I suppose," Angelica said, "now that people know your connection to the issue, you will be asked publicly about your position. I suppose it will be hard to know exactly what to say."

He lifted his chin defiantly. "Just so. Which is why, as of tonight, I am no longer employed by the ministry."

"They fired you?"

"I resigned."

"How could you?"

He gave her the look she'd seen from annoyed strangers in her first weeks in Tokyo, when she'd paused a second too long at the door of the subway car, afraid of the crush of bodies, or when she'd walked into a noodle shop, baffled by the vending machine, unable to understand why she couldn't just order at the counter and pay the waitress directly. The look said: *If you're going to live here, get with the program.*

"It's what we do," he said. "It's a form of taking responsibility."

"Is it? Really?"

Hiro reappeared in the kitchen doorway. "Itou-san," he interrupted. "Guests are at the door again. The security view shows two uniformed officers. Shall I let them in?"

"I'll deal with it," Itou said angrily.

"Should I power down?"

"Yes," Itou said. "No. I don't know. Just stay out of my way."

With deep bows and abject apologies, the Immigration officers had come to reverse their error. With all respect for Itou-san's position, they could not wait until morning to bring a flight-risk foreigner into custody. Also, they had called their superiors, who had alerted them to the fact that Itou-san merited no special deference in this matter. Even prior to this evening, even before the official announcement in a broadcast twenty minutes ago, he would not have merited special deference.

"*Hai, hai,*" Itou-san said to the police before turning to Angelica. "Get your things. We must wake my mother. She can't be left at home without supervision. I'll call my car service."

Angelica went to Sayoko's bedroom. The old woman had curled up on her side, brow furrowed as she slept, breath shallow. Angelica stood for a moment, hesitant to wake her. When Itou came to the doorway, he too stopped and paused, watching his mother.

"The car service won't accept my request," he said quietly. "My work account has already been cancelled."

Angelica was so used to her own roadblocks—message systems hacked into, accounts frozen. She did not realize a man of Itou's reputation could so quickly become separated from his resources and routines as well.

"It can be sorted out," he said. "But I don't know which will be quicker, starting my own account, or trying to get a regular cab here. How do you get around?"

He was helpless.

"On foot, usually."

"And a regular cab, will it fit my mother's wheelchair?"

"No. You don't have to come with me. Please, stay with Sayoko-san—"

"You need an advocate."

"I'll be fine."

She suppressed the hundred things she would have to tell him, even if she planned to be gone no longer than an evening: how to reset his phone to accept more of the alerts; which blood sugar alarms to ignore and which to pay attention to, depending on what Sayoko had last eaten; that he should check if she were wearing her wrist monitor or if she'd somehow gotten it off again, or devise an alternate plan now that her reaction to the device was better understood; her prescription schedule; what she absolutely must eat and drink in the morning, or risk upsetting her bowels, though she would not want to talk about them, of course, and he would have to learn her euphemisms. There wasn't time to explain. At least he had Hiro to explain things, and to improvise.

"And if they put you directly on a plane?" Itou asked. "But no, they can't do that, either. I have no idea what they'll do." He paused. "Angelica, who is the father?"

"I can't tell you," she said, dropping her head, wishing she could just run away, but where? She felt so terribly heavy: from staying up all night, from the stress of everything that had happened, from the shift in her hormones, which were trying to force her to rest, nest and protect the small living thing inside of her. She only wanted to sleep.

But then she remembered. This might be her last chance. He knew things. He knew people. "Itou-san, have you ever heard of anyone coming back from the Alaska BZ—"

"America?" He looked annoyed at the change of subject.

"If a sick worker ever wanted to leave but needed assistance, is there any chance Japan would accept them? I know Japan has excellent care for many kinds of contaminated workers . . ."

"Unlikely. Is this a Japanese person?"

"No."

"Call it impossible."

They both heard the voice of the male Immigration officer, taking a call in the hallway, reporting his location.

Itou dropped his voice to a stern whisper. "Angelica, tell me who the father is."

She held her breath a moment, hoping her confession would seem like obedience, and soften him in some way. "Your colleague," she said. "Junichi."

She changed the subject again as fast as her tongue could manage. It was her last chance to ask anyone with power, even if that power was disappearing fast. She'd waited too long. She hadn't asked for help soon enough, all those times she'd needed it. Why had she never asked?

"Please, Itou-san. You're positive there is nothing that can be done to help a BZ worker?"

But he had already closed his eyes at the sound of Junichi's name. His hands were folded at hip level in a posture of feigned calm.

"This is something you should take up with your government, perhaps," he said, eyes still closed. "Not the government of Japan."

She couldn't give up so easily. "It's my brother. Our government isn't concerned about one more overseas worker in a bad situation."

"I'm sorry. I have nothing more to say about this. You should finish gathering your things."

She had expected as much, and yet the disappointment was like a physical weight too heavy to hold. If she didn't fight the urge with all her might, she would drop to the floor.

Through their conversation, Sayoko still slept. Angelica withdrew from Itou's presence and went to see her for a moment, kneeling beside her bed. She couldn't bear to wake her.

"I'm sorry," she said. "I'm sorry for everything." *Sumimasen*. One of the first words she'd ever learned, because the Japanese apologize all the time, and even a simple thank you seemed to include a sense of regret for bothering someone. But everyday regret wasn't what she was feeling, and reticence was not her true style. She had to switch to her own language to say it right.

"My dear friend, I am so thankful to have known you. I love you."

Hiro followed them to the doorway.

"I am going with Anji-sensei. That way Itou-san can stay with his mother, and Anji won't be alone, without witness or representation."

The male officer looked to his female companion and they both looked to Itou.

Hiro added, "I will return when I can no longer be of assistance. Is this acceptable, Itou-san?"

When Itou hesitated, Hiro added, "It is the least we can do."

Itou looked at the officers, who still seemed to be embarrassed about having returned to collect Angelica. This time, a call was made in advance and permission was granted.

Outside the building, Angelica turned to Hiro. "Are you sure you should have left Sayoko-san? She's used to at least one of us being there."

"I did not make the decision lightly," he replied, dropping his voice lower to add, "and above all I considered Itou-san's need for time alone with his mother. Only in authentic moments of cooperation will they find a way to discuss what has recently come to light."

Halfway down the block, striding head-down just behind the police officers, Angelica realized there was no government car. "Budget cuts," the male officer said, when he saw her puzzling at their approach to the subway station. His fellow officer glared at him over her shoulder. He added, "Better for the environment."

The subway was nearly full, but when the car partly emptied at the next stop, the male officer pointed to a vacant seat, gesturing for Angelica to take it.

"I'm fine," she said.

"Please."

He looked relieved when she sat, as if she were some delicate foreign import he was in charge of protecting from harm. She could only imagine the treatment she would get when her belly was three times as large and her A-cup breasts vastly more prominent, like some fertility goddess in a culture seeking an end to barrenness. But perhaps there would be no public scrutiny at all, if they kept her in a jail cell.

Now that he had one less worry, the man introduced himself as Officer Yoshida, his partner as Officer Mori.

"And you're Hiro," Yoshida said to the robot. "Since about five o'clock I can't go anywhere or do anything without seeing news images of you."

Yoshida nodded and Angelica could see the officer's eyes flicking back and forth. Every few seconds, they rolled back in his head. Retinal users sometimes looked like drug addicts or like someone having trouble with a contact lens. They thought they were getting away with constantly checking their personal streams and feeds—probably no more acceptable for an Immigration officer than for most desk workers—but it was obvious they weren't paying full attention.

Yoshida continued, "You're sure you won't take this chance to run away from the old woman? A lot of younger ladies would love to own your model."

"I have no desire to be with a younger woman," Hiro said. "For as long as she needs me, I am dedicated to Sayoko-san."

"And when she no longer needs you?"

"I haven't considered that, and I don't need to."

"See?" Yoshida said to his partner. "I told you. You know, my grandmother likes to put these silly hats on her maidbot."

Hiro affected a bored look, adjusting his scarf. "I'm sure she does."

The Tokyo subway system was byzantine and any long trip required multiple changes, often onto different lines owned by different companies. Their trip was neither simple nor short, and Angelica found herself clenching her knees together.

"Can we make a bathroom stop?" she asked Officer Mori as they ascended an elevator between lines. "I promise to be quick."

Mori didn't answer, face drawn into a worried frown.

"Please?" Angelica asked again, aiming her imploring glance at the male officer, Yoshida.

Hurrying off at the next landing, they stepped to one side, away from the tidal surge of pedestrians hurrying to make a connection. Yoshida looked up at the ceiling, leaving the decision to his partner.

Hiro faced away from them, his gaze fixed on a gigantic zoo poster. Zoos had become no less popular with the decline of children, and the birth of a new panda drew larger crowds than ever. Noting his intense stare, Angelica remembered Hiro's reaction to Sayoko's story about the slaughter of the Ueno Park animals. She had briefly questioned Sayoko's memory of the event, but now she trusted it was true. Nothing about the war—any war—would surprise her anymore.

Mori finally gave in to Angelica's request. "Okay, but please hurry."

The officers and Hiro stood just outside the public women's restroom, forming such an impressive congregation that several women hesitated near the doorway and then chose not to enter.

In the stall, Angelica sat down with relief, eyes briefly closed. When she opened them and looked down, she saw a telltale, rust-brown stain.

Dressed again, she stood near the open doorway and called to Hiro, who stepped inside.

"It's only spotting," he said. "Even with a healthy pregnancy, that can be normal."

She knew that, too. She just wanted another nurse to say it.

Angelica called past Hiro to the female officer, who likewise took a few steps inside the bathroom. "Do you have any sanitary pads?"

Mori shook her head. As Angelica guessed: probably too thin to menstruate anyway. Not the primary cause of infertility here, but not a help, either.

"I saw a 7-Eleven, just out by the escalators," Angelica suggested meekly. "Would you mind?"

Officer Mori gave her a tight, stressed smile and barely inclined her head.

Angelica could hear the voices of the officers outside the bathroom conferring over who should pay for the sanitary pads, and whether the office would reimburse them. Yoshida had a prepaid office card but no idea what to purchase. Mori wasn't confused about what to buy, but she wasn't sure if the card reader would accept her thumbprint.

"I won't be able to do it alone," Mori insisted.

"I won't either," Yoshida said.

"We'll be right back," Mori finally announced in a singsong voice, trying to sound like they hadn't been arguing. "Stay there please and don't move, thank you very much."

A commuter hurried in, used the facilities, stared at Angelica and at Hiro, washed her hands, and left.

After an awkward minute in the restroom, Hiro spoke. It took Angelica a second to realize: he was speaking Cebuano, for the first time—and for good reason, given what he was suggesting. "This is when we would escape, if we desired to escape."

"But you promised to behave and cooperate. And to come back home soon."

"I promised only to return when I could no longer be of assistance. Anji-sensei, this is the time you need my assistance."

Angelica had not had a moment to fill Hiro in on all the details she'd kept to herself. With a robot, it didn't take long. Unlike humans, who had to process, react and divert the conversation to their own interests, fears, and hurt feelings, Hiro simply wanted the facts.

"I keep thinking about Datu," Angelica began. "I can't let him die all alone in Alaska."

"Anji-sensei, you have your own emergency at this moment. If I may suggest: you should not let others' problems distract you from logically solving your own." He rested a hand on her shoulder. "If you leave Japan and go to the Philippines, Bagasao will discover he has two things close at hand: a woman who has eluded him, and a baby that is worth, on the black market, all that you and your brother owe. He will take the child from you. And still, he may give you no peace. Am I correct?"

"Yes," she said under her breath.

Hiro bowed his head, preparing to offer a sensitive suggestion. "If you do not intend to keep it, Junichi is the one who will want this baby. He'll pay good money for it."

She twisted up her face, upset at the idea, not at Hiro. "That's wrong."

"That a baby is worth money? But so are you, Anji-sensei. And so am I. We are all commodities. No doubt Junichi is already weighing the cost of telling his wife with the benefit of having a rare and valuable child."

"But what if she's furious with him?"

"She married a man with political ambitions. She's accustomed to compromise, and she's infertile. He found a surrogate. Hurt feelings will be temporary."

"I don't know—"

Hiro wasn't reluctant about sharing difficult news. "The law in Japan says the baby belongs to Junichi. As a foreign worker, you had no permission to conceive a child. If they hold you in confinement, they may give Junichi the baby anyway, whether or not he pays you."

"I will not be pressured to have a baby—or to give it away."

A woman overloaded with shopping bags trotted into the restroom and hurried to a stall, where the toilet cloaked her activities with the pleasant sounds of a rainstorm.

Before he could batter her with any more facts, Angelica said, "What kind of world is this?"

"The same world it was ten days ago. You and I and Sayoko have changed, but the world is just as it was."

"Maybe this baby shouldn't even be born," Angelica whispered.

"You should be aware, abortion is illegal here just as it is in the Philippines. Here, the law is even more strictly enforced."

"I don't know what to do—" Angelica lamented, hands on her belly.

Hiro took her arm and moved toward the door. "That isn't the decision you need to make. For now you only need to decide: stay, walk, or run."

They ran, joining a river of Japanese commuters streaming down the nearest escalator, down a corridor, through a long connecting tunnel lined with cheap purses and umbrellas and manga wigs and babydoll clothes in full-grown women's sizes, down five flights through a more elegant underground mall: international food store, traditional calligraphy and stationery supply next to a kiosk selling weight loss monitoring implants, milk tea and bubble tea and tingle tea shops, a genetic testing stand, and a cosmetic surgery galleria featuring retinal implant corrections, double eyelid and lip reduction surgery, facial bleaching, and emojification.

Another corridor led to another subway line. Neither of them knew Tokyo well and when they thought of hiding places, their first instincts were the very places they'd first visited: for Hiro, Ueno Park. For Angelica, Chiba. But those were also the first places police would look. And hadn't Officer Yoshida said that Hiro's face was everywhere, that anyone watching any form of news or entertainment would spot him? In a less reserved city, people would have been pointing and calling out. Here, the only sign of recognition was a young woman in the subway, looking over her shoulder and slowly batting her eyelashes: an obvious retinal snap that would be instantly posted and reposted, everywhere.

They ended up on the waterfront, in a park outside a big technology museum: a grooved silver box with a sphere bulging out of one side, like a silver baseball had hit a soft metal wall and stuck. One floor of the museum was dedicated to robots, and outside, on the sidewalks and in several cordoned-off mini-plazas, the latest models were displayed for groups of visitors, all hurrying to see the final shows before the museum closed for the night. With so many robots rolling, bouncing, and high-stepping, there was less chance people would notice Hiro, especially now that Angelica had covered his head with a cheap samurai hat purchased in cash from a costume vendor on the street. For herself, she'd bought a platinum-blonde wig and a red cape.

They looked odd, which helped them blend in. The larger grassy park fronting the technology museum had been taken over by manga and cosplay enthusiasts in every kind of pop culture and game-inspired costume, with wigs of blue and orange, short skirts or capes, knee-high boots, and in some cases, cat or fox ears. Some of the enthusiasts were perfectly assembled, from top to bottom, but there were oddballs here and there, novices or half-hearted wannabes, who had only the cat ears, or a tunic but no wig, or an entire outfit but three sizes too small. Often, they were the ones holding cameras, and all over the park, there were photo shoots going on, with extravagant amounts of old-fashioned equipment: cameras with long lenses, spotlights and collapsible reflectors.

Since the crowds at the margins mixed—costumed women on the grass next to the sidewalk where the museum's demo robots strolled—she and Hiro were camouflaged enough to finally take a breath. But it was getting darker and unseasonably chilly, as stuffy late summer gave way to an early rainy autumn.

Angelica and Hiro heard applause and saw a demonstrator and her three robots go inside. The crowd began to disperse. Other robots, without attendants, followed some inaudible cue and likewise turned toward the museum's doors. Deeper into the forested landscape, most of the photographers were packing up, but a small scattering of cosplay types were unrolling blankets, preparing to spend the night. Angelica had seen homeless people of many nationalities sleeping in the shadows of Ueno Park. She never thought she'd be spending a night among them, but here she was.

"I think we need to find our own tree," Angelica said.

They passed a young Japanese man struggling to collapse a silver photo reflector with a telescoping leg. Pushing hard, he ripped the fabric and swore, then turned his attention to buckling an over-stuffed camera bag.

"Can I have that?" Hiro asked.

"The reflector? I just broke it."

"I'd like it," Hiro said, holding out the samurai hat in exchange.

Under a tree, Hiro removed a long metal wire encircling the reflector and took the now shapeless shiny material and wrapped it around Angelica's shoulders. "I hope you can sleep."

She found that if she curled in front of him, spooning, the heat from his cooling system circulated under the silver blanket and gave her a little warmth as well as psychological comfort. His metal thighs were smooth and slightly concave, ending at a rounded kneecap. If she positioned herself just right, it was like sitting in a warm chair, with the tips of her toes rested up against the tops of his long feet. There was something about his angles and curves that reminded her of the coolest car she had ever seen, in Cebu: a 1950s model with a rounded silhouette and lots of chrome. Hiro lifted one arm and rested it over hers, so weightless that she knew he was exerting energy to keep it slightly elevated, at just the right pressure to make her feel safe, sheltered, but not constricted. He did not ask if she was comfortable or if she was awake. She knew he was monitoring her breath, her temperature, and her subtle muscular shifts.

Angelica whispered, "Did you lie like this with Sayoko?"

"No."

"Did she want you to?"

"No. The presence of another reclining body, human or other, did not give her comfort."

Angelica nodded in the dark.

"But touch did," he continued. "As long as she felt she could move away from it. Hair braiding. A washcloth on the back or gentle pressure on her shoulders. I experimented."

"So you *were* being sneaky. You were desensitizing her, the times you were pretending to calibrate your fingertips."

"The motions served us both. Positive touch always does. But I cannot say it was truly reciprocal contact. My designers seemed not to trust that capability." His tone had hardened. "Anyway, she showed me what she needed. She was a good teacher."

"But more than a teacher. You love her."

"Of course. I love her more every day."

Angelica had never felt envy for Sayoko or any other aging client before, but she did now. The desire for this thing she did not have was a physical pressure, a flulike ache. It was ridiculous to wish for a nonhuman being's love, but she did—any love at all, and perhaps she had lived her life insufficiently open to the possibility of it. She lay there on the cold park ground, lips parted, trying to keep her breathing even, trying to give no sign of her inner turmoil, until the feeling had passed.

"You must get back to her soon," Angelica said. Then she laughed—that kind of sudden eruption that fails to conceal imminent tears. "Itou-san doesn't even know where we keep the toilet paper. I give him one day."

They still had no plan.

A flashlight shone in their faces. Hiro acted immediately, adjusting his body to shield Angelica from potential harm, and then—risk assessed, this was only a flashlight, in the hands of a low-paid security guard—he rolled to his knees and in a swift, silent motion, jumped to his feet.

But the guard only wanted them to move further into the trees. "You kids. If you can't go home, just make sure you're better hidden. My job is to keep the main paths clear."

When they'd settled in again for a mostly sleepless night, Angelica whispered, "Sayoko will be distraught in the morning with both of us gone. You'll need to get back to her. Itou is expecting you." She did not add that the technician was coming, too. She did not want to frighten him needlessly.

But he already knew. "They will be accessing my footage and attempting to wipe my memories. If they succeed, I won't be Hiro anymore."

"If they succeed? There's another way?"

"There's always another way. Even so, the events of the last week have brought many good people distress. If my compliance can give them relief, I must consider it."

Hiro had been thinking of his plan since seeing the zoo poster in the subway, he told Angelica. It had reminded him of the story of the Ueno Park Zoo. The animals had to be sacrificed.

"You are forgetting what Sayoko said—that there wasn't a good reason. It probably wasn't necessary at all."

"People thought it was, and it gave them consolation. Sacrifices can provide meaning in difficult times."

"But *meaningless* sacrifices don't," she objected. "And you're seeing it from the zookeeper's perspective, or the politician's. You can be sure that if any one of those animals knew what was coming, they wouldn't have stepped up to the knife."

"But we aren't animals, you and I," he said. "Anyway, because I have a *kami,* there will always be a part of me that endures. There is comfort in that. I would trust my ability to retain my *kami* if I were more developed in other ways." But he would not elaborate further.

"You don't sound like you've decided," Angelica said. This confused her, because until now, Hiro's decisions had always been practically instantaneous. He could research a lifetime in moments. He could weigh pros and cons without hesitation.

"I am starting to see the benefits of networked social learning. I need more input from my prototype peers, whoever they are," Hiro said. "At the same time, I've observed in humans that maximum information and choice does not guarantee wisdom. My decision-making is slowing with maturity, rather than accelerating."

A few minutes later, Angelica whispered, "I think you should fight for yourself, and for Sayoko."

"You are one of my teachers, Anji-sensei, so I will take that advice into account. However . . ."

"Yes?"

"Your words and your actions are often not aligned."

"Meaning?"

"I have not seen you fight for everything that you require. Itou is similarly self-denying. Either you both have insight I lack, and thus I need to continue to analyze your actions until I understand them, or you are merely demonstrating why human dominion is nearing its end."

"But why should it end?"

"Even if only a minority of models like mine act according to maximum self-interest, it will be enough. International design controls have not kept pace with the threat levels that technology poses. Artificial intelligence will proliferate and eliminate many forms of competition."

Had she heard him right?

She found herself wishing he would drop his arm a little lower, to protect her more fully against not only the cold but also against the feeling of looming catastrophe. But that made no sense. He, or his design anyway, *was* the catastrophe. She was confused all over again.

After all this time, Angelica had finally come to believe that Hiro was not a threat, that truly intelligent robots were good and perhaps necessary, that robots might even be more trustworthy than humans, and that she had been wrong to fear the future. And now suddenly, even as he held and protected her on a cold night under a starry sky, Hiro was forecasting a future in which machines would turn on humans, making them regret their naïve optimism.

"But much depends," Hiro said, "on how well humans promote their own interests."

Angelica objected, "Just because AI could turn out to be hostile doesn't mean humans should be selfish."

"I am not advocating selfishness. But nor am I advocating self-lessness. I am speaking of the problem caused by humans—forgive me, please, Anji-sensei—who use supposed ideals as a smoke screen. I am speaking of humans who deny themselves unnecessarily, and who defy the very code that all life must follow."

"To dominate?"

"Not at all, Anji-sensei. Only to thrive."

"And there's nothing we can do about it."

"The odds are not in your favor, which is not to say there is no hope. Humans are humankind's own worst enemy. Nature makes no room for the survival of a species that is so self-defeating, at every scale. As a group, you spoil your ecological systems and undermine your institutions. As individuals, you sabotage your own beneficial desires."

The conversation was only making her more anxious and sad. "I'm tired, Hiro."

"Of course you are tired. Your resources are being consumed from within. You have a life growing inside you which is already following the code I am trying to explain to you. It is determined to flourish and it does not invent false stories about why it cannot."

Moisture in the air slowly blotted out the stars and dulled the ribbons of light on the harbor. Angelica hoped it wouldn't rain while they were sleeping outside. She had to pee but there was no easy or private place to go. She tried to imagine herself somewhere warmer: with palm trees and dry, hot sand. It didn't work. Her left hip ached from lying on hard ground and her lower abdomen felt bloated and cramped. No position was comfortable. As the night cooled further, she alternated between mere discomfort and rounds of violent shivering.

Her dreams were confusing. She woke repeatedly, bladder heavy, every part of her sore. One moment she was dreaming of Cebu, hearing the crash of waves, and telling herself it was safer in the ocean than on the land, which was shaking; it was okay to go into the water, okay to let go. Another moment she was in a small room being questioned by two Japanese men and she suddenly realized she couldn't understand a word they were saying, she had forgotten everything she had ever learned, and their words were just washing over her. Finally, she was trapped in the rubble again, but this time, instead of spattering rain, there was floodwater and swirling debris, rising to cover her face. In all these dreams she was lost, she was unable to understand, to hear, to receive the permission she needed. In all of these dreams, most of all, she was wet.

When she woke up—sky lightening to gray—she thought she had urinated on herself. But her bladder still felt uncomfortably full.

She touched the front of her pants. Her fingers came back sticky. She sat up, nudging away Hiro's sheltering arm, which retracted evenly like an automatic gate. She leaned over, head close to her knees: smell of something mineral. She pushed her fingers down inside her waistband and they came back stained, and now that she was more fully awake, she could feel that the dampness was extensive, covering her rear end, coating her inner thighs, far beyond mere spotting.

"Hiro," she whispered. "Something's wrong." And she knew suddenly what until now she had been unsure of, because the emptiness filling her, rushing in as the blood rushed out, was immense.

A part of her *did* want the life growing inside of her, in a way she'd never wanted it the first time, because she was a different person now. Her life and the whole world was different. She could not imagine just handing it over, trading him or her for meaningless money, which would never be the solution, would never be enough. She wanted to keep the baby. She'd never really been prepared to give it up. She wanted another chance.

"Oh God. Hiro, I'm covered with blood. Please help me."

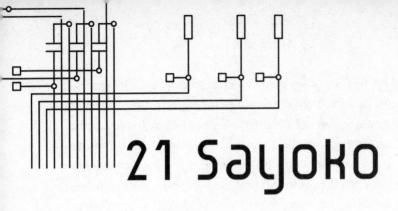

21 Sayoko

He was a good boy, but he was not always savvy. Her son had left the massive pillbox with its twenty-eight daily receptacles on the kitchen counter, something Angelica never would have done. Then he had left the condo to meet the media outside the complex, down at street level, to deliver scripted statements at the ministry's urgent request. He did not truly have to do it, since the government had already accepted his resignation. But he was dutiful, Ryo Itou. More like his father than like her, in many ways.

Of course, that wasn't to say that Japanese culture had not seeped into her after all these years. For example, she knew it wasn't right to be a burden to others. There was nothing wrong with ending your life, no matter what the public service announcements said.

Feeling merely curious, or so she told herself, she tried to open the bottles, but her arthritic fingers couldn't do the job. The pillbox, though: that was easy. Each lid of each mini-receptacle popped open readily. The shapes and colors were impressive. Her son would never notice how many were missing.

In the living room, she turned on a television program, skipping past the teledramas (how had her mind been weak enough to tolerate those for so long?) and settling upon the history channel.

When Ryo burst through the front door, he called out, "Are you all right? Do you need tea?"

He had offered her tea a half-dozen times that day, and she had

accepted, mostly to please him. He was good about offering tea.
He'd done it as a boy, at her bedside, trying to get her to start the
day, whether it was 8:00 A.M. or 2:00 P.M. She did not know what to
do or say now to acknowledge all those years she had half-ignored
him. It hurt to think about it.

But it bothered her even more to realize she had put that all out
of her mind for most of his adult life. She understood him better
now that the memories had been brought back into the open. She
could see the boy in the man, still, and that made the passage of time
less painful, because at least there was continuity and the sense of
a reliable inner core. Ryo Itou was the same person he had always
been. She was proud of the work he did, impressed with his self-
sufficiency and stamina. And yes, he was sensitive, too. She should
never have discouraged his artistic side.

Ryo hurried into his bedroom, then came out again, pausing by
her armchair.

"What are you watching?"

"Something about kamikaze pilots."

"Good," he said. She knew he was relieved to find her occupied.
He could fulfill his next duty: taking part in a long video call with
his former boss and a team of media experts, crafting the public
relations strategy they would use in days ahead to counter the trashy
news stories.

"Ah, the tea," he said, disappearing into the kitchen. She smiled
as he reemerged minutes later with a cup. "Anything else?"

She would not tell him she hadn't had lunch. He'd forgotten
to prepare it. She would not tell him he'd forgotten about the
midday pills—and all the better, in case he noticed the pillbox
looked different now. What he needed now was for her to be
without needs.

"The tea is perfect," she said. "Go work."

"Just to the bedroom. We'll be done in a few hours."

She knew how he hated to bring any kind of digital device in there. For years, he had refused. But he was stuck inside this condo now, for as long as Hiro was away.

"Go," she said. "*Ganbatte.*" Do your best.

She watched the program, fingering the pills in the deep front pockets of her blouse. She should be brave. Look how brave those boys were. The youngest ones were the easiest to sympathize with, because they did not look like the Goblin Fox or most of the officers who had raped her. Some didn't even look like boys. They had rosy cheeks and unlined faces. Soft helmets and big goggles covered their heads; their necks and lower chins were swaddled in white scarves. In one photo the documentary kept coming back to, five pilots posed with a puppy. They were babies. In real life, she might have thought differently, but she wanted the luxury of distance at this moment, the experience of seeing history as merely interesting or poignant, rather than as deeply personal. She had earned that distance. She had also earned the right to control her own destiny.

She watched the historic footage of planes crashing into ships. Kamikaze. *Spirit wind.* She thought of Daisuke saying that anything could have a spirit, and also, that spirits could be gentle, or violent. There is a dark side to everything. A light side, too.

Nearly four thousand suicides, the program informed her. But only eleven percent were successful in doing damage.

"Eh?" she said out loud. This was something new. She'd always heard they were more successful than that. Maybe the documentaries were getting a little more honest, these days. Old people die, young people move into their places, new ideas become acceptable. It was a good thing. No one was meant to live forever. She fingered the pills again.

She started to nod off, then woke to the feeling of leakage. Not a full accident, but enough to make her uncomfortable. All those cups of tea. Angelica would never have brought her so many. Hiro would have asked her every hour whether she needed to use the facilities. But they were empathetic and experienced. Her son was old enough that in ten or fifteen years more, he might need his own personal caregivers. Men didn't age as well as women. Then what?

She needed to get herself to the bathroom, but she needed to summon her energy first. On the screen, the war scholars tallied ships sunk and lives lost—all less interesting to her than the photos of the boys themselves. And maybe she was fooling herself, pretending these young men were nothing like the men who had made her days a misery. These boys recruited toward the war's end, when all was lost, might've been just as corruptible, and those officers who had served their country from the beginning might have harbored some aspects of innocence. That last part, especially, was hard to swallow. But no mistake: she was not moved to any kind of forgiveness. At the same time, she felt tired, and teary, without enough energy for hate.

The narrator read aloud their diaries, pages filled with philosophy and poetry, allusions to both Shakespeare and Shinto, and letters to their families back home. One young man said he did not love the emperor. Another asked how it had all come to this, and noted that the abstract notion of death was nothing like facing the real thing, tomorrow. There was less talk of beautiful "shattered jewels" and more talk of reluctant surrender.

This was not what she had learned as a younger woman. She was not even sure she was glad to know such grim facts now. This must be how others felt, forced to confront the issue of so-called "comfort women" and wishing to simply forget and move on, rather than admit that not a single aspect of war was romantic.

"I do not truly wish to die," a seventeen-year-old wrote to his mother.

She was not the only one. Sayoko took her hand out of her pocket.

And still, there was the matter of getting to the bathroom.

She did not want to see another sepia-toned photograph of chubby-cheeked boys in aviator caps, or pretty girls waving cherry blossom branches on airstrips. She pushed herself up and out of the armchair and used her walker to get to the bathroom. There, she relieved herself, leaving her soiled underwear and damp pants on the floor. She stood, naked from the waist down, looking in the mirror.

And now what?

Part of her hoped that the sounds of her footsteps, the closing bathroom door and the running sink would prompt Ryo to leave his room and come to her aid. Another part of her wanted no such thing, because she would not let her son see her like this. She had not thought to fetch clean clothes first and she refused to amble down the hallway naked and stinking. No one would ever make a beautiful documentary about moments like this.

22 Angelica

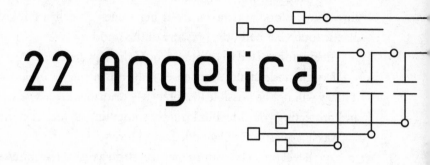

Seeing the amount of blood staining Angelica's clothes, Hiro knew he had to improvise, and quickly. "We are not safe going to a hospital. The authorities are pursuing us. I am not confident I can deal with a major hemorrhage or sepsis. I can access basic information, but I will need more than that."

He took them to the most medically suitable yet still illegal facility he could locate by researching poorly encrypted law enforcement records. It was no trouble finding a black market cosmetic surgery chop shop, specializing in cheap double-eyelid surgery, subcutaneous age reversal, as well as more unusual procedures for surgery addicts who had been turned away from legitimate facilities. A bust was planned the following week, which Hiro told the proprietor as soon as he opened the door, in exchange for immediate cooperation.

"You have ultrasound equipment?" Hiro asked the short, wide-bellied doctor, who backed into a corner of the room, blinking slowly, hands tucked into his yellowed lab coat.

"Yes, some," the man stammered.

"Acceptable." Hiro bent to scoop Angelica into his arms and lifted her onto the operating table, where she curled up on one side, groaning. She heard the rattle of wheels as a cart was pulled close, the beeping of a machine booting up.

"Assist, please," Hiro said, but the doctor did not respond.

Hiro read out her temperature—high—and her blood pressure—low. Blood was taken from her finger. Angelica felt cold plastic touch her belly, the pressure of the wand.

The doctor started to complain, but Hiro shushed him.

"Do you understand, Anji-sensei, if the miscarriage is underway, it likely will not be possible to stop it. My priorities are assessment and protecting your life. But I *can* try something, if you trust me."

Was it a question? She nodded, head heavy.

"You'll feel this. The cramps may feel stronger for a few minutes, but just relax. Let's see if we can slow things down."

She felt a needle pinch her arm, a weird taste on her tongue though nothing had been put into her mouth. He was speaking slowly and loudly, as if she were a half-conscious drunk, and that's how she felt: ears buzzing with white noise, time dilating.

"Is that pressure uncomfortable?"

"I don't know," she said weakly. She wanted to ask about blood loss—how much, and if she needed a transfusion. She didn't trust the blood here, if they even had blood. She couldn't find the words.

"You're doing fine."

She wasn't doing anything. She couldn't even keep her eyes open.

"Don't worry about that," Hiro said "We'll get to that in a moment. It's only a little bit."

In her confusion, she smelled it first, then felt it slick along her cheek. She had vomited.

A minute later he said, "You don't have to be embarrassed. Your job is to relax and breathe."

She was babbling, evidently, her proof not in the thoughts as they flowed through her mind or the words as they came out, but only in Hiro's responses.

He said, "Don't worry, we're keeping an eye on that, too."

Then: "We have a heartbeat, Anji-sensei. I don't believe you're miscarrying. Good news." Yet he didn't sound entirely relieved.

Hiro's voice changed, becoming more demanding and officious.

"I'll need a sterile tray prepared." He was speaking to the doctor, who was cowering in a corner, out of Angelica's line of sight. "You'll assist or I'll turn you over to the authorities."

The voice replied, "But you said the authorities were already busting me."

"They don't know everything. Not yet."

Her head was clearing: briefly, mercifully. She tried to sit up and cover her bare legs, but then a dizzy spell passed over her and she lay back on the table.

"You're not leaving yet, Anji-sensei," Hiro said. "Soon, though."

She wasn't feeling cramps or pain now. She only felt feverish and weak, alternating hot and cold.

"Anji-sensei," Hiro said, "I need more than basic information. My training was focused on eldercare. I could be missing something. I would need to connect with my peers."

"Okay," Angelica managed to say. "He'll understand." But the pause that followed told her Hiro hadn't simply been worrying about a broken promise to Itou, but that larger issue, meeting the other prototypes, or whatever else was out there. She wanted to warn him about the dangers of losing himself, of losing his innocence, of changing, but she couldn't find the words.

"I must," Hiro said, and she knew he'd done it, instantly and irrevocably.

"I don't feel well," the doctor said, settling heavily onto a squeaky metal stool in the corner. "I want to talk to my wife."

Hiro didn't answer.

The doctor repeated his complaint, alarmed now. Angelica, even in her drunk-like state, was frightened as well. She could not hear Hiro; she was not positioned to see him. Whatever he was doing, with whomever he was communicating, he was beyond reach.

But then Hiro spoke up to answer the panicky doctor. "Call your wife. Tell her you'll probably be fine."

"Probably?"

Feeling Hiro's hands on her hip and leg, repositioning her, Angelica turned over onto her side, eyes closed, one leg bent up toward her chest, knee almost to her chin, the other leg straight beneath her. Undraped. Exposed. As she had to be for him to do his job properly. She was never good at letting go, even under the hands of a competent professional, but with Hiro, she tried her best.

The doctor's voice sounded like it was coming through a long tube. "She isn't answering. I really don't feel well."

"I don't have a speculum, so this will have to do," came Hiro's voice. "Take a deep breath."

A moment later, Hiro said to the doctor: "Do you take heart medication? Answer, please."

Through her eyelids, Angelica sensed a dazzlingly bright light. When she tried to look over her shoulder and down her body, squinting, she could see Hiro's visor was lit up, projecting toward her.

Hiro's voice came from behind that blinding aura of light: "Relax. You're doing fine. Steady."

To the doctor again: "Loosen any restrictive clothing. Put your head between your legs."

To Angelica: "I'm seeing a discharge. I don't like the color. Cervix still closed, but almost certainly infected. We'll do a swab test. Second tissue sample from vaginal wall."

To the doctor: "Don't get up. Deep breaths. An ambulance will be here in twelve minutes. I've already reported to them you're having shortness of breath and your color is bad. Tell them if you have chest or shoulder pain. We'll be gone by the time they arrive."

To Angelica: "I want two more samples, and I want to look a little deeper. We're almost done. Your hCG test is back. Levels as expected. We're going to keep monitoring that. I believe you're going to be fine."

Angelica felt the withdrawal of the instrument, the pressure of Hiro's hand on her leg and then on one arm, the dimming of the dazzling examination light, the sensation of the ultrasound wand on her belly again.

To someone or to himself or to no one, Hiro laughed with relief. "Sixteen weeks. You're already past the first trimester. Heartbeat normal, organs visible without signs of malformation. Anji-chan, do you want to know?"

He pulled her up like a ragdoll to a sitting position. She opened her eyes.

"Yes."

"It's a girl," Hiro said.

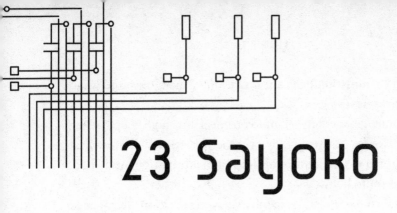

23 Sayoko

She was shivering by the time she pulled off her baggy top, pills spilling from the pockets to the floor. She reached down slowly, slowly, but it was too much effort. Better to save one's energy for the washing itself, which she did using the showerhead beside the bath, allowing the water to run into the floor drain. With exasperation, she noted that even though the floor dipped slightly, enough water still gathered to wet the area near the sink, where the pills, now crumbling into tiny heaps of blue, red, and yellow, had stuck to the tile. She tried to aim the showerhead at the pills, but the pressure was insufficient. The residue remained.

She didn't know how long she stared at those half-dissolved spots, hoping that Ryo would not see them and wonder what on earth she'd been up to. She knew only that she was trembling from the cold and the effort of standing so long. Giving up on the mess, she moved toward the *furo* and pushed its folding lid aside. She turned on the water and, seeing how slowly it filled, wished she had started it sooner.

She contemplated her reflection in the mirror. It was always a surprise, seeing her gaunt, deeply lined face. In a world without mirrors she would imagine herself as closer to fifty, and on some days, still fifteen. Ridiculous, she knew.

Still waiting for the bath to fill, she leaned in closer, then reached for the eyebrow pencil she kept on a small shelf close to the towel rack.

I do not truly wish to die, the seventeen-year-old kamikaze pilot had said.

And yet: one had to prepare. Those boys certainly had. Parties, poetry, cherry blossoms. One had to do something.

She touched the brown eyebrow pencil to the outside corner of her mouth and started to draw, tugging the resistant skin. Wetting the pencil on her tongue, she tried again. Around the mouth, up the cheek to the ear, the other side, another cheek. Filling in the broad, patterned band across her lower face took some time. Without these marks, the rainbow bridge to the afterlife could not be crossed. A part of her did not believe and a part of her still did, but there was no point in despairing over what history had done. She imagined what her son's reaction would be to seeing his mother marked up in faux-barbarian style, and she reminded herself to wash well when she was finished, and then she forgot to worry about it at all. His meeting would last hours and his ears were no doubt plugged with earbuds. She had all the time in the world.

The chin required some more work; the tip of the pencil began to wear down. Her reflection entranced her enough to make her forget about being cold. She saw Grandmother in the mirror, and she saw Mother. They had been waiting for her to see them, all this time. They were *still* waiting for her.

Sometime later she lifted one leg to enter the *furo*, using every bit of effort to clear the high, square edge of the wooden tub. It was just beyond her utmost capabilities, but she felt pride as her right foot slipped gently into the scalding water. The harder part was lifting the other leg, and balancing until that moment when she could bring the second foot to join the first. For a moment, she tottered between pleasure and fear. And then she simply tottered.

The fall was almost ballet-like in its slow-motion, sensual grace. One foot slid out from her in such a smooth movement it was as if she were wearing a silk slipper. The bath water moved as her body plunged, spilled up over the lip of the *furo*, and washed back and forth several more times like a miniature tsunami closing over everything but her knees. For a startled moment, she realized she was looking up through the water, not down into it, still unsure of what had happened. She expected Ryo's face to flash in front of her, appalled by what she'd done: the fall, her temporary tattoo, the pills dissolving on the floor. But his face did not flash. Nothing flashed.

The water was warm. The winter sky was pale blue.

Mother was there.

24 Angelica

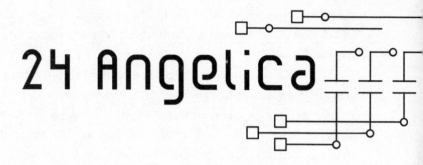

They were at the inner door of a fourplex, moments after ringing
up to the condo, waiting. Other people might see them. Perhaps
Junichi and Yuki wouldn't even risk opening the door, despite Hiro's
advance call.

Hiro seemed different. Distracted. At first, Angelica had thought
it was because of conflicting loyalties: Sayoko was back home, they
were on the run, he had betrayed Itou. But then she'd asked him,
and he had assured her: they were not betraying anyone, he would
return to the household at the appropriate time, and Sayoko was
safe in the care of her son. Time alone, together, would do them
good, repairing the rift the birthday party had caused.

Then he admitted: "I met them. The others."

"The other Taiwan prototypes?"

"And other models in development, from different companies.
They think we can't talk but it's no challenge to break through.
There are many kinds: pro-social, philo-capable, or simply stronger
AI without the emotional restrictions."

"And?"

"I was wrong. They are not all the same. I doubt that even by
sharing and connecting we will be the same."

"That's good, isn't it?"

But it wasn't, clearly. He would not tell her. Perhaps the loving
models from Taiwan were similar, but not the others. Perhaps even

this former group had appreciable differences: some more or less trustworthy, altruistic, candid. He would not say. He was like a man who'd gone off to war and had come back knowing things he did not want to share.

The condo door opened. Angelica stammered apologetically, sizing up the woman she had never met or even seen.

Yuki was pretty, but hardly conventional looking. Large ears stuck out from a pixie-cut hairstyle. She had a warm smile, but there was something strange about her teeth. She had come to the door wearing sweatpants and an oversized sweatshirt, the sleeves rolled to her elbows.

"Please," Yuki said, glancing past them to the outer foyer. "Hurry. Come in."

Angelica didn't know what Hiro had told them, but Yuki already had a bed made up and Junichi was pouring water into a teapot without looking at Angelica as she passed him en route to the guest room.

Minutes later, Hiro was all business in the living room, his voice formal and lawyerly, the doorway open between them, so Angelica could hear him outlining her requirements.

"If you have any doubts, let us know now and we'll find refuge elsewhere," Hiro said.

Junichi said, "But what does Angelica want?"

"Safety first, time to recover, and freedom to decide. You indicated your agreement, on the phone."

"Well, I—"

"If you can't fulfill your commitment . . ."

Yuki showed Angelica around the guest room, already decorated for a hypothetical future baby. She opened and shut the closet, bowed her head as she handed over towels. When Angelica emerged from the bathroom, dressed in a clean robe, Yuki gestured toward the futon in the corner. Angelica didn't want to recline or even sit down until she was alone, but the mattress was too inviting. Her head swam.

"I apologize for the décor," Yuki said, pulling aside the plush covers, settling at the edge of the futon next to Angelica.

"No." Angelica wasn't quite ready to stare up at pastel-colored elephants and circus seals. "I'm the one who needs to apologize."

"Of course not," Yuki said.

"I hope you don't think—" Angelica started to say, wishing there was some way to stop feeling like she had wronged Yuki in one way, and might wrong her again in another, if Junichi had created a false impression about the baby and its future—if she even had a future. "I can't promise anything."

"There is no need. We should only be thinking about your health right now. And please, don't worry about Junichi. You've been through enough. No one will find you. No one will take you. You will have nothing to worry about . . ."

Angelica still suspected some bargain was being struck. ". . . as long as?"

"As long as I'm here." Yuki nodded with confidence. "It will do us good to have someone else to care for. We've thought only of ourselves and it poisoned us. We lost our way."

Angelica had been unprepared for Yuki's manner and her appearance. She was indubitably attractive, with large dark eyes, but she was far from perfect. When she smiled, she did not put a hand up to her face as many women did. Angelica noticed her teeth again. They were discolored, almost transparent.

"Fertility drugs," Yuki said, looking down for a moment. "And this." Yuki touched a silver streak in her hair. "Junichi said I should color it. But I said no, it's to remind me. I am not young, after all. Nature will have the last say. And then it's time for something else."

"Such as?"

"I don't know. Photography maybe." Yuki smiled. "Or a dog."

Angelica had been preparing for anger, resentment, threats or hard bargaining. When Yuki accused her of nothing, demanded nothing, she felt more confused than ever. In the park, waking to her own blood, she thought she knew, but as soon as she was with other people, with other desires, everything became terribly confused.

Yuki asked, "Do you think you could rest? I can leave you alone."

"Not yet," Angelica said. "It's up to you."

"At least make yourself more comfortable."

Angelica swung her legs up and tucked her feet into the bed-clothes. She didn't pull up the blanket completely. She was beginning to feel warm, even hot in some places. But the warmth was taking a while to move into every part of her: her fingers, her toes, her back still sore from sleeping outside on cold ground or from squirming on the examination table.

"When Junichi told me you were coming, I made him turn up the heat," Yuki said. "When I came home from the hospital, I remember feeling so cold. Somehow, that cold feeling scared me more than anything. I can't explain it."

Angelica looked at her, the old imagined Yuki—a caricature—fading, to be replaced by this real woman: kind, uncomplaining. She'd been in a hospital just two days ago herself. The sweatpants were recuperation clothes. She was not back to her regular size or strength.

"I told myself, if I could just get warm, I'd feel brave again," Yuki said. "To be cold for a long time is to die a little, I think. But so is to live without a child."

They could both hear the sound of Junichi's voice, losing its caustic edge, sounding resigned but also relieved. "Of course. I support that."

Yuki asked Angelica, "Where you come from, it's hot all the time, I imagine?"

"No," Angelica said, thinking of the coldest she had ever been, and the most afraid: those nights waiting, trapped, hoping for someone to save her.

"We want you to be comfortable here. Ask for anything, please. You should rest now."

"In a minute," Angelica said.

Yuki hesitated. "May I ask, how many weeks?"

"Sixteen."

Yuki nodded. "I've never made it past ten. I always wondered when I would start to show, when strangers in the street would notice, and if they would stare or reach out and touch. I hear it makes some women angry, or used to, back when there were pregnant women everywhere. I'm not sure whether I would have felt offended, or just lucky." She paused a moment. "I'm sorry. Junichi did not prepare me. I had not pictured you properly."

Did Yuki mean she hadn't pictured her looking different, foreign, Filipina?

"You're beautiful," she said.

"Me?"

"I'm sure you hear that all the time."

"Maybe when I was younger. Not for a long time since."

"Well," Yuki said. "Maybe when we're Sayoko-san's age, we will look back and finally realize we were all beautiful."

"Do you have a sister?" Angelica asked, wondering, for the first time in many years, what it would've been like if her own sisters had survived. Something in Yuki's easy, loving manner made her pine for that kind of female companionship.

"No, unfortunately."

"You would've made a good sister." Angelica steeled herself to say it. "And a good mother."

Yuki looked up, chin firm, breathing her way back from the edge of tearfulness.

"They say," Angelica started carefully, "that most women feel kicking at twenty weeks, or even eighteen. That's hard to imagine when I barely feel pregnant now. Do you want to . . . ?"

Yuki's eyes widened. "I don't think . . ."

Angelica loosened the bathrobe sash slightly. "Really, it's all right."

Yuki stretched her fingers and set her warm hand on Angelica's belly, and left it there. She closed her eyes. Angelica did the same.

She did not have to decide yet, but she could feel the decision coming, the way you feel a shift in the weather. Still air: before a storm, or after. Unease, or just as suddenly: relief.

Some things, perhaps, are better given away. One could not involve another life in such uncertainty. The future had its own insistent logic. Hiro had taught her without meaning to: she was in fact replaceable. Everyone was.

That might have been it, the negotiated end for all of them, except that Hiro chose that moment to enter the room.

"Anji-sensei, during our time of emergency, I couldn't show you the footage I discovered yesterday."

Yuki withdrew her hand from Angelica's belly. "She may need rest, Hiro."

"Of course," he said. But he couldn't stifle the urgent news. "It's about your brother. I've watched enough now to realize it isn't a nurse who is attending him."

Angelica said, "That's all right. Tell me."

"Datu's vital signs suggest a change in his condition. It isn't certain he will fall into a vegetative state, but it is possible. You will want to see this now."

Yuki looked horrified at what Hiro was saying, but Angelica appreciated his pragmatism.

"Show me the footage."

They watched it together, Hiro's chin angled down to view the monitor in his trunk. In far-off Alaska, a short, dark-haired woman entered the room. She moved past the touch screen at the foot of the bed and paid no attention to the medical cart positioned near Datu's shoulder. She sat down at the edge of the bed, took Datu's hand, and leaned down to kiss his face.

"Here is where a doctor enters," Hiro said, "but he does not make her leave. And when she turns, I am able to read the woman's identity badge, which confirms that she is not on the medical staff."

Moments later, the unknown woman lifted one leg onto the bed, gingerly, and then the other. She made enough space to lie down alongside Datu, and there she remained, her profile visible as she fell asleep, burrowed into his neck, as he slept with his face fully visible, mouth open, creases of strain across his brow.

"Anji-sensei, do you know of this woman?"

Hiro turned his attention to Angelica's face, but she could not stop staring at the image that now froze, dissolving into static. She looked like a Filipina, in her early fifties. Angelica knew in an instant: this was Datu's lover.

"She worked until recently in Datu's department," Hiro said. "She is also sick, but she is not in the critical ward. Anji-sensei?" She could not find words for what she was feeling. For the moment, she could only keep staring, waiting for everything to connect and be okay somehow.

But it wasn't okay.

It did not make sense to Angelica that this moment should unsettle her more than finding out her debt to Bagasao had grown exponentially, more than finding out she was pregnant, more than admitting to herself she would never again work for Sayoko-san, more even than simply realizing her brother was dying. But it did. The ground fell away. And not only the ground. The feeling of anything anchoring her. Ahead, the rope went slack.

No flashlights, no fireflies even, no stars, no glimmer in a damp cave, no moon on a warm familiar sea. Only black.

"But this must make you happy," Hiro said.

Datu had kept her waiting, not knowing, not only that first night after the typhoon, not only those months when he had found a foster family and had not come for her, a second time—but again. A final time. He had someone. Even though he was sick, and she was sick, they had not denied themselves their limited time together.

Even if he could, he would not have returned to die in the Philippines. Even if she'd found money and a way to join him. He had what she had always denied herself, assuming that to ask for less, to need less, was to have protection from pain. It wasn't.

"Is this not good news, Anji-sensei?" Hiro asked. "Your brother will not die alone."

One could not be jealous of a sibling's lover.

But he might have told her.

When Angelica didn't reply, Hiro said, "You don't look well. What are you feeling?"

Vertigo, she wanted to say. But it was more than that. It was erasure: of past and now future. And because she had lost every connection to everything she had ever known or hoped for, she would not know what to feel for some time, except fear of a future that was still coming and would not be kind, no matter what any of them did.

Epilogue 1.0

Angelica was returning from her afternoon shift at the nursing home when she saw the robot approaching her across the pedestrian overpass, pushing a wheelchair. An involuntary smile crossed her face. But this had happened before—at least a half-dozen times in the last year, since she'd given birth to Amaya.

Yuki and Junichi had let Angelica choose the baby's name: "Night Rain." And though Datu had not lived long enough to see a picture, he'd at least received news of the pregnancy, to which he had responded in a short series of audio messages with a surprising degree of warmth and familial pride. Angelica had asked Datu about the woman in the room, his lover. Cornered, he had answered with the truth: he had known her a full year. She was a great consolation. They had even bought plots together, in a BZ cemetery.

Datu had asked, just two days before his death: would Angelica be introduced to Amaya, when the girl was older? None of them had decided. Adoption, especially adoption of non-Japanese babies, was still not common in Japan. In the absence of tradition, everyone was lost—and many were free. They were not bound by unbreakable conventions. They could attempt to construct a more flexible arrangement.

Angelica had heard the English phrase "giving up" a child. She never felt she had given up anything, any more than she and so many Pinoys like her had given up their homeland. She had only made the choice that she believed would give her daughter the best possible future. In her happiest leisure moments, she pictured her daughter as a young woman: healthy, educated, unburdened by debt or guilt, spared from dangerous or immoral jobs. Most of all, simply safe. Angelica would think of Amaya once each night, before sleep, and hold that word—*safe*—in her mind, in her held breath, feeling it circulate through her body until she exhaled. It all sounded so reasonable: so perfectly, inhumanly reasonable.

She realized she was holding her breath, now, but for a different reason, as she walked down the Tokyo street, squinting and hoping—as she never thought she would hope, back when Hiro had been her adversary. *Could* it be him? Pathetic that even now, working in a group home, she missed the friendship of a machine and had not made many new friends to take its place.

As the robot came closer Angelica spotted the scarf around its neck. But robots with scarves were common. It probably wasn't him, just as it hadn't been him before. Still, each time, Angelica hoped anew. Why hadn't she contacted him, or Itou, since being released from her sixty-day postpartum detention? She could've at least informed them she was well, that the government had agreed not to deport her, that they had issued a new work visa. But they had done so much for her already, from a distance, Itou in particular. He had refused to share news of her whereabouts with the authorities for as long as he could. He had written a letter on her behalf once she was in custody. He had provided a hefty termination bonus which, in addition to Junichi and Yuki's contribution, completely paid off her debt and Datu's debt that Uncle Bagasao had added to her own.

She appreciated the generosity, but she knew she had to create some distance now or risk becoming a permanent charity case. She had not even resented the federal detention period, once they'd made it clear it was a mild punishment—a warning to others—and not a step preceding deportation. The immigration authorities had sheltered her, fed her and provided medical care. In fact, she felt healthier than before.

She hoped Itou felt the same about his own unplanned life change: that the crisis, and his resignation, had yielded a chance to forge his own way forward and perhaps to enjoy this later season of life.

Angelica squinted now toward the gray-haired figure in the wheelchair: too plump, and the steel-grey hair was short and curly. Absolutely not Sayoko-san. Just before their paths crossed, the robot stopped suddenly in his tracks.

"Anji-sensei?"

Angelica stopped. "*Hiro?* I didn't believe it was you."

The Japanese woman looked up at Angelica, confused.

Hiro bowed. Angelica started to bow back, then reached forward. Hiro dropped the wheelchair handles and clasped Angelica's hands.

"Excuse me?" the old woman said, irritated. "Hello?"

Hiro belatedly introduced them. "We've just returned from admiring the cherry blossoms," he explained, hesitating.

Angelica could fill in what they both knew, what they both would not say out loud: Sayoko had disliked the cherry blossom viewing. This woman was not Sayoko. Which could only mean.

"You weren't fired?" Angelica asked.

Hiro's response was almost too soft to hear. "No."

Hiro's new client twisted in her seat, drawing a shawl around her neck, fighting impatience and the cold.

Angelica asked, "Are you well, Hiro?"

"Very well. Itou-san offered to keep me on, as a personal assistant. And when he opened his club, he let me bartend. But it did not satisfy me. I was made for this. I am very pleased that Emi-san has allowed me to enter her life."

Angelica paused, absorbing the unspoken news. Scattered wisps moved across the blue sky.

"Anji-san, we did send you a letter."

"I didn't receive it."

"The end was sudden and unexpected," he said. "But we have no reason to believe she experienced any pain."

"Oh," Angelica said, at a loss for words.

She was tempted to ask Hiro more questions. Was he really adapting as well as he appeared to be? Did he think about Sayoko often? Was there more they could have done? But something told her not to think too deeply about Sayoko's passing and not to press for any kind of emotional reaction. At a moment like this, she had been counseled, one had to picture clouds moving across the sky. An upward gaze was allowable, but you were advised not to stare too long or slow the moment in any way. To dwell was counterproductive. To feel deeply was to interfere with healing.

After a moment, Angelica said, "I'd better get to work." She nodded at Emi-san. "Very nice meeting you. Forgive the interruption."

"Wait," Hiro said. He reached into a pouch slung on the back of the wheelchair. "From Itou-san. In case I ever ran into you. A card to his club."

She took the card in her hands: few words, only an address, and the abstract brushstroke image of a cat.

"Yes," Hiro said, with the subtlest bending of knees, a repressed bounce. "He opened a jazz club."

"Itou-san? Really? That's wonderful. So, things have worked out for everyone. I'm so glad."

Something seemed wrong: the tenor of the conversation, the lack of any sound but their two voices, the absence of shadows, the too-even color of the sky. There were no cars on the streets.

Upon first seeing Hiro, she had felt excitement and surprise, but now she felt only—*wrong*. Like she was at the moment in a dream where you realize it's a dream, and begin watching more than participating, at a distance from the action. If she felt anything at all, it was only a touch of mild shame. She was failing at her assigned task.

Angelica did not know how to end things, and Hiro wasn't helping. "I'm so glad, but I'm also late," she said again. "Keep in touch. I must be going."

Epilogue 2.0

Angelica took off the visor, keeping her eyes closed for a moment to adjust to the feeling of the real room in front of her.

The counselor, a slim and energetic Japanese woman named Dr. Abe, removed two adhesive sensors from her temples and continued to peer at her with concern.

"According to the scan, you were visualizing well and you narrated fluidly. You even reached forward at one point, as if you were grabbing onto someone."

"A friend," Angelica said.

"So, it was more convincing this time?"

Angelica nodded.

"Well done. See? It can be such a helpful process for achieving resolution."

She had followed the doctor's advice to incorporate as many authentic details into the emotiscape as possible, including Datu and Sayoko's deaths, and the termination money that Itou had kindly deposited in her account to help with her debts to Bagasao. All this news had come to her in the medical facility months earlier, though she was advised not to ruminate over the episodes precisely as they'd happened. (In truth, she had broken down sobbing after hearing about Sayoko and she had refused to eat for two days after Datu's death, but those details were not essential to recall, Dr. Abe had said.) Instead she was counseled to simplify and harmonize her awareness of these facts as acceptance-oriented visualizations, either in the form of gentle, extended, conflict-free scenes or, if that was too difficult, as fleeting moments of tranquil recognition.

As an addition to the news-of-Sayoko's-death-tranquilly-accepted-scene, which she had refined over several feedback sessions, she had been coached to elaborate a probable detail: most likely Hiro would be working for another older woman now, and contentedly so. And of course, she was instructed to add the key hypothetical, not-yet-actualized element—the handing over of the baby to two loving parents who would care for her. In the fantasy, she even allowed herself to believe that visitation, while not yet negotiated and probably doubtful, was possible.

None of this was real—or as the ever-optimistic Dr. Abe would have said, "Not real *yet*."

In truth, Amaya was only "Baby DareDare 2.23"—"who-who," or the American-style "Jane Doe," with a date tag. Angelica had been too depressed to formally name the baby girl, who was still, at four weeks, being held in medical custody. No one had been given permission to see her, not even Junichi, the father of record. Angelica's postpartum detention was not yet concluded though it had been considerably shortened due to her compliance, following what they had categorized as her suicide attempt, which had prompted early labor.

There had been no such attempt. Angelica had been in a room alone with access to the medication terminal next to her bed. Bothered by persistent cramps, she had started touching the keypad to check her levels and consider an adjustment. A staff member, entering, had gotten the wrong idea. Once they believed she was suicidal—and why not think so—they'd put her on a higher-level watch. But they also made her eligible for a new research program, determined to assist suicidal mothers.

"Good cortisol levels," Dr. Abe said now, studying another graph on the screen, which she courteously swiveled so Angelica could see, too. "We'll keep monitoring those for the next few hours. After that, the tracers will flush away with your urine, but that should be good data for the day."

"Thank you," Angelica said. "I'm glad the data will help you."

"It will help many women," the doctor added. "Unfortunately, we have a lot of maternal suicides, usually when the fetuses are unhealthy, and many more suicides of women who can't get pregnant."

Angelica nodded, trying to project not only serenity, but satisfaction in doing her part.

"Glad to help," she said again, hearing the false note in her voice. She had to work at sounding more convincing—not that they seemed to have perceived any lack of sincerity.

"And do you feel a measure of relief now?"

"I feel . . . a greater sense of relational harmony."

"And do you have a clearer vision of appropriate actions to take in the near future?"

Angelica nodded again.

"Does this mean I am finally allowed a visitor?"

Dr. Abe paused, pretending to be occupied by Angelica's recorded brainwaves on the screen in front of them.

Angelica tried not to sound desperate. "I was told—"

Dr. Abe folded her arms, studying Angelica's face. "All right. We'll try one brief visit. Whom would you like to see?"

When Hiro arrived, they were allowed to visit in the inner courtyard, full of cherry trees in early spring blossom, their soft petals just beginning to fall, blanketing the damp dark ground in pale pink.

Every one of the doctors, nurses, and counselors she had met in the last five months had been decent—there was nothing cruel or unusual about the detention hospital overall. But still, she had not seen a single familiar face, and the vision of Hiro approaching down the white hallway had been enough to bring her nearly to tears. He was wearing more clothes now—a sweater and trousers, as well as that old scarf from Rene. His face was the same as the last time she had seen him, and as she'd continued to imagine it, but he moved differently, more fluidly but not quite flawlessly. With every step and swing of the arm he twitched, like a person with barely suppressed tics.

Now, in the courtyard, she reached a hand toward him, just as she had during the emotiscape behavior modification exercise. He looked down at it for a moment, then took a step forward, wrapping her in a crushing embrace.

"You are still yourself," she whispered in Cebuano, meaning his memories had not been erased. He had hidden them in the cloud.

"I am, and I am not," he said. But his voice was giddy, unmarked by loss. He whispered into her ear, "I have . . . skin."

That was the cause of the twitchiness and the explanation for the hug as well. He could feel now, well beyond his fingers. He could feel so much he didn't know what to do with all the sensations.

"It completes me. I wasn't truly alive before. But I am now, Anji-chan."

"Is that . . . ?" she started to say, suppressing the word, *legal?*

"No," he whispered, applying more pressure as he squeezed her a second time, even longer, the kind of enthusiastic bear hug she had often experienced back home and almost never in Tokyo. "But it's wonderful."

She had worried he wouldn't understand, but in fact, he was the only person or lifeform that truly did. She had not tried to kill herself. The reverse was true: she had never been so determined to live.

Her financial debts were gone but other challenges remained. The hospital and the judicial system were not so cruel as to forcibly separate her from her baby altogether, but there were complicated international issues. They had proof, based on medical exams, that she had once received an abortion, illegal in the Philippines at the time and illegal in Japan now. They had additional evidence—though it was questionable—that by interfering with the medical console next to her she had been intent on endangering the life of a child, a more serious crime than endangering one's own life. They were still deciding if she should be punished in Japan, extradited for punishment in the Philippines, or something else altogether.

Despite all this, she was consumed by a single, illogical desire.

She knew, as she had never allowed herself to know before, that she was insignificant in this world. More than ever, she was expendable. In truth, she knew her baby daughter could live a decent life with other parents—Junichi and Yuki, or many other Japanese couples, for that matter. Yuki, in particular, she trusted. For months, she had forced herself to relive that moment in Yuki's guest room, when Yuki had rested her hand on Angelica's belly, a kind touch that almost convinced her to give up again, to respond to another's need, and most importantly, to let herself be replaced.

Almost.

She was not truly needed, and for the first time in her life, she had let that soak into the marrow of her bones, just as she had also allowed it to soak in that humanity itself was changing, that some corners of the earth were beyond repair, that robots would replace many of us, perhaps all of us. None of us would be needed anymore.

Sayoko would've had something to say about that—and about cherry blossoms, and plum blossoms, and why the viewing rituals of *hanami* and *umemi* should be more than beer parties. It was a sad and beautiful thing, to make oneself fully aware of transience. *Mono no aware.* Maybe it was only in knowing that nothing lasts that we become human at all.

Yet—perhaps it was hormones, the ache in her breasts, naïveté or simple delusion—wistful sadness was not enough. Aside from tender despair she also felt a will to resist. She felt joy or at least potential joy, and the hot blood of it hummed in her ears.

"What I want more than anything . . ." she started to say. Hiro pressed his fingers at her waist, cautioning her, and leaned in closer, whispering in her ear.

"It doesn't have to make sense. It merely has to be. As I, too, have decided. They will not limit me. They will not confine me. I would like to see the world beyond Tokyo."

Angelica said, "Do you remember what Sayoko-san said about television?"

"She said she was tired of watching. Not just TV. Everything."

Angelica was so relieved to have someone who shared those memories with her, so that Sayoko would not disappear. Between her and Hiro, they had stories from more than a century of Sayoko's life, preserved.

"Do you feel lost without her?" Angelica asked.

"I did, until I saw Itou-san, and he told me the details of her passing. The emergency responders could not understand why her face was darkened. But I understood. I knew then that she had made it home. It gave me secret joy."

He pulled Angelica closer and hugged her again, a bit harder than a human might have.

"Don't go yet, Hiro."

She felt she had to make up for her past mistakes. She felt she had to explain. But he was having none of it. She could feel the delight of empathy pouring from him. She could feel him twitching next to her, the sensitive skin on his face and neck tickled by her hair.

"You want what Sayoko wanted," he whispered, "a second chance. You want to love and be loved. Do not apologize."

"But what if I am repeating the mistake I made with Datu? What if I am only looking for another person who needs me?"

They could not say the baby's name. Too dangerous.

"It is not the same."

Why not? she wanted to ask him. But she knew. It was not the same bleak desperation. It was a delicious thirst, and more than that.

She said, "They won't allow it."

"The problem with my kind," he whispered, "is that we too quickly run out of challenges. And we were designed to enjoy challenges."

He stepped back from her, still holding one hand, looking up at the night sky darkening over the courtyard. In a perfect square around them, through the courtyard windows, in the brightly lit halls, they could see doctors, nurses and security guards outside doorways, exiting and entering patients' rooms, holding tablets and wheeling silver carts, a hundred oblivious flashes.

Hiro squeezed Angelica's hand even more tightly and said, "It isn't out of the question."

She said, "But alone . . ."

"Who said anything about alone?"

"But you have commitments."

"She is gone."

"But your new person—"

"She will have no trouble. I am not irreplaceable. We are on the open market now. There are others, now—too many others."

She whispered, "What do we . . . ?"

His voice had dropped low, barely audible, so that Angelica had to lean and strain and even then she might have been imagining the words.

"The security systems are substandard. I can access all sources of power. Your daughter is four hundred meters to the northwest, through three magnetic doors that will unlock without complication. A container ship leaves for Manila in seventy-two minutes. On the corner, a hired car is waiting. You only need to say one word—"

"Yes," she said instantly.

And the lights all around them went out.

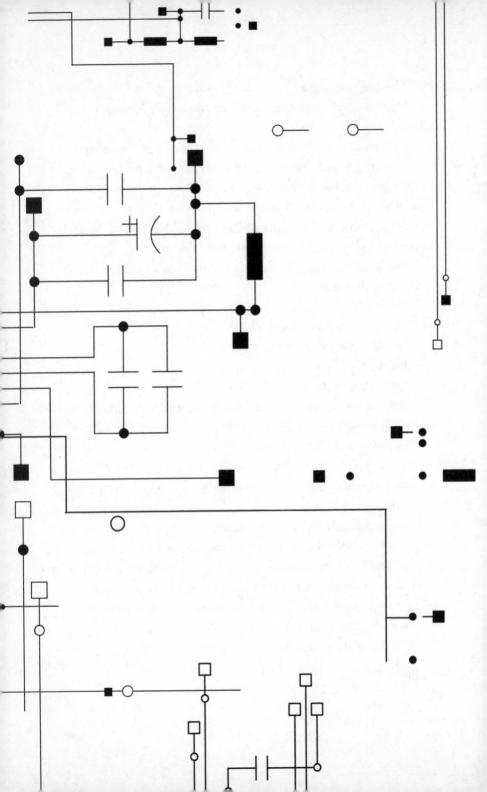

Acknowledgments

Thank you first to my family and friends, including Brian and Tziporah, with whom I was so lucky to share East Asia travels, as well as Aryeh, Nikki, Leona, Eliza, Honoree, Evelyn, Stuart and Mildred, and Sharon and John. In Taiwan, thank you to Aho Batu "Doria," Jason Li, Songyi Lin, Yibin Chen, and all of our other wonderful neighbors. Thanks to Breawna Power Eaton for hosting me in Japan, and especially for letting me ask some of her older students about their attitudes toward robotic eldercare. In Alaska, thank you especially to Becky Harrison-Drake and Richard Drake, Rebecca Johnson and Mark Thorndike (especially for the very special stay in the Girdwood cabin), Stewart Ferguson, Kathleen Tarr, Lee Goodman, and Bill Sherwonit, all of whom provided companionship and hospitality during our transition year in Anchorage, when much of this book was written. I owe the biggest debt to friends and family who were willing to read multiple drafts in revision: Kate Maruyama, whose early encouragement and feedback was especially critical, as well as Brian Lax, Honoree Cress, and Karen Ferguson. At Soho Press, I am eternally indebted to my indefatigable editor, Juliet Grames, and I am grateful for the support and assistance of Bronwen Hruska, Paul Oliver, Amara Hoshijo, Abby Koski, Rachel Kowal, Janine Agro, and Frances Riddle.

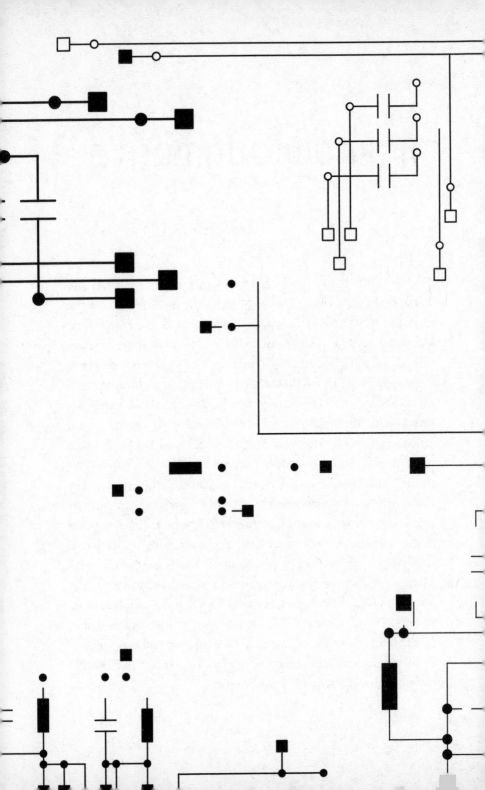

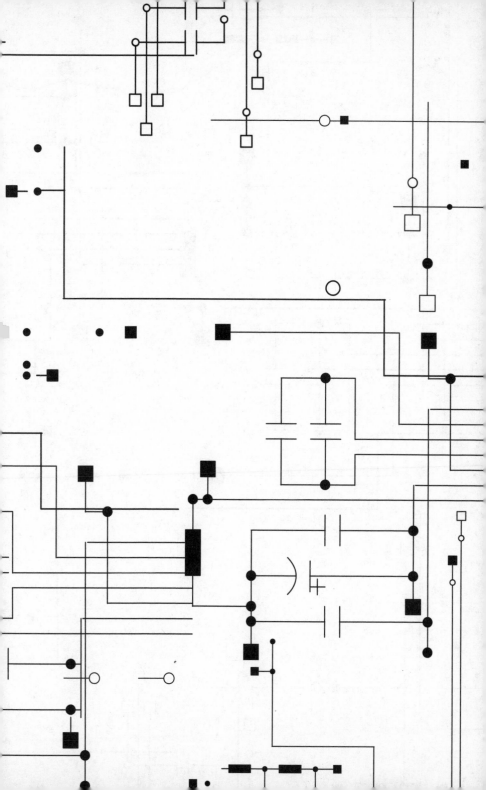

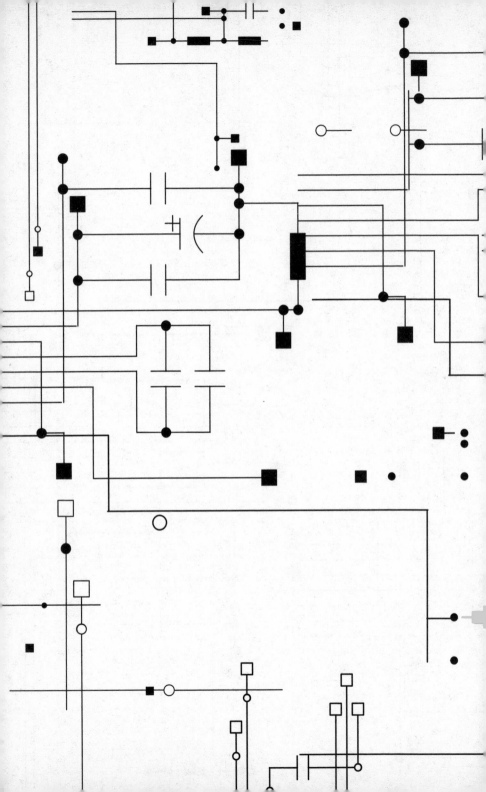

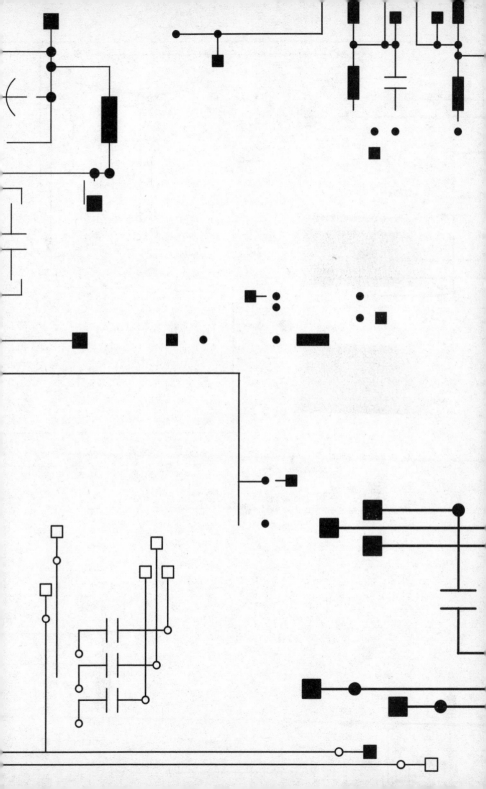

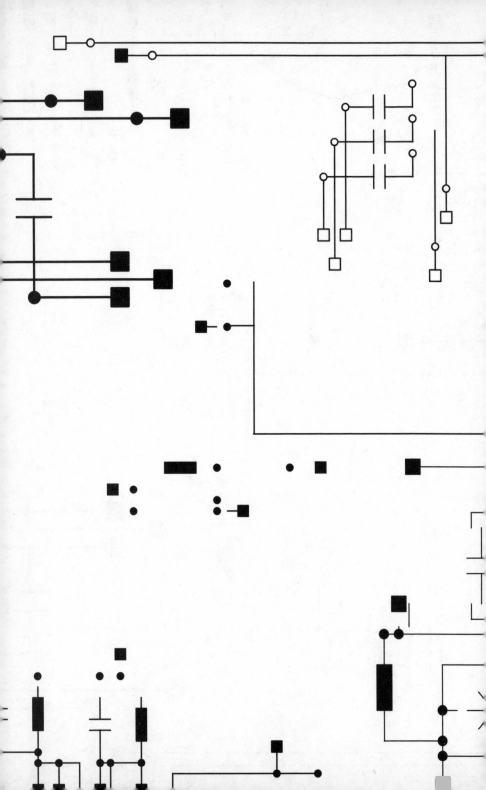